A Meeting With Murder

Miss Gascoigne mysteries: book 1

Caron Allan

Caron Allan

Dedication

To my family

Chapter One

Mildred Evans was looking dismayed. 'I'm so sorry, Dee. Believe me, my dear, I did try to reason with them. In losing you, I shall be losing not just an excellent modern languages teacher but also a very popular, very *dear* member of staff. But I'm afraid they are rather a bunch of old stick-in-the-muds. The collective view was that divorce—or even as in your case, a marital separation—does not accord well with the traditional values of Lady Adelaide Joseph's Academy for Young Ladies. Especially as Martin is still working here. You've scandalised them, my dear. I'm sorry.' The headmistress was on her feet and coming round to this side of her grand mahogany desk. 'You will, of course, be paid up to the end of the school year in July, if that's the slightest consolation.'

Feeling numb, all Dee Gascoigne could do was nod, and smile politely, and say of course, she quite understood, and thank you so much for trying to help.

She was on her feet too, and almost at the door before she even knew she'd moved from her chair. Mildred Evans handed her a small visiting card.

'Contact me, dear, if—well—if anything changes. Would you like me to ask around amongst my chums? I have a few acquaintances who are senior staff at *Secondary Moderns.*' Miss Evans lowered her voice on those last two words, and all but shuddered. 'Not ideal, obviously, but a job's a job at the end of the day, and in your present situation, you may find it hard to come by another place at a more exclusive establishment.'

Again, Dee could only nod and say thank you politely as her mother had taught her. She opened the door.

Miss Evan's hand was on her arm. 'I shall miss you, my dear. But for what it's worth, I think you've done the right thing. You've got to do what's best for you. As I said, let me know if anything changes.' She paused, uncertain, then added, all in a rush, 'That said, please my dear, don't go back to him, no matter what he promises. A leopard can't change its spots, you know. Keep in touch, won't you? God bless you, dear.'

Dee was relieved to make it all the way to her car before bursting into tears.

How many bridges had she burned? But the last time had been... the last time. She couldn't keep putting up with it, she couldn't take it anymore. She had been every kind of fool to take it for as long as she had. If her parents had known, her father or her twin brother... she shuddered to think of the scene that would have led to. Even so, after worrying about the situation for several months, she had come to her decision and packed her things all in a rush the day before, when Martin had been out. But though she couldn't possibly regret it, she felt a shimmer of fear at what the future might hold. She clamped down hard on the shimmer, saying viciously as she stamped on the accelerator, 'Nonsense,' in the time-honoured fashion of the women in her family.

Besides, her family would never let her starve. With nowhere else to go and all that she possessed already packed in the car with her, she headed for Hertfordshire and home.

Dee halted her car in front of the ancient family retreat *Ville Gascoigne* and steeling herself, grabbed her bag and suitcase then crossed the gravel drive to the front door. She had warned them she was on her way. They knew why, of course. That her mother had been looking out for her was clear as both she and the aged butler opened the door to Dee before she got anywhere near it. They were already coming down the steps.

'Hello Mother, hello Mr Greeley.' She sent a bright beaming smile in the direction of the ancient butler who winked at her and relieved her of her suitcase and jacket. Her mother was not in the least deceived by the attempt at cheerfulness.

'Oh Dee, darling! Are you all right? Oh you've lost so much weight! I'm so glad you're here.' Flora Gascoigne swept her only daughter into a tight hug. Tears threatened, and Dee pulled herself out of her mother's grip, turning away to fuss with her handbag.

'Gosh it was a horrid drive down,' she began, and concocted a story about an entirely fictitious traffic jam just outside London. She just needed something, anything, to talk about. Anything other than why she was here and what had happened.

'Come into the drawing-room. Your father's not here, he's off somewhere with his cronies, but he said he wouldn't be late. My goodness, you look so pale, dear, and so thin! I'm sure you girls don't eat properly.'

'God, Mother, no one eats these days. Don't fuss. I'm not a child.' Dee rolled her eyes. It was not easy to maintain her appearance of trendy self-sufficiency when all she wanted was to curl up in a ball and sob her heart out. Bloody men. 'Is Freddie here? I thought he said he would be.'

'Tomorrow, apparently. I think he's going out for a romantic dinner or something this evening. I only hope she's a decent sort of girl. That last one...'

'Lord, yes. Freddie can't half pick 'em. And what about Rob, is he home?'

'Oh of course he is. When does your youngest brother ever go anywhere?' Her mother sighed, and they went into the drawing-room.

As they came into the room an earnest-looking, bespectacled young man looked up from a book. He grinned at his sister. 'Deedee, about time.'

'Hello yourself, Boffin.' She flung herself down in the seat next to him and hugged his arm. Her baby brother. Her rock.

To her relief she managed to get through the rest of the day by fielding any further questions that came her way, or by skilfully turning the question around to get the other person to talk about themselves.

She had a feeling no one was fooled but she was grateful for their silence. She really didn't want to go into the whole sordid mess quite yet. At some point, she knew, she would have to tell them exactly what had happened, and what her plans were for the future. But tonight, she just wanted to turn back the clock, pretend she was still a kid and not an almost thirty-year-old unemployed woman who had just left her husband.

But when everyone else had gone to bed and it was just her and Rob, he poured her a glass of wine and brought it over, sitting down next to her, and saying, 'So what *are* you going to do?'

'Look for another job, obviously. Other than that...'

'I suppose they didn't kick him out on his ear too? It was only you who lost your job?'

'Of course they didn't kick him out. It's only bad if a

woman leaves her husband and wants to get a divorce. It's not bad for the man. Half of the male staff will probably want to take him out for a drink and tell him what a lucky dog he is. Women are supposed to stay married and be grateful for it, even if they aren't happy.'

'Yes, double standards are all too prevalent in any profession. Where are you going to live? When are you going to start looking for somewhere?'

To her shrug, he added, 'You do know it's going to be three years? Even then you'll have to take the blame for deserting him. Unless you've got proof that he is at fault. If you can prove infidelity, or marital cruelty, then...'

Crossly, she said, 'Oh Rob, I know all that. I don't want to think about it just now.'

He took a sip of his own drink. His light brown hair appeared almost black in a room lit only by firelight. His eyes shone brightly as he watched her. He may always have his nose in a book, she thought, but he saw everything. And he was a wonderful listener. There was no one better to pour your heart out to. She dearly loved all three of her brothers, but for some reason Rob, the baby of the family, was special; she was closer to him even than her own twin brother, Freddie. She always had been, perhaps because she had seen him as a living breathing doll when he was a baby and she was three, almost four years old. Now he was no longer a baby but a charming, good-looking, intelligent and sensitive man. She leaned against his shoulder.

'Rob, do you think I'm doing the right thing? The last thing I wanted was any kind of scandal or fuss, but it's all going wrong.'

He put an arm about her and she rested her head on his shoulder. In a meditative voice he said, 'The right thing?'

'Don't go all philosophical on me right now, I couldn't cope with that.'

He laughed. 'I wasn't about to. But let me see. Shall we examine the facts?'

'Yes, M'lord,' she murmured. He was definitely studying the right discipline; he'd make an excellent judge one day.

'Was he unfaithful?'

'You know he was.' Rob was the only one who knew it all.

'Were you?'

She turned to glare at him. 'What? No, of course not! What do you take me for?'

'Sorry. Had to ask. The divorce court will, so...'

She nodded. 'Of course. Sorry. No, I was never unfaithful.'

Perhaps not in deed, said the nasty little self-accusing voice in her head. Just in thought. She pushed out of her head the image of a man's face, along with those old Bible words, whosoever something looketh upon something something even in their heart, was an adulterer. Or words of that sort.

Rob said, quietly, gravely, 'Did he hurt you? Clarke?'

There was a silent moment. Then she heard the crackling of the flames devouring a log in the grate, and she said, softly, 'Yes.'

Another long pausing moment. Rob kissed her hair and got to his feet. He paced a little, a barrister through and through. In a very matter of fact manner, he said, 'I always suspected as much. In that case, yes, you are doing the right thing. If you had proof of either his violence or any adultery on his part, that would speed things up, otherwise you'll need to allow him to sue you for desertion or for infidelity.'

'What if he won't allow me to sue him?'

'I'll kill him for you.'

She looked at her tall, skinny brother. 'You?' She grinned.

He shrugged. 'Clearly I won't do the dirty work

myself, I'll contract it out. Obviously when I say I'll kill him for you, I mean, I'll do the organising side of things, but probably set Freddie onto him. Or Bill.'

She wriggled in her seat. 'Not Bill,' she said.

Rob nodded and said nothing. He didn't need to say anything. He knew how she felt, had always felt, about her 'cousin', Bill Hardy.

Bill wasn't really her cousin, of course, any more than Rob or Harry were her brothers or Freddie her twin brother. Dee was the lovechild of Diana Gascoigne and her married lover Archie Dunne. Her father having been murdered by his wife months earlier, Dee had been born in desperate circumstances, and her mother had died as soon as Dee took her first breath. Dee had been raised by her mother's brother and his wife, and to the outside world, she was the daughter of George Gascoigne and his wife Flora, and Freddie's twin sister, when in reality she had been born almost five weeks earlier to completely different parents. Flora's younger sister Dottie was the mother of Bill and his brother and sister, and so—whether a blessing or a curse, Dee wasn't quite sure—there was no blood relationship between herself and the attractive but annoying Detective Inspector Bill Hardy, though for the sake of convenience, she claimed him as her cousin.

He flomped into the chair opposite and they sat in silence staring into the fire.

Later, when the ancient grandfather clock in the hall chimed one o'clock, surprising them that the hour was so late, Dee thought she'd better get to bed. It would be odd, sleeping in her old room again after—what? Almost nine years?

She said goodnight to Rob suspecting he was at least half-asleep himself. As she was about to leave the room, he said, 'By the way, I've decided to go into business with JJ. We both qualify next year. We thought we'd set up shop together.

'Oughtn't you get some experience first? If you're both new to the job, how will you know what to do?'

'I've got a part-time position with Monty. I can use it as part of my coursework. It's only temporary. He's retiring.'

'Again? Didn't he retire about ten years ago?'

'Hmm, he did, yes, and a few years before that, too. This time he says he means it, he's almost eighty after all. But he said he wanted to stay on to give me some experience.'

'Can't he take on both you and JJ as juniors then retire in a year or two and let the two of you just carry it on for him?'

'Who knows? That is one possibility. But if he does stick to his guns, at least he'll have given me a bit of a start. It's dashed good of him.'

'I'm glad,' she said. M'dear Monty, as they all called him in the family, had been a staunch friend and ally of the family for many years. He'd even helped her aunt to avoid a murder charge once, back in the mists of time.

'So I was thinking, why don't you and I share a flat? I'll have to be in London, so it just seems, you know...'

That surprised her. 'Oh.' She thought about it. 'That's a fab idea. Just us? Or JJ too?'

'Just us. I think JJ is going to move in with Bill during the Easter hols in a couple of weeks.'

'Of course.' Again, she didn't want to talk about Bill. 'Well goodnight, Rob, thanks for the pep-talk. Sleep well.'

'Night Deedee. About Clarke. I'm relieved you're out of it. He wasn't worthy, my darling.'

As soon as she'd got into the hall, she reached for her handkerchief and scrubbed the tears from her cheeks. Enough was enough. Time to look to the future.

Three weeks later, Rob and Dee were searching for a vacant flat within easy reach of where Rob was studying, and M'dear Monty's offices. Yet it had to be somewhere central enough for Dee to get to most areas without too lengthy a commute. Always assuming that she managed to get another job to start when the new school year began in far-off September.

After viewing several properties, they found what they were looking for. Not as central as they'd planned, nor as cheap as they'd budgeted for, nor as modern as they'd hoped, but it was the best of all the properties they viewed, and the lease was a long one.

The flat was in an ordinary Victorian building, on the fourth floor. The sitting-room and dining-room were at the front of the building, overlooking a busy street, whilst the bedrooms overlooked the service yards and surrounding houses, and hopefully would be fairly quiet.

In many ways the flat was everything they'd decided against, but with their budget and time limited, it had become clear they couldn't afford to be too choosy. The outside of the building was unremarkable. But as soon as they stepped inside the flat, they knew it was just what they needed, being spacious, bright, and possessing that indefinable something extra that told you that you had entered not just a house but a home.

'It feels friendly,' Dee said to her brother. That was the only way she could explain how she felt.

He nodded. 'This sitting-room is perfect. I don't even mind that the front door leads straight in here with no entrance hall.'

'With all this open space, it'll be wonderful for parties,' she said.

He shot her a sideways glance. Parties were really not his thing.

She grinned at him. 'I know, I know. Not on a school night.'

There were three bedrooms, two bathrooms, a kitchen, a small rather dark dining-room, and an even smaller darker dressing-room that Rob immediately claimed for his office. And then there was this large, open sitting-room with three floor-to-ceiling windows looking out onto the late afternoon London traffic. The vehicles purred along beneath them, seeming far enough away not to be too much of a nuisance.

'And what does madam think?' the agent asked with a smarmy grin. He'd been standing in the middle of the room talking at them continually whilst they walked round him and ignored him. He seemed anxious to make them love the place. Rob wondered if it was his first day, whilst Dee wondered if there had been a murder in the flat which meant that he was desperate to get rid of it.

She exchanged a look with Rob then beamed at the agent.

'We love it. We'll take it.'

The agent tried, not very successfully, to hide his relief.

Dee said, 'It's not haunted, is it?'

'Hardly, madam,' he sneered.

'Good. When can we move in?'

'It'll take a day or two to do the paperwork and for your deposit to clear, but any time after that. Just call into the office to collect your keys. I hope you'll both be very happy here.' He left them to it, almost running down the hall, telling them to slam the door shut when they left, the latch would lock automatically.

Dee and Rob wandered about, talking, leaning against the walls and planning the layout of their small amount of furniture, then they just stood looking out of the windows.

'What a shame this block isn't one of the sort with the kitchen in the basement, sending hot meals up to our little kitchen in a dumb-waiter. That would make it just about perfect.'

'They used to be in the attic more often than in the

basement,' Rob told her. 'I suppose I shall have to learn to cook. If we rely on you to make our meals, we'll either starve or die of food-poisoning.'

'Well thank you very much! But I'm not doing all the domestic stuff just because I'm the girl, so yes, you had better learn to cook,' she laughed. 'And clean. And just to be very, very clear, I'm never going to wash your pants either, so that's another thing you'll need to learn to do.'

'Fine,' he sighed, pretending to be irritated. He put an arm around her shoulders. 'Are we sure? I mean, it's a lot of money.'

'It'll be fine. Mum and Dad will always help us out if we're stuck. And besides, everywhere's a lot of money these days.' She began to move about the room. 'I love this place. We're going to be so happy here.'

'I suppose you'll want a house-warming party.'

'A flat-warming, you mean.' She beamed at him. 'Yes!'

But the house-warming, or more accurately, the flat-warming party never happened.

Rob and Dee moved in three days later, and three days after that, Dee was struck down by bronchitis. She spent the following eight days in bed, and when she was finally able to drag herself out of bed and sit by the fire in the sitting-room, she was as weak as a kitten, with no enthusiasm for anything. It took all her energy to sit in the chair and stare at the fire. Easter was a washout.

Her doctor had declared her in need of complete rest. 'You've been overdoing it,' he told her severely, in the bossy manner of all doctors. 'You must try to get away somewhere quiet to recover. If you stay at home you'll be up and down every five minutes thinking of some little task that you simply have to do, and you won't get any rest at all. You're lucky you didn't get pneumonia,' he added, as if she'd been careless with her health.

Dee made the mistake of mentioning this on the telephone to her mother, who it seemed already had plans.

'I know just the thing. It's all fixed up. You're off to spend some time at the seaside. Remember our former maid, Cissie Palmer, Cissie Spencer as was?'

There was no opportunity for Dee to either accept or deny Cissie Palmer nee Spencer. Her mother hurried on:

'She's a widow now, poor thing. She is a post-mistress in some tiny place down in Sussex. And she has a cottage that she lets out to paying guests. Holidaymakers, that sort of thing. *People recovering from bronchitis.* It's right on the Sussex coast. The village is so picturesque, I'm sure you'd love it, dear. When she sent her card at Easter, I wrote to tell her about you, and she says that of course you must come down, and so it's all arranged.'

Just the thought of going all the way to Sussex made Dee feel worn out. She began a kind of exploratory, half-hearted refusal but her mother—all too predictably—simply said, 'Nonsense dear, it'll do you the world of good. Leave your car in the garage then all you've got to do is sit on a train for a couple of hours. It'll be a wonderful rest for you. Take a magazine and some Spangles or Opal Fruits, you'll be perfectly all right.'

Dee said, 'I hate Opal Fruits,' wrinkling her nose as she said it. She sighed. She'd known from the outset she would end up giving in. You always did with Mother. 'And Spangles. Oh, all right. I suppose I could do with a change of scene, and it will do Rob good to get some sleep without me coughing all night long in the room next door.'

'Excellent,' said her mother. 'I'll telephone and let Cissie know.'

'I thought you said it was all arranged?'

'Oh—er—well, you know, just in case... I mean...'

'You're a terrible fraud, Mother.'

'I just want you to get out of London and get some sea air into your poor lungs. You'll come back perfectly recovered and ready to start job hunting again.'

'Ugh, don't talk to me about that. I'm sure someone has blighted my good name. I've sent in four applications and not heard from any of them.'

'Well, you can worry about that when you come home. Now, I suggest you get the ten-fifteen to Redhill and from there...' Her mother broke off. 'Do you have a pencil and paper ready for the details?'

And so Dee found herself, on a Monday at the end of April, on the train to Sussex, off to stay in the cottage of Mrs Cissie Palmer, once the bubbly and devoted Cissie Spencer, maid for over ten years to Flora and George Gascoigne but now a solid and respectable widowed post-mistress who took in the occasional boarder.

She had to change trains at Redhill for the local service that visited all the smaller dots on the railway map of the south coast. She had never even heard of Porthlea before, let alone visited the place.

By the time she arrived, she was at the end of her strength and inclined to feel depressed and emotional. Damn this bronchitis, she grumbled to herself. All she wanted was to feel well again so that she could get on with her life and get back to looking for a job. She wasn't too concerned about money: her parents had been generous in that regard, but if she left it too long, how would she get back into things?

Stepping down off the train, she immediately saw the beaming face of Cissie Palmer. Cissie rushed forward to hug her in welcome and take her suitcase, leaving Dee with just her bulging shoulder bag to worry about.

'I'm so glad to see you, Miss Dee. How long's it been?

You were just a skinny young girl when I last saw you, though your mother's been kind enough to let me have a photo of you from time to time.' She almost said that the last one had been the wedding photo. It was on the tip of her tongue to say what a lovely bride Dee had made, but she caught herself just in time. 'Well, let's get on, shall we? It's only a short step, my dear,' Cissie said. And giving her a close look, added, 'Just as well by the look of you. You're as white as a sheet, my girl.'

Dee was beginning to feel better already.

Later that evening, from the phone box on the edge of the village green, she telephoned her mother to report her safe arrival, and to send Cissie's fictitious regards.

'Dear Cissie. Give her our love too, and tell her in confidence,' and here her mother dropped her voice to a whisper, 'that the new girl isn't a patch on her.'

Dee laughed. 'New girl? Etta's been with you since I was fourteen. It must be easily fifteen years.'

Her mother was shocked. 'Surely not?'

'She has, Mother. Right well, I suppose I'd better be going...'

'Dee, dear, there is just one small thing.'

Dee felt something go cold in the pit of her stomach. She held her breath.

'Martin has rung up twice. In a *very* bad temper. Oh, don't worry, we haven't told him where you are. Or about the flat. You know we wouldn't do that, but I just—you know—felt you ought to know.'

He didn't know where she was. Everything was all right. Pushing aside her fear, Dee nodded then remembered she was on the phone. 'All right, thanks for telling me. I hope he doesn't make a nuisance of himself.' Her voice sounded almost normal. To herself she joked, speaking of Martin, that is definitely 'one small thing'. She almost giggled and it made her feel better. They talked for a couple more minutes then said goodbye. She pressed Button B and got a penny back. Then she quickly called Rob to let him know that she had arrived and everything was fine, and she'd see him soon.

As she walked back across the green to the little terraced cottage where she was staying, she felt a cold wind coming up the road from the sea. It made her shiver. Goosebumps came out all along her forearms. She felt an urge to get indoors, and quickly.

Dee was up bright and early on her first morning in Porthlea. A good night's sleep that she attributed to the sea air meant that she was ready to go out and explore.

In the kitchen, she turned on the transistor radio she'd brought with her and made some toast and tea. Micky Scott was Dee's favourite breakfast show disc jockey, although some thought him smarmy. Dee liked him because he didn't talk as much and played more music than some of his colleagues.

'Without more ado,' Micky now declared, 'Let's get on to the next song—it's everyone's fave bad boy, Sonny-Ray Smith. You know you love to hate him.' Micky gave a snort of laughter. 'Now, I know what you're thinking, but no, this is not Sonny-Ray's controversial hit from last year, but a new release, or rather Sonny-Ray's version of an old release. Here it is, his cover of a smash hit from 1962, out on Monday.'

The first bars of the song began, and then there was Sonny-Ray, bad boy of pop, crooning a sickly-sweet rendition of Cliff Richard's *The Young Ones*. Dee wrinkled her nose in distaste. She wasn't fond of the original, but this was awful. She turned off the radio. Sonny-Ray would have to do better than that to stage a comeback after the debacle over his song *Need Someone* of the previous summer.

It was odd, she reflected. One moment the man was the darling of single girls, wives and grandmothers around the country, then one ill-judged, boastful comment in an interview had practically killed his career overnight. He had appeared on the Ted Greenway show. The notoriously prickly host had goaded him into admitting that the original lyrics of *Need Someone* had in fact been *Need Something* and wasn't about romance but his 'former' use of illegal substances to help him cope with his demanding schedule. This admission turned the tide of popularity against him incredibly quickly. All his TV appearances and public events had been famously dropped or postponed indefinitely.

Dee wondered what he was doing now. No doubt he was holed up in some rural retreat, licking his wounds whilst his agent and record company desperately tried to decide how to recover from this disaster.

She was ready. Grabbing her bag, she left the cottage. Then she had to run back inside for a cardigan. The sea air may be fresh and healthy, but it brought a slight chill with it.

*

Chapter Two

At forty-four, Meredith Prescott, with her handsome features, trim figure and excellent dress sense, was frequently taken for at least ten years younger than her true age. Not that she was in the habit of seeking out flattery, she told herself, for she was definitely one of those women who never thinks about herself, what she's wearing or how she looks. She was far too busy running errands for someone or other.

It was one of these errands that brought her out into the village street on a wet Tuesday morning towards the end of April. Relieved that it was no longer actually raining, she crossed the road by The Seagull public house, heading in the direction of the village green. She waved a greeting to old Mrs Hunter, to whom she read on Mondays and Thursdays. Mrs Hunter was being wheeled along to the doctor's surgery by her granddaughter Marlene, a plump, bad-tempered seventeen-year-old who reeked of cigarettes.

Meredith Prescott had almost reached the green when she collided with Major Reeves on the narrow bend. She apologised swiftly and conferred one of her sweet special smiles on him before moving on, leaving him staring after her with admiration and a resolution to ask her out for drinks, or dinner, or possibly the pictures.

Meredith Prescott, oblivious to the major's intentions, continued to the post office, and glancing in at the window as she went by, she was irritated to see at least three people already waiting. But there was nothing for it, she had to get the stamps, and the postal order that was to be the birthday present from her aunt to her late husband's nephew Edward which had to be sent inside the birthday card, and so Meredith went in.

One of the waiting people was Miss Fenniston. Of course, if Meredith had seen her sooner she would never have gone in, even though Edward's birthday was on Thursday, for if there was one person she always went out of her way to avoid, it was her brother's secretary.

Miss Fenniston nodded to her and said a cool, 'Good morning.'

Meredith Prescott felt irritated again, as if she had been condescended to, but she shook off the feeling and trying to force a good deal more warmth into her voice than she really felt, she replied, 'Good morning to you, Miss Fenniston. How are you? It's been quite a while since I last saw you.'

'Just about three weeks,' Sheila Fenniston responded, her tone still rather cool. 'But perhaps you forgot I was away with Jeremy for that conference in Brighton before taking my annual holiday?'

'Of course, how silly of me.' Meredith blustered a little, noting that the other occupants of the shop were taking in every detail, including the woman's very inappropriate use of Meredith's brother's first name. Really, it had to stop, this all-too-casual familiarity.

The person at the post office window moved off and

Miss Fenniston stepped up to carry out her business, making further conversation impossible. But Meredith continued to feel flustered and upset. She was relieved when, a few minutes later, Miss Fenniston left the post office with only a curt nod in Meredith's direction. Her feelings were further relieved when she came out and glancing up and down the street, found that Sheila Fenniston was nowhere to be seen.

Meredith began to relax. She pulled out her list to check what she needed to do next. Ah yes, library books. The 'library' was a single room at the back of the village hall, along by the seafront, and staffed by volunteers, but mostly by Meredith herself or the vicar's wife, Millie Edmonds.

By the time Meredith had arrived home, hung up her coat and emptied her basket on the side table in the morning-room, it was almost lunchtime.

Her aunt entered the room, leaning rather more than necessary on her stick. She proceeded to complain about the library books Meredith had selected for her, waving away Meredith's apologies and explanations, and gathering everything together in a wobbling heap, she went up the stairs very slowly, with every appearance of frailty. She carried everything to her private sitting-room, only to hurry down a few minutes later when luncheon was announced, accidentally leaving her walking stick upstairs. Another small task for Meredith.

Davies the maid came through from the kitchen, and ran ahead to open the dining-room door for Mrs Smithies, who sailed past her, putting Meredith in mind as usual of an old steamship entering a harbour.

'No Jeremy today?' Meredith heard her aunt enquire. Before Meredith could answer, Davies responded quickly with:

'Not today, Mrs Smithies. Mr Jeremy mentioned that he has a meeting with the gentleman from Italy today and is lunching at his office.'

'Ah yes, of course. So he did. Well, I can't bear cold meat, let us begin.'

'Yes madam, I'll bring it through immediately.' With a quick bob, she turned and left the room.

As soon as the door closed behind her, Mrs Smithies turned to Meredith and said, 'I do hope that odious Fenniston woman isn't lunching with him, it would not be at all appropriate. Men are so terribly lax about these things. Especially since the war.'

'Yes, Aunt Lucinda.' Meredith was not required to say more. Her aunt continued to expand on her main theme.

'It encourages the woman to believe herself on an equal footing with him. It arouses hopes that ought not be aroused. It is most...' and here Mrs Smithies felt about her for the right word, found an old favourite and pronounced it with finality. 'Inappropriate!'

'It is indeed, Aunt.'

'Perhaps you or I ought to have another word with him. I'm convinced he has forgotten everything you said to him last month about the position in which he is placing himself, and by extension us, when he acts so familiarly with this—this creature.'

There was a brief pause in which Meredith, on the point of responding in either the negative or the positive as required, suddenly had a presentiment of what her aunt was going to say next.

Mrs Smithies spoke again, distress in her voice. 'If only your uncle was still alive, he would know how to handle a situation of this sort. Indeed, the situation would probably have never arisen in the first place.'

About to agree once more, Meredith was prevented from doing so by the door opening and Davies coming in with a tray of covered dishes which she dispensed about the table and withdrew, leaving them to serve themselves. Thus distracted, Meredith had no opportunity of steeling herself or heading off the current in another direction.

Her aunt said, 'Perhaps you could have another word with him about it. Be more forceful this time. He must be made to get rid of the woman. I simply cannot endure the strain of her rudeness, nor her familiarity. She's so uncouth. She has no respect for us, she's an embarrassment. Speak to him this evening after dinner. That way you will have to get it over and done with, and he won't be able to do anything other than listen because we shall have guests to entertain. He won't risk causing a scene.'

Meredith's heart sank. There *would* be a scene, she knew it. She had been through a similar situation only a few weeks earlier, when last her aunt had tasked her with talking to Jeremy about his relationship with his secretary. It had been unpleasant in the extreme and he had sulked all the evening. At the time it had been difficult, but she had been comforted by the fact that he had appeared to take notice of their concerns. But now, after spending some time away together—*and who knew what that may have led to*—she could hardly bear to think of them dining together in the hotel, perhaps drinking a little too much—it was all too clear this had been just a momentary improvement and he had now slipped back into those objectionable ways. Did that mean that in another month's time, she would be facing the prospect of yet another talk with Jeremy about his precious Miss Fenniston? She had a horrid feeling that is exactly what would be happening. Her future life would be punctuated with such talks on a regular basis. She said:

'Do we really want him sulking all through tonight's dinner, when he should be setting himself out to entertain his guests?'

'That's why I said you should speak with him *after* dinner. Really, Meredith, I do wish you would pay attention. Wait until the gentlemen join us for coffee, then I shall entertain our visitors and you can take him into the morning-room for a quick talk in private, and there will be no time for him to make a fuss. We can't put it off any longer. The woman is making complete fools of us.'

It was all very well for her aunt to talk of 'we' but the task was falling to Meredith alone, and she dreaded bringing up the subject that had been so angrily discussed between her brother and herself only a short time ago. Once upon a time he had trusted her judgement and followed her advice. They had been so close. Not anymore. The evening ahead began to loom horribly in Meredith's mind, and she toyed with the possibility of a migraine coming on gradually during the afternoon. But she knew it wouldn't be any good. The dinner party was too important, her aunt would not permit any absences.

If the dinner had gone well that evening, that was all that could be said. In the drawing-room, Jeremy was witty and attentive. His guests clearly enjoyed themselves.

But beneath the host's perfect demeanour burned a bright, brittle anger and Meredith was all too aware of it whenever her brother should look at her. She was confident, however, that no one else detected anything amiss, even though some of his jokes were barbed. At least she could be sure he would wait until after their guests had returned to their hotel before he turned on her. Even so, she was not looking forward to that.

Miss Fenniston, passing around the cigarettes, bent near to Meredith and said softly for her ears alone, 'What on earth have you said to Jeremy? He's in a filthy mood.' Her eyes, bright with malicious enjoyment, rested on Meredith's before she moved on.

Meredith excused herself for a moment, though no

one even noticed her leave. Praying that her brother would not seize the opportunity and come after her, she made her way to the bathroom. She bolted the door behind her and leaned against it for a moment, relieved. It was cool in here, and quiet. She went to the basin and splashed some cold water on her wrists. Then she dampened the corner of the towel and applied this to her temples and the back of her neck. Immediately the delicious chill freshened her. Some of the tension lessened, though her head still ached abominably. Not long now, and the evening would be over, she comforted herself.

She looked into the mirror and saw how pale she was looking. She patted her cheeks vigorously several times to induce a little more colour into her face. Her aunt did not approve of rouge. But with so little colour, Meredith felt rather too much like a country mouse. Especially beside the painted face of Miss Fenniston, who was very much a town mouse.

She took a few deep breaths and felt a little better. She was as composed as she would ever be; besides, she couldn't stay in the bathroom forever. A glance at her watch told her it was just a few minutes before ten o'clock. If she was very lucky, their guests might leave soon. But she doubted it—they were all getting on far too well for the evening to end so early. Jeremy was in fine form, and Miss Fenniston—whom the guests so readily addressed as Sheila—was bubbling with friendliness and conversation. She was plying her knowledge of foreign languages to charm the German, French and Italian visitors, whilst ably discussing the latest in cinema and music with the Americans. It was too much to hope that they would all leave any time soon.

She left the bathroom. Crossing the hall, she met her aunt coming from the drawing-room. Mrs Smithies looked highly annoyed.

'What is it, Aunt?' Meredith's heart sank at the thought of some new offence.

'That woman!' her aunt snapped. 'Anyone would think *she* was the hostess, and not myself. Surely they know she is only a secretary? To hear them calling her Sheila, like that! It's too much. Laughing at her jokes. Fawning all over her. They include her in all their conversation and constantly ask her opinion. And the way she addresses Jeremy by his first name. It's insupportable. I thought I made it perfectly clear that you were to speak to him about her.'

'Yes, Aunt Lucinda, and so I did. You saw me leave the room with him.'

'Then a very poor showing you must have made of it. He's worse than ever with her. He actually put his hand on her arm. And now they're talking of going off to a *casino*, of all places. At this time of night!'

Meredith looked at her watch. Dead on ten o'clock. She looked at her aunt in dismay.

'But Jeremy will...'

'Yes, I know. I am quite aware of what Jeremy will do, thank you very much. You hardly need to tell me about my own nephew! We must stop this.'

At that moment the drawing-room door opened, disgorging the guests in search of coats and belongings, ready to take their leave. Jeremy, all smiles and triumphant looks, came over to kiss his aunt and sister, saying:

'Don't know what time I'll get back, so no need to wait up.'

Davies was suddenly there handing the ladies their wraps. The American gentleman, cigar clamped firmly between his teeth, was helping his beautiful daughter into her little fur cape.

'Oh Miss Niedermeyer, I do hope...' Meredith began, but Miss Niedermeyer wasn't listening. Nobody was listening to Meredith's anxious twittering. They were all

concentrating on Jeremy and the glamorous Miss
Fenniston who wore plenty of rouge, and all kinds of
other make-up, expertly applied. Under her aunt's
furious gaze, Meredith tried again. 'But surely it's rather
damp and chilly to be going out at this time of night?
Perhaps we should have some more coffee? How about
a nice game of Bridge?'

Once again, she heard the squeaking of the country
mouse in her voice and was embarrassed. Her aunt
glared at her. Meredith knew it had not been enough,
but what else could she have said?

'Gnädige Fraulein, I thank you for the plentiful
dinner you have made for us. I say at you great thanks
for the nice hospitality, and to you all ladies, good
night.'

The German gentleman, tall, blond and as
handsome at fifty-six as he had been in his thirties,
bowed low as he kissed first Meredith's hand and then
her aunt's.

Jeremy, with a malicious grin, sketched a wave in
their direction. The rest of the company took their
leave, Miss Fenniston and Jeremy ushering everyone
out ahead of them so they could bring up the rear, and
just as the door closed behind them, through the glass
Meredith saw Miss Fenniston tuck her hand into the
crook of Jeremy's arm.

Davies tsked. 'Well I never did,' she said, shaking her
head.

'Yes, all right, Davies, thank you!' snapped Mrs
Smithies. 'You won't be needed again tonight. You may
go.'

The maid left, still craning her neck to see through
the glass of the front door. Meredith and her aunt stood
alone in the hall, like children waiting for a party that
never arrived.

Mrs Smithies rounded on her niece.

'This is all your fault. I don't know why I put up with

your incompetence. I ask you to do one simple little thing, and you make a complete mess of it. Really, Meredith! After all I've done for you and your brother.' Her aunt whirled round to the foot of the stairs, resting her hand on the post in preparation for her ascension, her other hand gripping her stick, her wrap falling from her shoulders. 'I'm going to bed. Thanks to you I now have a migraine. We will talk about this *disaster* in the morning.'

Halfway up the stairs, Mrs Smithies bellowed in a most unladylike manner, 'Davies!'

Davies, used to being dismissed then immediately summoned again, came scurrying from the bowels of the house to follow her mistress up the stairs, collecting the trailing satin wrap as she went.

Meredith took in a deep, quavering breath and went to sit in the morning-room. She left the lights off so she could be still and quiet in the darkened room. She brushed a couple of tears from her cheeks, weary of always being in the wrong, exhausted from the humiliation of being outdone by a tart of a secretary, and cross with herself for giving way.

Clearly it was her aunt's intention to lay all this at her door as usual. But Meredith did not see that she could have done anything different. After all Jeremy was an adult. At almost thirty-eight, he should be completely responsible for his own actions. *Should be.*

What an idiot her brother was! She knew the casino idea must have been his, and was intended purely to spite her. She only hoped he wouldn't lose too much. Or get drunk and offend his business associates. But in drink, Jeremy was not known for his good sense. He was completely lacking in restraint, and his main mission in life had always been to have fun and to deal with the consequences later. Much later.

He came home at a quarter past four in the morning.

She was still waiting for him in her chair in the morning-room. She had dozed, off and on, and was cold and stiff.

But on hearing his key in the lock, she had roused herself, stretching her neck and shoulders. By the time he was actually stepping into the hall, she was standing in the doorway of the morning-room, watching him.

He saw her immediately.

'Here she is, my perfect big shishter,' he said, not troubling to keep his voice down. He slurred his speech. He was drunk again. His sarcastic tone cut her. 'Waiting up for me? Waiting to tattle to Auntie? More like, waiting to have another go at me! Tell me all my faultsh and where I'm going wrong in life? Eh? T-tell me how dishappointed you are with me? Your naughty b-baby brother.'

She didn't speak. He was roaring drunk. She could smell the alcohol on him from across the room. His face was red and slick with sweat, his tie unknotted and hanging down on either side of his crinkled collar. And was that a smudge of crimson lipstick on the white cotton of his shirt collar? He swayed as he stood there. Had he driven himself home in that state? She dreaded to think. She could only hope that the chauffeur, Rodericks, had done the driving. She would get no sense out of him now. In this state, all he wanted was to fight. He raised a wavering finger at her.

'Well I'm going to bed, sho there. You can jusht forget about h-having another go at-at me.'

And he turned and tottered up the stairs. His grip slipped on the polished wooden rail, he dropped to his knees on the step, teetered for a moment, then, having got his balance, hauled himself back onto his feet with the aid of the banister. Concerned, she watched until he made it to the top of the stairs and successfully negotiated the corner. A few moments later she locked the front door then went up to her room. At least he was home safely. Now she could sleep.

At eight o'clock her alarm woke her from a deep sleep. Her first thought was, I forgot to ask him, how much did he lose?

*

Chapter Three

Dee Gascoigne first met Meredith Prescott in the post office on the Thursday morning, two days after the disastrous dinner party.

That morning Dee had received a letter Rob had forwarded to her. At last! She was pleased that one of her job applications had been well-received: she had been invited to attend an interview in London in two weeks' time. She quickly penned an acceptance letter and hurried with it to the post office. She also needed some postcards to send to family and friends.

She had only been in the village for a couple of days but was already beginning to feel stronger in spite of the cough still disturbing her sleep. The briny air was doing her good, she was sure of it. And she was developing a routine. Each morning she went for a walk after breakfast. She began by going along the road to the tiny beach and from there she went into the churchyard via a white-painted wooden gate. Then coming out on the far side of the churchyard by another gate, she crossed a bridge and followed the river a short distance until she came back into the village on the far side of the green. Once back in the village, she could either pop into the post office for a short chat with Cissie, or if she was busy, Dee could go to one of the other two shops, or to the cafe, or go back to the cottage, depending on how she was feeling.

Today she had decided to do her duty and send postcards to her grandparents, her parents and of course one to her brother Rob at the flat. On an impulse she decided to send a card to Miss Evans and her former colleagues at Lady Adelaide Joseph's. She turned the revolving postcard stand and exclaimed aloud at a charming view of the beach, the sea an impossible shade of blue. The picture had been taken from the top of the hill, looking back through the churchyard gates down towards the water.

Her exclamation drew the attention of a woman who had just entered the post office. Dee glanced up and with a grin said, 'Sorry, I got a bit carried away. I really only need three, but these are so sweet, I can't make up my mind.'

Meredith saw a young woman, quite tall but very thin like girls were these days. She had a lot of long reddish brown hair held back out of her eyes by a wide stretchy hairband in bright blue. Her hair was straight but with the latest popular upward flick at the ends, and the girl had huge blue eyes well enhanced by the obligatory jet-black eyeliner and mascara, such as one saw on the screen at a cinema or on the front covers of magazines. She was every bit a pretty girl in the modern style. Meredith glanced at the stand and selecting a card after a moment, held it out to Dee.

'This one has a lovely view of the church with the little bridge and the river beyond.'

Dee took it, smiled and said, 'That is lovely! It doesn't help, I'm afraid, it's easily as nice as the others. Oh, I don't know which ones to choose!'

'Or what about this one? Perhaps you should buy a couple more than you need. I nearly always find I've forgotten someone.'

It wasn't an original thought, but it was the kindness behind it that counted. Dee smiled again. 'Good idea. Thank you. By the way, my name is Dee Gascoigne. I'm staying in the village for a while.' She held out her hand. The other woman pulled off her glove and shook it briefly.

'Then, it's lovely to meet you, my dear. I'm Meredith Prescott.'

Dee noticed the woman was smartly dressed and older than she, and that she was lovely in a tired, delicate way. There was no wedding ring on her hand, so Dee assumed she was unmarried. Though people might think that about her too, she thought, glancing down at her own bare fingers. But she pushed all thoughts of Martin out of her mind. He didn't belong here in this charming spot. She looked down at the cards in her hand. She had six now, plenty to be going on with, in case, as Miss Prescott said, she had forgotten someone, or just wanted to use them as bookmarks or something.

There followed one of those very British scenes where Dee and Miss Prescott each held back to allow the other to go to the counter first. In the end Meredith went up to the counter, although Dee had a feeling that she had wanted to let Dee go first, and not just out of kindness or courtesy. The friendliness she had shown towards Dee was now replaced by a tense, formal manner. Leaning forward over the counter and speaking softly, Meredith pulled a couple of pale blue envelopes from her handbag and pushed them across the counter towards Cissie.

Dee couldn't make out the words exchanged between the two women, but from her tone, Meredith was distinctly put out. After a few minutes, she abruptly concluded her business and left without a backward look, banging the door behind her and leaving the bell jangling.

Dee stepped up to the counter and handed over her letter and the six postcards. The hand that took them from her shook, and she searched Cissie's face. Cissie was flushed and wouldn't meet Dee's eyes. But there was no one else in the shop, so Dee, impulsively putting out her hand, said, 'Cissie, are you quite all right? You're not poorly, are you?'

Cissie seemed surprised and touched by Dee's enquiry. 'I'm quite all right, my dear, thank you. And it's very kind of you to ask. But it's nothing serious, just me being silly. Now then young lady, will you be needing stamps for all these?'

The attempt to continue being businesslike didn't work as well as Cissie had hoped, and she struggled to regain her composure. The urge to relieve her burden was strong. Dee asked for four stamps, so Cissie busied her fingers with extracting the stamps from the folder in front of her on the counter, and at the same time confided to her customer,

'I just wish *some* people would realise that I can't help what *some* people put in the post. It's not my fault if *some* people send *some* people spiteful letters. It's not as though I go through all the post and check what's in it before I deliver it to *some* people, though if I did, I daresay that might solve a number of problems round here. That'll be a shilling for the stamps, and the postcards are tuppence ha'penny each, so that's two shillings and threepence, thank you, dear. And if you can get them written straight away, I'll make sure they go in this afternoon's post.'

Dee handed over a half-crown and waited for her threepence change, biting her lip as she watched the post-mistress's face and wondering whether to say anything else. Clearly something had happened, and

Miss Prescott had taken it out on Cissie, and poor Cissie was still feeling indignant. Cissie counted the change into Dee's hand.

Taking the plunge, Dee said, 'I'm sure no one could possibly blame you for getting bills in the post. All of us hate getting bills, but it's not the fault of the post office. And after all bills have got to be paid, haven't they? I'm sure you do an admirable job, Cissie. This is such a busy little place, and you manage it all on your own.'

'Bless you, dear,' Cissie said with the ghost of a smile. 'No, it's not bills as Miss Prescott—um—I mean *some* people are complaining about. But never you mind. You're supposed to be getting yourself better, aren't you? Nasty thing, bronchitis. But you've got a bit more colour in your cheeks today, I'm glad to see. Deathly pale you was, when you got off that train.'

She seemed calm again, so Dee gladly accepted the change in subject and they chatted on happily for another ten minutes. Cissie issued an invitation to supper which Dee accepted with pleasure.

When she left the post office a few minutes later, she was still puzzling over the little scene between Cissie and the unknown Miss Prescott, and what Cissie had said about it. What sort of letters did people get that they didn't want, if it wasn't bills?

Dee decided to have a light lunch in the cafe opposite the seafront. The place seemed almost deserted. Though it suited her perfectly, she wondered if it was always this quiet. She still felt too wonky to be anywhere noisy or hectic, in addition to which too much activity still sent her into a coughing fit.

She chose a table near the window so that she could look out in either direction, at the village street or the sea, as she ate. Whilst she was waiting for her pot of tea and her plate of egg and chips to arrive, she wrote her postcards: the first one to her parents and brother

Freddie, and the second to her grandparents, Herbert
and Lavinia Manderson, still living in the same elegant
Georgian townhouse in London that they had moved
into as newlyweds in 1910. She then wrote the third
postcard, and addressed it to the headmistress, Miss
Evans and all her former colleagues at Lady Adelaide
Joseph's. As she wrote, she could already imagine the
postcard on the noticeboard in the smoke-filled
staffroom where everyone would see it.

Finally she wrote the fourth postcard to send to her
brother Rob back at the new flat. She crammed in as
much of her neat writing as she could on the 'news' side
of the postcard, telling him the sea air was wonderful
and the area pretty, and that she was feeling much
better. What else was there to say?

She put the cards away in her handbag to post later
and turned her attention to her meal. As she ate, she
gazed out the window at the view. Directly in front of
her, a seagull marched up and down in the middle of
the road as if on patrol. The café was a good central
spot, but Dee was not really conscious of the view. With
little else to occupy her, she was still puzzling over that
small scene in the post office.

Why would a well-to-do and well-educated woman,
clearly a pillar of the community, think that it was the
fault of the post-mistress when she got an unwanted
letter? More than one, in fact. Dee remembered at least
two if not three envelopes in Miss Prescott's gloved
hand. Two or perhaps three envelopes of a pale blue,
cheap paper, addressed in a neat but childish hand,
written with what looked like a splodgy fountain pen
rather than a biro or pencil.

Why be upset about something you received through
the post? It didn't make sense to Dee. She could only
think of one answer to the riddle. Because surely there
was only one kind of letter that people got that would
be upsetting? If it wasn't a bill as she had at first

Caron Allan

assumed, and these couldn't have been. Bills were an inevitable but less-than-welcome part of everyday life. She wondered if perhaps there had been a mix-up about the amount, and Cissie had somehow overcharged Miss Prescott? But no, that wouldn't be right. Cissie had been quite clear that Miss Prescott hadn't been complaining about a bill, and Cissie had definitely said the envelopes contained something 'spiteful'. A bill, however unwelcome, would never be described as spiteful.

And if the letters contained bad news, perhaps about a medical condition or a relative's health, or a job application, or... Dee shook her head as she mulled this over. No, that wouldn't work. None of that seemed to fit with the word, 'spiteful'.

In any case, she now realised as she pushed her empty plate aside and reached for her teacup, bills were not sent out in handwritten envelopes of blue paper. There were clerks who typed invoices and envelopes for customers of businesses. She had even done the job herself many summers ago during her holidays from college. Her typing had been awful, so she had never been in danger of giving up the idea of teaching to be a secretary or work in a typing pool. But some of the girls where she worked had typed so fast, their fingers had been a virtual blur on the keys; they had finished half a dozen addresses to Dee's one. But these envelopes of Miss Prescott's had definitely been handwritten.

Surely only one kind of letter was left when other possibilities had been discarded, and that was...

The door opened and a very smartly dressed woman came in. She sat at the other table by the window, sending a curtly dismissive nod in Dee's direction as she took her seat. Dee was left feeling prickled.

Lily Glover, the woman who ran the café, approached the newcomer with her pencil and pad ready to take down her order. But the customer waved her away with a rather rude, 'Oh just a pot of tea, Lily. I don't want anything to eat, I'm watching my figure.'

Dee wondered how the cafe managed to keep going in the quieter parts of the year when hardly anyone ordered anything more than a pot of tea.

The teapot and milk jug were brought over and deposited on the table next to the cup and saucer and the sugar bowl with its perfectly polished tiny tongs that had already been neatly set in the centre of the table, as on all the other tables. Mrs Glover retreated once more behind her counter, casting glowering looks at the smart woman.

Outside, a few people wandered past. One of them was a gentleman in a business suit that was far too well-cut and modern for this little place. He was good-looking in a conventional way, and Dee put his age in the mid-thirties, a few years older than herself. As soon as she spied him, the smart lady at the other table set down her cup in its saucer with a clatter and shoving back her chair, hurried to the door as fast as her high heels and the cluster of tables and chairs would permit. She threw the door open and called loudly to the gentleman in a manner Dee instinctively knew her mother would have set down as 'low'. Dee exchanged a look with Mrs Glover, who stood watching the performance from behind her counter.

'Jeremy! Jeremy, over here!'

The gentleman halted in his stride and turned. To Dee his expression did not indicate any pleasure in seeing the smart woman. However, she didn't seem to notice, and assuming a girlish coyness that Dee found grating, the woman said, 'Sorry, Jeremy, were you looking for me? Did you need me for something?'

It was perfectly plain from his expression that he had neither been looking for the woman nor did he need her for anything, but the woman persisted. He came over, no doubt to avoid her bellowing at him again. She stepped back in the doorway, and seemingly without being aware of what he was doing, he followed her inside.

'I'm just having a pot of tea, if you would care to join me. I know it's rather a dull spot, but there's little enough choice in this place. And it will do you good to get away from your desk for a while.'

Clearly, he had already been away from his desk, Dee thought, and it looked as though he had been on his way to walk to the church or the seafront. But for whatever reason, probably just out of politeness, he joined the woman at her table.

Behind her counter, Mrs Glover pursed her mouth at the implied criticism of her establishment of which she was no doubt very proud. The man took the seat opposite the smart woman who immediately began to chatter and gush at him, simultaneously holding aloft an imperious hand to Mrs Glover. Thus summoned, Mrs Glover approached the table for the second time in five minutes with her pencil and pad at the ready, only for the gentleman to shake his head.

'Oh, nothing for me, thank you. I'm about to go back to the house for lunch.' He glanced at the woman who had, to Dee's mind, practically dragged him into the cafe and said, 'Why don't you join us? I'm sure Meredith will be expecting you in any case.'

And so they left, pausing only for Jeremy to leave a few coins on the table to pay for the woman's untouched pot of tea.

When the door had slammed shut behind them, Mrs Glover came across to clear the table and to take the money.

'You're most welcome, I'm sure,' she said in the direction of the door.

Dee couldn't help remarking, 'Gosh, how very rude!' Her ready sympathy created an immediate bond between her and the proprietress.

'And no better than she should be, let me tell you,' Mrs Glover replied.

'Did she call him Jeremy?' Dee asked.

'That was Jeremy Prescott, chairman and owner of the wine business up the road, and a kind of Lord of the Manor.'

'Prescott?' Dee asked. 'I met a lady in the post office earlier, she had the same surname.'

'That would be his sister, Meredith Prescott. She's a lovely lady, and I do mean, a *lady*. Unlike that Miss Fenniston, Sheila, that was just here. She calls herself his secretary, but I don't think there's a soul in the village that thinks that's what she really is, not for one moment. She's after him, and she's that determined, she's sure to get him. He's proper spineless even if he is a gentleman. She's too fast for any of them and mark my words, it'll end in tears.'

Dee was thinking about this as she sat there with her drink.

That evening, Meredith ran into him at the top of the stairs. She concentrated on buttoning up her coat and said nothing, still angry with him about the dinner party. She couldn't help noticing, though, that his late-night revelries had left no signs on his face: he was as fresh and full of energy as he always was. She was even more annoyed that he could behave so badly, so childishly, yet still look so handsome. No wonder all the women threw themselves at him.

'Going out?' His tone was jaunty. Clearly he'd made up his mind to forget all about their scene after dinner, forget how furious she'd made him, she thought. She nodded curtly.

'It's Thursday. I'm off to read to Mrs Hunter, as always.'

'The old hag won't thank you for it. Just leave a few cheap magazines with her, let her entertain herself. We do enough for this place as it is.'

Meredith frowned now. 'You know she can't. Her eyesight's too poor. Besides, it's company for her.'

'She's got all the company she needs, cooking up trouble with that granddaughter of hers. And *she's* a real chip off the old block. The rumours I've heard about dear little Marlene.'

'I never pay attention to gossip,' Meredith snapped. Then, 'What do you mean, cooking up trouble?'

'What do you suppose I mean?'

'I don't know. How could I? But you sounded as though you meant something in particular.'

'Oh, you know. Just the things one hears when one listens to gossip.' He turned to walk away along the hall. Over his shoulder, his parting shot was, 'I think what surprised me the most was that either of them knew how to write.'

'What on earth do you mean by that?'

But he was gone.

*

Chapter Four

Mrs Hunter greeted Meredith with the words, 'You're late!' and a sly grin, saliva collecting in the corner of her mouth in a way that turned Meredith's stomach. Why was the old woman so vile?

Nevertheless, Meredith smiled, pulled out the upright wooden chair, which she knew would be so hard it would make her behind go completely numb within ten minutes. She placed the bag of apples on the filthy counterpane of the bed before taking out the book, and finding the place where she'd left off on her previous visit. 'Oh, I'm sorry about that Mrs Hunter, I'm afraid it was difficult to get away this evening. Now where were we? Ah yes...'

'Your aunt sending you on more errands, was it?' She gawped at Meredith with cloudy eyes, hungry for news, or better yet, scandal. For a nearly blind old woman, she seemed to see everything.

Meredith was conscious of a deep revulsion for Mrs Hunter. But she merely smiled, and glancing down again at the page said, 'To quickly recap, Miss

Armstrong had just met the consultant, Dr Phipps, in the corridor of the hospital, and he had some upsetting news to tell her.' The saliva was dripping slowly down the old woman's chin and onto the front of the none-too-clean nightdress.

'I expect her old mother's got some terrible wasting condition, and no doubt he'll be on hand to comfort that prim-and-proper Miss Armstrong. You know what men are.' Mrs Hunter gave a scurrilous meaning to the word 'comfort' and giggled to herself. Meredith tried not to frown and look disgusted.

'Er, quite. Well, we shall have to just wait and see. So then, chapter nine.' She opened her mouth to begin reading again, and the old woman belched and excused herself, then said,

'I could do with some handsome young doctor with a friendly bedside manner. That old beggar Bartlett is as boring as a Sunday sermon, and I reckon he's past it, don't you? We could do with some fresh blood in the village. Someone young and virile.'

Privately agreeing with Mrs Hunter's assessment of Dr Bartlett, Meredith nonetheless began to read. She made her voice warm and soft, keeping her tone even, hoping that by doing so, she would lull the objectionable old woman to sleep within a short while. That would make the hour go by far more pleasantly and give Meredith the opportunity to carry out her private errand.

Sure enough, within fifteen minutes, the old woman was snoring loudly, her mouth dropping open in sleep to reveal the bare wet gums. As quietly as she could, Meredith slipped from the chair, took up the shopping bag she'd brought with her, and left the room, easing the door closed behind her.

As soon as Meredith left the room, Mrs Hunter opened first one eye then the other, glanced about the room, and seeing she was now alone, she grinned to herself. Wait until she told Marlene about that. What fun they could have with this knowledge.

Meredith returned just a few minutes later, again opening the door as quietly as she could, and entering practically on her tiptoes. Then she picked up the book, found her place, and with a quick glance at the face of the sleeping old woman, Meredith began to read once more, keeping her tone soft and soothing.

The remainder of the hour had not passed quite as pleasantly as she'd hoped, Meredith thought ruefully as she closed the cottage gate and went home to the manor house later that evening. During her slumber, Mrs Hunter's corpulent frame had produced some astonishingly loud and unpleasant sounds, and the smell had forced Meredith to move her seat back several feet from the bedside. It had been utterly disgusting, and not for the first time. Sometimes it required an almost superhuman effort to make herself go to the cottage twice a week and do her good deed. Although in other ways the evening had been a success.

It irritated her that Mrs Hunter's predictions about the book had proved correct: Dr Phipps had indeed proceeded to offer 'comfort' to Miss Armstrong in a variety of ways, none of which had been hinted at by the bland cover or the recommendation of the vicar's wife who was volunteering at the village library that day. Meredith would definitely make a complaint next time she went to the library, it was her duty to ensure everyone knew the content of this book. No one wanted to read that kind of thing outloud to a geriatric.

And, 'Fanks for them apples,' the old lady had said, without an ounce of gratitude in her voice, and again, she spoke in that sarcastic tone that made Meredith feel so inept.

But she had done her duty to the poor and needy. She huffed to herself then put the ungrateful woman out of her mind. She was almost home now. She turned her thoughts back once more to her brother and his problems.

Norman Slough frowned over his pint of bitter in the bar of The Seagull public house. He was thinking. And he was drinking. The subject of his dark thoughts was Sheila Fenniston. He felt aggrieved.

Norman was in love with Miss Fenniston. Until recently he had thought that Sheila returned his feelings and that they had made a well-matched couple on the two occasions he had taken her to the picture-house in Sandneath. Then she had accompanied him to the dinner-and-dance at Prescott's. He felt that they looked very fine together but also that when his colleagues and the Prescotts saw them arrive together, her hand tucked into the crook of his arm, they also thought she and he looked very fine together, he was convinced of it.

Then, when he had walked her home to her rooms at Mrs Hunter's, she had permitted him to kiss her. The next morning there was a new respect for him in the eyes of his colleagues. At last they could see he was going to make something of himself, that he wasn't just another blue-collared member of the masses. Norman Slough had an attractive lady-friend and he was going to amount to something.

But that had been three weeks ago. Since then, Norman's happy little bubble had burst. And now he felt aggrieved.

He had even bought a car, admittedly second-hand but nevertheless very clean and smart, if not exactly the most recent model. He had wanted to be able to take Miss Fenniston—Sheila—about at the weekends. He had asked her to go and see the new film starring Raquel Welsh at the picture-house in Sandneath but he had been rebuffed repeatedly and with increasing impatience.

The chaps in the warehouse had been asking him when he was seeing Miss Fenniston again. *Sheila*, they all called her in stupid sing-song sarcastic voices, so disrespectfully. So now he had to keep inventing excuses to save face, but in their eyes he could see he had not only slipped back to his old, despised position but had actually fallen even lower in their estimation. He knew they all thought he had tried too high and fallen flat on his face. He was a failure.

She—it was clear to Norman now—she was still trying high. She was daily ingratiating herself and rendering herself more and more indispensable to Jeremy Prescott. Rumours abounded regarding events that took place at the conference they had attended together. Rumours concerning how many hotel rooms the company had been invoiced for, and how much champagne. A cold fury stirred in the pit of Norman's stomach. Now, finally, he could see her ultimate aim. She was aiming far, far higher than a mere warehouseman. Sheila Fenniston was intending to succeed where all others had failed—she was going to snare Jeremy Prescott, and elevate herself out of the workday crowd to a position of moneyed security.

Norman was not good enough for her. Norman's car was not good enough for her either. She aspired to something much newer, much bigger. He had been her plaything, used and thrown aside. Now he was a walking object of scorn: she cared not a scrap for him and everyone could see it.

Norman Slough took another draft of his beer and thought his cold thoughts.

Over a wonderful steak and mushroom pie, Cissie told Dee everything she knew. Dee found out all about the source of the Prescott fortune, all about Miss Prescott's lost love who had gone away just three weeks before their wedding and never been heard from again, leaving her to carry on sharing her late parents' house with her brother and their widowed aunt. She heard all about the old aunt, Mrs Smithies, and all her imaginary aches and pains, and how she made Meredith Prescott, who had the patience of several saints, run herself ragged to keep her aunt happy.

Dee also heard about the other inhabitants of the village, and about those mysterious pale blue envelopes she had seen in Miss Prescott's hand in the post office that morning, which gratified Dee's curiosity a good deal.

'She *is* a lady, I'll grant you that,' Cissie told Dee who had had no compunction about passing on everything Mrs Glover had told her following the incident in the cafe. 'She is a lady,' Cissie repeated. 'But as you saw for yourself, she can be a little imperious at times. Not that she fancies herself or gives herself airs, but it's just there in the breeding, isn't it? I will say it upset me at the time, but now I've thought about it, I don't think she really meant it the way I took it, it was just that she was upset about the letters.'

And little by little Dee got to the bottom of it, much to her own satisfaction. She hated not knowing things.

'That's three of those poison pen letters Miss Meredith's had, and there's been one to the vicar. And two or three to that smart piece, Miss Fenniston, and even Norman Slough, he's a warehouseman up at the Wines. He's had one too, of all people.'

Dee had walked past the warehouse with its huge sign proclaiming *Prescott's Wines: Second To None!* and bearing the legend underneath, 'Importing Superior Wines From Our Exclusive Continental Growers: from our cask to your table'. The warehouse, a sprawling unsightly barn-like prefabricated building, was situated on the outskirts of the village a few hundred yards beyond the manor house. Practically as soon as she had arrived, Dee had become aware that the

Prescott's wine business dominated the village. Every morning a steady stream of villagers walked along the road to the warehouse to begin a new day's work, and in the evening, back they came again, marking the end of another day. But without the warehouse there would only be a scattering of farms, the village itself with its four shops, church and village hall, which together would offer precious little work for those who lived in the area. As it was, she estimated almost all the local men were employed by the firm, along with at least one woman—Miss Fenniston.

'Why would this warehouse fellow get one?' Dee asked, puzzled. She quickly declined a second helping of the apple crumble and custard, reflecting it was one thing to be building up her strength but quite another to end up the size of the kindly Cissie. It had been a long time since she had eaten so well and so heartily, but there was not the remotest possibility of swallowing another mouthful. 'What do the letters say? What are they about? I always thought that sort of thing only existed in old films.'

Cissie looked at Dee. She was still quite young, to be sure, Cissie thought, but she'd obviously had some experience of the world and of life. There might be no ring on her finger, but Cissie knew the girl was still married. She'd chosen badly and had her heart broken, Cissie knew. But oh, to be that young again, almost your whole life ahead of you, with all its possibilities. It was such a shame to let real life spoil all that goodness and hope in the young lady. Cissie felt quite moved for a moment. Then her natural common sense reasserted itself. Dee had a good sensible head on her shoulders, and a kind, caring way about her. Given time she'd recover, and no doubt find a new love.

'Well dear, I haven't actually seen one of them myself, but I can imagine the sort of thing they contain. Any little bit of gossip, all bent out of shape, any little secret or sorrow, or shameful desire taken out of all proportion and made to seem dirty.'

Dee still shook her head. 'I just don't see why people get upset. I mean, why can't they just put the letters in the dustbin or on the fire and forget about them?'

Cissie smiled. 'Think about it like this,' she said. 'Imagine you lived in a tiny little place like this, where you knew everyone. Then imagine one day you opened a letter, you didn't know who it was from, for they never sign these poison pen letters. And when you looked at it, it said something like, 'I know you killed your mother to get all her money'. Think how you'd feel, to get something like that. And you'd know that somewhere in the village was a person who really thought it was true, but you didn't know who it was and you didn't know how many others they'd tell. And suppose you were frightened everyone would believe them, and that they were all looking at you too. Suppose your friends began to hear rumours and believed them. Suppose they stopped speaking to you and began to avoid you...'

Dee stared at Cissie and her delicate colour faded from her face so quickly Cissie was afraid she had gone too far to make her point. She felt cruel. She reached out a hand to pat Dee's arm. 'There, there, dear, don't let it upset you. I was just trying to explain...'

In a soft, distressed voice, Dee said, 'But that's horrible, I've never thought of it like that before.'

'Exactly, dearie. But that's the kind of wickedness these letters contain. Now imagine getting three like that in a fortnight. And everyone you know, everyone you meet, you'd look at them and think, was it you what sent me that? You'd feel like you was being watched, my dear, and you wouldn't know where to turn or who to go to, nor would you be able to sleep for fear of what the next day would bring, and you'd wonder if people knew and if they thought it was true. Even I've had one. Accused me of stealing money out of the birthday cards that were put in the post. And I've never stolen a thing in my life.' Cissie pulled her shoulders back and lifted her head, the very model of moral rectitude.

Dee stared at Cissie. Her eyes were wide and troubled. 'Of course you haven't. You wouldn't. Did you keep the letter?'

'No, my dear. I threw it in the fire where it belonged.'

'What about going to the police?'

'Ah well, any sensible person would go direct to them and have done with it. I suppose I should have done that. But as I said, I just threw it in the fire, and I haven't had any more of them, touch wood.' She briefly tapped the corner of the table. 'But of course, some people might not want to admit they've had the letters. They'd be afraid of losing face, or of people getting to know too much about them or possibly they'd think the police would believe what the letters said and make trouble. So most people just hide the letters away or burn them or something. But they don't forget what the letters say. It plays on their minds. And so that's why I feel more sorry for Miss Meredith than angry about her snapping at me.'

Dee, leaning forward, said with frank curiosity, 'So did you see what was in the letters Miss Prescott had in her hand?'

There was real regret in Cissie's voice when she set down her cup and said, 'Do you know, I'm sorry to say I couldn't make out a word of it from where I was. She had them all folded up inside their envelopes.'

Later that night, Dee curled herself up in one of the squashy armchairs in the sitting-room of the cottage and thought about the poison pen letters Cissie had mentioned. Dee was intrigued about what the letters might contain and couldn't seem to keep her thoughts on any other topic for long. Again and again she returned to the letters. She wondered how many people had received one. And who could possibly be behind them?

She longed to really discuss them with someone. Who was writing poison pen letters in Porthlea? Surely someone had to know more than she had so far discovered from Cissie.

She thought of the characters of the village that she had already come to know. Who was the type of person to enjoy the misery of other people? The first face that sprang to mind was that of Mrs Hunter, who lived in the cottage next door but one. Dee thought about her: an elderly widow, practically blind, and needed a wheelchair to get about. She was usually to be seen being pushed along by her granddaughter Marlene. Yet in spite of her several infirmities, Mrs H, as Dee privately called her, seemed thoroughly nosy and to enjoy a good gossip. I bet she knows everything that goes on in the village, Dee thought.

She reflected a moment and then mentally dismissed her phrase 'enjoy a good gossip' and changed it to, 'positively loves to gossip, especially if about something bad'. She had seen Mrs Hunter outside the pub commiserating with the vicar over the loss of his curate, an event which had happened a month or so before Dee's arrival. Whilst the vicar seemed upset and tried to steer her onto a new topic, Mrs H had been virtually drooling over the subject, her gummy mouth open in a wide grin, her large loose lips wet with saliva. It had made Dee feel as though she was observing something secret and foul and not meant for her eyes. She remembered Mrs Hunter's face. The old woman's faded blue eyes were cloudy and staring, seeing little, but her sharp wits meant she knew everything and believed the worst. Mrs Hunter enjoyed life in all its drama.

If anyone knows all the secrets, it's that nasty old woman, Dee thought.

At the end of an hour, she felt as though she had

watched a play as she revisited various scenes she had witnessed over the few days since her arrival, replaying everything she had seen and heard.

The smart middle-aged gentleman with his plump black Labrador. The vicar out on his rounds. Marlene and her boyfriend locked in an embrace on the corner outside the pub. Meredith Prescott. Cissie at her post office counter. The vicar's wife in the library, helping people to find a good book. The large American car that swept grandly through the village, its driver hidden by a tweed shooting cap and sunglasses.

It was as though the village of Porthlea was a play come to life, and the *dramatis personae* had been made flesh. But the characters all knew their lines, their cues, and she was like a member of the Greek chorus: not part of the play, but there at the edge of the stage, ready to watch and to comment on the action, or perhaps to learn a vital life-lesson from it.

Feeling drowsy now, she got up to go to bed. She wished the cottage ran to a telephone, she would have liked to talk to Rob. She knew he was not able to get down to the cottage this weekend, but he had said he hoped to come down the following weekend, and then after that it would only be two or three days before she was due to travel home again to London for the dreaded interview.

She undressed and put out the light, then opened the heavy curtains to let in the breeze. Getting into bed, she battered her pillows into the right shape, and lay back, gazing at the stars that shone in a night sky of the darkest blue. Presently she drifted off and enjoyed a dream in which she stood up in court and read to the judge from her exercise book. At which point, Dee turned into a child in school uniform, and the judge was transformed into Miss Evans, the headmistress of the school where she used to work, and Miss Evans had said, 'Very nicely read, Dee, dear. And what lovely neat handwriting. Two house-points to you.'

'Dear Miss Evans,' Dee thought as she turned over in bed and yet again rearranged her pillows. 'She's been so kind to me.'

She remembered this when she awoke to a fine, bright Friday morning, and she smiled at the thought of herself giving evidence in a courtroom. How ridiculous.

*

Chapter Five

On Saturday, the first day of May, a Spring Fair was held in the village. When Dee left the cottage that morning, preparations were well under way.

She was fascinated to see the stalls being assembled as benches were carried out and set up in the middle of the single main street. Snowy tablecloths were unfurled to cover the bare unfinished wood of the trestles that covered the entire green. Next signs, games, produce and flowers, streamers and banners all began to make their appearance. The fair was taking shape before her very eyes.

And all the while, music tinkled from an old-fashioned organ and people seemed to be everywhere, if not actually busy then they were watching and commenting on the goings-on. Surely there were already far more people present than the village actually contained?

Lily Glover, from the seafront café, had set up a tea stall near the supposed entrance. She'd already had half a dozen customers, even though the fair wasn't officially open.

Dee thought it odd that there was an 'entrance' when it seemed as if the whole village was already amongst the stalls. Getting out her purse, she went over and handed her sixpence to the distinguished-looking gentleman she had seen several times out walking with his dog.

He gave her a ticket and with a polite tip of his straw trilby, introduced himself as Major Reeves. She smiled and shook his hand, saying, 'Pleased to meet you, I'm Dee Gascoigne.'

Major Reeves beamed at her and said, 'I've seen you about the village, of course. Having a pleasant holiday?'

'Oh yes, thank you,' she said. 'I'm staying in one of the little cottages over there, the one belonging to Mrs Palmer from the post office. I'm recuperating really, although there's not much wrong with me now. But this is such a lovely spot.'

'Can't beat the British seaside, can you, for a lovely summer's day? Sorry to hear you've been on the sick list. Not down here all on your own, surely?'

'Oh—er—yes, at the moment. One of my brothers is coming down next weekend if he can get away from London.'

She noticed the major was surveying the growing crowds of chattering people who milled about, and she couldn't help wondering if he was looking for someone in particular. Her suspicions were confirmed as soon as Meredith Prescott came into sight. The major's expression softened and he grew a little pink in the face. He turned back to Dee and said, 'Very nice to have met you, Miss Gascoigne. Could I—could I possibly impose on you? Could you possibly mind the shop for me for just a few minutes? Only there's someone I must just catch for a quick word. Would you mind awfully?'

Dee smiled and said quite sincerely that she would be delighted. He pointed out the sign which laid out the terms and as he dashed off, boyishly excited, Dee turned to see Mrs Hunter and her grand-daughter Marlene waiting to pay their entrance fees.

They paid, ignoring Dee as they stared after the major. Marlene leaned forward to say loudly in her grandmother's ear, 'Look at 'im go. The galloping major. You were right Gran, he's in hot pursuit!'

'Wasting his time,' her gran pronounced. 'She's got no eyes for anyone but her precious baby brother. And we know who *he's* after, don't we?' She gave a wheezy cackle. As Marlene pushed the wheelchair onwards, Dee wondered whether the local children thought Old Mrs Hunter was a witch. She wouldn't be in the least surprised if they did. Something told her the old woman would relish the idea.

Dee had sold several tickets by the time the major reappeared, smiling outwardly but carrying with him an acute sense of disappointment.

'Didn't you manage to find her?' Dee asked.

'Yes I did. Thank you for asking. But um, sadly, the er—person—has other engagements at present.' He seemed to give himself a mental shake, and said more vigorously, 'Not to worry, always tomorrow, as they say, what? I say, you've taken a good bit of cash! Jolly good, jolly good indeed. And really *jolly* good of you to step in for me. But I mustn't keep you here all day. After all, you have already paid your sixpence!'

He smiled his kind smile and Dee felt sad for him.

She said, 'If you get a chance to speak to your friend a bit later, I'll cover for you here again.'

He patted her shoulder a little awkwardly. 'Thank you, m'dear. Very kind.'

There was a coconut-shy nearby. Dee was never able to knock the coconuts off their perches, but she always enjoyed watching the young men trying to win one for their girlfriends. She smiled as one lucky fellow proudly presented his trophy to his lady, and the stall owner, Mr

Higgins, sent sour looks after them as he filled the empty space with a new coconut.

The stalls were in full swing, with people thronging round them.

There was a used babywear stall, with several young mothers and some older matrons unfolding shawls and overalls and holding them up to get a proper look, as Millie Edmonds the vicar's wife, looked on, frowning at the disarray they were creating. Next to the babywear stall was a handicraft stall, laid out neatly with row upon row of various examples of all kinds of needlework, and overseen by the same Mrs Edmonds. But knitting didn't really interest Dee, so she turned from the handicrafts to the comforting sight of the cake stall.

The cake stall appeared to be under siege. Dee paused to lend a hand here too, working for several frantic minutes to wrap and hand over sticky buns or whole cakes and single slices of cake to the eager hands holding out pennies and sixpences. When the queue had gone, Mrs Higgins, Eddie's mother, mopped her face and neck with a handkerchief and surveyed the wreckage of her display woefully.

'Every year I makes more, and every year they is all sold by halfway through the fair. I can't keep up with demand.'

'It's your fault for making such delicious cakes,' Dee said. She leaned forward to tidy the table a little and brushed a few crumbs into her hand to tip into the rubbish-bin behind her. Mrs Higgins bent to reach underneath the table and draw out some large, covered baskets. Dee hurried to help her lift the heavy baskets onto the table.

'Good thing I kept a few cakes and whatnot under here. I never puts everything out all at once,' she said with complacence. Dee handed over a penny and grabbed the last slice of an iced cherry cake and ate it immediately from the paper bag.

'I wish I could still eat the way you young ones can,' Mrs Higgins said. 'And speaking of which, there's one as isn't as young as she makes out. Nor as classy neither.'

Dee followed Mrs Higgins's gaze to rest on Miss Fenniston, lighting a cigarette and looking about her with impatience, a deep frown drawing her brows together.

'Isn't that Mr Prescott's secretary?' Dee asked. A man she didn't recognise came up and began to speak to Miss Fenniston.

'If that's all she is, I'd be surprised,' Mrs Higgins said darkly. 'In my day we was told, a man won't buy the cow if he can get the milk for free. 'Course, I doubt she's actually giving it away for nothing.'

Dee said nothing. Relations between the sexes, as she knew to her cost, were very different from the idealised, romantic picture she had grown up with. But at the same time, she felt indignant that all the blame over any 'goings-on' fell only on Miss Fenniston's shoulders, and no guilt or shame was attached to Jeremy Prescott. No doubt his behaviour was considered to be perfectly normal, even acceptable. If Miss Fenniston had refused his advances, would she have lost her job? Dee strongly suspected that would be the case. She watched as the conversation between Miss Fenniston and this new man appeared to grow heated.

In the end, with a very audible, 'I said, no!' Miss Fenniston turned on her heel and marched away. The man, noticing at last that he was being observed, hurried off in the opposite direction.

'That wasn't Mr Prescott, was it?' Dee asked. 'I've only seen him once, but...'

'No ducks, that's her brother. That'll be tuppence please, my lovely.' Turning away to serve a customer, Mrs Higgins handed a paper bag of baked goods to a small child who skipped away happily with her treasure, having paid with sticky halfpennies. 'He lives in the next village, I think. Don't know what he does for a living though. Mind you,' she said, turning back to Dee, 'She's the type of woman as comes unstuck. The men fairly flock after her, that I do know. But for all her worldly ways, she's the type as always goes for a wrong 'un. Well, go on, missy, you don't need to spend the whole time helping me, you're supposed to be having fun!'

Dee smiled and promised to return if Mrs Higgins was inundated again.

She spent some time looking around, buying raffle tickets here and tombola tickets or homemade conserves there. She talked to everyone she met. Although it was still less than a week since her arrival, she already knew many people by sight, if not personally.

The fair was now well and truly underway, and business was brisk. Outside The Seagull pub, a man was shouting and waving a fist at someone he had bumped into. The other man told him in no uncertain terms where to go, and kept moving, and the drunkard staggered away in the opposite direction.

At half past eleven, the village children assembled for a demonstration of country dancing. They were more enthusiastic than graceful, but their enjoyment of the dances was evident and infectious. Families stood around, clapping and bobbing up and down in time to the music, mothers waved and fathers nodded proudly as their offspring passed, and the children's faces grew pink and hot with their exertions. Hair escaped from ribbons and clung to necks and cheeks, and the shirts of the little boys came untucked from their grey school shorts.

Dee admired the brightly coloured frocks the girls

wore, and the handsome waistcoats of the boys, no doubt the work of the mothers, grandmothers and aunts of the village children. Looking around her with fresh eyes, she saw as if for the first time all the work, the care, and the pride that had gone into the event.

All too often villages were disappearing altogether as the younger generation left to find work in the cities and the older generations died off, or cities expanded, swallowing up nearby villages and small towns into suburbia. But here it seemed as though nothing had changed for fifty years. Or perhaps a hundred.

Dee was roused from her introspection by the ending of the final dance. The judges, Miss Prescott and her aunt Mrs Smithies, and the vicar's wife, Millie from the needlework and babywear stalls, deliberated before stepping forth to announce the 'winners' of the several dances. Jeremy Prescott stood nearby, stifling a yawn and doing a poor job of concealing his boredom. His attention was wandering. He smiled and nodded to Dee. He also exchanged a smile from time to time with Miss Fenniston who was watching the dancing.

A large crowd had gathered to watch the children. Dee noticed that Mrs Hunter, her chair positioned right at the front, commanded an excellent view. Marlene was crouched on the ground next to her, and Dee could see her whispering behind her hand to her grandmother. The old lady was nodding. Not so deaf as she makes out, Dee decided. Beside them stood the major, whose eyes never left the object of his affection, his expression one of longing.

Miss Prescott looked cool and pretty in an old-fashioned tweed skirt, topped by a pastel blue twinset and pearls. Her light brown hair was caught back in a loose bun low on the back of her neck, and even from here, Dee could tell that Meredith wore no make-up at all. She was the epitome of a refined lady of the traditional country gentry.

By contrast, Miss Fenniston couldn't help but stand out from the crowd: her hair, an improbably bright red, was arranged in a beehive, adding easily six inches to her normal height. Her lipstick was over-bright. No one else was wearing lipstick of any shade let alone a vivid colour like that. The over-smart, short-skirted suit, and the precariously high heels all made her remarkable. Everyone seemed to be staring at her. Dee wondered if Miss Fenniston was aware of the looks she drew, and if so, how did she feel about it. Did she crave the attention or feel embarrassed by it? The young girls and women looked with envy at the hair, the make-up. The young men—and quite a few of the older ones—looked with thinly-disguised lust. The older generation looked at her with all the amused interest of spectators at a museum or art gallery.

How did it feel, Dee wondered, to be set so firmly apart from village life? Sheila looked as out of place as if she had been naked. She was staring at her employer with a fixed expression, although once or twice, Dee saw her turn to address a snapping comment to a man behind her. Dee could only make out a part of his shoulder, but she thought it was a different man to the one she had seen quarrelling with Miss Fenniston earlier—this chap's jacket was brown not navy. He moved slightly and now Dee realised this was the staggering drunk man from earlier. She saw his hand come up to Miss Fenniston's shoulder and he attempted to turn her to face him, but she shook him off impatiently and turned away, apparently intent on watching the children although Dee was sure Miss Fenniston was in fact once again gazing at Jeremy Prescott, her employer. Or more than that, if local gossip was to be believed.

Village gossip was, Dee thought, usually greatly to be relied upon. Her mother always said so. And as Nanny Minter had been wont to say now and again when she thought her young charges out of earshot, 'There's no smoke without fire.'

Jeremy Prescott appeared to be lost in his own thoughts, his smile was becoming rather fixed, and he was a little late joining in with the clapping each time a child came up to receive their prize. By contrast, his sister clapped enthusiastically and smiled, and had a word for each of the winners. Mrs Smithies was handing out the ribbons and the small, neatly wrapped package that was each child's prize. But where Jeremy was distant, Mrs Smithies was condescending, appearing as one who carries out an onerous duty. Dee was glad to see the children did not notice and were thrilled to the core to receive their prizes. Dee decided that Mrs Smithies was a bit too superior to be kind. But Meredith chatted with each and every child, sending them away with a happy smile to go with their prize. Dee's heart warmed to the woman, and she wondered if there was any way she could somehow direct Miss Prescott towards the very much smitten Major Reeves.

The prize-giving was over. As the audience dispersed, many decided it was time for refreshments. There was a noisy straggling queue for the fish and chips now being served from a caravan parked in front of the pub. Dee spent twenty frantic minutes on each of the tea and cake stalls, at the end of which the cake stall consisted of a displaced cherry and one solitary rock-cake.

Just as Dee was about to purchase this last item, the vicar came over and requested it, saying, 'That will do nicely for my tea.'

'You take it, my dear Vicar,' Mrs Higgins said. 'There's no need for me to charge for the last one in the shop.'

But the vicar, although pink with pleasure and embarrassment, insisted on paying. Then he asked Dee if she would care to accompany him to listen to the band, and although it wasn't really her cup of tea, she felt it would be churlish to refuse.

'Callum Edmonds, vicar of this parish,' he said with a great deal of enthusiasm. Dee thought he looked rather like an overgrown boy scout.

'Dee Gascoigne.' He shook her hand vigorously, then she was disconcerted to find him taking her arm in a tight, almost possessive grip as they turned to head towards the band. She wondered where his wife had got to, and whether she would mind her husband grabbing the arm of a young woman.

Mercifully the band only played for half an hour before taking a break, and so Dee was able to murmur an excuse and slip away. The vicar, standing politely when she got up, did not seem to mind her leaving him, and he once again ensconced himself in his deckchair ready for the second half.

The fortune teller's tent was much more in Dee's line, having an irresistibly romantic allure for her. She spotted the previous customer, an older woman, leaving as she was about to go in. Not just for the young, then, Dee thought.

Dee paid her sixpence and even though she knew it was all nonsense, she couldn't help the flutter of excitement in her stomach as she went in and took her seat in the dim interior.

But if she says anything about me meeting a tall, dark, handsome stranger, Dee thought, I shall know she's not even trying to do the thing properly. After a millisecond, she added, not that there's anything in it anyway.

She didn't recognise the woman in the gypsy get-up. Was that because she didn't know her, or because her disguise was so good? The costume and make-up, whilst not particularly original, were extravagant and gaudy. In a breathy, vaguely 'Romany' voice the woman asked Dee her name and what she wanted to learn from

'The Fates'.

Dee said the first thing that came into her head.

'I want to know about my future.' It seemed that more precise details were not necessary. Doubtless everyone said the same.

She was told to place her hands palm-upwards on the table in front of her and to close her eyes.

She did so. She had to resist the childish desire to giggle, especially when the woman said in a sing-song voice, 'And now I want you to quite relax, quite reeeelax and empty your mind. Theeenk only of the sound of my voice.'

Dee bit her lip to keep from laughing and tried to concentrate on the woman's voice. It wouldn't do if she giggled; one had to go along with the charade, after all.

'What is eet you wish to know? Tell eet to me, whisper eet to me. What is it you seeekk?' the gypsy woman intoned.

Dee wasn't sure whether to visualise the thing in her head or put it into actual words. She wasn't sure if she should open her eyes yet, so she kept them closed and said in a clear voice, making herself speak the words and not accidentally sing them back at the woman, 'I want to know what to do with my life.' Then she added, 'Job-wise I mean, of course. Thank you. I mean, please.'

She thought she heard a slight snigger, but she wasn't sure. There was a silence, then the gypsy woman began to speak rapidly in a foreign-sounding tongue, and Dee felt something softly touch her hands. The touch was so light and cool she couldn't tell if it was breath or water or cloth, but she dared not open her eyes in case it spoiled the spell. However, she flinched slightly, then felt the gypsy's hands on her wrists, firmly holding her hands in place on the table-top, and the woman said in a much more normal voice, 'It's all right, dearie, it's only rose petals.'

Dee relaxed in her seat once again, and whether the

scent was truly there or whether it was the power of suggestion, she didn't know, but her nostrils detected the soft scent of roses. There was a pause. Dee heard the sharp sound of a match being struck. And straight away the smell of sulphur tickled her nose.

'Open your eyes.'

Dee did so, and saw a lit candle was now on the table in front of her, her hands resting on either side, filled with rose petals of the palest pink.

'Blow out the candle, and as you do so, you will see the answer to your wish.'

Dee did so, and felt a twinge of disappointment at the lack of anything in the form of a vision or enlightenment. No bangs, no flashes. She stood to leave, feeling foolish. Well, that's that over with, she told herself. Then she thought, well so what, everyone goes to the fortune teller at a fair, it's no different than the coconut shy, just one of the attractions. Everyone knows there's nothing in it.

The gypsy woman threw back the flap of the tent, and sunshine flooded in, blinding Dee and making her duck away from its brilliance, and as she did so, for the briefest of moments she saw an image of herself standing in a courtroom, giving evidence in a clear, confident manner, just like in her dream. Except Miss Evans wasn't there. And Dee herself was as she was now, and not a child in her school clothes.

Dee turned to the gypsy woman, surprised and unsure whether to say anything, but the woman held up her hand to stop her, saying, 'It's for you alone.'

Going through the gap and out into the real world once more, Dee turned again to thank the woman. The woman smiled back and said, 'Most women want to know about love, whether or not they will meet a tall, dark, handsome stranger.'

Dee blushed guiltily but said nothing. The woman touched her arm and said, 'But you will never meet a man like that,' and before Dee could analyse her deep sense of disappointment, the woman continued, 'There is a man in your life, or about to come into your life. He is both dark and handsome, but he is not a stranger. He is not the film-star type. He will never be rich, but he will make you happy. He will be first a friend, then a lover. Your love will last forever.'

With a swish, she was gone, the tent flap closing behind her and Dee was left standing there alone, her thoughts in a whirl, feeling suddenly emotional with a lump in her throat, and her arms prickled with gooseflesh.

'Nonsense,' she told herself firmly, shrugging away a mental image of a very familiar face.

*

Chapter Six

Dee realised she was standing there alone doing an impression of a goldfish so she did what anyone would do: she tidied her hair and shut her mouth.

'Beware a sea-voyage and you will meet a tall, handsome stranger?' said a voice. Dee turned to see Miss Prescott nearby, smiling. Miss Prescott was carrying a variety of items that appeared to be rapidly getting the better of her. Dee ran forward to try to help.

'Miss Prescott. How nice to see you again.'

'Did you get your postcards written and sent off?'

'Fancy you remembering that,' Dee said. 'Yes, I did, thank you. Duty done to the family.'

'Our families do make these demands of us, don't they? One always has to do one's duty. Family always comes first, doesn't it?'

On closer inspection, Dee decided that Miss Prescott appeared pale and weary. As an impulse, Dee suggested they took a seat and had a drink or an ice-cream and listened to the band. 'It's rather warm this afternoon. Those last couple of seats are in the shade.' She hadn't really expected Meredith to agree, so she was surprised and pleased when Meredith accepted.

They settled into the seats in the back row. The band had resumed playing but the music was not quite so trying the further one got away from it, and an old oak tree provided a delicious shade. Meredith sank into her seat with obvious relief and Dee was a little alarmed by how pale she looked now. She reiterated her suggestion.

'Shall I get teas, or would you prefer an ice? Which do you think would be the most reviving?'

'Oh, ices, I should think,' Meredith said with her gentle smile. 'Shall I come with you?'

'No, of course not. You look done in. Anyway, one of us should stay and guard our goodies.' Dee hoped Miss Prescott wouldn't object to being bossed about by a relative stranger years younger than herself. She added, 'If you don't mind of course.'

'Not at all, it's very kind of you. But look, you're doing all the hard work, so let me pay for the ices, it's the least I can do.' She handed the money to Dee who hadn't the courage to argue, but hurried away.

When she returned, Major Reeves was standing beside Meredith, but with a curt, 'It's all right, I'm not staying,' he strode off.

Meredith smiled. 'Funny little man!'

Dee held out Meredith's ice to her, drips running down the cones onto their hands.

'Gosh, how sticky this is!' Dee said. Then, 'I think he's rather keen on you. It's a shame he left.'

'I'm glad he did, he seems to way-lay me everywhere I go. He's rather a nuisance. Funny little man,' she said again.

Dee said nothing, feeling very sorry that the apple of the major's eye didn't seem to reciprocate his feelings. They ate their ices in silence, largely unnoticed by the milling people around them. The band stopped again for their next break, finishing to a smattering of applause before going in search of refreshments. People got up to wander and talk with friends. Dee wiped her fingers on her handkerchief and asked, 'Do you have the fair every year?'

'Oh yes, I'm afraid so. Though fortunately it's not usually as hot as it is this year. Who'd have thought it, and only the beginning of May. Usually we get rained off. Someone clearly forgot to do their rain-dance, blast them!' Meredith gave a wry smile.

Unable to think of a nicer way to spend the day, Dee said, 'Oh don't you enjoy it?'

'It's all right, I suppose,' Meredith replied. 'It's just the endless pretence of good humour, it's so much work. One always has to attend, regardless of how one feels. There are always competitions to judge, and sweaty hands to shake, and sticky babies to kiss. And one needs so much tact! Later this afternoon, for example, there's the Bonny Baby competition, with three categories. There's the under six months, the under one year, and the under two years. And as there have only been six babies born in the village in the last two years, it's not going to be much of a competition. I predict Mrs Jameson will collect two first places, one for her four-month-old and the other for her eighteen-month-old, so that's two of the three categories finished with before we've even started, just to one household. Much to Mrs Ford's chagrin. She is still awaiting the arrival of her baby, it was due ten days ago, and she had been hoping to enter the poor little mite into today's competition.'

'Oh dear,' said Dee. There was little else to say. She could quite see that judging any kind of baby competition would be a feat of diplomacy in a village.

Meredith continued, 'Then there is the flower competition and the vegetable competition. Again, so few entrants means the winner is practically a foregone conclusion. But at least my brother has the burden of judging the veg, so I can relax for a few minutes. But it is shockingly hectic every year, and to be honest I'm always so relieved when it's over. It might surprise you, but honestly, being Lady of the Manor is a full-time job. What with reading to Mrs Hunter twice a week and listening to all her grumbles and complaints... that was her daughter Harriet Grayson who was the gypsy fortune-teller, by the way. Did you recognise her? She is awfully good.'

Dee shook her head, saying she hadn't met the woman, though she knew Mrs Hunter and Marlene, of course.

'One could hardly spend five minutes in the village without getting to know those two,' Meredith said wryly. 'And then I have to visit Muriel Higgins once a week at the Higgins' farm. Muriel's grandson Eddie is 'walking out' as they say, with Marlene Grayson. And then I have to help Millie Edmonds with her blasted needlecraft group, not to mention my shifts at the library. It's a wonder I have any time for myself. And my brother is no use whatsoever. He just tells me to get on with it. Like this dinner tonight, yet another one we are hosting for the visitors from the Continent.'

Dee couldn't help feeling surprised. This wasn't at all what she'd imagined. She still couldn't see how anyone would think it anything other than wonderful to be involved with all this. But then she didn't have to deal with it every day like Meredith. No doubt it was different if you were actually on the spot. But at least Miss Prescott felt comfortable enough to be able to really speak her mind.

Dee said, 'I have three brothers, two of them younger than me. But age doesn't matter, does it, they boss me about no end.'

'Three brothers? Oh dear, how awful for you!' Meredith laughed. 'I'm sure I find one brother is quite enough.'

'Exactly! Don't you find brothers such useless creatures?' Dee smiled back. 'My twin brother Freddie is quite incapable of dealing with the simplest task without me. Left to his own devices, he'd get into no end of trouble, I'm sure. And as for girlfriends! He's such a fool for a pretty face. He has no idea about suitability. My mother gets in such a state about him.'

'Hmm,' said Meredith, gazing into space. 'I know exactly what you mean. My brother is also younger than I, but you'd think he was ten years older, the way he tries to boss me about. And he really is so immature and thoughtless and...'

She broke off as her brother came into view at that point, and on his arm hung Miss Fenniston, scarlet-lipsticked and laughing uproariously at some remark of his.

Meredith stiffened immediately, her Lady-of-the-Manor persona firmly back in place as her eyes narrowed and her lips pressed together in a straight, firm line.

'Isn't that...?'

'Yes. Yes, it is. Will you excuse me, Miss Gascoigne? I've just remembered I need to catch my brother. I have an important message for him. It's been lovely sitting here, but I'm afraid...'

'Call me Dee, and yes, of course, I quite understand.'

Meredith grabbed her belongings and hurried after her brother. Unashamedly eavesdropping, Dee could hear the fury in her tone as she snapped at him, 'Jeremy! Jeremy, I must speak to you in private. No, not later, immediately, right this minute!'

On seeing his sister, his face took on a somewhat sheepish look, like a small boy caught raiding the cake tin. He murmured something to Miss Fenniston who stepped aside, rolling her eyes rather noticeably.

Meredith Prescott bore her brother away at top speed without so much as a backwards glance.

Miss Fenniston looked around her and saw Dee watching her. Doubtless Miss Fenniston would have stalked off, but Dee's sympathetic smile and her, 'Oh dear!' brought Miss Fenniston over and she dropped down into the seat that Meredith Prescott had just vacated.

'My God, that woman gets my back up,' Sheila Fenniston said and fished in her handbag for her cigarettes and a lighter. She offered her cigarette packet to Dee, who smiled and shook her head.

'She does seem determined to keep her eye on him,' Dee suggested. She waited to see what Miss Fenniston would say next.

'Absolutely obsessed with him, if you ask me. It's not as though he's a child. She doesn't need to keep him on leading-reins the way she does. She's just frightened of me getting my claws into him, that's all.'

'Why should she be?' Dee asked, with a pretence of ignorance.

'Exactly.' Miss Fenniston took a long drag of her cigarette and momentarily closed her eyes, tilting her head to catch the sun on her face. Her beehive was starting to come down with the heat and bustle, with long lifeless-looking wisps of hair hanging here and there. She looked old, Dee thought with an odd stab of fear. From a distance Sheila may look twenty-five but Dee could see now that she was probably another fifteen years older than that, almost the same age as Meredith Prescott herself. The heavy make-up couldn't quite hide or disguise the lines around the eyes. Nor those on the forehead, or the deep creases from the corners of her mouth down to her chin with its suggestion of jowls, the sagging skin no longer in its first fresh bloom.

Miss Fenniston took another puff on the cigarette and sent Dee a shrewd look. 'Well of course, I'm not the right sort. 'Not like us', as they say. And I'm also his secretary. Though she'd like to see me out of that too. She hates us going anywhere together. Like that conference a couple of weeks ago. And she hates the way he depends on me. That's perfectly normal for a manager and his secretary, but it's all just too scandalous for poor Meredith. She always imagines the worst. Really, her mind is a sewer.' There was a brief pause as she took a draw on her cigarette, blew out the smoke then directed a knowing look at Dee. 'Though I'd have to say, she'd die of shame if she knew what really went on when we were away. Whatever she imagines, I doubt it's anywhere near as bad as the truth.'

Astonished, Dee didn't quite know how to respond to this, but she knew that sometimes silence produced more information than an outright question, so she sat back in her seat and waited.

'Haven't I seen you around? I'm Sheila by the way, Sheila Fenniston. As I say, I work for Jeremy Prescott.' She transferred her cigarette to the other hand to shake Dee's hand in a quick warm grip.

'Dee Gascoigne. Yes,' Dee said, 'I've been staying in one of the cottages just over there since the beginning of the week. I'm getting over bronchitis.'

'Nasty. But sea air's good for that, or so they say. Though it's a bit dull round here for a youngster when you could have gone to Brighton or Bournemouth or— well, pretty much anywhere along the south coast would have been livelier than here. Southend in Essex in nice.'

'Oh, it's all right here. I wanted somewhere small and quiet. I'm not one for amusement arcades and loud music.'

'So what do you do? Are you at work?'

'I'm a teacher. Although, I'm between jobs at the moment. I shall need to find another one to start in September.'

'Gosh, how worthy. What do you teach?'

'French. And when necessary, a bit of art too. Art was my first love, but they say you can't make a living at it. Luckily I also love languages.'

'You've obviously got talent, then. If you speak a language, you'd be wasted as a teacher. Unless you like working with children, of course? Some women do, peculiar, I know.'

Dee wrinkled her nose and hesitated but before she could reply, Sheila Fenniston butted in with a laugh and said, 'You don't seem completely besotted with the idea.'

'No, I am, I *do* love teaching.' But there was still reserve in her voice, and Miss Fenniston just smiled and quirked an eyebrow at her. When Dee said nothing more, Sheila said,

'I'm afraid a woman with brains is not something that goes down too well in this place. I should know. I've given two years of my life to organising that man. Really, left to himself he couldn't organise a... well, he really is completely hopeless. And of course it helps that I've learned a bit of French and German, obviously, for when we deal with our contacts on the Continent. Take my advice, make use of your language skills in the business sector. We won't be an island nation forever, and Europeans absolutely love it if you can string together one or two sentences in their language. That goes a long way in business, I can tell you. And the salary must be tons better than a teacher's.'

'Most salaries are tons better than a teacher's,' Dee said wryly.

Sheila laughed, and warmed to her theme.

'It's not just Prescott's. You'd be surprised how few of the top bods in any British business can speak a foreign language. Jeremy's hopeless. But I can say, in terms of currying favour with our overseas people, a little attempt at French or German goes a very long way, and now I'm trying to pick up some Italian too, just to spice things up a bit. Fortunately, I seem to find that sort of thing quite easy. I believe my father may have been an Italian sailor. We'll probably never know. My mother can't remember.

'Anyway, it's so frustrating. Everyone expects me to just stick to typing up the odd letter or ordering foils and seals, when I've got all these ideas just buzzing around inside my head. Ideas that could help build up the business. And one minute Jeremy is lapping it up and talking about expansion. Then the next, Madam has poured cold water on his ideas—and mine—all because she has the usual conservative views and absolutely no vision or imagination. Or business sense. The stupid cow is living in the past. She thinks all this,' and here Sheila Fenniston waved her hand to include the fair, the people, the whole village. 'She thinks all this will last forever, never changing, and that she'll just be able to carry on living her life in her own little corner of Ye Olde Englande.' Sheila leaned to one side and viciously stabbed out her cigarette in the grass, immediately reaching into her handbag for another. She clicked the lighter and lit it, disappearing once again behind a cloud of steel-blue smoke.

'And won't it?' Dee asked. Her question held a gentle attempt at a challenge, but Sheila didn't seem offended.

'If they don't do something soon to really woo their overseas contacts, they're going to see their precious company go up in flames. The family spend far too much, especially Jeremy. He relies too much on doing things how they've always been done, and makes no effort to move with the times or to try anything new. I've tried to persuade him to find new suppliers or to try new retail outlets, but it's gone nowhere. These days, you've got to go out there and *find* the clients, *win* the orders. And develop relationships with the wineries, or those wine producers we buy from are going to realise there are other ways to get their wine into the restaurants, hotels and dining-rooms of this country, and Prescott's will be left out in the cold. The days of everything just falling into the Prescotts' laps because of their position as a County family are over.

'That's what this dinner tonight is all about, wooing and winning. But if the Prescotts and their damned aunt start acting all pompous and condescending again, they are going to offend everyone. The growers could very possibly decide to look elsewhere. As I've pointed out to them numerous times. And will the Prescotts listen to me? No! It's so bloody infuriating!'

She seemed to suddenly recollect herself and taking a calming breath, in a softer, more conventional tone, she said, 'I'm so sorry, I don't know why I'm rambling on like this. You won't say anything, will you? They'd be furious if they knew what I was saying. I bet you're bored stiff, anyway. Tell me about your boyfriend, is he a teacher too? You must have a boyfriend.'

Fortunately, Dee didn't have time to answer the question for at that moment, along came Marlene wheeling her grandmother. At Mrs Hunter's raised hand, Marlene stopped the chair as they drew level with Sheila and Dee.

'Nice day for it,' the old woman wheezed.

'Yes, isn't it?' Dee said politely. Sheila was taking another pull on her cigarette and watching Marlene and Mrs Hunter closely, her foot bouncing impatiently. Mrs Hunter turned her attention to Sheila.

'So, Sheila, are we going to be hearing wedding bells soon?'

This was greeted with a frown. 'I hardly think so, Aggie. Don't keep asking me.'

Dee glanced from Mrs Hunter to Sheila and back again, but said nothing.

'Oh? I thought Mr Prescott relied on you to do every little thing for him. Thought you'd have had him eating out of the palm of your 'and by now... But then again, perhaps you've got better fish to fry now?' Mrs Hunter smirked. Once again, Dee wondered just how much the old woman knew about everyone in the village.

Sheila treated the old woman to another frown and didn't trouble to make her tone polite.

'You really shouldn't believe everything you hear, you know. Things are not always as they seem.'

'No, true,' Mrs Hunter admitted with a nod. 'Nor people neither.'

'Indeed.' Sheila was sizing Mrs Hunter up as she looked at her, Dee thought. As if she was trying to work out what the old woman really knew. Marlene was looking bored and cross. In a moment they'd be going, Dee suspected.

'What about that German fellow? He seems pretty keen too, if you ask me.'

That surprised Sheila. She smiled a tight-lipped humourless smile.

'Ah well, you have to let me have some secrets, you know. It wouldn't do if you knew everything.'

Mrs Hunter held up a hand, partly in reconciliation and partly to alert Marlene that she was ready to move on again. 'Oh no, no, I didn't mean nothing by it, no call to fly off the 'andle. Come on Marlene, let's get a move on.'

And move on they did.

'Nosy old bag,' Sheila snapped. 'She's got a nerve, I must say. I wish I could find somewhere else in the village to lodge, she sticks her nose into everything.' She extinguished her cigarette on the ground by her shoe. She sighed. Then reached into her bag for another cigarette. 'Now then, what were we talking about? Oh yes. You were about to tell me about your boyfriend. You must have one, surely? You're very pretty. I bet the men are queuing round the corner to take you dancing.'

Dee didn't mind the change in topic, she felt she had learned quite a lot during the course of their conversation, and so she began to tell Sheila about leaving her job, which of course led to her explaining that she had also, a few days before, left her husband after a little less than three years of marriage.

'I met him at work,' she explained. 'He's a chemistry teacher at the same school as me. But of course, his career always had to come before mine. Not that that was the main issue with our marriage...' She left the sentence hanging, suddenly aware that it was a deal too private to discuss with a stranger, especially amongst the crowd of villagers.

'Was he a brute?' Sheila asked with surprising candour. 'I expect he was. They so often are. We women don't need to stand for it anymore. Just because our mothers put up with being treated that way, doesn't mean we should do the same. Why should we put up with misery or worse, just because they did? When I think of what my own mother suffered...'

Dee hadn't planned to say more but found herself telling Sheila all about it: about how disloyal she had felt, how wicked, for leaving Martin, for turning her back on her marriage and her vows. It had lost her a good job, but now she saw that she couldn't have gone on any longer.

'So you've been hating yourself for it, I expect? But you know, it's pointless to keep on with something that makes you so miserable. You did the right thing. It'll all work out in time, I'm sure.'

Dee nodded and murmured something non-committal. In the pause that came, she suddenly seemed to have a further revelation about her life. Seeing him at work as well as at home had been too much, especially after any of their violent disagreements. That sarcastic look he gave her if she met him in the corridor at work, when he saw she'd covered up the bruises with a bit of make-up. And so often she'd wondered if any of his colleagues knew, or even if they approved, perhaps encouraged Martin. Wives had to be kept in line, after all. It had become a daily battle to make herself get up and go to work. Why had she sent a postcard, she asked herself now, when she hated it so much? But there had been some good and kind colleagues. Chief among them her mentor, Miss Evans. Dee now wondered if Miss Evans had guessed what was going on at home. That remark of hers, 'For what it's worth, I think you've done the right thing.'

The breeze ruffled her hair and brought her back to the present and to her companion. Sheila was smoking yet another cigarette. There was silence as they looked around them and tried to think of something to say.

Then Sheila glanced at her wristwatch and declared she had to dash. 'It's been lovely chatting, Dee. You won't tell anyone what I said, will you? I was just letting off steam a bit really, and I probably said more than I ought. I hope you'll be around a bit longer. We must get together for a cuppa in the cafe soon, it's been such a relief to talk to someone normal. Or perhaps I could wangle you an invitation to the next Prescott extravaganza. If nothing else, it'll be a laugh watching Dear Meredith and Widow Twanky attempting to be polite to the European visitors.'

Dee laughed and said something vague, knowing it wasn't a genuine invitation. She watched Sheila go with a mixture of awe and relief. She'd expected Sheila to be a bit brainless and even mercenary from the little she had heard about her. But Sheila had turned out to be warm, clever and obviously talented. She was attractive to men and made no apology for that, and she was confident. But she was also far too up-to-the-minute for this little place; she was brassy, pushy, outspoken and a little unrefined. She was definitely not one to suffer fools gladly, but perhaps the Prescotts, in their complacency, needed the shake-up that Sheila

Fenniston was determined to give them.

What Dee would have given to attend that evening's dinner party. It sounded as though it would be very interesting indeed.

*

Chapter Seven

Later that evening, Dee settled herself in the armchair and watched as the storm clouds rolled in at the end of the hot day. Quickly the village was shrouded in darkness and the air was heavy and still with the expectation of rain.

She couldn't concentrate on her book. Instead she carried her radio into the sitting-room to listen to music. She lay back in the chair, sinking into the cushions, humming along vaguely with any song she recognised as she always did, and soon she was lost in her thoughts.

She revisited the day, remembering all the small unimportant events that were the threads weaving the tapestry of village life. And she thought about Meredith Prescott that evening, presiding over her brother's business dinner, and the irking presence of Sheila Fenniston. Sheila, who would glitter like a Christmas bauble at the refined table. Sheila, who could address friendly and useful comments to the guests in their own languages. Sheila with her innovative ideas and her confidence and her determination to breathe fresh life into Prescott's Wines and make it competitive in the modern market. Sheila, to whom Dee had confided things that she hadn't told anybody, not even Rob. If nothing else, Sheila Fenniston was a good listener.

Beside her, Dee instinctively felt, Meredith would appear as a dull, ageing spinster with little to offer except out-of-date charm and her sense of familial duty, and even, though it pained Dee to say it, her outmoded sense of entitlement.

She felt a twinge of unease, yet sorry for Meredith who could not resist the tide of progress. She saw a fleeting, nonsensical image of Meredith, her gown billowing in the wind, seated on a medieval wooden throne on the little beach just a hundred yards down the road, holding up her hands desperately trying to compel the sea to turn back, like Canute. Dee thought back to her schooldays and to Shakespeare's play *Richard II*, to Richard's 'rough rude sea' that he believed was insufficient to wash off God's anointing balm from the king. But in the end, he too, had lost his crown. God had turned away from Richard's arrogance and another man had taken his place.

She roused herself, getting up to go into the kitchen to make a cup of tea. A flash of lightning briefly illuminated then plunged the room back into darkness.

Meredith did not see herself as an anointed queen, Dee chided herself with a brisk shake of the head. That was ridiculous. It was Jeremy who ran the business and he alone would decide on its direction and its future. Unfortunately for Meredith, she was powerless. All she could do, in the traditional feminine style, was to watch and wait.

Dee took her tea back into the sitting-room. Just then thunder clapped, shaking the house, and lightning dazzled her eyes. She set her tea down hastily and ran to wrestle the old sash windows closed against the heavy rain now driving at the glass. Who would have thought only a few short hours ago, the fair was still in full swing and bathed in bright sunshine?

She ran up the steep staircase and groped her way to the front bedroom window, slamming it shut and shaking some rain from the curtains. Hopefully they'd dry out soon enough. She went to the back bedroom too, and checked the bathroom window was also closed.

Lights were going on in the other houses. She was vaguely surprised. For some reason she had always thought lights couldn't be lit during a storm. It would be a comfort, she was nervous, alone in a house during a storm for the first time. The streetlamp outside the post office flickered into orange-glowing life. Presently it would be brighter, but now its glow was largely ineffectual though reassuring. As she stood there, she made out two figures, Marlene and that boy Eddie from the farm, scurrying under the flimsy shelter of his coat in the direction of the churchyard.

Dee felt sure there would be no service on tonight, and even if there were, she didn't think Marlene, or Eddie for that matter, were the kind of young people to go to church. More likely they would be looking for a quiet corner in the churchyard for a spot of hanky-panky. Even so, thought Dee, ever practical, it would be horribly wet and cold out there in this weather.

She returned to the sitting-room. From her transistor radio, Donovan was singing about trying to catch the wind, another song she loved. Singing along with the lilting chorus, Dee turned on the light, closed the curtains, and then sat back down in the armchair to sip her cup of tea and think.

Still taken up with the curious triangle of Meredith, Sheila and Jeremy, she pondered. And the more she thought about it, the more she became convinced that Sheila would have to leave or make her peace with her position and settle more demurely into the role of secretary. Otherwise, clearly, Meredith and her fearsome aunt Mrs Smithies would certainly combine forces to oust Sheila and install a secretary who met their standards far better. No doubt someone older, without Sheila's sex appeal, and with a meeker disposition.

Up at the big house, the dinner party was flagging a little as everyone tried to force themselves to laugh at yet another humorous anecdote from Herr Kostner or Signor Bocci, translated a bit at a time by Sheila and so losing most of its entertainment value. Jeremy countered with a fishing story, but his delivery was too technical and long-winded to allow the guests either to fully comprehend what he was saying or to find any genuine amusement in the finale.

Meredith had a headache. She was tired from the long afternoon at the fair, with all its social demands and the noise of the crowd, and now to sit here wreathed in polite smiles with Frau Kostner on her left hand and the elder Monsieur Truchet on her right... She was exhausted from having to think of simple things to ask them, and uncomplicated observations to make, such as, 'We have bad weather tonight.' To which these guests politely agreed, adding, 'But also it was much sun today,' the veracity of which no one could deny.

The dining-room was well glazed and curtained from the storm outside, and only now and again did the thunder intrude upon the meal, or the lights momentarily dim as the lightning cracked overhead. With so many guests at the table, the volume of conversation drowned the complaints of nature.

Mrs Smithies added her own contribution to the discussion with a very loud, over-enunciated, 'Have you been to Eng-er-land bee-fore?' It was the same—and only—question she had asked them on their previous visit. Her question also involved quite a lot of pointing and nodding as she attempted to make her meaning clear. Her nephew briefly closed his eyes in embarrassment. Miss Fenniston softly tutted to herself then in fairly fluent Italian, her voice pitched at a normal level, asked Signora Bocci if she ever attended the fashion shows in Milan or Rome.

Mrs Smithies had confused her guests with the use of the word 'before', or possibly with her pronunciation of it. Quizzical brows furrowed and the guests searched one another's faces for clues. It seemed the two French gentlemen could speak German and Italian, and the Italian and German couples could also speak the other languages.

'But virtually no English,' Mrs Smithies said to herself in exasperation. 'Why come here if they can't speak the language? How do they expect to get on?'

Halfway along the table, the Americans confined themselves exclusively to conversation with Meredith seated opposite, which meant of course that Meredith was not helping with the European visitors. Mrs Smithies promised herself a stern word with Meredith at the end of the evening.

At the other end of the table, Miss Fenniston quickly translated Mrs Smithies's original question, and the puzzled faces were bathed in comprehension. Sheila turned back to interpret and slightly edit Jeremy Prescott's story and the German gentleman and his elegant wife laughed with real, and loud, amusement. Jeremy looked pleased, and to Meredith's chagrin, poured himself yet more wine. For a few minutes talk became technical, as the wine was a new one from Herr Kostner's vineyards. When he thought no one would notice, Herr Kostner raised his glass in a small, secret toast to Sheila Fenniston, and she smiled back and nodded. But Lucinda Smithies's eyes missed nothing. It was just one more thing to discuss.

Eventually even the longest evening must end, and

in spite of the storm that was still in full spate, Jeremy offered to drive the visitors back to their hotel himself. Meredith, catching his arm, drew him to one side.

'Surely Rodericks can do that, there's no need for you to go out in this. Rodericks gets paid to chauffeur people about.'

'Don't be an idiot,' Jeremy said with a frown. 'Of course I'm going to drive them myself, it's a nice gesture. Anything else would be an insult. And we need to stay in their good books if we don't want to lose their interest, especially with these new wines they are developing.'

'But...'

'I'm driving them and that's that. And when I get back, I'll drive Sheila back to her digs, too, there's no need for her to get soaked going home on foot.'

Again Meredith attempted to dissuade him. At the very least, it meant she had to entertain Miss Fenniston for another hour until he returned, and of all the people to dump on her...

'I don't see why she can't walk home, it's only five minutes away. There's really no need to keep her hanging about all that time.' Because if he took Miss Fenniston home, would he come back again that night? Then Mrs Hunter would really have something to gossip about. And her loathsome granddaughter. Meredith couldn't help wondering if he had already spent the night at the cottage, in Miss Fenniston's room. She felt a sense of dread inside. What if she was the only one who didn't know, and it was already old news? There had to be a reason why the village was so convinced of an intrigue between Jeremy and Sheila. And Aggie Hunter was always dropping hints about what she might know.

'It's raining cats and dogs out there! Really Meredith, you are so thoughtless! She'd be drenched to the skin in no time. Anyway, there's still the odd bolt of lightning about, I don't like the idea of a woman walking home alone at night, no matter how short the distance, and this weather makes it downright unacceptable. Surely you can entertain her until I return, it's the least you can do.'

Then he was gone for the car, leaving Davies and Sheila to help the guests on with their coats, to locate a strayed handbag and Monsieur Truchet senior's walking-stick, whilst Meredith hovered ineffectually and Mrs Smithies stood impatiently at the foot of the stairs, her hostess smile fixed and fading rapidly.

When Jeremy drew the car up and come over with the huge umbrella, everyone began to hurry out. The last guest to leave, Monsieur Truchet junior, briefly patted Jeremy's shoulder as he went past him, and Jeremy grinned back, putting out a hand and saying, 'Jean-Marie, after you.'

The moment the door closed behind their guests, Mrs Smithies said a curt 'Goodnight,' turned and fairly ran up the stairs to her room with Davies on her heel, leaving Meredith and Sheila watching each other warily.

'You can go up to bed too, if you like,' Miss Fenniston said, 'I really don't mind. It's not as if I'm a guest.'

'True,' said Meredith curtly, 'but I promised Mr Prescott I'd entertain you until he is free to...' She didn't quite like to say 'see you home' as it very markedly implied an intimacy she had no inclination to encourage, so in the end she settled for, 'until he is free to drop you off.'

'He doesn't need to,' Sheila insisted, 'I could quite easily walk.'

'I know you could,' Meredith replied, her voice cool. 'But for some reason, he feels a duty to see his staff safely home.' She felt quite pleased with that one, it set Miss Fenniston firmly in her place, and Meredith felt a small sense of triumph when she noticed Miss Fenniston looked upset as she turned away.

'We may as well wait in the small sitting-room,' Meredith said, taking the lead. 'He'll be at least an hour, so we may as well be comfortable.'

They whiled away the time by silently flicking through old magazines, although it is doubtful whether either of them was aware of the content of the pages. Not a word was exchanged between them in the ninety minutes they waited.

When at last they heard the sound of the front door banging open then closed again, there was an acute sense of relief in both women's hearts. Jeremy Prescott's footsteps approached across the tiled floor of the hall.

He appeared in the doorway, swaying slightly. He's drunk, Meredith realised in astonishment. When he saw them sitting there looking up at him, he beamed at them, a happy man.

'There you are, my two best girls.'

*

Chapter Eight

Monday morning was not going well for Norman Slough. It was only a quarter to eleven, but already he'd been rebuffed by Sheila Fenniston. He'd met her quite by chance in a corridor and, seizing the opportunity, had attempted to ask her yet again to go to a dance. But her response had been cold and quite definite: 'I'm sorry, I don't think we're at all suited. Please don't keep bothering me like this, Mr Slough.'

Unfortunately for Norman, some of the men from the warehouse had been passing by just then, and his humiliation had given them a great deal of amusement. A few minutes later he had seen a couple of them looking in his direction and sniggering. Like schoolboys, he thought, and told them sharply to get back to work. But as he'd walked away he'd heard one fellow saying to the other, 'Please don't keep bothering us like this, Mr Slough!' This had been followed by gales of laughter. By tomorrow, Norman was certain, it would be all over the warehouse. He would be a laughing-stock. How could he ever hold his head up again? And it was all her doing!

Norman burned with fury. He felt an overwhelming need for action. She needed to know how much she had hurt him. She had snubbed him at the fair, and now this. She had to be made to know how it felt to have people laughing at you every time you passed them in a corridor. She had led him on, making him think she really liked him, making him think he was special, making him hope and plan for the future, and now this: humiliating him, making a spectacle of him in front of his colleagues, making him a laughing-stock. Leading him on, and all the time planning to throw him over and laugh about it with her precious Jeremy Prescott, no doubt, at one of his smart dinners at the manor house, with all their overseas guests in on the joke too.

It made Norman shake with rage to think of how she had spoken to him in that soft, sympathetic way, pretending to like him, pretending to be interested in him, pretending to care. But she didn't care. Not at all. She didn't care tuppence for him or his status or what people thought of him, he saw that now. To her he was nothing, and now, thanks to her, he was nothing to everyone else too. She had got to be made to see what she had done. Calling him 'Mr Slough' in that bored, rather despising tone.

And then, at a quarter to twelve there came the summons from on high. Prescott wanted to see him in his office immediately. This was bad. Prescott never saw people in his office. Except to sack them.

Norman was relieved that Sheila Fenniston had absented herself from the outer office when he went up. At the back of his mind, he was wondering if she had anything to do with the summons. If she had made a complaint to Prescott, well, Norman wouldn't be at all surprised. He felt certain she was behind this.

The door to Prescott's office was standing ajar, and Norman could see through the glass panel to where

Prescott sat at his desk. Norman tapped on the door and Prescott immediately called out a stern, 'Come!' rather like a headmaster. Norman entered the office and shut the door behind him.

He was only in there two and a half minutes. As soon as he stepped inside, and Prescott barely glanced up from his papers, Norman knew he was being dismissed. Prescott looked uncomfortable as he always did in these situations. He didn't invite Norman to take a seat. He didn't waste time on pleasantries. He shifted in his seat and dropped his gaze to the back of the chair that shielded Norman Slough. Norman's grimy fingers gripped the back of it.

'Thing is, Slough, this is the third time now. We can't keep letting it go. I'm sure you understand, we've been very patient with you. But I can no longer turn a blind eye to you being drunk on duty.'

And here it comes, thought Norman, Sheila Fenniston's little bit of poison dripped into the boss's ear. But he was wrong.

Jeremy Prescott continued, 'It's the muddled orders and the breakages. Twice you've promised to pull your socks up, to pay greater attention to what you're doing. You're costing the firm an arm and a leg with your carelessness. We can't afford to just throw money away. And as I've already said, this is the third time now you've been drunk on duty. So I've made my decision. You'll be leaving at the end of the week. Toe the line until then, and I'll give you a decent reference. Hopefully you'll find something that better suits your abilities. And for God's sake, get some help with the drink problem, man. I'm sorry, but that's my final decision.'

When Norman came down to the warehouse again it was twelve minutes to twelve. Almost lunchtime. For twelve minutes Norman fumed and fussed with some paperwork in his corner of the warehouse. When the clock struck twelve and everyone began to drift off to take their lunchbreak, Norman, still flushed with unrelieved temper, swept the papers onto the floor, turned on his heel and walked out of the warehouse.

'And don't expect me back at one o'clock!' he yelled, though no one was paying him any attention. 'I'm not coming back.'

Norman took himself off into the village, going directly to the public bar of The Seagull. He ordered a pint of Best and positioned himself at the far end of the bar. There were a few little knots of men from the warehouse, but no one bothered him, which suited his mood perfectly. He drank his pint down in three long draughts and ordered another. By the time he had drunk his third pint, he was feeling a little calmer, but still a resentful wrath simmered against Jeremy Prescott and especially against Sheila Fenniston, who would surely know by now that he had been dismissed. He began to think perhaps he hated her. Sheila Fenniston, of whom he had harboured such hopes, and now she was the mistress of his downfall at Prescott Wines. He kept on drinking.

At five minutes to one o'clock, his colleagues glanced back at him as they headed out of the door and back to work. But Norman Slough was not budging. He ordered his sixth pint of Best and he thought about exactly what he would like to do to Jeremy Prescott and Sheila Fenniston.

At the time Norman Slough received his summons to Jeremy Prescott's office, Dee Gascoigne was on the way to the front door of the cottage to answer a knock.

She turned the catch and the door swung slowly open to reveal her husband, Martin Clarke. Dee gawked at him, her stomach churning, her brain refusing to work. How on earth had he found her?

Without waiting for her to speak he shoved the door

wide and entered the house, coming forward so quickly
that she had to leap back to allow him room to pass. He
stood on the threshold of the sitting-room just three
feet away whilst she remained by the front door, as if
she were the visitor and he the resident.

He stayed where he was, looming over her, his large
frame filling the space. Her tentative smile faltered as
she realised he had been drinking and had worked
himself up into a fury. Somehow it seemed worse that
he spoke softly and carefully, his well-bred accent
clearly enunciating each and every word. She couldn't
help wondering how she had ever thought him fun and
easy-going.

'Remember me? Your *husband*? Oh, you do, do you?
You remember me? *Do you, Diana*?' He was a step
closer now. Making an odd hollow sound as he did so,
he stabbed the centre of his own chest with his
forefinger to emphasise his words, still so softly spoken.
Her confusion was replaced with a new, unsettled fear.
She tried to smile, to step forward in her old friendly
way to laugh him out of it. But at the expression on his
face, and as his fist came up, she found herself
shrinking back into the corner by the door, her heart
bumping in terror. Beyond him, in the sitting-room, the
radio was playing a cheerful pop song, ironically at odds
with the present situation.

As The Supremes asked someone—a lover,
perhaps—to stop in the name of love, purely out of
instinct Dee put her hands up to protect herself, as
Martin's fist pounded home—on the wall three inches
from her cheek. In desperation she wailed, 'What is it?
What have I done?'

Martin gripped her by her shoulders and dragged
her close to leer into her face. The stench of alcohol and
stale cigarettes on his breath, and seemingly oozing
from every pore made her almost gag. His face was red
and sticky with sweat. Her stomach lurched with

nausea. Wrapping his fist in her hair, he yanked her head back, forcing her to look into his eyes.

Softly he said, 'How long have you been down here?'

The whites of his eyes were fully red, giving him a crazed, furious look. His teeth were yellowed from the cigarettes. She tried to look away. How had she ever let him kiss her? Or to touch her? She couldn't believe she had ever thought he would be a loving husband, let alone a good father.

'Um, well, just over a week.'

He jeered at her, wobbling his head as he imitated her voice in a high, squeaky pitch. 'Oh just over a week? Is that all? Just over a week?'

He released her so abruptly that she fell to the floor. He turned away for a second only to swing his fist back again with full force, breaking through the plaster of the wall. As he grabbed her shoulders then threw her back down again, he bellowed at her, 'I noticed you found time to send a postcard to 'my dear much-missed former colleagues'. It was pinned up on the bloody noticeboard! What was I supposed to say when people asked me about that, Diana? Did you just forget you were *married*? Did you forget to wonder what it would be like for your *husband* to see your lovely little card telling all his colleagues about your lovely little holiday down here in Sussex? Well? Is that it? Were you so busy enjoying your lovely little holiday you forgot all about your husband slaving away to keep a roof over your head? Did you, Diana? Did you?'

Dee trembled on the floor, the stink of his breath in her face. His mouth was twisted in a snarl, his brows pulled down, bristling and threatening, his whole body shaking, though whether from rage or the drink, she didn't know. Never, ever had she seen anything like this. She'd seen him drunk before, seen him furious and he'd even hit her a few times. But this... When she'd left him she believed she had already seen him at his worst.

But not for one moment had she ever imagined... She hardly dared to take a breath.

Then everything stilled within her. She looked up at his reddened face. Saw the bloodshot whites of his eyes. She heard the ragged gasps of his breathing. Her fear calmed and left her. Slowly and carefully Dee got to her feet. She dusted her hands on her skirt. She turned to look at the man towering over her. And before he could think of anything else to hurl at her, she said, 'That's quite enough, I think. You'll give yourself a stroke or something if you carry on like that. It's not good for you. I believe you will have seen my letter. So you know what's happened, and you know why. My brothers will come looking for you if you don't leave me alone.'

He snorted derisively. 'Your brothers! What, precious little Robbie? He'll hurt me, will he, that pansy? What will he do, hit me with his handbag?'

'And my father and my cousins will be right there with him.'

'Oh your cousins! I almost forgot. Darling Bill-the-copper? I bet you can't wait to see him again. You'll be panting all over him the second he gets here. But he'll never marry you, you know. Cousins can't marry.'

That was the fatal flaw in his argument. It was her turn to sneer.

'It's not illegal. In any case, you know perfectly well I'm not really his cousin as I was adopted by my parents.'

She'd been a fool to drop her guard though. He came at her again, his fist raised.

'Well cousin or not, I'm sure you won't mind whoring it for him. Got you where he wants you, hasn't he, instead of at home where you belong. Filthy, cheating nympho!' He lunged at her throat, hands outstretched, snatching at her skin. She leapt back and he fell flat on his face. She ran to the door and held it open.

'It's time for you to go. I'm not your scared little wife anymore. And I never will be.' She folded her arms across her chest for confidence, hiding her shaking hands, staring coolly back at him. She had to conceal a smile at the almost bovine bewilderment in his expression as he hauled himself upright once more.

Taken aback, he attempted a sneer. 'What are you on about? You're still my wife. You always will be. Don't think you can get away that easily. And you'll be sorry when you've calmed down and you realise what you've done. Don't burn your bridges, Diana darling. You'll soon come crawling back. Think about it, you stupid cow. I won't take you back if you change your mind!'

'I won't,' she said. He wasn't making sense, but she no longer cared, she just wanted him out of there. 'This is the best decision I've ever made. It's over. We're getting a divorce. You will be hearing from my solicitor. Now please go. I don't ever want to see you again. And if you don't leave right now, I shall call the police.'

What if he didn't go? What if he attacked her again? She had nothing to defend herself with. She had no idea what to do if he decided to stand his ground. But he went. To her astonishment he straightened his tie and walked out of the door slowly and meanly, as if he was going on his own terms when they both knew it was just a charade. In the doorway he paused, just as she had known he would, for a last theatrical flourish. Turning back he said again, 'You'll be sorry.'

Dee put on a brave smile. 'I don't think so.' She reached a hand to shove him the rest of the way out of the door, then banged the door shut behind him, bolted it for good measure then flicked the catch. Then she sank down onto the floor and wept, her hands over her face, shaking from delayed reaction, appalled at the enormity of what had just happened.

She expected him to pound on the door. She expected to somehow have to run to Mrs Hunter's house for moral support or safety. It was a more than ten minutes before she was able to compose herself. She got to her feet and carefully made her way to the sitting-room window and looked out, keeping well back behind the curtain, just in case. Thank goodness the windows had all been shut. She would not have been surprised to see him lurking there, but apart from a couple of children playing, the street was empty. She could hardly believe it. Martin Clarke had gone. And the Rolling Stones were belting out, 'This will be the last time...' in what seemed like the acme of perfect timing.

She went to wash her face then combed her hair. She added a swipe of the palest of pale pink lipstick and a dash of blusher. Then, to top it off, put on heavy black eyeliner and a generous sweep of mascara with a none too steady hand. That felt a little better. She made herself a cup of tea. She was calm now, though still rather shaky. She wished there was a telephone in the cottage, how she would have liked to speak to Rob at that moment, or Bill Hardy, whom she knew had disliked Martin on sight and never seen the need to revise his opinion. It was a good thing Martin hadn't realised there was no telephone in the cottage when she'd threatened him with the police.

She spent an uneasy afternoon and evening, afraid to go out, at every moment expecting him to return and to bang the door down, shouting and threatening. Her fear increased as darkness came; she was alert to the smallest sound, her heart in her mouth. But by ten o'clock there had been no further sign or sound, and so Dee, exhausted, went up to bed with a sense of relief. She expected to toss and turn all night, and to start at every creaking board. But she slept deeply until morning.

Her marriage was truly over.

*

Chapter Nine

Early on Tuesday morning, Dee got up and got ready, had breakfast then ran back up the steep stairs to brush her teeth in the bathroom. The window was wide open, the sky was blue, the birds sang. It felt like a fresh new day, and a great burden had been lifted from her shoulders. There was no going back now. She felt free.

Until ten minutes later when there was a knock at the door.

Keeping well-hidden behind the curtain, she peered out of her bedroom window, afraid it was Martin again. But she couldn't see who was there—the visitor was concealed inside the porch. Whoever it was, they knocked again, a gentle, polite knock. Martin would have hammered, pounded and yelled if she didn't open the door immediately, so she was reasonably sure it couldn't be him. She tiptoed down the stairs and hesitated in the hall.

She was braced for confrontation, in case it was him after all, planning to slam the door in his face and quickly lock it. She eased the door ajar by a bare three inches. A middle-aged female face beamed at her, and beside her was the man Dee had seen playing the piano for the children's dancing at the fair, and who had then taken her to listen to the brass band. He was now sporting a 'work' suit of dark jacket and trousers, and a light grey shirt along with the white dog collar he'd worn at the fair. His wife Millie was dressed head-to-toe in pink florals, topped by beads obviously made of dyed macaroni by children in an art class. She was looking at Dee closely, assessing her.

Dee leaped back and threw the door wide. Relief made her almost laugh in her hurry to welcome them.

'Vicar. And Mrs—er...?' Just for the moment the surname escaped her.

'Edmonds,' she said, walking past Dee and into the sitting-room. She handed Dee a small fern in a papier mâché pot painted a vivid pink. 'Call me Millie. It's not too early, is it? We like to do our calls first thing.'

'We've come to formally welcome you to the village,' the vicar explained, taking a seat beside his wife. He beamed at Dee, holding her gaze in an intense stare.

'How nice to see you. And how thoughtful, thank you.' Dee smiled back and placed the fern in the centre of the coffee table. Knowing what was expected, she bustled off to the kitchen to make tea, bringing it on a tray a few minutes later. It looked as though she'd have to wait a while for her walk.

'And how are you settling in, Miss—er...?'Mrs Edmonds immediately piled sugar and milk into both cups, stirred them vigorously then handed one cup to her husband and took one for herself. They both began to drink the hot brew straight away. Dee wondered if she should warn them how hot it was, but they seemed to have asbestos mouths and throats.

'I've seen you at the library and at the fair, of course, but I'm afraid I didn't catch your name.'

'Oh I'm sorry. I'm Diana Gascoigne,' she said.

'Though everyone usually calls me Dee. I think you may be under a misapprehension,' she added. 'I'm only renting Mrs Palmer's cottage for a couple of weeks whilst I get over a bout of bronchitis. I'm afraid I don't plan to stay here permanently.'

From their crestfallen expressions it was clear they had indeed taken her for a new 'recruit'. She attempted to cheer them up by extolling the virtues of the village, ending with how much she had enjoyed the fair.

'Oh it's a grand event for everyone,' Mrs Edmonds agreed.

'Did you grow up in this area?' Dee asked, noting the Irish twang in Millie's voice.

'No indeed. Millie was over here from Belfast to train as a nurse just after the war,' the vicar said, smiling fondly at his wife. 'I was studying divinity at Canterbury, and was learning the ropes, so to speak. We met when I was at the hospital with a patient who sadly passed away.'

Millie beamed back at him. As 'how we met' stories went, Dee thought it wasn't terribly romantic but she said,

'So some good came out of the sorrowful event.'

But they were far more interested in Dee's life and family background. As soon as they heard that her grandfather was *the* Piers Gascoigne de la Gascoigne, their interest deepened still further. After elaborating a little on the births, deaths and marriages of the family, she waited, readying herself for the inevitable question.

The Edmondses seemed quite determined to find out absolutely everything about her. The expected question came now, as Millie poured herself and her husband a second cup of tea.

'No young man in your life, then?' The look directed at her was sharp and all-seeing. Dee knew she was blushing as she said, feeling terribly guilty at the lie,

'Oh no, I'm all on my own.'

It was clear from Millie's 'Really?' that she didn't believe her. Dee wondered if Mrs Edmonds had heard something in the village. Or worse still, seen Martin either arriving or leaving and put her own construction on that. The vicar was more interested in taking another Bourbon biscuit.

As he dunked it in his tea, he said, 'Young fellows these days! A perfectly lovely young lady, right under their noses...'

Dee had heard this kind of thing a hundred times before. She knew he meant it as a compliment, but it was as if a woman shouldn't be allowed to live her life on her own terms. Surely, people seemed to say, an adult female could only be happy cooking, cleaning and having babies? Most men, and indeed most women seemed to think women had to be 'saved' from spinsterhood by some kind man. Dee knew her smile had cooled slightly, but she couldn't seem to help it.

Dimly aware, from something she'd heard, that there had been a recent scandal about the curate, she said with a little thrill of malice, 'Do you have a curate to help you oversee your flock, vicar?'

The Edmondses exchanged a look.

Millie said coldly, 'No, we do not.' Doubtless she would have left things there, but her husband, terminally truthful, continued:

'Alas, I'm afraid our curate had to leave us, well, two or three months ago now. I'm afraid he—er...'

'Fell somewhat short of his responsibilities,' his wife finished for him. 'And it was only six weeks ago, dear.'

The vicar was blushing, but with a grateful smile agreed, saying, 'My dear Millie has a wonderful head for details. Yes, I'm afraid it was felt that it was best all round if young Henry moved to a new area.'

'Oh dear, what a shame,' Dee said with assumed innocence. 'So I expect you now have twice as much to do.'

Millie set down her cup a little too sharply. She directed a commanding look at her husband. 'Callum and I must be going now, Miss Gascoigne. We just wanted to pop in to welcome you to the area, but sadly it seems we won't have the pleasure of your company for long.'

Callum, taken by surprise halfway through a gulp of tea, was already standing up as he quickly slurped down the last of his drink. Millie cast a sad glance at the fern they had wasted on Dee. Dee wondered if she ought to offer it back to them but decided to see if Millie had the gall to ask for it. She didn't. They left at once, Dee smiling at them from the front door and thanking them again for their kindness. They walked back across the green in the direction of the church.

Mrs Hunter was on her way past the house, propelled as ever by Marlene.

'Paid you a visit, did they?' Mrs Hunter wheezed with laughter as she drew level with Dee.

'Yes, that's right. To welcome me to the..."

'Wanted to save your soul, I don't doubt, or more likely they was just sussing you out. Single woman. Want to know what you're up to. Tell you about that there curate?'

Dee shook her head.

'They won't never neither,' Mrs Hunter said.

'What happened?' Dee asked, curiosity getting the better of her manners. Mrs Hunter held up an imperious hand for Marlene to halt, even though Marlene had already pulled the wheelchair back a little so they were standing beside Dee.

'When?' asked Mrs Hunter.

'When the curate left?' Dee prompted.

Mrs Hunter shook her head and tapped the battery of her hearing aid. Dee knew this was just a charade and waited. Mrs Hunter would never miss out on a chance to gossip.

'One o' they poofters,' Marlene announced, pre-empting the old woman's response. 'Wasn't he, Gran? One of them fairies?'

Her gran, having no trouble at all hearing this, nodded vigorously.

'Weren't he just,' she said, grinning broadly. 'Proper shocked, the vicar was, when he caught him canoodling round the back o' the church with that there driver chappie, Rodericks, from Lady Prescott's.'

'Meredith Prescott is Lady Prescott?' Dee asked, surprised.

'No, that's just Gran's joke. On account of that she gives herself airs,' Marlene explained with a laugh.

'Oh, I see.' Dee could see that the two of them, with an age-gap of easily sixty years between them, both enjoyed the joke. 'So the curate was carrying on with the Prescotts' chauffeur?'

'S'right. How that Rodericks kept 'is job, I don't know. I did hear as he had one o' them poison pen letters.' Marlene gave Dee a sly look as she said this, as if testing to see just how up to date Dee's knowledge of local gossip was.

'I imagine he did,' Dee replied calmly. She fancied Marlene looked disappointed by her response. 'I imagine quite a few people have had them,' she added, hoping they'd be able to tell her a bit more.

'Oh quite a few, quite a few indeed, miss,' Mrs Hunter repeated, chuckling to herself. She waved to Marlene to start walking again, and over her shoulder as they moved away, she said,

'You'll be getting one too, if you're not careful. No telling who'll get one next, and you a single young lady, new to the village.'

Half an hour later, a little nervously, Dee left the safety of the house and walked along to the post office. There was still no sign of Martin. She went into the call box on the corner and phoned Rob. In a few short sentences she had told him all that happened. He was furious.

'I'm getting the next train down. I'll be there by dinnertime.'

'Rob, there's no need, everything is all right. He's gone.'

'No, DeeDee. I'm coming down. It's only a few days early in any case. Monty won't mind. And if I bump into that—*that so-and-so*—well, he'll get a bloody nose, that's what.'

Dee couldn't help smiling at that. The very idea of Rob doing anything so manly as punching someone was too much. She managed to persuade him to leave his arrival until the following day, and arranged to meet him at the station. She rang off, already looking forward to seeing him again.

As she stepped out of the call box, she became aware that Cissie was outside the post office and standing on the edge of the green wringing her hands, a gaggle of villagers around her. They were all looking immensely excited about something, and there in the thick of it was Mrs Hunter and Marlene. Dee could only hope it had nothing to do with Martin or herself. And she remembered she needed to tell Cissie about the hole in the wall where Martin had punched it. That would make another hole—this time in her savings, Dee thought ruefully, wondering how much the repairs would cost.

'What's happened, Mrs Higgins?' Dee asked the farmer's wife who was nearest to her.

'Oh Miss Dee, you'll never guess. Such a terrible thing,' Mrs Higgins said, and as she saw that Dee was waiting for the information, she added, 'It's that Miss Fenniston, the wine works secretary. We think she's dead. She was found a few minutes ago by Marlene's mother, Harriet Grayson. They think Sheila's done away with herself. Can you believe it! Harriet went for the doctor, but he's out on a case and so no one knows what to do, so she's gone to the vicarage to ask the vicar to come and help.'

'I did a first aid course at work,' Dee immediately said, turning to cast anxious eyes at the front door of Mrs Hunter's cottage. 'Are they certain, do you know? I mean she might just be unconscious?'

Mrs Higgins called out, 'Oi, Marlene, tell your gran Dee thinks Sheila might just be unconscious. She says should she take a look?'

Dee hadn't said quite that, but she found herself being propelled by Mrs Higgins towards the open front door. She turned back to see Marlene folding her thin arms over her bust and saying in a loud sulky voice, 'Well I ain't going in with her, I already seen for myself, thank you very much, and once was enough.'

That sounded rather worrying, Dee thought. She could see Marlene was a lot paler than usual, and her skinny frame was trembling noticeably. She was smoking a cigarette in rapid puffs.

Mrs Hunter motioned to be wheeled closer, afraid of missing something as always. Mrs Higgins left Dee on the threshold of the cottage, saying, 'Straight up the stairs and turn left, you can't miss it.'

Everyone waited for her to go in, expectant, crowding around the door. Cissie with her hands to her mouth, Mrs Higgins looking worried, Marlene looking as if she might be sick, and her grandmother definitely looking excited. A few other villagers had joined the mob in front of the terrace of old cottages. With them all standing there watching her, Dee felt she had no choice but to go inside. Because obviously, someone had to make sure. Sheila might just need a glass of cool water and an aspirin. Or, or something...

Just as in Cissie's cottage, the stairs were right ahead of her as she entered the house. But where hers was bright and welcoming, here the interior was dim; only the first three or four stairs were illuminated by light coming in at the open front door. With a pause to allow her eyes to adjust, and to get her nerves under control, Dee placed her hand on the panelled wood of the enclosed staircase and began to ascend. The steps were steep and shallow, and with no rail on either side, it was a precarious climb in the near darkness. How on earth did Mrs Hunter manage, she wondered. Perhaps the old lady had a bedroom downstairs? At the top, she paused and took a deep breath. She turned to the left and walked across to the door standing open, spilling a little pool of soft buttery light into the hallway.

She felt a deep reluctance to enter the room. Already she knew this was no ordinary moment. There was a musty stale smell, and something else besides. The metallic scent of blood on the air. She was still puzzling over the idea of there being blood as she went into the room. After all, no one had said anything about...

She stopped dead. Staring at the scene, her brain scrambled to make sense of the picture in front of her. Someone—Sheila, yet not Sheila anymore—was seated in an armchair beside a circular dining-table. On the table was a wine bottle and a single glass with a small amount of wine left in it. Beside the wine bottle, the radio was still playing softly, the music was an old danceband tune that seemed hauntingly out of place in the circumstances. The goosebumps stood out down Dee's arms.

Unwillingly, yet knowing it could not be avoided, Dee forced herself to look at Sheila Fenniston. She had fallen slightly to the side, leaning against the edge of the table, and her head lolled back, her eyes half-open, her gaze fixed upon something Dee couldn't see. Sheila was wearing a long nightdress of a surprisingly demure variety. She held her hands in her lap, and along the forearms and on the lap of her nightdress was the brown sticky mess of blood. It had run down on either side of her and formed two puddles on the thin aged carpet. And there by her right foot, glistening softly in the half-light was a razor, dirty with blood.

Dee put her fingers to Sheila's neck, knowing it was pointless. The skin was cold. There was no pulse. Dee backed out of the room, groping her way down the stairs. She closed the front door behind her and said, her voice faint, 'No one can go in. Sheila's dead. We must get the police immediately.'

*

Chapter Ten

After the long wait, everything seemed to happen very quickly and noisily.

The doctor arrived, and emerged almost immediately, shaking his head sorrowfully. Villagers surrounded him, and he held up his hand to appeal to them to step back and allow him to pass.

There was a collective gasp, then Dee saw what they all saw: blood on the cuff of his jacket sleeve. He glanced down at his arm, frowned, and as if it was the fault of the onlookers, he grumbled, 'It's up to the police now. I can do nothing more.' And he pushed his way through the throng to walk back to his house.

If anything the crowd increased over the next ten minutes as they awaited the arrival of the police. They heard them long before they saw them, arriving in a clanging jarring mass of two cars and an ambulance.

A man of about fifty, dressed in tired tweeds, went into the house, closely followed by a younger man who was looking much too excited.

In just a few minutes the younger man ran out of the

house and was violently sick in the roses on the corner of the green. The onlookers, turning to nod at one another and mutter, shook their heads a good deal about this, but Dee felt for the fellow. Obviously he had seen few dead bodies in his short career. She was feeling pretty queasy herself.

When he had composed himself, his general enquiry at the front of the crowd led to them pointing at Dee, and he came over to speak to her. She told him who she was and what she had found, and he wrote it all down in his little, black-bound notebook. She also told him where she was staying, anticipating that in due course, the senior officer would need to speak to her and no doubt, ask more questions. The young policeman just nodded, put a piece of gum in his mouth, and said,

'That's fine, thanks, doll. You can go.'

Dee hated being called 'doll'. She blamed popstars like Sonny-Ray Smith for this revolting new trend. She narrowed her eyes. 'So, you'll contact me later for a statement?'

He shrugged. 'Doubt it. We won't need it. It's just a suicide.' He sniffed loudly and walked away.

Irritated, Dee returned to the cottage. She waited in all the rest of the day, but no one knocked on her door. The police left well before the ambulance.

The next morning, Dee waited at the railway station to meet Rob's train, hopping from foot to foot and glancing frequently over her shoulder, still on the lookout for Martin, half-expecting to see him lurking behind a tree or the telephone box. Not that lurking had ever been part of Martin's *modus operandi*. He was more of a direct-action sort of chap.

It was a huge relief when the train pulled into Porthlea, and there was Rob, already letting the window down so he could reach outside to open the door. As soon as he got down onto the platform, he hugged her and she felt as though all her worries were behind her. Nevertheless she hugged his arm tightly as they set off for the cottage, Rob swinging his weekend case as they went. She told him hurriedly of the previous day's events, the memory of it making her shudder.

Outside Mrs Hunter's a small knot of onlookers had gathered beside a large well-polished dark car, the same one Dee had seen arriving the night before. It seemed the police were back for another look at Sheila's room, or possibly to talk to the Graysons or Mrs Hunter. Dee yearned to know what was going on. If she had been alone, it would have been tempting to join the waiting group and see what she could find out.

As soon as she and Rob were inside her cottage, his jacket hung up, his case ready at the foot of the stairs to be taken up and unpacked, Dee went through to the kitchen to set the kettle to boil. She braced herself for the inevitable. It came at once.

'My God!' Rob exclaimed from the hallway. 'What happened to the wall?'

'Oh that,' she said, attempting to sound casual. 'Martin, obviously. I've told Cissie about it, she'll need to get it fixed, of course. I feel terrible. Her lovely house. I've only been here just over a week but the place is already suffering wear and tear. I've asked her to let me have the bill as soon as she gets it, I don't want her to be out of pocket.'

He wasn't going to leave it at that, but he could see she needed a few minutes. Just one glance had shown him she was fragile. He'd never seen her so pale. And there were deep hollows under her eyes. Why had they let that swine marry her? He wanted to hug her but knew that would just make her more emotional. So he asked again about Sheila Fenniston, and she told him everything again in more detail.

'And they really didn't realise she was already dead? Horrid for you, Deedee, having to see something like that.'

'I don't really know what anyone thought,' Dee admitted. 'From the way they were talking, I'd imagined her on the floor having just fallen and bumped her head or fainted or something—I really didn't expect her to be genuinely dead. In fact, I didn't even think she'd be seriously hurt. Oh, it was just awful. I can still hardly believe... And even now, I keep thinking...' Tears prickled her eyes. She couldn't go on, so she simply shook her head and whispered, 'Poor Sheila.'

'And you had that swine Clarke to deal with too!' He couldn't help it, he was still boiling with a mixture of rage and fear on her behalf. That hole in the wall... it could so easily have been his sister who had been on the receiving end of that fist.

She sighed. 'Yes. That was the afternoon before. It was my own fault, though. I so proudly sent off my postcards and completely forgot that he was practically guaranteed to see the one addressed to everyone at Lady Adelaide's. He must have got the train straight down on Saturday, or perhaps even Sunday, though the Sunday service on this line is shocking. Then somehow, he found where I was staying.'

Rob looked furious. He shook his head, 'I imagine he only had to ask the first person he met. In a place this size, he'd find you pretty quickly. Everyone would know about the nice young lady from London staying here to get over her illness.' Drawing her into his arms for a comforting hug, he asked softly, 'He didn't hurt you, did he? Seriously I mean?'

She could only shake her head, then she wriggled free before she gave into the urge to sob on his shoulder.

He didn't look any happier. 'Tell me all about it. Do I need to unleash Freddie and Harry?'

She busied herself with making the tea, and Rob, still enjoying being manly, carried the tray through to the sitting-room. As she curled up in her favourite armchair, she replied, 'Luckily, I haven't seen him since. I'm hoping he's gone back to London. He's got his job to consider, after all. But I must admit, for the last couple of days, I've been pretty jumpy.'

'It sounds as though you put him in his place, at least. Well done, Dee, I'm proud of you.'

The inquest into the death of Sheila Fenniston was held on Friday morning in the main room in the village hall. The place was packed.

Dee, attending an inquest for the first time, couldn't help but feel a flutter of excitement as she and Rob took their seats about halfway back, amid the buzz of chatter and the scraping of chairs on the highly polished floor.

But it was with a sense of profound sadness that she listened to Mrs Hunter's daughter Mrs Grayson—who was indeed the 'gypsy' from the fair—explaining how she had found Sheila's body, then Dee was called forward to briefly explain her presence in the dead woman's room.

The doctor who had attended the scene was called to give his evidence, adding that he was Miss Fenniston's own doctor, and that he had known her professionally for about two years, but not at all acquainted with her socially.

Then they heard the inspector from the area police headquarters at Sandneath tell the coroner what little was known of Sheila Fenniston's life. He suggested she had been somewhat wild in her youth, that she had been cautioned for shop-lifting at the age of seventeen, and had been fined for being drunk and disorderly in a public place at the age of nineteen. He continued by saying that she enjoyed going up to London for the night-life, where she went to bars, nightclubs and private casinos. He finished his evidence with the statement that it was believed there had been a large number of boyfriends whom she sometimes saw concurrently.

It all seemed too awful, Dee thought. The bare bones of Sheila's life were being laid out for the crowd to pick over like last Sunday's roast chicken. All Sheila's mistakes and failings were brought out into public view but none of her strengths or achievements. Her small, ordinary hopes and plans, confided so recently to Dee, seemed all the more pitiful for being normal.

The pathologist explained that Miss Fenniston had taken a large quantity of sleeping pills together with three or four glasses of wine before slashing her wrists with an old-fashioned straight-edged razor. He confirmed that only Miss Fenniston's fingerprints were found on the glass and the handle of the razor. He gave the time of death as somewhere between ten o'clock on the night of Monday 3rd May and one o'clock in the morning of Tuesday the 4th May. He had based his conclusions on the condition of the body when it had been officially examined by himself some four hours after the police had been notified, which was itself approximately thirty minutes after the deceased had been discovered on Tuesday morning.

When the coroner asked if the wine was from Prescott's stock, Jeremy Prescott came forward to state on oath that it was. There was then a discussion of whether Miss Fenniston had been seen by anyone taking the wine or whether it had been purchased in a shop or received as a gift.

It quickly became clear that although there was a slight chance of Miss Fenniston obtaining a bottle from a hotel or restaurant in London, it was too slim a chance to be considered likely. It was known that she had not been to London for some months, having recently only left Porthlea in order to accompany Mr Prescott to his conference in Brighton. Then the deceased had taken her own two-week holiday immediately afterwards. It was established that Miss Fenniston had gone to Southend for her holiday, and although she had changed trains in London in order to reach her destination, there was no evidence that she had visited a hotel and purchased a bottle of Prescott's wine.

Jeremy Prescott emphatically denied that it would have been given as a gift by anyone from Prescott's management. He managed to suggest that Miss Fenniston had somehow obtained the wine herself from the warehouse. He admitted there were occasional discrepancies in the stock, that a few bottles went missing annually, 'But,' he maintained, 'not a large number.' Most of the discrepancies could be explained by breakages or routine tasting, but he was forced to admit not all missing stock could be explained in this way.

'May we assume Miss Fenniston had access to the warehouse and therefore to the wine stored there?' the coroner asked.

Prescott nodded, and said clearly, for the whole room to hear,

'Oh yes, Miss Fenniston was a trusted member of staff. She was certainly free to go wherever she pleased within the premises, and from time to time, I sent her into the warehouse to fetch me some wine. There would be nothing remarkable in Miss Fenniston going into the warehouse or being seen carrying a bottle of wine.'

'They're making her sound like a common thief,' Dee whispered furiously to Rob. He nodded, and replied, keeping his voice low,

'And why are they focussing on the wine rather than the open razor with which she supposedly slashed her wrists? That's not a common thing to have lying around the place these days. Twenty years ago, perhaps. But not these days... And the character assassination!'

Questioned on the subject of his involvement with

Miss Fenniston in a romantic relationship, Prescott flushed pink. His tone was rather defensive as he said, 'There was no question of my being involved in a relationship of that kind. Miss Fenniston was a trusted secretary. I found her efficient and reliable if a little overly emotional. She gave excellent administrative support throughout the time she worked for Prescott's and we are all very sad that this horrible thing has happened.'

He was thanked and excused by the coroner and as he turned to go, Prescott added, 'I find it impossible to believe that she had any hopes in my direction. That would hardly be appropriate. No, if Miss Fenniston was unhappy in love, there must have been some young fellow who had—hurt her.'

Rob leaned to murmur in Dee's ear, 'I don't believe he's being completely truthful. He knows something.'

Dee had been thinking the same thing.

Prescott was permitted to return to his seat. The doctor who had attended Miss Fenniston briefly returned to the front of the hall to attest that he had never treated Miss Fenniston for depression or anxiety, nor had he ever prescribed her sleeping pills. He stated that he could not account for them being in her possession, but that the brand was a common one and available on prescription from any pharmacist. The police inspector once again bobbed up to inform the coroner that he was satisfied no one else was involved in Miss Fenniston's decease, and that he was satisfied that Miss Fenniston was depressed due to the realisation that Mr Prescott was not in love with her. The coroner announced he would retire for a short while to consider the evidence before giving his ruling.

Within half an hour, the coroner returned to his seat, banging his gavel and calling for order. The villagers quietened immediately. Dee bit her lip, trying to tell from his expression what his findings would be.

The coroner gathered his papers and prepared to give his verdict.

'I am satisfied that Miss Sheila Fenniston died by her own hand, due to being depressed over a failed love affair.'

Dee was horrified to hear sniggering from a number of people seated around the room. 'How could they,' she whispered to her brother.

A man who had been sitting three rows behind them suddenly leapt to his feet and shouted, 'He as good as killed her. He turned her head. She fell for all his fine words and look what happened to her. It's all his fault!' He waved a fist in the direction of Jeremy Prescott.

Dee stared, caught between embarrassment and fascination. Conversation erupted loudly all around her. But the coroner pounded his gavel several times, demanding silence, and the man was hauled out by a couple of policemen whilst all around people jeered and shouted:

'Go on, Norman, you tell 'em.'

'Oh give it a rest, Norman, she was nothing but a cheap tart.'

The coroner banged his gavel on the table in front of him once more. At the front, Prescott stood up and turning to face the crowd and lifting his voice, he demanded that they settle down. 'Or I will have a week's pay from every man Jack of you!'

That threat brought the room to order far more quickly than the coroner's gavel. With the shouting man now gone, and Prescott resuming his seat, the coroner, with a stern look for the 'audience', continued his summing-up, and in a few short minutes, it was all over.

Back at the cottage, with a pot of tea and hot buttered crumpets in lieu of lunch, Rob and Dee discussed the inquest and the coroner's findings. Rob began by saying, 'They sat in judgement of her morals, and on the slimmest of evidence. They tried very hard to make her sound emotionally disturbed, sexually immoral, and foolish. They made it sound as though she was an habitual lawbreaker, and used that as proof of lack of moral rectitude which led to her committing suicide. Suicide should no longer be viewed in such terms. It was no better than taking her character away.'

Dee was desperately unhappy about the whole thing. It wasn't so much the result—that was just as she had feared. It was the evidence that bothered her. Rob had more experience of courtrooms and coroners' inquests, so she asked him,

'Do you think it's possible the Prescotts have hushed things up? I thought at first they were such nice people, but now I'm beginning to think they are rather self-serving. For Prescott to suggest the attraction was all only on Sheila's side... Well, I don't know if that's true. Everyone in the village was certain he was carrying on with her. It was all anyone talked about.'

'Are you saying you think Prescott killed her to avoid a scandal and made it look like suicide?'

'What?' Dee sat up so quickly she almost upset her tea. 'No, I'm not saying that! What on earth made you think...? Of course not. No, I just meant, everyone in the village believes Miss Fenniston and Mr Prescott were carrying on, but the evidence we heard today made it sound like she had a silly schoolgirl crush on him that he knew nothing about, and that he believed she had another boyfriend. And that may possibly be true, because there was a man who pestered her at the village fair—it was that Norman fellow who stood up and shouted at the end of the inquest.

'But later on at the fair, there was another chap who was trying to speak to her. I saw her walk away from him. In fact she tried very hard to get away from both of them—at the fair I actually heard her saying to the other man something like, 'I said no', and she said it quite loudly. Admittedly Sheila seemed to be flinging herself at Jeremy Prescott. I'd seen them together a couple of times. And if, as the Prescotts say, there was nothing going on between Sheila and Jeremy Prescott, why did Meredith act the way she did at the fair—she was furious to see him laughing and joking with Sheila. The second she saw them, she rushed over and dragged him away, presumably on some concocted pretext or another. Then it was Sheila who was furious.'

'Was his sister worried about his reputation, perhaps? Or was it just a case of Sheila's wishful thinking, and his sister wishing to save him or the family from embarrassment?'

But Dee was still trying to puzzle out the inquest. 'I'm doubting myself now. Perhaps it *was* all just on her side? I can't remember actually seeing anything very much... the first time I saw them both together, she practically summoned him off the street to join her in the beach-front café. He looked a bit irritated by that, but he didn't give her the brush-off, He did what she wanted, and even invited her back to the manor house for lunch. But—it's funny—the more I think about it, the less sure I am that there was anything on his side.'

'I suppose the police, the coroner and the doctor all know their jobs,' Rob said. 'They must have heard the stories about Sheila and this Jeremy Prescott, possibly from the Prescotts themselves, and dismissed them as just that: stories, rumours.'

'Perhaps she was just fooling herself, or they may have had an affair and he'd ended it a while before,' she added, her brow furrowed as she pondered it all. 'Or they may have had an affair and *she* ended it, and his pride won't let him admit it.'

'The police and coroner must have been sure. They wouldn't have come to their conclusions if they weren't absolutely certain. So in spite of my reservations about the way the inquest was handled, we don't actually have anything to show she didn't take her own life.'

She murmured her reluctant agreement. 'I suppose it's just one of those sad things that happens now and then,' she said. 'Perhaps it was what happened at the fair with Meredith grabbing her brother and taking him away. Perhaps that was when it finally hit Sheila that the family would never let her marry Jeremy. Poor Sheila. I wish I had known that she was so unhappy. She seemed perfectly all right that afternoon at the fair. More than all right. She was enjoying her job, even trying to persuade me to give up teaching and go in for that sort of thing myself. Although she was chain-smoking rather a lot. That's said to be a sign of unhappiness, isn't it?'

'Only if you don't usually chain-smoke. Some people do it all the time.'

Dee shook her head. 'I never dreamt she was so miserable. It must have just come over her out of the blue and been too much to bear.'

Rob nodded. 'Yes. So much for life being a bed of roses.'

They spent a quiet evening at the cottage. Rob told her all his news—not so very much, after all, but after the last few days, it was pleasant to receive good wishes from her family. She was not at all surprised to hear that their brother Freddie had already been given what Rob described as 'the great heave-ho' by his latest *amour* after just three dinner dates.

Dee could only shake her head and say, as she always did, 'Freddie can't half pick 'em!'

Their other brother Harry was as dull and reliable as ever, spending most of his time tying fishing flies or standing up to his waist in cold water clad in waders.

'Poor Harry. I keep hoping he will do something more interesting with his life,' Dee murmured, leaning back and taking another sip of the wine Rob had brought with him. She felt as though she was relaxing at long last.

'As a trainee stockbroker,' Rob responded, 'He says he gets more than enough excitement at work. He doesn't want it at home as well. Though he did catch a really large trout the other week.'

Dee rolled her eyes. 'I know, but he's only 28, why is he so boring already? He should be doing something exciting with his life!'

'Well, he's making a heck of a lot of money, so...' Rob said.

'True. But he's got no one to spend it on. Surely he should have lingerie models flinging themselves at him by now?'

'He'd be terrified. Though, strictly on the QT, I think he does have a bit of a thing for a daughter of one of the top bods where he works. Apparently she is doing a few weeks' paper-shuffling before going to university. In his own eloquent words, she is the very personification of feminine beauty.'

Dee raised her eyebrows. 'My God, did he really say that? He has got it bad. I wonder if she is allowed to use her brain too?'

'Probably not,' Rob said, taking another sip of wine. 'Otherwise she'd realise that under that posh suit, he's a bit of an old fuddy-duddy.'

'Well I shall rely on you to keep me informed.' She watched him over the rim of her glass, and seeing that he looked tranquil, she added a sly, 'What about you, Robert Charles, any new gorgeous young thing in your life?'

He frowned briefly, but then his features relaxed into a smile. 'No, my darling, there's no one. I shall be an old maid at this rate.'

'What happened about Jeffrey Kent? I thought he was utterly smitten?'

Rob's face fell. He sighed. 'Gone back to his wife.'

There was a long pause. He really did look upset about it.

Dee reached out to touch his arm. She said softly, 'I'm so sorry, sweetie. I didn't realise he was still... I know he meant a lot to you.'

He shook himself and sat up. 'He *said* they were finished. Said they were going to be divorced. Said that it was me he loved, and that we'd be together always. Well. Obviously, that was a lie. I suppose that's what happens when one breaks the eleventh commandment or whatever and falls for a married man. Thou shalt not covet thy neighbour's gorgeous husband.' He gulped down half a glass of wine and poured himself another. 'Bloody men, they always go back to their wives, it seems. Blast them. Top-up for you, Deedee?'

'Better not.'

*

Chapter Eleven

On Saturday, they took a train and went on an excursion to the bright lights of Sandneath. It was even less exciting than they'd anticipated, and they were back by twelve o'clock. They went for a lunchtime drink in the village pub but failed to find out anything new about Sheila Fenniston. Everyone was talking about the woman and her death, but it was all the same stuff they'd already heard.

On the way back, Dee introduced Rob to Mrs Hunter, out for an afternoon 'walk', propelled along by Marlene who appeared to be in a very bad mood, even for her. Until she saw Rob, that is, then she straightened up, patted her hair and adopted a deeply interested expression, appearing to drink in his every word of the short exchange of pleasantries with her grandmother. Dee wished she could tell Marlene she was wasting her time. Instead, she turned to the old lady.

'Will you be having any more lodgers, Mrs Hunter?'

'That'll be up to my daughter. 'Tis her what rents the

place from the Prescotts. I just lodge with her.'

'Oh I see.'

Mrs Hunter fixed her with a blank stare. 'You was pretty thick with Sheila, wasn't you?'

Dee shook her head. 'Not really. I only really spoke to her once at the fair. But I liked her. She was clever.'

Mrs Hunter nodded.

Seizing the opportunity, Dee asked, 'Did she have many friends in the village?'

Leaning back again in her chair, Mrs Hunter shook her head. 'Not really.'

Dee thought the old woman seemed a little wary. But why? 'Was it true what they say, that she had three boyfriends at once on the go?'

Mrs Hunter bridled with offence. 'Who's been saying that? Taking away her character after she's dead and can't defend herself. Tell me who it was!'

Dee was forced to hedge. She was glad Mrs Hunter was prepared to defend Sheila, but didn't particularly enjoy being on the end of the old woman's wrath. 'Oh, I'm afraid I didn't catch their name.'

'Hmm.' Mrs Hunter's expression was suspicious.

But here, Marlene craned forward over the handle of the wheelchair and said, 'There was only that Norman, wasn't there, Gran? And she'd already got shot of him. Wasn't good enough for her. Can't say I blame her, neither. Big drip.' She beamed at Rob, who was frowning at his shoes.

'Shush, you!' Mrs Hunter snapped. 'Yes,' she said turning back to Dee, 'Sheila was seeing that Norman chap. The mummy's boy. A complete drip. But then she had a better offer, as you might say.'

'Jeremy Prescott?' Dee asked.

Mrs Hunter's mouth widened into a gum-revealing grin. 'I know that's what people think, but no. He's more in your line,' she said with a nod at Rob, who looked completely taken aback. She turned back to Dee.

'No, missy, Sheila had an offer from one of they foreign chappies.'

'Really?' Dee was astonished. She leaned a little closer. 'I don't suppose you know which one?'

Mrs Hunter looked annoyed with herself. 'No I don't, mores the pity. If you find out, will you let me know?'

Dee had a sudden idea, and leaning forward, she asked in a slightly lowered voice, 'I don't suppose you know if there were any poison pen letters found in Sheila's room, do you?'

The old lady looked at Dee. She seemed surprised, and that wary look was back. Dee was practically holding her breath.

Mrs Hunter shook her head, 'Sorry, I don't know nuffin about that.' She motioned to Marlene to start pushing again.

As they parted company, Dee smiled to hear Marlene speak to her gran, then heard the old lady say something that ended with a witch-like cackle, then Marlene said, 'What? No, he can't be, he's so good-looking!'

Rob gave Dee a rueful look. 'I always thought I blended in well with the—er—country gentlemen?'

To his annoyance, she burst out laughing.

That evening they had dinner at Cissie's. Rob brought along another bottle of wine and got the post-mistress a little tipsy. The evening was spent in reminiscing and looking at old photos. When Rob and Dee walked back to the cottage, they enjoyed the gentle breeze and felt quite at peace with the world.

As they stood in the porch of the cottage, Dee was trying to find the door key in her bag, and a large car drove slowly along the village street. Rob said softly,

'Did you see who that was?'

'No, idiot, I'm trying to put the key in the door. Get

out of the light.'

'I think it might have been that Prescott fellow. Posh bloke sitting in the front next to the chauffeur.'

'No doubt he's been out entertaining his visitors, or has just taken them back to their hotel. Hardly earth-shattering.'

'Except that he had no tie or overcoat on, and I could see that he was doing up his shirt.'

Dee turned to stare at him. 'What? Coming back from an 'assignation', I assume you're suggesting? He certainly got over Sheila quickly.'

'Didn't he just.'

'What was it Mrs Hunter said? Something about him being one of your lot?'

'I bet she knows everything. She's like an old soothsayer or something.'

'I was thinking the same thing. And she said that about Rodericks the chauffeur too.'

'Perhaps she thinks all men are bent?' Rob said.

They went to church the next morning. Dee had insisted. Rob groaned and moaned and wanted to know why, especially given the 'ungodly hour' she dragged him out of bed. It was just on nine o'clock when she gave him his tea and toast.

'Because in a village this small, everyone will be there. It might be useful.'

'Useful? How?' Then realisation hit, and Rob rolled his eyes. 'Oh, I see. Still playing Miss Marple, are we? Oh very well, if we must. Though I don't see why you need me to come with you.'

The church service was dull. Callum Edmonds might be a friendly neighbour and keen fan of brass bands, but he was no sermoniser. Several people, including Rob, were blatantly asleep.

But outside the church, they hovered, hoping to exchange greetings with a few people. Their patience was rewarded: Meredith Prescott—the sole representative of her family—came over, and in no time at all, Rob was introduced to her and they received an invitation to dine that evening.

'Half past seven. We don't Dress, so just come as you are,' Meredith said. She seemed quite taken with Rob, Dee thought.

They arrived promptly, taking with them the pot plant that the Edmondses had given Dee. It was the only gift they could think of. There seemed to be little point in taking a bottle of wine as a hostess gift to a family of winesellers. They were greeted by Meredith herself. She smiled broadly and welcomed them, relieving Dee of her shawl, and then taking in her mini dress with a slight compression of the lips. Dee presented the plant.

'Oh thanks.' Meredith seemed rather nonplussed by the gift, and left the plant on the bottom stair, presumably for disposal later. 'It's lovely to see you again.' Meredith hesitated, looking back over her shoulder. She lowered her voice. 'I just thought I'd let you know, some of our visitors are still here. My aunt is not at all happy about it. They were supposed to leave two days ago.'

'Ah,' Dee replied and exchanged a look with Rob. They followed Meredith into the drawing-room, where Mrs Smithies and Jeremy Prescott were waiting. Three other men and a woman were standing slightly apart and looking uncomfortable.

'May I present Miss Dee Gascoigne and her brother Mr Rob Gascoigne. They are staying in the village for a short while,' Meredith announced to the room at large. Mrs Smithies inclined her neck with stiff formality, no smile relaxing her lips, but Jeremy came forward, his hand outstretched and said he was delighted. Dee thought his two or three furtive glances at Rob were rather telling, and her thoughts set off in a new direction. It should be an interesting evening.

'Where are they staying? Surely not at the public house?' Mrs Smithies asked her niece. Meredith's glance at Dee and Rob was hesitant.

Thinking it was rather rude of Mrs Smithies to ask Meredith about their arrangements, Dee said, 'Oh we're staying in Mrs Palmer's cottage. She's the post-mistress.'

Mrs Smithies inclined her neck once again but said nothing. Clearly she was not happy about their accommodation.

Dee rushed on to add, 'It's very cosy and pleasant, quite a little home from home.'

'I don't remember the Palmer woman asking for permission to let out her cottage,' Mrs Smithies remarked.

Meredith, looking worried, said with a placating smile, 'Oh, but it's just an informal agreement, Aunt, I'm sure we can overlook it just this once.'

'Humph,' remarked Mrs Smithies.

'I'm not paying any rent,' Dee assured them, worried on Cissie's behalf that the Prescotts thought Cissie was cheating them. 'It's was just a favour to my mother to let me borrow the cottage for a few days...' Her voice trailed off.

'Never mind all that,' Jeremy laughed as he crossed the room and hurriedly drew them over to the other guests, saying as he did so, 'Come and meet everyone. I'd like to introduce Monsieur Jean-Paul Truchet and his son, Monsieur Jean-Marie Truchet.'

Dee and Rob came forward, and politely greeted the two Frenchmen in their own language, Rob's accent almost as polished as his sister's. Jeremy said nothing but smiled and raised an eyebrow. Then he introduced them to Herr and Frau Kostner, and once again, Dee said good evening and that it was a pleasure to make their acquaintance, once again speaking in their own language. All four of the visitors were now beaming and came a little closer to engage Rob and Dee in conversation, the two French gentlemen speaking with Rob, and the German couple with Dee.

Glancing behind her, Dee saw that Meredith looked taken aback, and Mrs Smithies positively displeased. Oh well, Dee thought, it was just too bad. The Prescotts and their aunt really ought to move with the times.

The maid Davies came to the door and announced that dinner was ready. With Mrs Smithies leading the way, they crossed the hall to the dining-room. Dee was pleased to see she was being seated beside Frau Kostner, whilst on the other side of the long table, Rob was between the younger M. Truchet and Meredith. It was a shame there was an odd number of guests, Dee thought. It would have been ideal if there could have been someone else between the older M. Truchet and Mrs Smithies, who refused to so much as make eye-contact with the poor man who had to do with watching the conversation along the table from him, able to contribute only the occasional remark.

Mrs Smithies presided over the head of the table, and at the opposite end was Jeremy Prescott. The instant they were all seated, various dishes began to appear in rapid succession, carried in by Davies and Marlene who was wearing a uniform two sizes too big for her.

Dee enjoyed a light-hearted conversation about travel with Frau and Herr Kostner, whilst across the table, Rob and the younger M. Truchet enjoyed a friendly conversation in simple French, due to Rob's language skills not being as advanced as Dee's, but she could hear enough to know they were discussing a play they had both seen. Meanwhile, Mrs Smithies addressed herself only to Meredith, and ignored M. Truchet senior completely. Dee took pity on the gentleman, whom she took to be of a similar age to her father and turned to ask him a few questions about his family and his vineyard. Soon, he was smiling and chatting, a happy and charming man. The meal went by quickly enough. And if the hosts lacked warmth, the food was excellent.

When the meal was over, Mrs Smithies rose and led the other three ladies back to the drawing-room. Dee exchanged a smile with the rather nervous-looking Frau Kostner. No doubt I shall have to interpret every sentence from one person to the other, Dee thought. She was relieved to find that Frau Kostner spoke a little English and appeared to understand quite a bit more than she could put into words. Dee heard the clock strike nine and sighed inwardly. The evening was just dragging along.

The men joined them within twenty minutes, and Davies brought in coffee with small squares of Turkish delight and some tiny wafer biscuits.

There was a little stilted conversation, then at ten o'clock on the dot, Davies came in to say that Rodericks was there to return the guests to their hotel. The guests rose eagerly and began to say goodnight. As they prepared to leave, Frau Kostner thanked Dee, whispering that her presence had made the evening bearable for the first time of the fortnight's visit.

'It's been horrid, hasn't it? I don't know how you've put up with it,' Dee replied, and Herr Kostner threw back his head and laughed at this. Mrs Smithies, her eyes narrowed suspiciously, glared in Dee's direction.

'It is a terrible shame about Miss Fenniston,' Frau Kostner murmured, even though she didn't really need to lower her voice as she was speaking in German. 'We were so looking forward to working with her, she had some very fresh and interesting ideas. We liked her.'

But before Dee could ask the German couple any questions, they had to leave with the others.

Once they had gone, Dee wondered how soon she

and Rob could also leave, then Mrs Smithies surprised Dee by actually speaking to her.

'So why exactly are you staying here in Porthlea?' Her imperious tone could rob even a pleasantry of any warmth, and the query had the impact of an interrogation. Dee replied in the affirmative.

'Dee has been unwell, Aunt, and her doctor advised her to convalesce by the sea,' Meredith explained.

'I had bronchitis,' Dee explained.

'Probably merely a cold. Doctors these days know nothing.' Mrs Smithies added dismissively, 'You seem all right to me.'

Startled, Dee was unable to deny that she was much better.

'And what do you do?' Mrs Smithies demanded.

Dee began to explain that she was a modern languages teacher, but too late she realised that the great lady had finished speaking to Dee and turned her countenance upon Rob.

Mrs Smithies's manner could not have been better calculated to irritate Rob, and Dee could see he was annoyed. Which usually made him 'difficult'. Rob took his time answering, taking a drink of his second cup of coffee, then carefully leaning forward to set the cup down on the little side-table. He flicked an imaginary speck off his tie before replying. Mrs Smithies was noticeably irritated, whilst Meredith looked embarrassed and Jeremy... Jeremy was hiding behind a glass of port but Dee thought he was smiling.

'I'm studying law, in my final year as a matter of fact, currently working in a practise in London on a six-month placement,' Rob drawled.

'I see. Of course they tolerate all sorts nowadays one understands. I'm afraid standards have fallen shockingly since the war.'

'I imagine that's true,' Rob agreed with a smile, adding, 'In all walks of life, no doubt.' He sipped his wine. Mrs Smithies, unsure if she had been insulted or not, didn't seem to know quite how to respond to that. Meredith hid her face behind her handkerchief.

'And what does your father do?' Mrs Smithies demanded.

'As little as possible, most of the time.' When Mrs Smithies raised an offended brow at this, Rob went on to say, 'He leaves the running of the estate to our older brother Freddie in the main.'

'The estate?' This seemed to mollify Mrs Smithies somewhat. She tried unsuccessfully to disguise her interest.

'Just a few thousand acres in Hertfordshire, not a huge place.' Rob waved it away as if it were nothing. 'Been in the family since the days of the Conqueror. I believe someone or other of our ancestors did the fellow a good turn.'

There was a long silence as the Prescotts and Mrs Smithies mentally adjusted their attitudes.

Making the most of her chance, Dee said, 'It was terribly sad about poor Miss Fenniston.'

'We do not mention that woman in this house.' And with that, Mrs Smithies got to her feet and walked out of the room.

An awkward silence filled the void. Dee, horrified by her own power, hastened to stammer an apology. They heard Mrs Smithies going up the stairs.

Meredith jumped up and hurried for the door, saying over her shoulder, 'Please excuse me for a moment.'

Dee and Rob exchanged a look, and Dee hesitated on the brink of another apology. Jeremy Prescott waved it away.

'Please don't worry about it, Miss Gascoigne. It is I who should apologise. I'm afraid my aunt was very rude. These trying times have taken their toll and we are all very much shaken. I'm afraid our nerves are a little frayed with all the questions we've had to face from that blasted policeman from Sandneath. My sister will be back shortly, I'm certain. So let's talk about happier topics.'

And turning to Rob he asked him if he enjoyed fishing or shooting.

Meredith returned ten minutes later smiling, and it was clear the reviled topic was behind them. She invited Dee to step outside onto the patio.

'It's a little too dark for a stroll around the garden,' she said. 'But it will be pleasant on the patio. It's still quite warm out.'

Eager to make amends for her clumsy question, Dee accepted with as much relief as enthusiasm. As they rose to leave the room. Jeremy was asking Rob if he would care for a cigar. She was surprised to hear her brother say he would love one, and she fixed him with a puzzled frown. He never usually smoked.

The second they were outside, Dee turned to Meredith and said, 'I'm really so very sorry, I never intended...'

But Meredith immediately held up her hand, saying in an echo of her brother, 'No. It is I who should apologise. I invited you both to dinner and my aunt has allowed the fact that she is feeling rather tired to get the better of her. You have nothing to apologise for. It is we who should... My aunt has been unwell, she's not as young as she was, and we've had a few difficult days.'

They had headed towards a table and chairs at the far end of the patio, lit by the light from the drawing-room window. Meredith was right, Dee thought, it was still warm out here and the breeze was soft and pleasant.

Meredith continued, 'It's entirely my fault. Unfortunately, following recent events, my aunt had been looking forward to a quiet family dinner, and then

found our guests were still here, and that I had invited
both of you. Between you and I, she was a little put out.
And matters were just made worse by the foreigners
still being here. Can you possibly forgive us for our
awful behaviour? I don't know what you must think of
us.' There was a momentarily pause, then Meredith's
voice shook as she added, 'The pressure we've been
under—you have no idea! Everyone blames us, I know
they do, I feel them watching me when I go into the
village. And then the letters... But anyway, the
scandalmongers are loving every second of our misery.
I tried to be kind to the poor woman, but what can you
do when someone falls in love with her employer? It's
completely unreasonable and such an impossible
position to place us in.' Her eyes filled with tears, and
she began patting frantically at her sleeve.

Dee remembered she had seen the handkerchief fall
onto the floor earlier. She fished a clean handkerchief
from her evening bag and handed it over, saying, 'Don't
upset yourself. It's perfectly all right. I understand. You
ought to have sent a message to cancel, we would have
understood perfectly.'

'You're so kind,' Meredith said, still dabbing at her
eyes and attempting a smile. 'At the fair when I was
tired, and now here. And I'm so grateful to you for
talking to our visitors during dinner. That made things
so much easier for us. That's another thing that's been
an absolute nightmare.'

Dee looked out at the garden just below them, lit by
the drawing-room lamps, and the moon and stars.
Between them, all these lights created a very pleasing
effect on the lawn and surrounding shrubs and trees.
The evening was cooling, but not yet cold, the leaves
rustled gently. It would be lovely to sit here with a
sweetheart, Dee thought.

Meredith appeared to be calmer, and she had tucked
the handkerchief away in the waistband of her long

black skirt, promising to get it washed and returned to Dee as soon as she could.

'When do your overseas guests go back?' Dee asked. She hoped this would be a subject change for the better.

'Soon, thank heavens! The Americans and the Italians went back yesterday. We've got the Germans and the French for two more days, then they will be leaving too, and we can all give a sigh of relief and get back to normal. The Americans were all right, obviously, and the Germans are too. At least they are polite. And the older French man is pleasant enough. But the younger one, his son... Oh he's been just awful.' Meredith got to her feet again and with Dee following suit, meandered across the patio to sit on a stone parapet above the lawn. Meredith idly leaned over to pick a flower and played with it as she spoke.

'Aunt Lucinda and I were beginning to think they'd never leave. But thankfully Jeremy saw the first lot safely to the airport yesterday morning. And no doubt, he'll take the others as well. He insisted on driving them everywhere himself, even though we have a chauffeur. And even on the rare occasions Rodericks did drive them, Jeremy still felt it only right to go along, and dance attendance upon our guests. To be honest, he is rather hoping to get some contracts which will be very advantageous to Prescott Wines. But all the same, they were just so demanding! Really it's a huge relief to see them gone.'

'It must be difficult,' Dee hazarded. 'I suppose they all spoke good English?'

Meredith laughed. 'Oh, if only! I mean, you saw for yourself this evening just how hopeless it is. Sometimes it's absolutely painful to try and have any kind of conversation with them.'

Dee tried a change of subject. 'Sorry. Of course it must be a nightmare for Mr Prescott at the moment. And on top of that, he hasn't got a secretary to help him out. Is he looking for someone else?'

'Thinking of applying?' Meredith asked, her tone wary. Dee hastened to set her mind at rest.

'Heavens, no! I'd be utterly hopeless. I can't do shorthand to save my life, and my typewriting is of the two-fingered variety. No, I was just thinking there must be loads of work that has just simply ground to a halt, and then there are all your visitors. No doubt he'd be needing a new secretary pretty quickly.'

'Hmm. I can't deny that in many ways Miss Fenniston's demise has been a dreadful inconvenience for us. Jeremy is having to manage everything completely on his own. And as you say, just at this crucial time with our visitors, too. But he has already been in touch with an agency so hopefully it won't be for much longer. I do hope he gets a man this time though, I can't be doing with all that over-familiarity again, not to mention the way she mooned over him all the time, and the endless gossip in the village and around the warehouse. Ah well, there it is.' She glanced about her, and Dee knew the conversaton was at an end. 'Shall we go back in? I expect the men will have finished their cigars by now.'

They had. The four of them chatted about this and that, and soon Rob and Dee rose to leave. Jeremy offered to drive them back to the cottage but was clearly relieved when they declined, saying it was a lovely evening for a walk. At the front door, Dee shook hands with Jeremy and performed an uncomfortable kind of kiss in mid-air beside Meredith's ear as they said goodbye.

'I've got an interview for a job, which means I'll be going back to London with Rob right after Sheila's funeral tomorrow, so we probably won't meet again.'

Was it her imagination, or did that odd light in Meredith's eyes signal relief? The Prescotts stayed by the front door waving until Dee and Rob turned the bend in the drive and the house was lost behind the trees.

'Well, what a peculiar evening,' Rob commented as they went out into the street to the village. It was fortunate that it wasn't far to the cottage. Dee was bursting to tell Rob what Meredith had said, and to find out if he had found out anything interesting from Meredith's brother. She wanted to know what Rob made of the family who had hosted such an odd dinner.

She made hot chocolate and got out a packet of garibaldis. Once they were settled on the bouncy sofa, she leaned towards him, her eyes shining, and said, 'Well then, tell me everything!'

Rob frowned, remembering.

'Did Jeremy have anything interesting to say after we 'ladies' left you to your cigars?'

'Not really. Most of what he said doesn't bear repeating, he really does seem to have a one-track mind.' He paused for a few seconds, reflecting. 'But... Oh I don't know. I just felt that it rang false somehow. Like he thought those were the kind of things he was expected to say. The off-colour jokes and the sex talk. And of course, the two French gentlemen had little to say to Jeremy other than polite nods and smiles, and the German gentleman, Herr Kostner, went over to look at the books on the small bookcase there. He made no attempt to even try to join in the conversation, and I can't say I blame him. It's a shame my German is practically non-existent, I bet he's a very interesting fellow.

'But Prescott did make it pretty clear that any attraction was all on Sheila's side. He admired her business-sense and the way she helped with their visitors. From that point of view, he's really missing her. As to the other, he as good as told me he flirted with her to persuade her to do longer hours and things that weren't really her responsibility, that he led her to believe he thought a lot more of her than he really did to make life easier for himself. I wonder how much he actually promised, knowing he had no intention of honouring his promises. He said flattery gets you everywhere in business, so long as things don't get out of hand and the girl doesn't have too many expectations.'

'Which it clearly did. Get out of hand, I mean,' Dee pointed out. Rob nodded.

'Oh definitely. I said something about that. A bit more tactfully of course, though I'm not very good at that old-boys'-network, men-of-the-world stuff. He just laughed and said, 'Most unfortunate, leaves a bad taste in one's mouth, what? But I never thought she would take me seriously. She ought to have known better than that.' The idiot. Anyway, he is about to get a replacement, apparently. He told me his aunt and his sister want him to get a male secretary to replace Sheila, but he's got no intention of doing that. 'What's the point of a secretary with no nice figure or pretty face to brighten up the place,' he said. So I can only assume he plans to carry on the same way. To quote his own words, 'Business always goes down better with a pretty girl in the room."

'He's such a...' Dee couldn't think of anything sufficiently bad to describe how she felt about Jeremy Prescott. Rob set down his cup.

'He's a dog. And I don't think your friend Meredith is a lot better. Such snobs, all out for what they can get. And then closing ranks when it all goes sour. Although Sheila Fenniston must have been rather naïve if she believed he would keep any promises he made.'

'I don't think she was naïve. I liked her,' Dee said. 'She was a bit outrageous, and of course far too modern and gaudy for this little place, but she was clever. She had ideas, she worked jolly hard, and she was fresh and determined. She just seemed so—honest and open. I'm not too sure she hadn't already begun to see through Prescott and was making other plans. But then why take her own life?'

'Poor woman,' he said again, shaking his head. 'Did you find out much from your friend Meredith?'

'Will you please stop calling her my friend? After tonight I don't think I shall ever think of her as a friend. She was just the same as Jeremy. It was all about how Sheila's death has made everything so awful for them. How difficult things are, how much they've suffered, what people might be saying about them. How inconvenient everything has been for them. She complained several times about the nuisance of entertaining their winegrowers from overseas. Who are presumably helping them to make their fortune so they can carry on living in their lovely big house in their lovely village just like they probably did before the war. It's practically feudal.'

'Or at least, they seem to think it is,' her brother agreed. 'They are completely out of touch with the real world. I don't think we do things like that on our estate, do we? Dad's always been pretty scared of upsetting our tenants and gives them almost anything they ask for.' He fell quiet for a moment. Dee could tell he had something on his mind. After a short pause, he said, 'There is one thing I need to tell you.'

'Oh? That sounds serious.' Dee was all attention, waiting. He seemed reluctant to speak, given that he had just brought up the topic. 'Well?' she prompted.

He took a breath. 'Well. Actually—er—there was a point towards the end of the conversation when he offered me another glass of port, and I went over to join him by the drinks cabinet, the others were on the other side of the room looking at a painting on the wall and out of earshot. And, well... Dee, he turned to me and said, 'Are you a friend of Mrs King, at all? I believe you may be acquainted."

Dee felt a momentary internal jolt, as if she had been going downstairs and missed a step. Rob had told her previously that this was one of a number of phrases used among men looking for a male companion as a means of identifying one another, a kind of secret code, like Polari. Mrs King meant a Queen, meaning a homosexual man. There was a slight pause before she said, trying to sound calm, 'My goodness. And what did you say?'

'Well, what could I say? I could hardly give the usual response of, 'Oh yes, I love the Queens' or something of that sort, so I said, 'I'm sorry I'm afraid I don't know the lady.'' He was watching her closely. This was something he rarely spoke about openly, but if he did, it was with his sister, who just seemed to somehow understand. He saw her take another steadying breath, and knew he'd upset her. 'Sorry, Deedee. I don't really know how he guessed... I don't know if he believed me. He didn't pursue it. But it's really got me wondering.'

She let out the breath she had been holding. Keeping her voice calm and even, she said, 'Well, never mind. But you need to be careful. I don't want you to get arrested and mess up your career before it even gets started.'

'Neither do I, if it comes to it. And I'm certain I didn't say or do anything to—you know—give myself away. Perhaps sometimes people can just tell. Like old Mother Hunter. And you.'

'I'm your sister, I know you too well for you to hide something like that. Anyway, at home you've never had to hide it, we all know your—preference—and accept it. But out in the big wide world that's another matter. It's dangerous to confide in the wrong people. Besides, I've always known you have no interest in women. Don't forget, I've seen the way you look at the same handsome, dark-haired, muscular men that I'm attracted to. But unlike me, you're not in a position to either openly ogle or to take one home to meet Mother. Crikey, though, this puts a different slant on things, doesn't it? I suppose he wasn't just testing you? Or joking?'

He shrugged. 'No idea. I'd quite like to find out, though, it might be useful for the case.'

'The case!' She almost laughed, but was determined to make her point, worried about him. 'For heaven's sake, be careful. I don't want you to get caught. Think how Mother would feel if you went to prison, she'd be devastated.'

'It's all right, Dee. Don't fret. I don't intend to go to prison,' he laughed.

She felt a rush of maternal anxiety which she automatically disguised as annoyance, and shook him off crossly. 'Don't be an idiot. No one ever 'intends' to go prison. They go to prison due to carelessness, stupidity, greed, or thinking they know better when they don't, or just being in the wrong place at the wrong time, with the wrong man.'

'Ah,' he said. 'The wrong man. We're all looking for him, aren't we?'

Dee couldn't in all fairness deny the truth of that. She brought the conversation back to Jeremy Prescott. 'But about Prescott. I noticed he kept looking at you. That was what made me wonder. What if he isn't the lothario everyone thinks he is? What does that mean for our case, as you call it? Is he, or isn't he?'

'I don't know. It really looks as though your old witch of the village, that Hunter woman, was right. But you needn't worry, I didn't react. In any case, he is definitely not my type. They are a thoroughly unpleasant lot and I don't mind if I never see them again, any of them.'

'I'm sorry to say you're bound to.'

'What? Why?'

'There's still Sheila's funeral on Monday to get

through. They're bound to be there, it would look jolly strange if they weren't.'

'Blast!'

*

Chapter Twelve

Dee was down to breakfast bright and early on Monday morning, and immediately saw a pale blue envelope lying on the doormat beneath the letterbox. She grabbed it and went into the kitchen, her heart pounding. So Mrs Hunter's 'prediction' had come true: this, surely, had to be one of the famous poison pen letters.

She noted there was no Sandneath postmark, nor a stamp, the letter had to have been hand-delivered. The addressee was 'Miss Posh from London'. Dee smiled a little at that. So that was how it was, was it?

She ripped the envelope open and pulled out the rather stiff folded sheet, with cut-out magazine letters stuck all over it. The message was unsubtle and brutal.

'*What you doing down HEAR you posh bItch? I know youve got something to Hyde. The plice will be glad to know your we'er boute. Every 1 nose a-bout all them men visiting you. How much DO they pay you?*'

'Not exactly the work of a criminal mastermind, it seems,' Rob said from behind her. He had just brought their luggage downstairs. Pointing over her shoulder, he said, 'And look, it's still wet here and here from all the glue they put on it. Done last night or first thing this morning, I should say.'

'Hmm. Interesting, isn't it?' She replaced the letter in the envelope and put it away carefully in her handbag. As she turned her back to go to the sink and fill the kettle, Rob said,

'I hope it hasn't upset you?'

She laughed. 'God, no! I've been expecting it. It's interesting to see one in the flesh after discussing them with Cissie. And either one soon-to-be ex-husband and one brother constitute 'all them men', or they are just guessing about what might offend me, or what might be a terrible secret I need to keep private.'

The village's tiny churchyard was packed with mourners as the body of Sheila Fenniston was laid to rest later that day. The sunny morning seemed at odds with the sombre occasion.

Dee and Rob walked the short distance up the hill, Dee in her navy coat and skirt, Rob covering up his light shirt and trousers with a dark overcoat then regretting it immediately as he sweltered inside the heavy wool. On their way they fell in step with a little gaggle of people from the village clearly going the same way. As they walked, they exchanged pleasantries with Cissie and Lily.

The sky was blue and the light breeze ruffled the trees. Birds sang, whilst insects buzzed contentedly among the flowers. To Dee, it didn't seem like the right kind of weather for someone to be buried. If this had been just a few years earlier, Dee thought, Sheila Fenniston would have had to be interred somewhere that wasn't consecrated ground. Even so, the stigma of suggested suicide remained.

Though Dee was in two minds about the coroner's

verdict. If Sheila had been incredibly unhappy and unable to see any way out of whatever it was that had grieved her, Dee could imagine—almost—her taking the pills. But the razor? To use that too? To cut her wrists deeply. To cut first one, then, in spite of the pain, the blood and the effect of the pills she had already taken, to pull back the sleeve of that old-fashioned nightgown and cut the other wrist too, swapping the razor to her other hand to do so. Then to sit there with her hands in her lap and meekly wait for death. It seemed unthinkable. Dee shivered. Sheila had seemed to be a determined woman, and must have overcome many trials and disappointments in her life. Why had this last, admittedly unknown, trial been the one that was too much to bear?

No one had much to say, but she was touched that so many had turned out to pay their last respects to the woman who had lived and worked among them for two years. Although Rob's cynical, whispered remark that it was the only thing going on in the village made her wonder just how many of the mourners were only there to see and be seen, or to gossip and exchange speculations.

Whatever the reason, at least they were there, and they amenned the prayers led by the vicar as the coffin was lowered into the ground. Cissie nudged Dee and pointed out Sheila's brother. Michael Fenniston, seemingly her only family, and hollow-faced with grief, came forward just then to throw a handful of soil onto the shiny wooden surface. He stood there, hands folded as if in prayer, head low, eyes fixed on the ground.

Dee recognised him as the man she had seen arguing with Sheila on the day of the fair. So that was one small mystery solved. As she studied him, Rob nudged her and whispered, 'Your friends aren't here!'

She frowned. She risked a surreptitious glance round at the assembled people, reflecting that if he didn't stop calling the Prescotts and their aunt 'her friends' soon, she would have to give him a dead arm, which she hadn't had to do for fully five years.

But he was right. Among those gathered to mourn at Sheila Fenniston's graveside, there was no sign of Sheila's employer, his sister or Mrs Smithies. Not even Davies, their housekeeper was present in the crowd. Dee exchanged a look with Rob.

Beyond her brother, through a break in the crowd of onlookers, she caught sight of a man standing on his own. She wasn't certain but she thought it was Rodericks, the Prescotts' driver, though there was still no sign of Jeremy Prescott himself. But now she became aware that people were moving away. Sheila Fenniston's funeral was over.

Dee watched as one or two people approached Sheila's brother and shook his hand, murmuring a few words of condolence. He accepted their attention with a composed nod, his head bent in contemplation of the grave with such determination that Dee felt moved. A sideways glance and a nod at her brother told him she was going to go over and speak to Michael Fenniston.

'Hello,' she said softly. He glanced up, and his gooseberry-coloured eyes roved over her whole being in a way that made her feel most uncomfortable, but regardless of that, she remembered his grief and ploughed on with her words of comfort.

'I can't imagine what you're going through,' she said, 'and I'm so, so sorry about Sheila.' As she spoke, he dropped his gaze again to the hole in the ground just a few feet in front of him, saying nothing but clearly waiting for her to continue. A strange reluctance overcame Dee and she seemed unable to express the sorrow she had wanted to convey to him. She floundered.

'So sorry for your terrible loss, old man,' said Rob. He stepped forward and somehow managed to surprise

Sheila's brother into a handshake. 'Very, very sad indeed. Can I buy you a drink at all? We've got a train to catch, but that's not for another hour.'

Dee was relieved that Rob had stepped into the breach when words had failed her. He seemed surprisingly at ease in delicate situations.

Sheila's brother brightened immediately and nodded.

'Don't mind if I do,' he said and turned from the graveside without a backward look. 'The Seagull? That do you? I haven't got anything laid on. For some reason I thought them up at the big house might have the common decency to do something for her, but well, as you see...'

'Rob Gascoigne,' said Rob holding out his right hand, 'and this is my sister Dee.'

'New to the village, aren't you? Pleased to meet you both, I'm sure. I'm Michael Fenniston, Sheila's brother. In fact, I'm pretty well her whole family. Shall we...?'

They began to walk back in the direction of the village pub, pausing briefly in the gateway of the churchyard while Michael shook hands and mumbled his thanks to Callum Edmonds. Dee noticed Millie was standing a few yards away, stealing a surreptitious look at her watch.

'Everyone seems to have cleared off pretty quickly,' Fenniston observed, and the others could hardly help agreeing. The village street was deserted apart from Marlene slowly wheeling her granny home. Marlene halted briefly to say something to Mrs Hunter, something too quiet for Dee's ears to catch. The old woman, staring across at Michael, Rob and Dee, nodded, watching them closely.

Dee fidgeted over the idea of going to the pub with Michael Fenniston and wondered if she could get out of it. He reminded her a little too much of Martin. She sympathised with him over his grief, but instinctively

Caron Allan

disliked him. If only Rob hadn't suggested going for a drink with him. And they still needed to get their things and say goodbye to Cissie before catching their train back to London.

As they approached the public house, Dee was convinced she caught sight of Meredith's face in the dim interior of the post office. The bell was still softly jingling inside as though someone had just opened the door, and with no one else in sight, Dee wondered if Meredith had seen them coming and had ducked into the post office to avoid them. She was there, half-concealed by the revolving stand of postcards, presumably thinking she was safe.

On impulse she excused herself and went in to the post office. She went up to the counter where Cissie was already back behind her desk and banging a rubber stamp on some counterfoils...

She ignored Meredith who was definitely there hovering in the corner, and went right over to the counter.

'Come to say goodbye?' Cissie looked up from her work with a smile.

'That's right. We're popping into the pub first then catching the two-thirty train. We've left our luggage at the station, Rob took it down earlier. So here's the door key, by the way, thank you so much for letting me stay in your lovely cottage. And don't forget to let me have that bill for the wall repairs, I'm sorry about what happened.'

'Well you're looking much better, I must say. She was quite peaky, wasn't she, Miss Prescott, when she first arrived?'

Meredith came forward then, and agreed with a smile that didn't quite reach her eyes. Dee knew she was annoyed at being 'given away' by Cissie.

Cissie came out from behind her counter to give Dee a hug, saying, 'Now you just take good care of yourself,

146

my dear. And give my love to your dear mother. And
good luck in your interview, too. I'll keep my fingers
crossed for you.'

Dee kissed her cheek, 'Thank you. You take care of
yourself too. Right, got to dash. Bye-bye!'

As she left she smiled at Meredith who was
pretending to be busy with some packets of tea.

She went into The Seagull's saloon bar and found
Rob and Michael Fenniston engaged in drinking their
beer in total silence.

*

Chapter Thirteen

The interview that Friday was something of a disaster.

To begin with, she was twenty minutes late due to a collision between a taxi and a very beautiful Rolls Royce that had come out of a side street a little sooner than advisable. By the time Dee reached the premises of the Norman Smith Secondary Modern for Girls, she expected to be turned away. Her usual cool calm demeanour had been replaced by that of someone who felt as though she'd left a tap running in the kitchen.

It was a relief—and she thought, very decent of them—that they agreed nonetheless to interview her.

'Take a seat, Miss...' He consulted his paperwork. 'Ah, my mistake, *Mrs* Clarke. I do apologise, Mrs Clarke.' He clasped his hands on top of the papers in front of him and took a good look at her. A slight frown tightened his lips as his welcoming smile disappeared. 'Ahem, now then, we'll just begin with a few questions.'

The first and second questions, 'How did you hear about the position?' and 'What experience do you have in the field of modern language teaching?' were easy enough to answer.

Dee kept her responses short, to the point and remembered to smile just enough but not too much. Both the men, the one on the left and the one on the right seemed fairly pleased so far. The woman seated between them had frowned at her from the outset.

Perhaps, Dee thought, the woman didn't know she was frowning. That happened sometimes. Dee did it herself from time to time. She gave the woman a beaming smile and got an even deeper frown in reply.

'And what does your husband think about you possibly taking a full-time job, Mrs Clarke?' the woman asked.

Dee hesitated. If she said, as she wanted to, 'It's none of his damned business', she would definitely not get the job. But if she said, 'I've left my husband and I need a job to support myself', she would probably still not get it. She settled for, 'I've been working as a full-time teacher for a number of years, so it won't change my circumstances.'

'Do you have any children, Mrs Clarke?' the man on the left asked.

'No.' She felt that sounded too abrupt so she added another bright smile.

'Suppose you start a family,' the man on the right said. 'We couldn't take someone who might leave after just a few months.'

'I have no plans to start a family,' Dee assured him. Mentally adding, not that it's anything to do with you.

The raising of his eyebrows and his exchanged glance with his female colleague indicated that they were all too aware that families sometimes started without much planning. Dee began to feel irritated.

'Why did you leave your former position at Lady Adelaide's? I believe you have already left?' This was the woman again. Clearly it was her job to ask the difficult questions. And although Dee had expected this one, she couldn't remember what she'd planned to say. Something noncommittal about a change in her personal circumstances, but what was the exact phrase she'd...?

They were staring at her. She'd taken too long to answer, and now, to make things worse, she realised she was frowning at them.

Floundering she said, trying to keep her voice bright and interested, 'I'm sorry, could you repeat...?'

The woman could, and did, with the addition of a further frown.

Dee said, 'Oh well, er, you know...' Her voice died away. She bit her lip. She knew she'd lost her opportunity to win them over. Now she stared at them. The smiles had gone, and they stared back at her severely.

Did she really want to work here with colleagues who glared at her like that? She began to think she didn't want this job after all.

'Why aren't you wearing your wedding ring?' the man on the left asked suddenly.

She looked down at her left hand as if she'd never seen it before. She choked back another unsuitable response, another 'How is that any of your damned business?' Really she was becoming quite foul-mouthed and aggressive. Again she stared back at the panel of interviewers, doing her best impression of a goldfish.

All at once, snatching inspiration from the ether, she blurted out, 'It's at the jeweller's!' Then more calmly, ignoring their expressions of disbelief, she added, 'Sorry, I forgot for a moment. But it's at the jeweller's. It's got to be made smaller. I've lost weight, you see, and it's become rather loose. Wouldn't want to lose it, ha ha!'

She could see they still weren't deceived. Mercifully there followed several questions about where she did her training and asking for details of the kind of lessons she had taught, and other skills or interests she had. These helped to calm her nerves as the answers came more readily. She felt she had made a good recovery, until right at the end, the woman asked again about her husband, this time with, 'And where does your husband work, my dear? Will you be able to share transport with him?'

Once again, Dee's difficulty with telling the absolute truth let her down. So she embroidered:

'He's a police officer at Scotland Yard. He has his own car, of course, being an inspector. He may be able to bring me to work from time to time, but I am perfectly happy to take the bus. As I did today.' Too late she saw her mistake.

'I seem to remember that your late arrival led to a rescheduling of this interview,' the woman said coldly. She exchanged a look with each of her colleagues, they nodded then rose to their feet practically as one, and the man on the right extended his hand.

'Well, it's been very—ah—pleasant to meet you, Mrs Clarke. As soon as a decision has been made, we'll be in touch, of course. Though I should warn you, we still have a number of candidates to see.'

He's letting me down gently, Dee thought. She smiled back, shook his hand—hot and sticky—very briefly, and said thank you, like a polite child leaving a birthday party.

Outside the air seemed fresh and clear. She hadn't realised how stuffy it had been in there. In more ways than one. She headed home.

She was restless. The initial relief of being back in London in her own, very comfortable flat had dissipated within a day or two and been replaced by a vague feeling of dissatisfaction.

On Saturday morning, still in her pyjamas, in the small spare room that Rob had claimed as his study,

Dee was sitting at her brother's desk, her sketchbook propped open in front of her. Open but the page was still blank. A range of pencils lay neatly by its side, like soldiers standing to attention.

She couldn't think of anything to draw. Her muse seemed to have deserted her now that she had seemingly all the time in the world to concentrate purely on her art. Just lately nothing seemed to capture her imagination. Nothing *sparkled*.

But inspiration, often to be found as she browsed her previous work, both polished sketches and raw unfinished doodles, did not come. Dee got up from the desk and began to wander about the flat.

She gazed out of the window. She knew she should go and get dressed. She knew she ought to go out and buy milk and bread, but somehow she couldn't seem to motivate herself. She didn't know what she wanted to do, she only knew she had to do something.

The postman was just pushing letters into the letterbox of the block of flats over the road. Dee watched him as he turned away from the door and hunched his shoulders against the unseasonable sudden torrent of rain. He hurried to cross the road and entered the front door of Moncrieff Mansions.

With a deep sigh, Dee got up and went to wash and dress.

In the foyer, by the front door the post was still strewn over the mat. She gathered everything up and rapidly sorted the mail items into the various labelled pigeonholes on the foyer table. Those for herself and Rob she put into her bag to deal with later, then she hauled open the big front door and skipped down the steps and into the street.

On the corner, she arrived at the same time as the bus. She scrambled up to the top deck, clutching the rail as she tottered up the stairs for the bus immediately lurched away at full speed to join the moving traffic.

She handed over her sixpence to the flirty Jamaican bus-conductor, as he moved with practised ease from seat to seat collecting fares without losing his balance once. She fixed him with a big smile and asked for Millbank. He gave her a wink as he wound out the strip of paper that was her ticket.

She spent the morning walking around the Tate Gallery. She had been there so many times over the years. She had come there as a child with her parents and with her beloved Aunt Dottie, and her grandparents. Aunt Dottie greatly admired the Pre-Raphaelites, and Dee too had been smitten from an early age by their bold use of colour and their themes. There were many she did not especially care for, but one she had always loved was Millais' *Ophelia*. As a child Dee had never been able to understand how Ophelia had managed to drown when she had been floating so serenely on her back in scarcely-moving water. Why hadn't she simply stood up and stepped out of the water, Dee had asked the grown-ups.

How innocent I was then, she thought. Sorrow seemed to fall about her shoulders. The loss of naiveté, the opening of the child's eyes to the reality of the world around them was a thing that couldn't be recovered. The sorrow added to her own sense of restlessness and oppressed her.

She sat on a bench to view the painting. The gallery was busy, but at least it wasn't quite as crowded as it would be in the height of the summer tourist season. In spite of the other visitors coming and going about her, she quieted her mind, concentrating on the painting, its colours, its textures, and gradually inspiration began to move in her soul.

Refreshed, she had a sudden recollection, a brainwave. Almost in disbelief she thought, I forgot to ask Mrs Hunter about the poison pen letters. She had meant to ask the old woman if she knew who had received one. Or more than one, recollecting what Cissie had said about Meredith Prescott. If anyone knew anything about these letters, it was sure to be Mrs Hunter. And if the old woman herself was behind the letters, she would surely betray herself.

A little later a large crowd came in together on some kind of art tour, and the place seemed crammed full. When Dee got tired of waiting for the other visitors to stop blocking her view, she decided to leave.

Yet she felt exhilarated. The stroll round the gallery—for once without the pressure to sketch or analyse or capture, but simply to gaze and enjoy—had done her good. She felt as if something in her had been appeased.

As she boarded her bus home, the sun broke through the clouds and shone down on Dee, illuminating the London streets and bringing the colours to life once more.

It was twenty-five past eleven that night when Dee remembered the morning's post was still in her handbag.

She had gone to bed early, drifted in and out of sleep, then she had remembered the post and had been suddenly wide awake. With a groan she turned onto her side and glared at the luminous hands of her alarm clock. The post would just have to wait. She turned her back on the clock, pummelled her pillows into plumpness and squirmed down amongst the covers once more, determined to go back to sleep.

But a little voice insisted there could be something vital amongst the mail items. Ridiculous, Dee told herself. There won't be anything there that can't wait until morning. I'm not getting up. I'm sleepy. I'm comfortable.

Ten minutes later she was pulling on her dressing-gown and pushing her feet into her slippers. She went into the sitting-room, turning on a small lamp on the writing desk, anxious not to disturb her brother who had an early start the next morning. Reminding herself yet again that she was being a complete idiot, she sat at the desk and rummaged through her bag for the post. She also hauled out her unused sketch book and pencils.

There were four items of post. One official-looking envelope was for Rob, one with a neat, schoolgirlish handwriting was for her, the third was a circular addressed to 'the esteemed lady of the house' recommending a new store to buy bespoke curtains and other household linens at a lower price.

The fourth was addressed to Mrs Diana Clarke, and was a short, curt note thanking her for attending the interview on Friday but stating that they felt that she was not quite what they were looking for. They wished her well in her search for a new position. She was surprised by the strong wave of relief that came over her on reading this. It was hardly a surprise that they didn't want her—everything had gone wrong from the very start. Who knew if this was not some sort of portent? Whatever it was, fate or just purely the luck of the draw, she was glad not to have to go back to the dreary boiled-cabbage-smelling halls of the Norman Smith Secondary Modern for Girls. She folded the letter back up and returned it to the envelope, throwing it aside as she was already turning her attention to the other item of post.

The envelope was plain and of an everyday sort, the writing neat but rather like Dee herself had written at school aged about fourteen. The stamp bore a Sussex postmark. Her heart pounding as she ripped it open.

A slip of paper fluttered to the floor. She bent to retrieve it, and saw it was a news cutting. The headline read 'Second Tragedy In A Week For Wine Village'.

Almost too afraid to read further, she shrank back onto the chair, her hand to her mouth, her heart pounding. She unfolded the rest of the cutting and read:

Little more than a week after the death by Suicide of Secretary Sheila Fenniston, residents of the village of Porthlea, Sussex, home of the prestigious Prescott Wines, awoke on Thursday morning, the 13th, to the shocking discovery that once again a member of their community had been found Dead.

Mrs Hunter, an 85-year-old invalid, was believed to have suffered a seizure or succumbed to faintness during Wednesday night and was found the following morning at the foot of the stairs of her home by her daughter, Mrs Harriet Grayson. Sadly Mrs Agnes Hunter was beyond assistance. The coroner will give his decision on Monday 17th May, but it is expected to be accidental death, as advised by the investigating police officer.

Mrs Hunter was dead. Dee sat for some minutes, absorbing these details. She was shocked, though not as shocked as she had been when she had found Sheila Fenniston dead. Gradually the shock dissipated and she was relieved that it wasn't anything worse, though she wasn't sure what she had been expecting. She read the news story a second time. It was a while before she remembered to look in the envelope for the accompanying letter. Drawing it out, she saw it consisted of a single page of ordinary notepaper, folded in half. She unfolded it and immediately looked at the bottom of the page to see the signature. It was from Cissie Palmer. She had written:

'My dear Miss Dee

'I'm sure you will be sorry to hear that Old Mrs Hunter has died. You will see the cercumstancies in the bit of newspaper I sent you. Marlene insists that her grandmother wouldn't be up and about in the middle of the night without her walking sticks and there

wasn't no sticks found with the body, they was right there by her bed, next to the invalid chair. Marlene was that determined, they do say, as the coroner, what was all set to follow the police's desicion that it was a sad accident, has adjurned the case until it's been gone into. There's meant to be police coming down from London. Would that be your dear cousin Mr Hardy? He was such a sweet boy, I remember, though he could be cheeky too, but no nastiness with it...'

Glossing over the nice things Cissie had to say about Bill, and what a sweet little boy he had been, Dee read the last little bit Cissie had added:

'I really think Marlene might be right, you know, for all she's a brassy young piece that will get herself into trouble one of these days. But why would Aggie Hunter be out of bed when she could call out or bang on the wall and get Marlene to help her? Marlene thought the world of her gran and would do anything for her, as you know. Anyway, trusting this letter finds you well recovered,

'Yours sincerely
Cissie Palmer.'

Dee sank back in her chair, leaving the news cutting on the blotter in front of her. She pondered her earlier idea about the poison pen letters. She had left it too late to find out, it now seemed. She shook her head in sorrow. Mrs Hunter had been a malicious old woman, but she had enjoyed life, and her family had loved her, and would no doubt miss her terribly.

She heard a sound and looked to see Rob coming down the hall, tying his dressing-gown belt around his waist. His hair was rumpled, his eyes screwed up against the relative brightness of the lamp.

'Can't you sleep?'

She shook her head. 'No. Sorry, I didn't mean to make a noise.'

'Don't worry. I wasn't really asleep. I kept dozing

then waking up. I'm getting some cocoa, do you want any?'

'Yes, please.'

When he returned five minutes later, she hadn't moved.

'Look at this,' she said, and held out the letter and cutting. 'I've had the post in my bag all day, I completely forgot about it. As a matter of fact there's one for you.' Then as an afterthought she said, 'Oh cripes, I hope it's not anything important. As I say, I completely forgot it was there.' She pointed to the envelope.

He set down the mugs and she scolded him for not putting them on the blotter, then pulling out a chair, he sat down beside her at the desk.

He read Mrs Palmer's letter then the cutting. He let out a long, low whistle.

'Well, well. So what do you think?' he asked, laying the papers down and picking up his mug. Dee shook her head.

'I don't know. I mean, she couldn't walk without help, so I should think she could quite easily have fallen down the stairs. It's horrid to think of her lying at the bottom of the stairs. Poor Mrs Grayson, just finding her mother there like that. Mrs Hunter wasn't a very nice old lady, but you know, it's a horrible way to go. As you saw for yourself, Marlene used to push her everywhere in that wheelchair. They were thick as thieves, those two.'

Rob nodded. Then he opened the envelope addressed to him. He quickly read the letter, some of the tension in his shoulders seemed to fall away, and he looked up with a smile.

'Well, now I've only one more assessment, then an exam, and my *viva-voce* standing between me and qualification. My latest assignment was awarded a distinction.'

She smiled broadly and leaned across to kiss his cheek. 'That's wonderful! Well done, baby brother. I always knew you were an absolute genius.'

They sat back in silence. Dee's eyelids were feeling heavy, the cocoa was doing its work. She got to her feet.

'Thanks for the drink, I'm going to toddle off now, I can barely keep my eyes open.'

'So what are you going to do about the Tragedy in the Wine Village?'

'Nothing.' She stifled a yawn. 'The police obviously believe it was an accident, even if, according to Cissie, London police are being sent down. After all, how else could the old lady have died if it wasn't an accident? Who would kill an old woman? I'll write a quick note back to Cissie in the morning. Nighty night.'

Sunday dragged. All day Dee pondered what Cissie had told her, restless and unable to settle to anything. Following an almost sleepless night, on Monday she woke late to find her brother was about to leave for the day. She had just time to say,

'I'm thinking of going back to Porthlea.'

He didn't seem the least bit surprised. 'If you can wait until Saturday, I'll come with you. I'll ask for a couple of extra days. We could stay at the cottage again, I'm sure Cissie won't mind. I doubt it'll be for long.'

Dee smiled. 'I think I can wait until then.'

Once he had left the flat, however, Dee felt the weight of the long day dragging on her. There was a little cleaning to do, not that she felt much like doing it. She flicked the duster here and there then ran a carpet-sweeper over the bit of carpet in the dining-room and in the sitting-room then gave up. The laundry had been packed and sent off, there was no shopping to get. She looked through her sketchbook again, but the brief spark of inspiration she had felt had already evaporated. All she could think about was the death of

Mrs Hunter. She took out Cissie's letter and reread it. Almost without her even thinking about it, her mind was made up. She couldn't possibly wait until the weekend.

So she packed her suitcase for the forthcoming trip to Porthlea, cramming in as many clothes as possible around her little radio. Saturday was too far away. As soon as Rob came home that afternoon, she told him she was going down the following morning. He wasn't at all surprised. The wonderful thing was, she didn't even need to explain anything, he just understood and accepted it all, and promised to join her there on Saturday.

*

Chapter Fourteen

As Dee arrived at Porthlea's railway station late on Tuesday afternoon, a little over a week since she'd left, the heavy shower stopped as abruptly as it began, and the sun came out. Her heart felt light, her spirits lifted. Swinging her small suitcase, she hurried along the lane towards the post office.

Just ahead of her was Davies, the maid from the manor house. How odd, Dee thought, to be known to everyone just by your surname, especially for a woman. As Davies hurried along, Dee watching her rigid back clothed in sensible navy gaberdine, and wondered what her first name was. Esmeralda? Guinevere? She giggled softly, guiltily, at the thought of someone being called Guinevere Davies. That would be rather daring.

Was Davies married? Dee knew that at some point she might meet Davies and need to address her and it went against every instinct for good manners to call an older woman by her surname without the courtesy of the title of Miss or Mrs. No doubt her parents' generation would have thought nothing of it. Times have changed, Dee thought to herself. And I'm glad about that.

The post office was just closing, but Cissie had been keeping watch for her and chivvied her inside with her usual welcoming smile, flipping the sign around and dropping the catch on the lock, and seemingly at the same time, enveloping the young woman in a hug.

'I've already got the kettle on, so in you come and get that jacket off.'

With scarcely a pause for breath the postmistress scuttled off ahead, saying over her shoulder, 'Well and what do you think of this latest thing then? Not that she was what you might call a pleasant sort, but all the same...'

'I hope she didn't lie there on that cold hard floor in pain,' Dee said, hanging her jacket on a hook by the door and following Cissie into the kitchen. 'I mean, no, she wasn't a very nice old lady, but all the same, I wouldn't have wanted her to suffer.'

'I suppose we won't ever know, will we? The doctor said he thought she might have knocked herself out with the fall and not known any more about it. Let's hope that's how it was. Sugar?'

'No, thank you. Ooh, this is just what I need.'

Returning to the topic of Mrs Hunter, Dee said, 'I have to admit to being rather shocked. Coming so soon after Sheila Fenniston's death, it seems almost sinister. But there's something else I was hoping to discuss with you.'

'What's that, my dear?'

'About those poison pen letters?'

Cissie was all attention.

Dee leaned forward. 'I had one on the morning of Sheila's funeral. It implied I was rather free with my favours. It was a silly thing really. It didn't upset me, it just made me wonder who had sent it and why. Do you know who else has had them? I know about Meredith

Prescott, and Sheila of course. Have there been any others?'

'Well I've had another one myself.'

Dee stared. 'Never! When?'

'The same day as yours, it was. I was on my way out to Sheila's funeral and there it was, just pushed under the door. I meant to keep it, to show you. But, well, to tell you the truth, it upset me more than I expected it to, and I just wanted to get rid of it.'

'That's awful. I'm so sorry you've had another one.'

Cissie fixed her with a wry expression. 'I suppose you want to know what was in it?'

'I do rather. Do you mind? You needn't talk about it if you don't want to.'

'Oh it's all right. I was silly to let it upset me. Well, first of all, just as you'd expect, like the first one, it was written using bits of cut out words.'

'From a newspaper or magazine.' Dee nodded as if she'd dealt with hundreds of them before.

'I should think so. Not only single letters though, there was whole words too. And they was gummed onto that blue writing paper like Miss Prescott's.'

'And what did it say? What could they possibly accuse you of? Was it the same as last time?'

'Well,' said Cissie, and she sounded quite put out now, 'Not exactly, This one said as I was meddling with people's letters, steaming 'em open to get the gossip. As if I've got time to do that!' she shook her head, indignant.

'Was that all?' Amused that the worst thing from Cissie's point of view was that she was accused of having too much time on her hands, Dee added hastily, 'Though that's quite bad enough, obviously, and I'm sure no one would believe you'd do such a thing.'

'And saying I was making money out of people by threatening to tell their secrets.' Cissie leaned back and folded her arms, her tale told, and her indignation ebbing away. 'I hope you're right, my dear. I'd be mortified if anyone thought I'd really stoop to such a thing. Oh, it was silly of me to burn it, I could have shown it to you.'

Dee patted her hand across the table.

'Never mind. And no one would believe it for a second, and at least they've moved on from accusing you of stealing people's birthday money,' she said. Then, 'Anyone else?'

'Well, I told you the major had one, didn't I? I got that from Mrs Slough, she cleans for him.'

'Any relation to Norman Slough?'

'His mother.'

Dee nodded, making a mental note.

Cissie continued, 'And of course, Miss Prescott's had two or three as you said. And Sheila Fenniston, God rest her, had at least one if not two. And I think the vicar had one, but I'm not certain about that, it was just some comment Mrs Edmonds made, though I can't remember exactly what she said. And now, the major's had one too. It was probably something about him mooning over Miss Prescott, I imagine.'

'He's certainly got it bad,' Dee agreed. 'Even Mrs Hunter said as much to me.'

'O' course, if anyone would know anything about it, it would have been old Aggie Hunter. She always knew everything that was going on.'

Dee nodded. 'Yes, we've lost a useful source of information.' She thought for a moment. 'But if Marlene's right... well, perhaps that was why...'

'To shut her up, do you mean? But who?'

'I would love to know the answer to that.'

Cissie's eyebrows slanted up in the middle as her face grew sorrowful. 'But that would mean it was one of us. One of us villagers.'

'But you knew that was likely, didn't you?'

'I suppose so. It's just...'

'I know,' said Dee and patted her hand again.

Dee promised to come back later after she had settled
herself back in at the cottage. She left the post office
and went straight across the green to the telephone box,
reaching into her bag for her purse and fishing out
some change ready for the call.

'Hello Mr Greeley. It's Dee here. How are you?'

'My dear Miss Dee!' Greeley had a smile in his voice.
It warmed her. She remembered the piggybacks he'd
given her when she was little. Those, and the mint
humbugs. 'I am very well, thank you, young miss, apart
from a touch of rheumatism.'

'And I presume you'll be wanting to talk to your
mother, miss?'

Dee said yes please, and waited for him to call her
mother. Why the old folks didn't get a phone put into
her mother's sitting-room, she didn't know. That would
save poor Mr Greeley miles of walking every day. No
wonder the poor old chap had rheumatism, with the
mileage he walked everyday just around the house. Dee
hummed a tune and examined her nails, leaning against
the cool glass of the wall of the phone box. Soon, just as
Dee fed another coin into the slot, she heard the rattle
of someone picking up the receiver, then her mother's
voice, loud in her ear, was saying,

'Dee, darling, How lovely to hear from you. Robert
tells me you've gone back to Porthlea. Whatever for? I
thought you were better?"

Dee said she was, but that she had decided to stay
another week. She would have said goodbye at that
point, but her mother had other news to impart:

'Your Aunt Dottie tells me they have finally met Bill's
inamorata. Blonde. Busty. Her name's Barbara, and
she's very pretty, apparently. A secretary at The Met.
Dottie thinks they make a lovely couple, although he
won't say how serious things are.'

Dee's sharp intake of breath headed that particular topic off. Her mother's quick, 'Oh well these young romances never last, do they? She must be the third this year,' ended the subject.

But their next topic wasn't any better. Quite the opposite.

'Dee, darling.' Her mother's low tone warned Dee to be on her guard. Dee fed more money in to keep the telephone call going.

'What is it?' She knew she sounded brittle but couldn't seem to stop herself. Her heart pounded hard enough to choke her.

'Well I don't want to upset you...'

'Mother, for God sake!'

'Oh, sweetheart, I don't mean to worry you. I'm afraid we've had Martin here, banging on the door, shouting and swearing, and demanding to see you. Blind drunk, of course. Your father was furious and told him in no uncertain terms what he thought of him. Poor Mr Greeley was almost knocked over. Dee? Are you still there? Dee, are you all right?'

Dee said, 'Oh my God,' over and over again. She suddenly felt hot and sick.

'Dee?' her mother was still saying.

'I'm all right, Mother. I'm... Don't fuss... Oh dear.'

'Is Robert coming down to join you again? Perhaps I should send Freddie down too?'

'No. It's quite all right. I mean, he's not even here, anyway. Martin I mean. No, don't worry, I...'

'But Rob, dear. When is he...?'

'Saturday. Only a few more days. And I've got Cissie here, and, you know, everyone. So don't worry, I'll be quite all right. Look darling, I've got to go, I'm all out of change.' She put her spare coppers back into her purse.

'Well, let me call you back...'

'No! No, I told you, it's all right. There's nothing else to say. I just wanted to let you know I've arrived, I'm fine, and I'm having dinner with Cissie this evening. She spoils me rotten. And she sends her love. Take care. Speak soon, bye for now, bye.'

And cutting her mother's protest off mid-flow, Dee hung up the phone, fairly raced to the cottage, fumbled the key into the lock, bolted up the stairs and just managed to reach the toilet before vomiting. She sank onto the floor beside the bath, trembling and shivering.

It took her a while to calm down. First of all, she made herself a cup of tea. She added some pieces of shortbread from a box that was a very welcome gift from Cissie. She sat at the small round table in the kitchen. The strong tea and the sugary biscuits helped to steady her nerves. Then she carried her cup and saucer to the sink and washed them very carefully. She dried them and put them away, concentrating with all her might on this small mundane task.

Next, upstairs, having tidied the clothes from the bed where she'd thrown everything on arriving, she forced herself to lie on the bed and read a magazine until it was time to get ready to go to Cissie's. She reminded herself that Martin had gone when she stood up to him, and that she had no reason to think he would return to Porthlea when he had to go to work.

By the time she went to Cissie's, she was feeling a good deal recovered.

Cissie gave her lamb cutlets, lots of vegetables, and buttery mashed potatoes for dinner. Dee's appetite was restored by Cissie's motherly good sense. Dee had poured out the whole story, just to get it off her chest.

Cissie then began to apologise profusely. 'It's all my fault he found you!' she said, her hands to her mouth, a stricken look on her face. 'Why last time you was here, this good-looking young fellow came in here, and as nice and polite as you please, he came up to my counter, and said, 'I'm hoping you'll be able to help me,' and he gave me this story about picking up a lady's make-up purse on the train, and running after her, then losing her when the ticket inspector asked to see his ticket. Anyway, he described you to a T, and of course, I already sort of knew it was you he was on about, because who else could it be? And knowing as how you young ladies can't manage without your make-up... But he gave me this cute puppy-dog look and the sweetest smile and said that confidentially he was hoping to ask the young lady in question if he could take her out one evening, and well... Oh Dee, I am so sorry, I never dreamt...'

Dee said, 'Don't fret about it. He did that puppy-dog look with me a few times in the beginning. We always fall for it, don't we? We get taken in. And if you hadn't told him, someone else would have.'

Cissie still looked upset. Dee patted her arm.

'Really,' she said. 'It's not your fault. Look, let's go to the pub. Dinner was lovely, but I think I could do with a Babycham or two. How about it?'

Cissie looked half scandalised, half tempted. A little extra persuasion meant that the tempted half won the battle. She grabbed her front door key and her handbag.

Arm-in-arm and heads down for protection from the rain, they hurried the short few dozen yards to The Seagull. Inside it was warm, smelled of hops and there was a pleasant background hubbub of conversation.

'I'll get these,' Dee said.

Cissie settled herself at a table. When Dee came back with their drinks, they clinked their glasses together but couldn't think of a toast. Dee giggled, but then an idea struck her and she said,

'To absent friends.'

Cissie gave her sad smile, then repeated the toast. 'To absent friends.'

The street door opened and someone came in. In fact

two someones. Dee immediately recognised Marlene, and her companion was a young man Dee had only ever seen from a distance, but whom she surmised to be Eddie Higgins, son of the farmer who had the property just beyond the manor house.

The publican, alerted by the bell on the door, came out, saw the youngsters and stopped in his tracks.

'Oi! I've told you two before, I'm not serving you, you're both underage. Hop it.'

'Relax Grandpa,' Marlene said, scornfully. 'We only want a fizzy pop and a bag of crisps. We'll even have 'em outside in the rain if we 'ave to.'

The publican humphed about that but served them. 'You can sit in here, but only for half an hour. And keep out of the public bar. I've told Joan not to serve you either.'

'We know, we know. Wouldn't want to risk running into my old man, anyway,' the young man said, slamming his money down on the counter.

'None of your lip, young Eddie, or I'll go straight through there and tell him,' the publican warned, shaking his forefinger at them.

Still grumbling, the youngsters moved away from the bar. Catching sight of Cissie and Dee watching, Marlene said,

'We should of sent one of you two up to the bar. He'd have blinking well served you without giving you any fuss.'

Dee was tempted to point out that the reason she and Cissie got served was because they were over eighteen, but instead she said, not very truthfully,

'Marlene, I've just heard about your grandmother. I'm so very sorry.'

Immediately the girl's whole demeanour changed, and she dipped her head as she mumbled something. Eddie put a protective arm around her shoulders and replied for her.

'She says thanks. She's still upset, as you'd imagine. She was very close to the old bat. Gawd knows why.'

Marlene slapped him, 'Shut up you, you never liked her anyway.'

'Because she never liked me, that's why.'

'Who can blame her? Anyway, she reckoned as you'd get me into trouble, that's why,' Marlene retorted. There was a sulky silence, and they looked as though they were going to move away.

Desperate to keep the conversation going, Dee said, 'Did many people go to the funeral yesterday? I'm afraid I missed it.'

Marlene scrunched up her nose as she thought about it. 'Not really. She wasn't really all that popular. No one much liked her apart from Mum and me. There was a few people from the village, that was it. Mrs Palmer went. And Mrs Glover from the café. And His Nibs from the manor house. That was near enough it. There was more people at the inquest.'

'That was Monday, wasn't it? Marlene, I'm so sorry about your grandmother,' Dee repeated. 'I expect Miss Prescott will miss her too, she used to spend quite a bit of time with your grandmother, didn't she?'

'Oh, Her Ladyship used to pop in a couple of times a week to read Gran something improving. Gran liked a nice murder mystery or a romance but that Prescott woman always used to turn her nose up. Sometimes Gran used to get to hear something interesting, but mostly it was nice little stories about nice people living nice lives. Boring stuff. It used to send poor Gran to sleep. Anyhow it was all about her, Lady Muck, doing her bit for the poor, wasn't it? But Lady Muck didn't come to the funeral. She wasn't even there for the inquest, though *He* was, and half the village.'

'People like the excitement of an inquest. They always think something exciting is going to happen.'

'Well, they got a disappointment, I can tell you. It

got put off. They've got to go into it a bit more. The police down here said it was most likely an accident. Now they are sending some top bods down from London to go into it. Me and Mum were that mad they tried to make out it was just an accident. But them coppers never listen, made their own minds up long before the inquest, that's what Eddie says.'

'Them owners of the means of production never listens to the workforce,' Eddie said by way of confirmation.

Ignoring this, Dee turned to Marlene again with a pretend air of surprise. 'Why? What do you think happened?'

'She was pushed, obviously,' Marlene said. 'I don't know why. But someone got into the house and shoved her down the stairs and killed her.'

*

Chapter Fifteen

On Wednesday morning Dee repeated what she now thought of as her 'routine': she took a slow walk around the village, sitting for a while here and there to relax and enjoy the peace and quiet. There was no reason to rush, after all. In a way, she was just proving to herself that Martin was not in the village, and that she was safe from sudden violent confrontation. Having assured herself of this, she ended up at the café in a much brighter mood and in perfect time for lunch: it was spot on twelve o'clock.

She was the only patron and had her choice of tables. She chose one at the farthest end, by the window. She set down her handbag, her hat, and the white-framed sunglasses that she was seeing everywhere now that they were very much 'it'. Then she went over to where Lily Glover was standing behind the counter, a hopeful expression on her face.

'Nice to see you back here,' Lily said by way of a greeting. 'Does this mean you like it so much you want to stay?'

Dee laughed. 'Well, Cissie's cottage is very sweet and cosy.' She ordered her food. Then, a few minutes later, when it was ready, Lily brought it over to the table and said,

'Would you mind terribly if I brought my own lunch over and joined you? Just say no if you'd rather not, I'd understand if you preferred some peace and quiet, I know you've been ill.'

But Dee said she'd enjoy the company, adding, 'I'm completely over my bronchitis now. You probably get a bit lonely in here. If you don't mind me asking, is it always this quiet?' What she really wanted to ask was, how on earth do you manage to make ends meet, but she didn't quite have the temerity to ask such a personal question.

Lily came back with her plate—a ham sandwich—and a glass of fizzy orange. She sat opposite Dee.

'It's been awful for the last few years,' she admitted. 'I don't know how much longer I can keep going. I've had this cafe for more than twenty years, and I think it stopped making a profit about five years ago.' She shook her head, and Dee could sense the discouragement coming off her like a wave. 'For years now I've been telling myself it's the last year, that it's pointless. Even so, every March the first, I open up again, like a bloody fool, clinging to the hope that this season will be better. But...'

'Tell me what it was like twenty years ago,' Dee prompted. 'You must have been practically a child.'

Now Lily laughed. 'Oh go on, you!' Then she thought for a moment and said, 'Actually you're right. I was just twenty-one. I thought I was as old as the hills back then, so grown up and mature. But really I was not much more than a kid, now I look back. I'd been to college to learn catering, then I worked for a couple of years in a school canteen. Then the old fellow who ran this place died, and I heard about it and decided it was time to come home. I'd been away for four years. I'd been glad to get away. My father—well, he drank. My mother left when I was fourteen—ran off with a travelling salesman—not exactly original. And I didn't blame her, I just wished she'd taken me with her. Anyway...'

'So it seemed like a good opportunity?' Dee prompted again.

'Yes. There's a nice little flat above here, too small to have room for my father, which was lucky, but perfect just for us. I loved it. It was such fun in those days. And as I say, it was busier. Mr Prescott senior, Jeremy and Meredith's father, used to come in most days for breakfast, and then once or twice a week he'd have afternoon tea or lunch with Jeremy and Mr Smithies too, he was still alive then. And a lot more local people used to come in, sometimes just for a cup of tea and a slice of cake, or for lunch, or their morning coffee. But with the older generation dying off and this place not being smart enough for the likes of Jeremy or Meredith Prescott, everyone has more or less stopped coming. Oh, Vi comes in once or twice a week, but she only has a cuppa to keep me company. And Joan from the pub and Cissie too of course.'

'Vi?'

'Violet Davies, Mrs Smithies' housekeeper-cook.'

Violet. Dee smiled at her own musings on the lady's name just the day before. Violet was much nicer than Delilah or Guinevere.

'It's good of them, of course, but not enough to make the cafe profitable, I imagine,' Dee hazarded.

Lily nodded. 'Exactly.' She sighed. 'Oh, I can't fool myself any longer. It's taken all my savings to keep going these last few years. When I hear how much I could earn working in a factory, it sounds like an absolute fortune. At least then I could go home at the end of the day and forget about everything.'

'And you'd get the weekend off,' Dee agreed. 'Do you own this building, or...?'

'No, I rent it from the Prescotts. They own almost everything around here, as you'd expect in a little place like this.'

'I see.'

They lapsed into silence, concentrating on their food. Dee suspected that Lily would have very little capital to start a new life elsewhere if she decided to give up the cafe.

'If you left here, where would you go?' she asked, pushing her empty plate aside a few minutes later.

Lily shook her head. They sat in a companionable silence, gazing out at the sea that rippled and sparkled in the sunlight and looked impossibly blue.

'I've always wanted to go to London,' Lily said suddenly.

'Really?'

'The truth is, I love the museums. When I was a girl, history was my favourite school subject. They used to take us on trips sometimes. Usually to some museum or another. Oh, I loved it! Not the kings-and-queens type of history, no. What I liked was how ordinary people lived. What everyday life was like for normal people hundreds of years ago. I loved seeing the old kitchens, the bathrooms and even the servants' quarters. But my father said I had to learn a practical skill, so that I could get a proper job.'

'You didn't fancy being a teacher?'

Lily shook her head. 'I wasn't good enough for that. But you're a teacher, Miss Dee, aren't you? French, isn't it?'

'French and German. But art is my real love, and I love standing in for the art teacher when she is away for any reason. Used to, I mean. I don't work there now.'

'And you loved it? Teaching, I mean.'

'I used to. But now... I don't know. I had an interview

last week but to be honest, I rather messed it up and I
didn't get the job. I've got another interview next week,
but...'

'You're not keen anymore?'

'No...'

'But, begging your pardon for being nosy, but do you
need to work?'

Dee laughed. 'Yes, unfortunately I do. I'm lucky in
that I get an allowance from my parents. It's very
generous of them, but it's not quite enough for me to
live on. And please Lily, you don't need to call me Miss
Dee. We're friends now, aren't we? If you keep calling
me Miss, I shall go back to calling you Mrs Glover.' Dee
thought about what she'd just said, and added, 'Do you
mind me asking, what happened to Mr Glover?'

'All right, Dee it is then. About Mr Glover?' She
blushed and laughed a little self-consciously. 'I'm afraid
I made him up. I told everyone I'd got married straight
from college but that he died of scarlet fever after a
year. But the truth is... Well, you see I came back with a
little girl, so...'

Dee did see. 'Of course. And where is your daughter
now?'

'She's in service at a big place in Sandneath. I see her
once a week on her afternoon off. I get the train in, and
we go to a matinee together and then get fish and chips.
Or if it's too cold or wet or we just don't fancy going
around the shops, she's allowed to take me back to
where she works to have supper there.'

'Is she happy there?'

Lily screwed her nose up. 'Not really. I mean, it's
work, isn't it, and the money isn't bad. But the boss is a
bit handsy, if you know what I mean.'

'I know exactly what you mean. What a shame the
two of you can't have a business together. Run a bed
and breakfast somewhere busy...'

Lily laughed. 'Now that would be something! Though

I still have a fancy for London.' She gave Dee a measuring look. 'I know it's a bit of a cheek. But if you were to hear of anything but might do for someone like me...'

'Oh, I'll definitely let you know, of course,' Dee assured her.

'Thank you.'

They sat for a while not speaking, then Lily said, 'So why did you come back down here?'

Dee shrugged. 'I don't know, really.'

'Are you a private detective?'

Dee was taken aback and stared at the other woman. 'What? What on earth gave you that idea?'

It was Lily's turn to shrug. 'I heard your brother teasing you the other day and calling you Miss Marple. So I wondered... Especially with you coming back again. I thought it might be to do with Aggie's death.'

'I see. Well, no I'm not a detective. I just wanted to know more about Mrs Hunter's death. I know it's awful of me. I'm not usually one of those ghouls who enjoy other people's misery. But Cissie said that Marlene was so adamant that it couldn't have been an accident. So I got to wondering, and I felt like I just had to know.'

'Marlene and her mother, both. Poor Harriet Grayson was very close to her mother. She's been saying how she's got to know what happened. She just can't get over it.'

'Well, I suppose it did only happen a few days ago. It's bound to take a while to recover from the shock of finding her mother like that,' Dee said, ever practical. 'It must have been terrible.'

'That, and the back door standing wide open. And Harriet not knowing if she forgot to lock it or someone broke in, or even if they were still there. Anything could have happened. She thinks it's all her fault.'

'Really? My word, I hadn't heard about that. Poor Mrs Grayson.' Dee was shocked.

Lily said, her voice tinged with disapproval, 'Didn't tell the police, did she? Was scared they'd tell her off for keeping the spare key under the flowerpot right there by the door where anyone could get it.'

Dee leaned back in her chair. 'Well. That would put a different complexion on things if the coroner or the police knew, surely? It would certainly call into question the whole idea of an accidental death.'

'True.' Lily smirked at her behind her almost empty glass of orange. 'And so you're definitely not a detective, Miss Marple?'

Dee laughed. 'Confidentially, I'd love to do that. But I don't think it would pay the bills.'

'Probably not,' Lily said. 'You'll have to join the police. Become one of those WPCs that makes the tea and hands out the hankies.'

'I'm not very good at being subservient to higher ranks though,' Dee said, crinkling her nose, thinking of one specific police officer who annoyed her immensely. 'On a completely different topic, now that you know how nosy I am, do you know of anyone in the village who has had one of those poison pen letters? Did you even know people have been getting them?'

The bell over the door rang.

'Just a minute,' Lily said, getting to her feet.

Glancing up, Dee saw a woman she didn't recognise just coming into the cafe. Lily went over to take her order then having taken it to the customer, Lily disappeared through a door at the back of the café. Dee caught a glimpse of a dark staircase, very like the one in the Graysons' cottage. The floor of unrelieved stone reminded her of Mrs Hunter. Dee clutched her coffee cup for the little warmth that remained, shivering to think of the old lady falling to her death on that chilly unforgiving surface. If she had fallen. Or was Marlene right? Had someone pushed her?

The bell jangled again as Millie Edmonds entered the

cafe. She said a rather loud, 'Good morning to you, Miss Gascoigne.' But fortunately, she went directly to the counter and stood there waiting for Lily to return. Dee heard the sound of footsteps on the stairs, and looked round to see Lily approaching.

'Here,' Lily said softly. 'I had the top one just before Christmas, and the other one sometime around Easter. Look, sorry, I think my lunchtime is over. But you will come again, won't you? It's been so nice having someone to talk to.'

'I will. And thank you for these,' Dee said, putting them into her handbag. 'I promise I'll keep them secret. No one will hear about them from me.'

'Oh, don't worry too much. Actually, it's nothing people don't already know about me. And my daughter. After all these years, it's hardly a secret anymore.' Lily shrugged, and moved away to attend to Mrs Edmonds.

Dee finished her drink and said goodbye, managing to skirt past Mrs Edmonds with a quick, 'How nice to see you again.'

That evening, Dee looked at Lily's two letters, mulling over them long and hard. She knew them by heart now. Not that there had been much to learn, both were short and direct.

The first one, in the usual style of cut out words or single letters from magazines or newspapers, said simply, *'Your seCREt shame will NOT be a secret no lONger.'*

The second, more recent one, said, *'Your bAstard cHILd will pay for YOUr sin.'*

The word bastard had been made up from several sections of type: the *b* was a separate letter, then the *Ast* were together, presumably formerly part of a longer word. The next *a* was a single letter again, then the final two letters, *rd*, were once more part of the same word, and likewise, the *YOU* of your was formed of a word in capital letters with an extra lower-case r added to the end.

On the one hand, it was laughable that anyone would think this was still a scandalous secret in the modern era, especially as Lily had indicated that the truth was widely known. But on the other hand, Dee remembered what Cissie had said to her when she first explained about the poison pen letters. It must have been a shock, Dee decided, for Lily to open the envelopes and find these letters inside. To think that someone who knew her, someone familiar whom she no doubt spoke to on a regular basis, had composed these spiteful notes. It wasn't the content of the letters, it was the fact that they'd come from a friend or neighbour in the village, and intended specifically to cause unhappiness or trouble.

She sat for a long while pondering the letters. At last, she put them away, neatly folding them and slipping them into the zip-up mirror pocket of her handbag for safe keeping. She decided to have an early night.

*

Chapter Sixteen

Over bacon and eggs on Thursday morning, Cissie said, 'Did you know there's bingo on at the village hall tonight?'

Surprised, Dee admitted she didn't, adding, 'Are you going?'

Cissie nodded enthusiastically. 'I always go,' she said. 'Me and Joan from the pub, and Lily from the café, along with Eddie's mum, Ada. In fact, near enough everyone comes. The women, I mean. The only man that comes along is that Rodericks. And then there's our local celebrity, he's the caller.'

'Who's that?'

'You'll never guess.'

Dee grinned at that. 'I can't imagine who it might be. You'll have to tell me.'

'It's that Sonny-Ray Smith,' Cissie said. 'Oh, he's ever so good-looking. Though you can tell he knows it. A bit too pleased with himself, that bloke.'

'*The* Sonny-Ray Smith?' Dee echoed, hardly able to believe it. Surely Cissie was teasing her?

'The very one,' Cissie responded. 'He's the vicar's half-brother, apparently. Does things to help out from time to time. But I think it said something in the papers about a scandal?'

'Yes indeed,' Dee said. 'I can't believe it. I wonder if he's hiding here until the dust settles? He caused quite an outcry a few months back.' After a moment she added, 'I think I've seen his car about.'

Cissie nodded sagely. 'Big flash American job.'

'That's the one. Well, it sounds too interesting to keep away. Sonny-Ray Smith. Well, I never.'

'And if you come along,' Cissie pointed out, 'You might find out a bit more about the poison pen letters too.' She gave Dee a knowing grin. 'I know you're curious, it's no use denying it.'

Dee smiled. 'What time does it start?'

'Seven-thirty sharp. Be there or be square.'

Dee laughed at this. 'I'll be over at seven-fifteen.'

'You might win five pounds,' Cissie said.

The village hall was packed. The folding tables had all been set up by Millie Edmond's team of helpers: Rodericks, the vicar and Mr Higgins with a reluctant Eddie, whilst Millie herself filled and turned on the urn for tea in the interval. There were about twenty tables, each with four chairs.

Dee was doubtful that there were that many people in the village, but as with the fair, she quickly discovered that the event drew people from all over the area.

Cissie grabbed her arm as they entered the hall and dragged her to a table right up the front which they 'claimed' by putting their jackets over the backs of the chairs. They were joined almost immediately by Lily and Ada. Dee had to borrow a fat charcoal pencil, as she was the only one who hadn't come prepared, and it was clear from the outset that the ladies took it very seriously indeed.

Rodericks was at the next table with Davies from the manor house, a small shrew-faced woman Cissie said was Mrs Slough, and Marlene.

Dee was on edge to see if the 'local celebrity' caller really was Sonny-Ray Smith. Surely it couldn't be, and yet...

The lights dimmed briefly, and a voice, obviously Callum Edmonds, spoke into a microphone, 'Please welcome your host, Sonny. Ray. Smith!'

The lights went up again, as the applause broke out wildly all around Dee as the audience screamed, shouted, clapped and whistled. She was practically deafened by the din, and hardly able to believe her ears. Had the vicar really said...? She was holding her breath, waiting to see...

And there he was in his sparkling evening jacket, purple satin bowtie, pocket handkerchief, and his trademark purple winkle-pickers.

The applause was, if possible, even louder, and he was lapping it up, she could tell. The bad boy of pop, acting as bingo caller at a tiny village in Sussex. How the mighty are fallen. It just didn't seem real. Just a year ago, he had been performing in concerts all over the world, and now...

The noise died down and he began his patter: ingratiating, self-satisfied, and always a little too close to the mark with his double-entendres, she noticed. After a couple of minutes, he said, 'But you lot didn't come all this way to listen to me...'

To which the audience predictably responded, 'No, we didn't!' with gusto. She thought he seemed a little taken aback by their enthusiastic rejection of him, but he opted to take it as a joke, laughing heartily, and adding an 'Ooh missus!' in the style of a popular comedian. Then as Callum Edmonds came forward holding up a fan made up of several white slips of paper, Sonny-Ray announced,

'Without further ado, let's see what you're all playing for tonight. It is of course, a five-pound postal order for each person to correctly finish her—oops, I should have said *his or her*—sorry Kelvin.'

Sonny-Ray glanced across to where Rodericks was sitting, arms folded across his chest. He shook his head, smiling as if to say no offense was taken.

Sonny-Ray said in a snarky voice, 'Actually, it's only Kelvin, so I could have just stuck with saying 'her'.'

There were a few jeers and catcalls at that, and Kelvin Rodericks was not looking quite so happy now.

Hurrying on, Sonny-Ray repeated, 'So without further ado, let's get on with the first game.'

While he'd been speaking, Millie had been going around the tables collecting everyone's threepence fee and giving out the bingo cards. Once she'd finished, she gave him a wave then she went through to the back room of the hall, and Sonny-Ray began to call the numbers.

'Eyes down, everyone, good luck.' Obediently everyone in the hall fixed their eyes on the cards in front of them, pencils poised. 'To kick you off, our first number of the evening is eighty-eight. Two Fat Ladies. You and your mother,' he added with a cheeky grin.

Gales of laughter greeted this and the fortunate few crossed through the number with their pencils.

'The next one up, twenty-nine, rise and shine.'

And so it went on. Dee forgot to mark off half of her numbers as she stared around the room, lost in her thoughts.

There was a tea interval after forty-five minutes, and Mrs Higgins and Cissie went off to join the queue for drinks. Lily leaned forward, and almost shouting to make herself heard above the surrounding noise, said, 'Well, Miss Marple, and how's your investigation going? Seen anything suspicious this evening?'

Dee laughed and shook her head. Lily had to lean

forward again as Millie Edmonds stood behind her chair, speaking quietly to Rodericks. She had to practically put her mouth to his ear to make him hear what she was saying. Dee watched closely, wondering what Millie could be telling him. As Millie straightened up, she turned to smile in welcome at Dee even though she'd already seen her when she collected the money and gave her the bingo cards.

Millie went away again, and Lily was saying something Dee didn't quite catch, but just then Cissie and Mrs Higgins reappeared with four cups of tea and a handful of pink wafers biscuits. And when Dee leaned forward to grab one, laughing with Cissie and putting the wafer into her mouth, she glanced up and saw Rodericks was staring at her. He looked away as soon as he saw that she had noticed.

In the end the prizes were won by Mrs Higgins, Mrs Slough, Rodericks and two women from other villages.

'See you all in two weeks' time! In the meantime, don't do anything I wouldn't do!' Sonny-Ray had bellowed at the end, to tumultuous applause, then he had saluted and hung up the microphone.

'And a good time was had by all,' said Mrs Higgins, getting up and putting her postal order into her handbag. There was a great deal of good-humoured joking and chatter, but eventually they were out in the street and calling goodnight to one another. Mrs Higgins and Cissie walked back along the street together, whilst Dee went with Lily to the café. Lily invited her in for a while, and they went up to the upstairs flat, where they sat talking and enjoyed a small brandy each.

By the time Dee left to walk back to the cottage, it was dark, and a misty drizzle had started. Drawing the edges of her cardigan closer about her, she put her head down to stop the rain wrecking her make-up, and she hurried as much as her high heels would allow.

It was a good thing she hadn't far to go, she thought. As she drew close to the cottage, there seemed to be something odd about it. It took her a moment to realise that the front door was standing open.

Shocked, and a good deal annoyed with herself for forgetting to lock the door behind her when she came out earlier, she went inside, groping for the light switch and wondering if Cissie had seen the door open and been cross with her.

As she turned to try to find the switch, a darker-than-dark shadow seemed to shift in the narrow hallway, and before she could react, a pain seared though her head and she fell to the floor, just barely aware of someone stepping over her and carefully closing the door behind them as they left.

Dee's next thought was that someone was really annoying her by trying to lift her up. Why couldn't they just leave her alone, she was so comfortable here. That light hurt her eyes too. Why did they have to keep shining it in her face like that?

'Idiots,' she grumbled.

'Now then, young lady, you're lucky you weren't badly hurt. How much have you had to drink?'

'Ugh,' Dee said. 'Not that doctor chap again.'

Then she realised what she'd said. Her sense seemed to return to her from wherever it had been, and she sat up, stammering an apology and reaching for her head, aware of an abrupt, vomit-inducing pain.

'Where am I?' she asked, then was cross for saying what every fool in every detective film said on waking from unconsciousness.

'You're quite all right,' said a soothing, rather patronising voice. It was Dr Bartlett, and she hoped he hadn't taken her words to heart.

'What happened? Did someone attack me?'

'Just a bit tipsy, I should think. You'll be perfectly all

right. Take a bit more water with it next time.'

'I'm not drunk,' Dee said indignantly, 'I only had a cup of tea this evening. Ask Cissie, she'll tell you. Someone was here.' She looked about her. The sitting-room of the cottage seemd crowded. Besides herself and the doctor, Cissie was there, looking pale and anxious, and Millie Edmonds with an excited expression on her face, then behind her there were Meredith and Jeremy Prescott too, standing in the doorway, Jeremy looking bored and Meredith looking irritated.

'Someone was here when I came back from the bingo after saying goodnight to Lily. The door was standing open a little, and at first I thought... Well, I assumed...'

'Assumed what? Tell us, Daphne,' Meredith urged.

Dee retorted, 'I am trying to tell you. And you know perfectly well it's Dee, not Daphne.'

Meredith didn't say anything else, just waited.

'Yes,' said Dee. 'That's it. I assumed I had forgotten to lock the door, and I was cross with myself. But I wouldn't have left it standing wide open like that. Anyway... I came inside, and as I turned to close the door, something moved in the darkness, and I felt this awful pain in my head and... well then I woke up and you were all here.'

She looked around at them. Did they see the suspicion in her eyes? Why were they were all here? Cissie came forward to pat her hand. 'I've made you a nice cup of sweet tea, my dear. Just you have a drink of that, it'll help with the shock.'

Dee could see that no one believed her. Not that she cared. She just wanted them all to go. She said, 'I'm so sorry for worrying everyone. It was kind of you to make sure I'm all right. But now I'm going to go to bed, so I'll just see you out, if that's all right.'

'Oh no you don't, my girl, you're going to hospital for an x-ray,' Dr Bartlett told her. 'I'd drive you myself but I'm afraid I might be called out by someone else, so I think it's best if I send for an ambulance, if you don't mind waiting.'

'No need for that,' Jeremy said, 'I'll call Rodericks. He'll drive Miss—er—in the car, it'll be quicker that way.'

'Really, I'm sure I'll be fine without...' Dee tried to stand but her head swam, causing her to sink back down onto the sofa.

Bartlett nodded to Prescott. Prescott said, 'Rodericks will be here in two ticks. I'll go and get him now. Come along, Meredith.'

They left. Dr Bartlett stood up, scribbled something on a notepad, and tore the page off to give to Cissie. 'Perhaps you'd go with her to make sure she's all right and give them this at the hospital.'

Cissie took it and glanced at the page of near-indecipherable script. 'Yes, doctor.'

Reaching for his hat, Bartlett turned back to say, 'And as for you, young lady, be more careful! Goodnight.'

That just left Millie Edmonds.

'I'm sorry you got caught up in this, the poor vicar must be wondering where you've got to,' Dee said. It was as strong a hint as she could muster. Millie Edmonds just shook her head.

'Oh, it's quite all right, Callum will be sound asleep by now, he's always an early bird. I'll stay with you until the car comes, just in case.'

In case of what, she didn't say. They all sat down to wait for Rodericks. Dee sipped some of the tea Cissie had made; it certainly helped to bring the bits of her scattered brain together. The pounding in her head wasn't lessening at all.

A minute or two later, really he was very quick, Dee thought, there was a knock on the door, and Rodericks let himself in, peering around the door to say,

'I understand someone is at death's door and needs

an emergency lift to the hospital in Sandneath?' He grinned down at her. 'Been in the wars?'

She set her cup down and got up, feeling much steadier now. She managed to grin back at him and said, 'Something like that. Thank you so much for doing this.'

'It's no bother,' he said. 'Now who's coming with us?'

It came as no surprise to Dee that Millie Edmonds won out of sheer determination, and Cissie, shaking her head and retreating, called through the open door,

'I'll look in to see you in the morning, dearie.'

It turned out that Millie was quite useful. She bullied her way into the hospital, demanding immediate assistance as if Dee was there with a limb hanging off. As an orderly came over to guide Dee to the right department, Rodericks said softly,

'I'll be in the car outside.'

Dee just had time to nod and whisper, 'Thank you.' Then Millie was bundling her into a wheelchair she had found and fairly racing her along the corridor.

Back an hour later with aspirin and a hot water bottle, Dee heaved a sigh of relief, glad to be alone at last. She'd resisted Millie's offer to put her to bed, and persuaded the woman to go home. Dee went upstairs to bed, treading carefully and clinging to the banister.

In her bedroom, the wardrobe door was standing open, and the drawers had been pulled out of the chest. All her clothes and other belongings were all over the floor and bed.

The room had been thoroughly searched.

It was a good thing she hadn't undressed yet. She immediately went back downstairs, and out to the green to call the police, waiting shivering on the front door step for the sergeant to arrive.

The next morning, before opening the post office for her usual hectic Friday, Cissie let herself into the cottage with her spare key, and finding Dee was not yet downstairs, called up to her from the hall.

'Dee, it's only Cissie. Just wanted to make sure you're all right.'

Dee appeared at the top of the stairs in her dressing-gown. Her face was as white as a sheet.

'I'm all right, thank you. Just feeling...' Her voice was low, as if she had no strength even to speak.

'I can imagine. Best if you spend the day in bed.'

'Oh, erm...' Dee dithered on the landing, unable to decide what to do. Seeing this, Cissie said decisively,

'Now then, young lady, you take yourself back to bed this instant. I'll bring you up some tea ad toast in just a tick.'

Dee tottered back to bed, her head pounding. She piled the pillows up to prop her back, got in, and pulled the eiderdown up to her chin.

'My word, you look like death warmed up!' Cissie declared a few minutes later. She set down the tray on the bedside table. 'Now then, there's tea and buttered toast, aspirin and a glass of water. Is there anything you need?'

Not trusting herself to shake her head, Dee said, 'Thank you. You're so good to me, Cissie.'

'Don't you go fretting yourself, now, you need a good rest after last night,' Cissie said, sitting down on the side of the bed. She looked about the room, only now noticing the mess. She knew Dee would never leave the place in this state. 'Has someone been in here?' Her voice was high with shock.

Dee nodded, then as a bolt of pain shot through her head, she clutched it and yelped. She said, 'Yes. That must have been why they were in here last night. But what could they have been searching for?'

Cissie shook her head. 'You'll need to tell the police.'

'I rang them last night when I found everything like this. That sergeant from Sandneath came out and made a note of it, but he didn't seem very interested. Said it was an opportunistic thief looking for valuables that were easy to sell.'

'Hmm,' said Cissie, not at all happy. 'Right. If you've got everything you need, I'll leave you to get some rest. I'll come over at lunchtime to see how you're doing and clear up this place.'

'There's no need to trouble yourself, I'll be fine once I've had a little nap. I'll come over to you at lunchtime, if that's all right.'

'Of course it is, my dear.' Cissie got up. 'And I'll lock the door when I go out, so don't worry about that.'

She kissed Dee on the cheek and left.

Dee didn't expect to sleep again, but after lying there for a while puzzling over who had broken into the cottage, she found her mind drifting. The bed, no longer a bed but a rowboat, was rocking gently on a lake. All was calm and peace. Somewhere a long way off, a bird was softly singing. Dee was content to float on the water, until it occurred to her suddenly that she was asleep, which woke her up.

'They didn't break in, they had a key.'

*

191

Chapter Seventeen

At New Scotland Yard that Friday, eyebrows were being raised and heads shaken over the coincidence of two unexpected deaths taking place within two weeks, and now a common assault just the night before, all in the same small village on the Sussex coast. Their general opinion was that it didn't 'feel right'.

Chief Superintendent Morris Asquith came out of a senior staff meeting with a headache. He leaned against the wall beside the office door, loosened his tie and undid his top button.

This was not the kind of case he liked to get involved with. Morris Asquith was excellent at budgets and well above average at policies. He didn't enjoy being involved in criminal investigations, not even at arm's length.

The problem with sending his men to some other area to assist with an investigation—or two or even three, for that matter—was that, if you didn't find something 'off', as he put it to himself, the local chaps, police, journalists, council members would have a field day, claiming red tape gone mad, or an oppressive system of supervision from the nation's foremost police authority who fancied themselves so far above the local forces.

On the other hand, if you *did* find something 'off', those same locals would go on the defensive, claiming that their home-grown police had too much on their plates, insufficient staffing levels, or that budgets were too constrained to permit full investigations. Before you could say 'Not my patch' there would be articles in The Times accusing everyone from the local desk sergeant to the chief constable of incompetence or corruption, or both.

Morris Asquith was glad he had been promoted far enough up the chain of command that neither the initial nor the ultimate responsibility rested with him. He mopped his brow with a large, blue-spotted handkerchief. Well, if the Assistant Commissioner wanted The Met down on the spot to 'make sure' the local inspector knew what he was doing, Morris could think of two annoying officers from different departments who seemed destined to work together. What he liked to think of as a two-birds-one-stone strategy.

Thinking immediately of young Hardy, not even thirty yet and promoted to the rank of Detective Inspector just three months ago, quite against Morris's recommendations, and without doubt purely as a favour to his father, who was the Chief Constable of Derbyshire, he decided this would be a perfect opportunity to take the young fellow down a peg or two without anyone realising that was what he was doing.

And he knew the perfect sergeant to partner him with. He wasn't in CID. Yet. But had been asking about moving across to that department for several years. What was his name? Something Biblical, wasn't it? Matthew? Mark? Morris tried all the apostles he could think of but none of the names seemed to fit. But the man was a permanent pain in the neck, a bit too good to stay a constable, but not many of the men would work with him, a man of his *background*, since he'd been made up to sergeant. Passed his exams top of his class, after all, so no matter how one felt about a man of that background... the Commissioner was always saying they had to move with the times, had to remember that society was made up of many different cultural strands.

Morris Asquith lost this train of thought. The door began to open and he hastily straightened up and rebuttoned his collar. Two more men came out, they nodded at him and carried on along the corridor, deep in a discussion about the new road safety initiatives being implemented in the nation's schools.

Asquith returned to his office, dark, small, at the back of the building. Sharon, his typist, was nowhere to be seen. She was no doubt gossiping with those filing girls in Records. Women in the police force! He tutted, shaking his head. Sometimes it seemed as if the world had gone mad.

Behind his desk, he reached for the phone.

'Tell Hardy in C Division I want to see him immediately.'

He sat back. Yes, Hardy, and the other fellow, Whatshisname, would do perfectly. If everything went well, it could only reflect well on Morris. If it was all a mare's nest, or worse, well, it wouldn't be his fault. A glance at the clock convinced him there would be time for a game of golf so long as the weather held. He couldn't actually see the sky from his office, but hopefully the sun was still shining.

There was a knock at the door.

'Come,' Morris commanded. He always thought he said that in a very masterful, authoritative way. He smiled. Then he had to stop himself smiling. It wouldn't do for Hardy to think he'd done something well.

'Ah Hardy. Come in. Sit down. Got a new case for you. You'll need to book train tickets for tomorrow to Sussex. And you'll need a new sergeant on hand to assist you. I've got just the fellow in mind.'
He began to tell Hardy about the job he had for him.

The two men eyed one another warily and shook hands. Victoria station as packed with weekend travellers, and they were jostled left and right, before Hardy explained where they were headed. Hardy cast two or three secret, assessing looks at his new colleague as they made their way to the platform gate.

They'd never worked together before, though Hardy had heard of Nahum Porter. The man had been newly promoted to the rank of sergeant, and this would be his first experience working in CID. Hardy wasn't particularly surprised that the promotion was not a popular one. It was generally considered at The Yard that the job should have gone to a better man, a *white* man, such as Charlie Eastman, a man whom Hardy would rather transfer to the moon than work with.

And Porter was a little older than most men coming to the position of sergeant. Hardy had checked his file. He was forty-four years of age, to Hardy's twenty-eight, but had been in the force since he was eighteen. The rumour mill had nothing to say about the man that wasn't related to the colour of his skin. And his file showed a bland, unexceptional career that may indicate a lack of brilliance or ability, or it might mean a lack of opportunity. On the other hand, it might be that the man had been unfairly judged by harsher standards than his peers. He had been highly commended once early on in his career: he had been awarded a medal for bravery, receiving it from the hand of Princess Elizabeth in 1947. He had gone into a burning building to rescue two small children and a dog. That alone, in Hardy's opinion, showed all the qualities of an excellent police officer.

They discovered their train was not due for forty-five minutes. They found a bench and sat down. Hardy looked at his watch. Then he looked about him and saw the buffet along the platform. He turned to Porter and said, 'Perhaps a coffee would be a good idea? This journey will be fairly tedious, we'll need something to keep us awake.'

'Of course, sir,' Porter straight away responded. He placed his hands on his knees preparatory to rising. Seeing this, Hardy put out a hand to indicate he should stay put. Hardy got up.

'These are on me. Tea or coffee?'

Porter tried unsuccessfully to hide his surprise. 'Er...'

'Usually railway tea is terrible. I mean, the coffee is too, but terrible tea is worse than terrible coffee, in my experience.'

'Coffee it is, then, sir. Would you like me to...?'

'Not at all. Sugar? Milk?'

'Both please, sir... I...'

Hardy nodded and went along to the buffet.

On the train, Hardy sat apparently absorbed in his newspaper, leaving Porter plenty of time to covertly observe his new senior officer. Porter had heard of the 'boy wonder', Bill Hardy, on a fast track to the stars by all accounts. Although this was the first time he'd met the fellow. He was even younger than Porter had expected. But he seemed self-assured, with no need to bluster and shout.

Critics of Hardy said he was riding his father's coat-tails up the ranks, that nepotism guaranteed him success. But two or three of the men who actually knew him had said that he was a good officer. And he'd been told the man was a stickler for the rules. Porter had worked with several men who made up their own rules when it suited them, and had expected him to look the other way. He wasn't good at doing that. For Porter, integrity was essential. The police should never consider themselves above the law, he believed. But he would withhold judgement on Hardy until he knew him better. It boded well, although being a stickler for the rules didn't necessarily mean he was a good copper.

But this was the first time an inspector had ever bought Porter a cup of coffee.

In the police station at Sandneath later that day, Hardy was not invited to sit. The detective inspector was glaring at him across the desk, his every part bristling with offence. In his hand he held Hardy's warrant card, and this he threw across the desk at him now.

'Get out,' he said.

Hardy, astonished, said, 'Not until I've learned everything you know about these cases.'

'These cases!' the detective inspector snarled. He glanced to the side. If someone else had been standing there, Hardy knew the man would have said something along the lines of, 'Can you believe this?' but no one was there, and there was no one else for the man to take his anger out on, so he turned back to Hardy. He leaned forward, his hands firmly planted on the desk.

'There's no 'cases', all right? It's bloody open-and-shut. Nothing for the likes of you. Coming down here, telling me how to do my job. I'll have you know I was a copper when you were just a twinkle in your dad's eye! Coming down here... I worked my way up to inspector by sheer effort and hard work. You come along, only been in the job five minutes, trying to make yourself seem important...'

He glared at Hardy then at Porter. If anything, Porter's pleasant face and respectful attitude seemed to annoy him further. But unable to fault him in any other way, he resorted to a personal attack. 'Seems they let all sorts into the force nowadays.'

Caron Allan

Pulling out a chair and sitting down, Hardy indicated
to Porter that he should do the same. Porter moved his
chair back a little from the table. Hardy, with a quick
glance at Porter, said calmly,

'Could you take notes, sergeant. I may need to refer
to them in my report.'

'Of course, sir.' Porter got out his notebook and
pencil, dated a clean page and waited.

The detective inspector was red in the face and
growing redder. 'Bullying me in my own station!
Threatening me! You can bloody get out—right now!
I'm instructing my men to refuse any assistance...'

'Look,' Hardy said, keeping his voice steady and calm
as he cut across the other man's rant, 'We've been sent
here to do a job. I can no more refuse my senior officer
than you can yours. If you don't cooperate, I shall be
forced to ask my senior officer to contact your chief
constable. Just give me your case files, that's all I need.
Oh, and an office.'

Without a word the other inspector strode to the
door and yelled for a constable. 'Get me everything for
the three cases in Porthlea this month.'

'Yes sir.' The constable retreated, sneaking a
backward look at the other men.

'Take them, and get out. You can wait outside.'

'What room can we...?' Hardy asked. He was only
asking to provoke the man; he already knew no office
would be made available.

The DI's language in response to this shocked even
Porter, who'd served more than twenty years walking
the beat in some of the more demanding suburbs of
inner London. Hardy nodded at Porter and they left the
room. The detective inspector threw at them as they
went,

'You won't find anything! There's nothing to find.
Coming down here, telling me how to do my job. I'm
going to put in an official complaint, your career will be

over before it's even begun.'

The constable came over to hand three thin card folders to Porter. Hardy turned back and said, 'I appreciate your cooperation, Inspector. Good afternoon.'

The Detective Inspector slammed his door.

Hardy looked at Porter. 'You needn't think you'll get such a warm welcome everywhere we go. Not everyone is so helpful.'

Porter, torn between the desire to come back with a witty quip, and the need for a good strong cup of tea, just nodded, bemused.

'Right let's get back to the railway station. There's a train to Porthlea in ten minutes,' Hardy said. 'We're staying at the pub in the village. Nice and central.'

As they walked back to the railway station, Porter said, unable to hide his anxiety any longer, 'Sir, I'm not sure I can manage the room rates even at a small local pub.'

Hardy looked at him. Porter held his breath. He hoped he wouldn't get sent straight back to London, but he had no choice but to be honest. But now he had a sinking feeling.

Hardy clapped him briefly on the shoulder, and said,

'Don't worry, sergeant. It's all on The Met. Room and board, and a meal allowance, and any travel costs. I'm sorry no one explained that to you sooner, I wouldn't want you to worry about things like that. I need you to keep your brainpower for the real work. All right?'

'Yes sir.' Porter's spirit soared. Free food! And staying in a pub at the seaside. It was just like being on holiday.

*

Chapter Eighteen

Apart from a tender spot on her left temple, Dee felt completely recovered from her ordeal, and was up bright and early on Saturday morning. She had plenty of time before meeting her brother's train that afternoon. She had her breakfast, then humming along to a song on the radio, she tidied up the cottage as usual. She braced herself for tackling the mess in her bedroom created by the intruder, and was glad that it wasn't as upsetting as expected. At least everything was tidy before her brother arrived. She would need to think about how to tell him what had happened. She went for her usual walk, then in the afternoon, she spent some time lying on the sofa reading.

By the time she left the house to go to meet her brother's train, her equanimity was restored and she was eager to see him, eager to tell him everything she'd learned. She came out of the dim interior of the hall into the dazzling afternoon sunshine and walked directly into a man going past the cottage.

Then as he gripped her arms to steady her, helping

her to stay on her feet, she saw who it was.

'Oh!' she said, covering her sense of shock by becoming angry instead of flinging herself into his arms. 'So Scotland Yard finally turned up, did they? A bit late in the day.'

The tall man in the smart and very modern suit— surely too smart and modern for a little place like this, Dee decided—took a couple of steps back, clearly as shocked as she was at having literally walked right into her as she came out of the door as he and the other man were walking by on their way from the railway station to the pub.

Just seeing him was enough to set her heart singing, much to her annoyance. Meanwhile he was frowning down at her with what was known in the family as the Hardy Frown, his dark brows drawn together over long-lashed hazel eyes that were just like his mother's.

'What the hell are you doing here? You'd better not be interfering in my investigation. I'm not like my father, I don't allow private citizens to meddle in official police business.' He was holding his forefinger up in a lecturing manner.

'Oh shut up, Bill, you're so bloody pompous,' Dee said and stormed off.

Hardy sighed.

'I take it you know that lady, sir?' the sergeant asked, eyes wide with curiosity, following the lady as she went.

'You could say so, sergeant. Listen to me. On no account are you to tell that woman *anything* about this case. Don't give her documents to read. Don't accidentally leave your notebook lying around for her to just 'happen' to find and snoop through. Don't answer any of her questions, or tell her our line of questioning, or anything about our suspects, or—just—anything. She comes from a long line of nosy women. Do you understand me, sergeant?'

'Ye...' the sergeant began.

'Because if you do any of those things, believe me, I shall make your life a living hell.' Hardy caught himself and stopped. Then added, with just a hint of a smile, 'Not that I won't anyway, I expect you're thinking.'

'Oh sir, as a mere sergeant, I'm not paid to think.' Porter risked a grin at the inspector.

Stifling a laugh, Hardy said, 'I'm very glad to hear it. Now come on, we've got things to do.'

Still seething from the encounter, Dee approached the steps to enter the railway station to meet Rob's train just as Major Reeves was walking by with his Labrador, who was carrying two tennis balls at once in her mouth, her tail wagging vigourously.

Dee was a little surprised that the major hailed her, as they had rarely exchanged more than a smile or a 'good morning' apart from the day of the Spring Fair. In fact she was doubtful he remembered who she was, but this was evidently not the case as, when she turned to greet him, he immediately raised his hat and said, 'My dear young lady, I'm delighted to see you looking so well! Is it our sea air that has done that, or was it the chance to nip back up to London for a spot of shopping? I expect you've heard about our latest tragedy. Not that I shall miss the old... er... Well. Very nice to see you again, my dear.'

Dee smiled at him, wondering if the village grapevine had told him about the attack on her. But he said nothing about it, and so she didn't either. As she fussed the slobbery, excitable dog, her bad mood evaporated entirely, but the train came in at that moment, and the major simply said,

'Meeting your brother? Very good, very good, I won't detain you.'

She had no time to do anything other than nod, surprised he knew who she was meeting. But it seemed that even when there were other, more interesting things to talk about, mundane news travelled fast in the village.

The major continued, 'Perhaps you'll bring him round for drinks tomorrow evening? If you haven't anything else planned? Shall we say half past eight? Should be a nice little group of us. You know Meredith Prescott of course, and the vicar and his wife? And that pop star chappie will be there. Sonny-Ray. Ridiculous name, but the fellow's all right really. Splendid. Well, got to take Maybelle for her walk. We both need to walk off a few pounds.' He patted his stomach and laughed heartily, adding, 'Well, toodle-oo.'

Dee relayed the invitation to Rob five minutes later as they headed back to the cottage. He immediately nodded in satisfaction.

'It'll be interesting to get the major's perspective on the recent events, and the Prescotts'. So far we've only really heard from the women who work in the village.'

Dee smiled at his use of the word 'we' but agreed with him: so far they had learned next to nothing from any of the local men. 'But I should warn you about tomorrow night. They'll probably only want to talk about recent events. And as the major is madly in love with Meredith, I should think he's likely to spend most of the evening trying to flirt with her, though he usually gets the cold shoulder.'

'Really? He loves Meredith Prescott?' Rob sounded astonished. He was not the kind of man to understand the appeal of a quiet, attractive country lady, she reminded herself. 'And does she reciprocate his feelings?'

'Sadly not. Oh, and another thing. The Fuzz are here at long last.' She kept her tone neutral, but he looked at her closely.

'Any particular Fuzz? The locals from Sandneath? Or?'

She rolled her eyes. 'Who do you think?'

'Not Scotland Yard?'

'The very same.'

To her surprise he laughed heartily at this, which made her cross again.

Porter was pleased to find he had his own room. His half-expected them to be sharing. The view from the window was at the wrong angle to get a proper look at the sea, but if he leaned out a little and craned his neck to the left, he could just about make it out. And he could hear it, which was the main thing. He was looking forward to lying in bed that night listening to the sound of the sea as he fell asleep.

He unpacked his overnight bag, wishing he'd brought more clothes with him. It seemed they could be here for a few days, he'd not expected that. It was a learning experience, he reminded himself. Next time he would know to expect the unexpected, and bring more stuff with him.

He was boyishly excited. This was far better than processing drunk-and-disorderlies or mopping out cells. It was like an adventure. And what he was saving on groceries he would use to buy his mother something she needed. He might be able to buy treats for her more often if he stayed in CID. But even if he didn't, he thought, erring on the side of caution, he would not forget this trip, or this investigation. His first time ever out of London, and here he was at the seaside. If he had a spare moment, he'd love to get down on that beach and look for a nice shell to take back to his mother. He decided to go to the phone box on the green and call her to let her know he'd arrived safely, she'd worry if she didn't hear from him.

Porter came out of his room just as Hardy came out of his.

'Ah,' said Hardy, halting in his tracks.

'Everything all right, sir?'

'Yes, fine. Er—thanks. And what about you? How is your room? I know it's a bit basic, not exactly the Ritz.'

'It's very nice, sir, thank you.' But Porter couldn't hold back his enthusiasm completely, and he added, 'I can hear the sea!'

Hardy grinned then, looking about seventeen. 'I'm glad,' he said. He looked at his watch. 'Right, I was thinking we should get some dinner at about seven, if that suits you. That gives you just over an hour to—er—relax, or... I'll meet you in the dining-room downstairs at seven o'clock. Then perhaps after we've eaten, we'll take a proper look at these folders our local detective inspector so graciously gave us.'

'Certainly, sir.'

'And if you need anything to drink, please stick to tea or coffee, or... Well, it just wouldn't look good to be having a lot of alcohol. Though I think we can get away with a half to go with our meal. Just put anything you order on the tab. Is there anything you wanted to ask me, sergeant?'

Porter thought Hardy seemed ill at ease, then it came to him that this was possibly to do with a certain young lady staying in the village. He wondered if Hardy was rushing off to see her now, perhaps that was why he was giving Porter some free time.

'No sir. I think everything is fine. I will see you later, then. Must just go and let my mother know I got here safely.'

'Lord, yes, do. Don't let me keep you. See you downstairs at seven.'

To Porter's surprise, Hardy turned and went back into his room, picking up a case file as he closed the door.

*

Chapter Nineteen

Rob threw his things on the bed in the front bedroom of the cottage, not particularly interested in tidying them away right now. When he came downstairs, Dee was making coffee. As she got the drinks ready, she told him about her phone call to their mother a few days earlier, adding,

'I can't believe Martin tried to shove his way in like that.'

'Well if he turns up here,' Rob said stoutly, 'He'll get a punch on the nose. So he'd better just leave you alone, that's all I can say. No wonder you're looking pale and wishy-washy.'

'Thanks very much!' Dee smiled but said nothing more. If it came to a fist fight, she imagined she would have to protect her brother, not the other way round. But just having him here with her made her feel safer. She was on the point of telling him what had happened on Thursday night, guilt at keeping it from him eating away at her, yet at the same time she didn't want to worry him, and as she deliberated, he changed the subject, saying,

'So Bill is down here from Scotland Yard? I wonder what that means?'

She nodded. 'I literally walked into him and his sergeant on my way to meet you. I've already had a row with him. He warned me off his investigation! Can you believe it? It's as though he thinks I'm some sort of amateur sleuth. He didn't even wait to see... I mean... it's not as though he caught me in the middle of doing anything sleuth-like. He's such an idiot.'

Rob simply smiled at her, eyebrows raised.

'What?'

'Oh nothing,' he said. 'Nothing at all.'

She leaned her elbows on the table in a manner greatly frowned upon at home, and said, 'Come on, what?'

'Well you are, aren't you? Sleuthing?'

'I am not...'

'And the women of our family do have something of a reputation for that very thing.'

'Only Aunt Dottie—*his own mother, mark you*—she is the only one who... all right, our mother sometimes helped her out. And probably still does, if we knew but half of it. As did Father. And no doubt other members of the family too. But that's all. That's no grounds at all for... Why he should assume that just because I am here it means anything. I'll never...'

'But you are, aren't you? Here, I mean. And you came back here because Mrs Hunter died and you wanted to know why and how. And, from the very second you heard of her death, you didn't believe it was any kind of accident or attributable to some natural cause.'

'Oh shut up, Rob, you're as bad as Bill.'

'In that you love us both? Or that we are both handsome and intelligent? If so, yes, that's very true.' He smirked at her.

'I love my whole family,' she insisted, glaring at him and daring him to contradict her. But she couldn't resist adding a grumpy, 'Including you two. God knows why.'

After they had finished their coffee, Rob leaned forward, his elbows on the table.

'So, what have you found out?'

Her irritation once again forgotten, Dee mimicked his position, their heads almost touching above the shiny oak surface of the table. She loved being in cahoots with her baby brother.

'Apart from Cissie and myself, and Marlene and her mother, no one seems to be upset about the old lady's death,' she told him. 'I mean, yes, they are quite shocked, but it doesn't seem as if anyone liked her very much.'

'She was rather an old ghoul,' Rob reminded her.

'Well, yes, I suppose she was rather. I'm not so sure she was as deaf as she made out. She always seemed to know what was going on, especially if it was something bad. She really enjoyed other people's misfortunes.' She paused for a moment, thinking, then said, 'I'm afraid she was not at all a nice old lady.'

'She certainly got the measure of me,' he said. 'No one else seems to be aware of my—er—'persuasion'. Not bad for a deaf and blind old woman. So no one is sorry?'

'Only her family and one or two others: Lily Glover from the café, and Cissie. Even Marlene's boyfriend Eddie doesn't seem particularly upset. Though that might be because Mrs Hunter warned Marlene about being too involved with Eddie.' She was still thinking about what Rob had just said. 'Remember what you told me Jeremy Prescott had asked you?'

'Of course.'

'Do you think he is? Of that, what was it you said, 'persuasion'? I know everyone says he is a notorious womaniser, and his family say he is going to settle down with someone appropriately 'County'. And let's face it, he probably will. But the entire village seemed to think he was carrying on with Sheila Fenniston, but what if that was all just a smokescreen? I mean, some of your friends have got wives, haven't they? I don't just mean Jeffrey,' she added hastily, seeing his expression.

'You're right, of course. It happens rather a lot. The men need a smokescreen as you call it, a kind of cover story to protect their reputations, especially those in the professions. I mean no one worries about an artist or a writer being a bit of a pansy, it's practically compulsory. But when it's some businessman, or a government minister or even a copper, things are very different. All the while intimate relationships between men are illegal, we've got too much to lose if things became public. And some might even go to prison if their—let's call them exploits—came to the attention of the police.'

'So what do you think about Jeremy Prescott?'

He sighed. 'All I'd say is, it's possible.'

'Did he seem disappointed when you pretended not to know what he was talking about?'

He grinned. 'I'd like to think so. But perhaps he was just surprised. Am I really so very obvious?'

'No, not really. But you are very pretty, you know, those big brown eyes, those cheekbones, and you've got fabulous skin. So no, I wouldn't be a bit surprised if he was genuinely disappointed.'

'I'd like to think so,' he said again. 'I wonder if there's a way we could find out?' he murmured, sinking back into his own thoughts.

'You could try your fatal charm on him, see what happens, but for heaven's sake, be careful. I've also found out a bit more about the poison pen letters,' she said, and opened her bag to get out the ones Lily had given her. She quickly told him what she now knew about Lily as he looked at the notes.

After a few minutes, he said, 'You know, these are quite vicious, aren't they? I mean I had dismissed it all as a bit of a childish prank, but this,' He tapped the letter in his hand, 'This is horrid. How is the poor woman? Do you think she's frightened?'

Dee shook her head. 'She's a bit annoyed, I think, but other than that, she didn't seem particularly upset. Mind you, she's had them several months now, so I suppose she's had time to get over the initial shock. And with no more coming since these two, I expect she's stopped worrying about it. Also, she said her so-called 'secret' is pretty well common knowledge, so she's not afraid of it getting out. At that awful dinner party, Meredith Prescott almost let something slip, she mentioned something about letters, and then said something else, but in any case, we already know that she's had some. And Cissie told me she'd had another one too.'

That annoyed him. 'Really? Poor Cissie.'

'Yes. She said it upset her at first, but she's now quite all right about it. She threw it in the fire though, which is a shame.'

Dee told him everything she'd learned so far.

Later they decided to go to the pub for dinner and a drink. Dee had just got into the bath when Rob shouted through the door,

'I've just remembered, I promised to let Mother know when I arrived and to tell her how you are. She doesn't trust you to look after yourself.'

'Well, why don't you go on ahead,' Dee called back. The water was deliciously hot, and the bath oils were doing wonders for both her mood and her skin. 'I shan't be too long. I can meet you at the pub, in say, twenty minutes? Get me a Babycham will you?'

'All right. Just don't keep me waiting too long, or I shall eat without you, I'm ravenous.'

Dee bathed quickly, then got dressed. A glance out of the front bedroom window showed her that Rob was still in the telephone box on the green. That meant she had plenty of time to do her hair and put her face on.

Finally satisfied her hair was perfectly smooth but with a nice upward kink at the ends, she experienced a moment of gratitude that nature—or more likely, genetics—had supplied her with a large amount of thick hair that she back-combed carefully in the modern manner. According to the doctor at the hospital, her plentiful hair had saved her from a far more serious injury. She gave it another spritz with the hairspray.

She applied her favourite nude-coloured lipstick, tidied up her heavy eyeliner that had smudged during the course of the day, adding a little more at the outer corners. She ran down the stairs, grabbed her shoulder bag and a jacket, pushed her feet into the marginally more sensible of her shoes and headed for the door.

It was raining again. She threw her jacket about her shoulders without bothering to push her arms into the sleeves. She was only a minute away she reminded herself, though all the while she kept looking over her shoulder, suddenly nervous. As she passed the telephone box, she could see a woman was inside. Rob must be already in The Seagull.

She crossed the green, hurrying to reach the pub, and pushed open the side door. And in the lobby, next to the door to the bar, she paused for a deep breath, relieved to be inside and in a brightly-lit place. She quickly checked her hair in the mirror so thoughtfully provided, tucking a few stray strands back in place, and ran her fingers through her hair until she was satisfied. She puffed out her cheeks as she exhaled, turning her head to the left and right, apparently checking her hair and make-up but in reality just giving herself another minute.

'As good as it's going to be,' she said aloud.

'Pretty nearly perfect,' called a male voice behind her.

She spun nervously then attempted a relaxed smile

when a certain tall man strolled into view, coming in out of the street to shake the raindrops from his jacket and his dark wavy hair like so many tiny jewels.

'Bill. I might have known. I suppose you're domiciled at the pub for the duration. We must be going in the same direction.'

'No doubt.' He nodded curtly, unsmiling as ever, but as he reached past her to wrench open the door to the bar, his lips grazed her cheek, and he said, 'Good evening, Dee. It's lovely to see you again. Tell me, is there a skirt to go with that belt you're wearing?'

Looking down at it, she said, 'It is a bit short, I suppose.'

'You look very nice.' He almost smiled, she noticed. That was likely to be as good as it got, he wasn't a light-hearted, gregarious man. He held the door open for her to enter first. Saying nothing, she went inside. Even in high heels she was easily still six inches shorter than him. To her relief she immediately spotted Rob sitting at a table by the window, with another man beside him, full glasses of beer in front of them both. Rob waved to her, and she hurried forward. Both men got to their feet politely.

Rob said, 'This is Sergeant Porter, Bill's right-hand man. I've just been telling him we are Bill's cousins.'

She turned to smile at the police officer, now changed into casual clothes and looking more relaxed. He held out his hand and she shook it.

'We almost met earlier, I think,' she said with a grin.

'A pleasure to meet you, miss. I'm Nahum Porter,' he said, and in a lilting Trinidadian accent added, 'But most people call me Nat.'

'Pleased to meet you, Nat. I'm Dee. Rob's sister. And cousin to that ogre you call your boss.'

'Shall we go through to the dining-room?' growled the ogre, suddenly right above her left shoulder, closer than expected, his voice prickling her ear. She practically leapt out of her skin, then gritted her teeth and fought the urge to shout at him or slap him. Instead, she rolled her eyes, and Rob, behind her, laughed, guessing exactly how she was feeling.

*

Chapter Twenty

When Dee and Rob arrived at Major Reeves' cottage on Sunday evening, they found the Reverend Callum Edmonds and his wife Millie at the door, having just arrived. In the lane outside the major's house, a large American car gleamed in the evening sunlight. Dee heart sank. Sonny-Ray Smith was here. She only hoped he had left the purple bowtie and winkle-pickers at home.

'We've already knocked,' Millie informed them, looking Dee and Rob over in that assessing sort of way Dee had noticed previously. Dee wondered if she was surprised to see them there. Callum gave them both a vague smile and a nod. As before he seemed as if his thoughts were on higher things.

The major opened the door just then and welcomed them all into his home. In the background the Labrador was thumping her tail against the stair post in welcome and Rob paused to scratch her behind the ears. The dog flopped onto her side, wagging her tail madly, and again, Dee marvelled at her brother's ability to get along with anyone and everyone.

'Ah, you've got a friend for life now!' the major laughed heartily and directed them into the sitting-room.

There were a few other people already there. Sonny-Ray was there, sitting in a chair in the most prominent place, smiling and nodding like a guest on a television show, but keeping his seat, not getting up to greet the ladies in the conventional polite manner. Dee felt a growing sense of irritation towards the man who clearly enjoyed the weight of his popularity.

She had already met Dr Bartlett twice, but tonight he was accompanied by his wife, a short but forceful-seeming woman. The doctor appeared to be wearing the same suit she had seen him in previously, and Dee wasn't particularly surprised to see his large leather bag by his feet.

'Are you expecting to be called away?' she asked. His wife rolled her eyes.

'He's always expecting to be called away! This is why, when we have a holiday, we have to go right away out of the area. Otherwise, I'm sure he'd be called out, regardless of whether he was on duty.'

She sounded thoroughly put out, though everyone chuckled as though she had made a joke, and the doctor himself looked as if he had heard this complaint too many times before to care.

The major was taking orders for drinks. The doctor, the major himself and Sonny-Ray all had Scotch. Millie Edmonds and Dee opted for tea, and Rob for a glass of sherry, which prompted Millie Edmonds to change her mind and ask for a sherry too, then her husband asked for the same. It was several minutes before everyone was settled with their beverage.

'No Miss Prescott?' Dee asked, watching the major blush at the sound of her name.

'Er, not yet, no. She did promise to come though.

Perhaps she'll be here a little later.'

Dee nodded and smiled, feeling sorry for him all over again.

They talked in a general way, discussing the relative merits of living in such a small community. Seizing her opportunity in a roundabout way, Dee began,

'There must be times when it's inconvenient to live in such a small place. It can't always be a good thing to know everyone so thoroughly and to be known. I mean, for everyone to know every least little thing about you. All those secrets brought out into the open, whether you want it or not.' She added a smile, to keep it light-hearted.

'Makes life interesting at any rate,' Sonny-Ray said with a laugh. 'Not that I've got anything to hide, babe. My life is an open book.'

He was staring at her chest quite openly, making her wish she had at least two more layers on. Dee decided she hated him. She wondered if he had received any of the poison pen letters. Surely few people were more likely to targeted than a pop star. Especially one who was widely known to be having problems relating to drug use. In any case, she thought, he practically deserved it.

'Everyone has secrets,' the major remarked.

'Good God, what secrets!' Millie Edmonds gasped rather melodramatically, whilst at the same time, Mrs Bartlett declared,

'Then, what I say is, people shouldn't have secrets they are ashamed of.'

Dee had already decided she disliked Mrs Bartlett and her brisk manner. The group was rapidly being divided into two camps in Dee's mind, those she liked, and those she very much didn't.

The vicar nodded and gave a rueful smile. His wife was beginning to recover her poise and she now gave a little laugh, saying, 'Well, with old Aggie Hunter gone, it will be a lot easier for everyone to keep their little secrets once more.'

'Millie!' said the vicar in a half-hearted attempt at reproof. Everyone else was laughing and nodding in agreement.

'You think the same, you said so only yesterday. It may be wrong to speak ill of the dead, but Agnes Hunter was a mean old woman who enjoyed upsetting people and seeing them miserable.'

'I did rather get the impression that she loved a good gossip,' Dee said, thinking back to the day of the fair, reflecting that almost every time she had seen Mrs Hunter, it had been in the context of her enjoying someone else's misfortune.

'Oh, she did,' Major Peter Reeves said. 'She took great delight in the unhappiness of others, as does her granddaughter, Marlene. The mother's all right, Harriet Grayson. She works at Prescott's, in the warehouse.'

'And she's our cleaner,' Millie chipped in, looking round the room with a smile, as if she felt very clever and wanted them to applaud. Peter Reeves nodded and continued,

'But the grandmother and the granddaughter were certainly co-conspirators with but a single thought between them. To spread misery.'

Dee and Rob exchanged a look. Dee expected the vicar to reprove the major, but the clergyman was nodding sadly in agreement. He finished his sherry before saying,

'You know, confidentially, I've often wondered if it was Mrs Hunter and Marlene who were behind those poison pen letters that were going about a few weeks ago. I would dearly love to know if anyone has had one since Mrs Hunter died.'

Sonny-Ray rubbed his hands together gleefully and said, 'Oh really? Poison pen letters? How very Agatha Christie! All right, 'fess up, who's had one?'

Rob said with a laugh, 'Dee had one just before we went back to London. Accusing her of all sorts of things.'

'Oh you mustn't let it upset you,' Mrs Bartlett commanded with more vigour than kindness. 'Mustn't let whoever it is think they've won. Though perhaps you could wear slightly longer skirts in future. It doesn't do, you know, to dress quite so cheaply.'

Ignoring this, Dee said, 'I wasn't especially concerned. Though I should think it could be quite upsetting for some people, getting one of those. Or more than one.'

'Depends what it said, babe,' Sonny-Ray pointed out.

If he called her 'babe' one more time, she'd be tempted to throw something at him, Dee thought. With his hair thinning at the crown and his greasy skin, he was no Donovan, that was for sure.

'Just the work of some dried-up old spinster, I should think. Bitter. Got nothing better to do with her time.'

'That's rather harsh coming from a vicar,' Dee said with a gentle laugh to take the sting out of her words, but underneath it all, she was fuming.

Millie laughed. 'Oh he doesn't mean it, really.'

But Dee, making the most of this opportunity, said, 'And are there any dried-up old spinsters in the village? Apart from me, of course.'

'Dear lady!' said the gallant major in protest. His eyes were bright with interest. She noticed them returning several times to glance at her legs, revealed by the skirt Mrs Edmonds had condemned as too short. He was getting rather pink in the face. Dee hoped he didn't suffer from high blood pressure.

The vicar, singularly failing to be as gallant as the major, simply mulled this over and said, 'Hmm. Not really. There's Davies, perhaps. She's been a bit peculiar most of her life. Or perhaps the old woman at the post office.'

'It couldn't be Cissie!' Dee said immediately. 'I can guarantee that.'

'You can't be too sure, you know, my dear. You've only been in the village a short while, don't forget,' Millie Edmonds pointed out.

'Cissie Palmer has been a dear family friend since before I was born,' Dee stated, and her voice brooked no argument. That was clearly news to them all.

'Oh, er, well, you know...' said the vicar.

Rob leaned forward. 'But definitely a woman, you all think?'

'Woman's weapon, don't we usually say?' the major said. He leaned back in his seat, comfortable, confident.

'That's poison itself, not poison pen letters,' the doctor reminded him.

The major shrugged. 'Poison. Poison pen. All the same. Secretive, mysterious. Women's wiles.'

Dee sighed theatrically, shaking her head. Millie Edmonds smiled too.

Sonny-Ray said, 'Well, don't look at me, I haven't had any. Like I said, an open book, me.'

No one *had* been looking at him, Dee thought.

'Got one myself,' the major said.

'A poison pen letter?' Millie Edmonds sounded politely disbelieving. 'Why on earth should you?'

'Accused me of carrying on with Miss Prescott.' The major looked a little hot and bothered. Meredith Prescott. His Achilles' heel. Dee felt sorry for him yet again on that score. 'Said I was sneaking into her room at night.'

He received a dig in the ribs from the doctor, who added a wink and said with a guffaw, 'If only, what?'

The major couldn't help but laugh. 'Well...' he said, growing even redder. 'All the same, not nice. Imagine how Miss Prescott would feel if she found out. Most distressing.'

'Callum had one, didn't you, dear?'

Callum Edmonds nodded briefly but left it to his wife to continue. Which she did with relish.

'Accused him of pocketing the donations from the collection plate. As if he would do such a thing!' Millie was quite indignant, Dee noticed, whilst Callum simply gave a helpless shrug.

'Oh well, you know. Envy, hatred, and malice, and all uncharitableness.'

'Oh, er, quite. Well look on the bright side, vicar, at least it wasn't choirboys,' the doctor pointed out helpfully.

Bartlett's enjoying this, Dee thought, and he's not taking it particularly seriously.

But Millie Edmonds blushed a deep puce, and Callum said, 'Oh I say!' in a protesting voice. The doctor apologised, trying to defend himself.

'It's not me saying it. It's the kind of thing someone might write, someone who wanted to shock people, or upset them.'

Rob nodded. 'I should think if I stay more than a day or two, I'll get one too.'

'Probably accuse you of being a shirt-lifter or something,' Sonny-Ray said, lazing back in his chair, watching everyone through half-closed eyes. Dee thought the man gave every appearance of being relaxed, but in reality his hand was tense on his knee, the fist clenched, the knuckles white. He was on edge, watching them all, weighing what was said. She wondered why that was. Perhaps after all, his life wasn't quite the open book he'd claimed.

'Good lord, I hope not!' Rob immediately said. His good-natured laugh sounded so natural. He'd spent years covering up his true persuasion until it was completely normal for him. Dee thought it was unlikely anyone would guess his secret, although there had been that question from Jeremy Prescott a couple of weeks ago.

'It's all done for the shock value,' Dr Bartlett said.

The doctor had a point: the letters were designed to shock, or shame. But who had appointed themselves judge over this small community?

'And has nobody any theories about who the writer of these awful letters could be?' Dee asked again. Around her, heads shook sorrowfully. Callum Edmonds murmured,

'No, sorry,' whilst his wife just stared into space.

After a moment, in an abstracted kind of voice, she said, 'Well up until dear Sheila's demise, I'd always thought it was her.'

Dee found that rather surprising. 'Really? Why was that, if you don't mind me asking? I only met her once.'

Millie shrugged. 'I just thought it was her, that's all. She was an outsider, and she could be quite determined. She liked her own way, was far too 'flighty'. And well, frankly she was a bit too much for a place like Porthlea. She was just bored with this place, and angry and full of malice. I thought it was the sort of thing someone like her would do.'

The others all murmured in agreement but at that moment the major began refreshing everyone's drinks. It seemed as though the theme had run its course.

'I saw Marlene in the pub the other evening with her boyfriend, though they're both underage,' Dee said. Millie Edmonds nodded.

'That would be Eddie, son of a local farmer. A nice lad, actually. I do so wish it hadn't been Marlene who got her claws into him, she leads him astray. Poor Callum is always having to chase them out of the churchyard. Honestly, the things they get up to would make most of the inhabitants of the churchyard turn in their graves!'

'Oh now really, Millie!' the vicar protested.

'Well, dear, you can't deny she has left her knickers

behind on more than one occasion when you've chased them out.'

The men laughed but Dee felt rather embarrassed. The vicar, also clearly uncomfortable, admitted it was true.

'I really must have a word with young Eddie before things go too far,' he said.

'I don't see that things could go much farther,' his wife snapped, but then remembered she was in company and hurriedly turned on her cheery social smile.

Rob spoke. 'Well both deaths in the village seem a bit odd, don't they? Miss Fenniston seems a most unlikely type to have killed herself. And Marlene may be flighty, but she seems very sure her grandmother couldn't have walked from her bed to the top of the stairs unaided.'

'It ought to have been prevented,' Millie declared hotly. 'I've told Harriet time and time again, as I said, she cleans for me to earn a bit extra on top of what she gets at Prescott's. I said, that house is not suited to the needs of a disabled old woman. It's a death trap. But would she listen?'

Mrs Bartlett murmured something Dee couldn't quite catch, then Mrs Edmonds was off again, laying down the law.

'There was no handrail, no proper lighting.' She was counting the issues on her fingers as she spoke. 'Her wheelchair was kept upstairs, so how could she have got downstairs if she wanted to? I told Harriet and that daughter of hers that the wheelchair should be kept downstairs, and that Mrs Hunter should use walking sticks upstairs.'

Dee wondered how any of these measures could have possibly prevented Mrs Hunter's so-called fall, but she said nothing. In any case, there wasn't time. Millie was off again.

'It's terrible to think of that poor old lady falling down all those stairs, frantically trying to scrabble for a handhold and finding nothing. Really it was an accident waiting to happen. Meredith agrees with me. I've told Harriet in no uncertain terms that it should have been avoided. I'm afraid she got rather upset and I had to let her go home again.'

Dee was angry. Surely Millie should be offering comfort rather than accusations in Mrs Grayson's time of sorrow? Though Dee was surprised to hear someone else describing Mrs Hunter as a poor old lady for probably the first time ever.

She was saved from having to think of a new question to ask by a knock at the front door just then. The major, excited and blushing again, leapt to his feet, excusing himself. Dee groaned inwardly, certain something vital had just slipped out of her grasp. It would be difficult to reintroduce the topic with a new guest and all the distraction that would go with that.

A minute later he was ushering Meredith Prescott into the room. Dee had the sense that Meredith held back momentarily upon seeing her and Rob but if she had done so, she recovered immediately and came forward with a smile for each of them.

'Daphne, dear, how lovely to see you again, and looking so well! And you too, Roger, how do you do? It's so nice to welcome you back to our little village.'

Dee and Rob murmured something appropriate, avoiding each other's eyes to keep from laughing, then Meredith turned to greet the Reverend Edmonds, and received a kiss on the cheek from Millie and a glass of sherry from Major Reeves. She treated the Bartletts to a mere nod. At last Sonny-Ray remembered his manners, getting out of his chair to come over and kiss Meredith on the cheek, his actions clearly taking her by surprise, and it was not a welcome surprise, either, Dee judged. Meredith seemed to bristle slightly with offense at his familiarity. Clearly the bad boy of pop had a lot to learn about village social etiquette.

'We were just talking about the recent unpleasantness,' Millie Edmonds explained to Meredith.

'Then perhaps it's time we talked about something more pleasant,' Meredith said. 'How are your chickens coming along, Millie? I'm afraid mine are disappointingly slow so far. Only three of them have given any eggs.'

'They should be laying by now,' Millie said. 'Perhaps they're past it? If they don't lay soon, I suggest you put them in the pot and get some new birds.'

'Oh dear,' Meredith said with an uncomfortable laugh. 'I'll need to get a man in to do that, I'm afraid I'm rather squeamish.'

'Nothing to it,' Millie said. 'I always have to kill ours, Callum won't do it.' And with an unpleasant mime, she demonstrated her technique. Dee exchanged a look with Rob, who looked equally revolted. We are definitely city folk, Dee reflected ruefully.

Sonny-Ray and the major began to discuss cigars, whilst Dee and Rob chatted with the doctor and his wife about village life. Later the major, aided by Millie, brought in coffee and cognac and there was an opportunity to turn the conversation again. Fortunately the change wasn't provided by Rob or Dee. It was the major himself who returned to the earlier subject.

He said, 'I hear the police are in the village. I can't help wondering when life will get back to normal.'

'Or if...' Sonny-Ray added with a sarcastic twist of a smile. He'd already drunk his cognac but not touched his coffee.

Meredith looked put out by this but said nothing. The major shot her a worried look and smiled a non-committal smile. Millie Edmonds, seemingly always rushing in where angels feared to tread, said,

'My word, yes! And one of them is a... you know...'
She nodded her head a couple of times as if that would
make her meaning clear.

Dee looked nonplussed. 'Is a...? Is a what?' She knew
exactly what Millie was complaining about. She
wondered if the woman would have the gall to be
honest about it.

Inclining towards the rest of the company, Millie
whispered, 'A *black* man.'

Mrs Bartlett gasped in horror. Dee wanted to laugh,
or perhaps to cry at this ridiculous behaviour. How
dared they! She was about to speak when Rob said,

'That would be Sergeant Porter. An excellent man. A
very experienced, very intelligent officer. Highly
thought of at the top level, you know. Once saved Her
Majesty from a startled horse. He'll go far.'

They all stared at him, astonished, then nodded and
huffed to themselves as they rearranged their opinions
in the light of this new information. Perhaps the fellow
wasn't so bad after all, Dee could see them thinking.
She was the only one who knew her brother well
enough to recognise the brittle tone that meant he was
angry at their bigotry.

Major Reeves said, 'You know him, do you?'

Rob leaned back and preened a little. 'Oh, I've come
across the fellow once or twice in my profession.'

Her eyes narrowing, Meredith said, 'I thought you
were still training to be a barrister?'

Rob sat up again, blushing. 'Oh er, yes, I am. But you
know, almost at the end of my course now. Been doing
a lot of work with top barristers in London. I know
quite a few now I've been at the courts so much,
watching how it's done.'

Dr Bartlett accepted another tot of cognac from
Major Reeves, and said, ignoring his wife's sour look,
'But surely they are not letting a sergeant—wherever he
comes from—run some kind of secret investigation in

the village?'

'Got an inspector with him. Though he looks like rather a young fellow. Can't have much experience. Perhaps it's not what we think. After all, who'd want to kill an old woman? They must be here about some other matter,' the major responded.

'Who knows,' Meredith dismissed the topic once again. 'But now, do let's talk about happier things, and not this tired old scheme. Millie, have you done the library rota for next week yet?'

The remainder of the evening continued in the same boring manner. At least it was fairly good-humoured. That is, until Dee and Rob were getting ready to take their leave, following the others outside. Meredith had been offered a lift home by Sonny-Ray in his huge car, even though both of them lived merely a few minutes' walk away. Under the guise of saying goodnight to Dee, Meredith leaned towards her to kiss her cheek and said in a low voice, 'I'd advise you to stop tattling about recent events in the village. As an outsider, you will only make yourself look foolish. And you wouldn't want people to laugh at you, would you? I'm sure you understand.'

Dee was left staring after Meredith as she mulled this over. Sonny-Ray opened the front passenger door for Meredith, then once she was seated inside the car, he ran around the front to get into the driver's seat, the car roaring away almost immediately, the horn sounding several ear-splitting times whilst Sonny-Ray waved through his open window. Dee noted that Meredith simply stared straight ahead as if no one else in the world existed. Behind Dee, standing by the front door of his cottage, the major looked very disappointed and ruffled indeed.

'Phew, what an evening! I'm exhausted,' Dee said as soon as they reached the cottage. She waited by the front door for Rob to put the light on, then, with the nice safe brightness lighting the hall, she let out the breath she had been holding, came in and shut the door. 'My goodness, though, what about Millie Edmonds?'

'Terrifying, wasn't she? Brisk, efficient.'

'But not kind. I'd rather someone was kind than did everything perfectly. And that Mrs Bartlett was difficult to like.'

'Absolutely! And as for the local gossip, I think we could have learned more if Meredith Prescott hadn't turned up and ruined everything.'

'Hmm. It seems that the only person in the village who doesn't want to talk about the so-called 'unpleasantness' is Meredith.'

'Interesting, don't you think?' Rob hung up his jacket and took Dee's from her and hung that up too. He wandered into the sitting-room and threw himself down on the sofa. Dee followed close behind, kicking off her shoes and wiggling her toes in relief.

'Oh, I don't know. It's hardly a surprise. She knew both victims well. I know she didn't like Miss Fenniston, but even so... She used to go in and read to Mrs Hunter twice a week, don't forget. She must have been fond of the old woman.'

'More likely she is fond of being the Lady of the Manor, dispensing good works and charity, just as Marlene said,' Rob said. Dee stopped and turned to stare at him.

'I agree with you about her wanting to be seen as the Lady of the Manor, but are you saying you think Meredith had something to do with the two deaths? Surely not, they were so grisly and horrid. Or at least, Sheila's death was very grisly and horrid whereas Mrs Hunter's death was just... vicious.' She shook her head. 'Leaving an old woman to die on the cold stone floor like that? That seems so callous. I could almost imagine

Meredith putting a spot of arsenic in someone's sherry. But nothing really messy or cruel. I'm sure that wouldn't be her style. I don't think Millie Edmonds is right that her suggested 'measures' would have saved Mrs Hunter's life. It's so hard to believe it was just an accident. But in any case, what I keep coming back to is, why? Why kill an old woman?'

'I don't know what I'm saying. I agree she doesn't seem a likely murderer. Like you, I can't imagine her wielding the razorblade and coping with a lot of blood. Though on the other hand she does always seem to rise to the occasion. Stiff upper lip and all that. And I think she's a fake.'

'So you think that because she doesn't enjoy talking about the deaths, she's our number one suspect? What do you mean, she's a fake?

'She likes being kowtowed to. She likes being the one who matters. She loves her status and enjoys martyring herself to do all the good works she does, not because she really cares and wants to help people, but because she wants everyone to admire her and notice that she makes a lot of sacrifices. She wants everyone to think she's wonderful.'

'Well...'

'Look at the way she complained to you at the fair about how much hard work it was.'

'Oh, that doesn't count. She was just tired—understandably—and was making conversation. Anyway, she's been brought up to think a certain way. It's entirely unconscious. Though she did try to warn me off this evening, warned me against prying too much into the deaths.' And Dee told him exactly what Meredith had said.

'She seems to enjoy putting you down, Dee.'

'Oh that's tosh. Although she probably is afraid of a scandal. They all are really. Even that headmaster who seemed to enjoy talking about it tonight. It's just

Meredith's clumsy way of trying to warn me to be careful about listening to gossip.'

'Well for such a good friend, she doesn't seem able to remember your name, does she?'

'Oh shut up Roger.'

'Cocoa, Daphne?'

'No, I'm going to bed. Goodnight.' She kissed his cheek. 'By the way, I liked the story you made up about Sergeant Porter.'

'Ugh,' said Rob. 'Could you believe their reactions? *A black man*. Hide your pearls! Lock up your daughters! God, it makes me furious. Next, they'll be telling him to go back to where he came from.'

'I dare say he will go back to London when he's finished here. As will we. And only too glad to go. Night-night,' Dee said and went up.

*

Chapter Twenty-one

'But,' said Dee as she munched toast the next morning, 'How are we going to find out who did it? How can we find clues and information?'

'Bill might tell us what they know,' Rob suggested. He had a full plate of bacon and eggs, tomatoes and fried bread in front of him and was making excellent progress through it. They had decided to treat themselves to a 'proper' breakfast at The Seagull instead of the usual cereal or toast.

'He would rather die than let us mere citizens meddle in his investigation,' Dee said. She had already taken care of her scrambled eggs, and was finishing her first slice of toast. Every time the door of the small dining-room opened, she was on edge, expecting to see her cousin coming in. So far she had been disappointed three times, and was now beginning to worry she might not see him at all. What if he'd already decided there was nothing to investigate and gone back to London?

By the time the landlady came through to clear away, Rob had finally finished eating his meal. He thanked her profusely and they said goodbye. Outside, Dee persuaded him to take a walk around the village. She told herself she definitely didn't expect to bump into any policemen in pursuit of their enquiries. That was the last thing she wanted to do.

They followed Dee's usual route, stopping for a brief conversation with the major, out with Maybelle, and thanking him for his hospitality the previous evening.

They walked on a little further and at the gate into the churchyard, spied Sonny-Ray Smith, deep in conversation with someone. The two men broke off as they saw Dee and Rob approaching. As he turned to face them, they saw the other man was Rodericks, the Prescotts' chauffeur, for once not in his smart uniform. Sonny-Ray introduced them. Rodericks smiled pleasantly at Dee and shook her hand but his eyes were fixed on Rob. Dee noticed the man stared at Rob almost without blinking for a whole minute.

Sonny-Ray said frostily, 'Well, don't let us keep you. No doubt you're seeing the sights of the place!'

'Not that it will take long,' Rodericks added, smiling at Rob. 'We'll be in the pub later, if you fancy a lunchtime pint. In the lounge bar, of course.'

They said goodbye and carried on with their walk. By mid-morning they were at the cafe and ready for elevenses. They ordered coffee, and Rob ordered a massive slice of Victoria sponge. A minute later, Lily brought it over and stayed for a few minutes' chat. Glancing over her shoulder and lowering her voice, she said, 'Well Miss Marple, have you heard that the London police arrived on Saturday? I think they're reopening the case.'

Dee laughed at the nickname, and said they had already seen the officers. She added, 'I'm not sure if they're looking into the deaths or not. We couldn't find out very much, the inspector has warned me to keep my nose out of his case.'

'That seems to suggest it is an actual case though,' Lily said.

Dee nodded. 'It's annoying they won't tell us what they think. The inspector's our cousin, so you'd think he'd have a bit of family loyalty.' She was joking, but all the same she wished that police investigations did work like that.

Lily excused herself to attend to another customer.

Dee and Rob drank their coffees in silence, gazing out of the window at the street that led down to the beach. Just a few minutes later, Inspector Hardy and Sergeant Porter walked by, deep in conversation. At last, Dee thought.

The two officers came into the cafe, and Rob immediately waved them both over. Hardy went to the counter to give their order, and the sergeant came to sit down.

Dee smiled at Porter and wished him a good morning.

'How are you getting on with your enquiries?' she asked.

'Not very well, miss. So far we've been turned away from Prescott's Wines due to Mr Prescott being far too busy to see us. Then we were turned away from the manor house, by a woman who said that neither Mrs Smithies nor Miss Prescott were 'at home'. It's been a wasted morning all round,' Porter told them. 'No one is concerned in the least that we're police officers in the prosecution of our duty, and...'

'Sergeant!'

Bill Hardy loomed in his usual light-blocking manner, eyeing the sergeant severely and snapping, 'Do I need to remind you about my instructions when we arrived?'

Porter immediately lost his smile.

'No, sir. Sorry, sir,' he mumbled.

Hardy sighed. 'Oh, it's all right, sergeant. You're not

the first.' He pulled out his chair and sat down. Glaring at his cousin he added, 'She has that effect on men. Just don't tell her anything else. Think of her as the enemy.'

Shortly after one o'clock, Rob pushed open the door to the public bar of The Seagull. Although still fairly early on the weekday evening, there was already a crowd. A thick band of blue-grey smoke appeared suspended a few feet from the ceiling, the result of everyone smoking their favourite cigarettes or cigars, and as he looked about the room, for a few moments Rob's eyes stung with it.

Rodericks was unfortunately nowhere to be seen. But there was someone else Rob hoped to see. He spied his quarry on the far side of the bar, hunched on the end of the counter, alone, his fingers wrapped around his half-finished pint, all his attention apparently focused on the liquid's surface where a few tiny bubbles drifted in a steady stream.

Rob had hoped to get into conversation with Norman Slough almost by accident, planning to pass himself off as an amiable stranger visiting the area, with whom Slough would be glad to share a drink and unburden his soul.

But the man's position at the bar made that impossible, Rob could see that now. There was nothing for it but just to be open and hope that would be enough to win the man's trust and encourage his confidence.

'How about another one of those?' Rob suggested as he settled on the stool next to Norman. Slough glanced up, seemed to take in every detail of Rob's appearance in that brief appraisal and then turned back to his drink.

'No thanks. I've still got this one. And it's my last.'

'Sure? I'm having one myself, and I'd be glad to buy you one.' Rob signalled the barman.

'No,' said Slough. He added, 'But thanks,' as an afterthought without he sounding especially grateful. Rob shrugged, and unable to think of anything else to say, turned to take his pint from the barman and handed over his money. Then Slough said,

'You're one of those London coppers. You've got it in for me, you lot.'

Rob was surprised. He quickly denied it, saying, 'No, I'm not a copper. But I would like to talk to you.'

'Wanted to ask me more questions about Sheila Fenniston.'

'It must be infuriating,' Rob said. 'After all, you hardly knew the woman.'

Norman Slough drank the remainder of his pint down in one long gulp. He got off the barstool and attempted to loom over Rob.

'So if you're not a copper, what are you?'

'Just a private citizen,' Rob said. The man's breath was hot and sour on his forehead.

'Private citizens should mind their own business,' said Slough. 'But as you're *so* interested, let me tell you. She was a calculating gold-digger, always waiting for someone better to come along. I wasn't good enough for her once the boss started to take notice. I got the sack because of her. I wish I had killed her, but she saved me the job and done it herself. Good riddance. That everything you wanted to know, Mr Private Citizen?'

And staggering slightly, Norman Slough marched away, squaring his shoulders and clenching his jaw as he struggled to maintain his dignity. He banged the door behind him.

Rob sighed. Dee was not going to be very pleased with him.

The barman, hovering nearby, made a show of wiping down the counter, moving all the mats out of the way and then replacing them after smearing the surface with a grubby cloth.

He wants to talk, thought Rob and felt proud of his deduction. We'll make a detective of you yet, my boy, he told himself. He took a swig of the beer, repressed a shudder, sighed appreciatively then set the glass down.

'You don't get good beer like this up in London,' he told the barman.

'It's a good one, all right,' said the barman. 'Brewed by my brother-in-law, over the other side of Sandneath. He could tell you every single thing what goes into one of his pints. Not like them big companies what use chemicals and such like. Yes, that's a proper pint you've got there, and no mistake.'

Feeling called upon to lavish further praise, but running rather low on ideas, Rob said, 'And such a nice colour.'

'Ah well, let me tell you about that colour,' said the barman, leaning on the bar. Rob leaned towards him, taking another drink as he did so. He wondered how much of this stuff he could bear to take. Somehow this didn't seem like the kind of establishment where a chap could ask for a glass of red wine without upsetting someone.

'Go on,' said Rob by way of encouragement.

'See, when they first started making it, my brother-in-law and his brother-in-law,' began the publican.

Rob furrowed his brow as he attempted to sort this out in his head. What a lightweight he was. A few sips of beer and he wasn't able to think straight. In the end he decided it was a variation on the phrase 'my enemy's enemy is my friend' and therefore that the publican was actually talking about himself. Either that, or possibly someone else.

'Go on,' Rob said again, pleased with this second deduction.

'When Les and Norm—not that Norman what just left here five minutes ago,' he said with a jerk of the head in the direction of the door, 'a different Norm—

when they made their first batch, it tasted just right but for the life of them they couldn't get the colour to come out right. It was too pale, like old lady piddle, it was. And colour's very important when it comes to a pint—or why else'd they serve it in a glass?'

Rob found it impossible to fault the publican's reasoning here, and at the same time, he hurriedly revised the relationships in his mind.

'So what do you think they did?' The publican sounded excited, expectant. This was his big build-up. Rob could see he was expected to come up with something, but the beer was beginning to take its toll, and he just couldn't persuade his mind to function. He shook his head.

'Sorry. You'll have to tell me.'

The barman stood up and with a broad grin on his face announced: 'They only went and put treacle in it!'

Rob stared at him.

'See, it darkens it up,' the publican explained, still watching Rob's face with that look of childlike anticipation.

'That's incredible,' said Rob in all truth. The publican laughed and nodded vigorously. 'Absolutely amazing,' Rob went on, warming to his subject, 'I would never in a million years...'

'Me neither, mate. But them two's geniuses. Treacle! I ask you!'

Rob nodded and forced an astonished-sounding laugh. Pushing aside the mental image that he was holding a pint of the urine of an elderly lady in his hand, he took a great gulp of his beer, detecting now the strong, treacly favour. He set the glass down, certain he wouldn't be able to drink another drop. In any case, he was beginning to feel a little unsteady.

'He's a sour bloke, these days. Always was, I suppose, but even worse now.'

'Pardon? Your brother-in-law?'

'Your mate what just left. Norman Slough. Took it bad that woman chucking him over for her boss. And his boss too, I suppose.'

'Ah. Yes, so I've heard. He didn't seem to want to say anything to me.'

'Not Press, are you?' the barman asked, pausing as he wiped a glass with the same grimy rag.

'Press? Oh, no, no, I'm not Press.'

'Ah,' said the barman. Rob felt he was a little disappointed, and by way of compensation said,

'Actually I'm a barrister.'

'A barrister? What, like a lawyer, you mean? From London?' The barman's eyes lit up.

'Oh yes, big practise in—er—Pall Mall.'

'Oh-oh. Pall Mall, eh? I bet you charge people a fair whack for your services?'

'Oh yes, a very big—er—whack—very big indeed.'

'For all them years what you studied, I suppose. That's fair. I expect you know Latin?'

'Ye-es. A little Latin. And—er—a little Greek. And French.'

The barman nodded, clearly impressed, and began to wipe another glass with the filthy rag that Rob wanted to snatch out of his hand and fling onto the floor.

'Say summat in Latin.'

Rob stared. 'Sorry?'

'Go on, show off a bit. Say summat in Latin for us.'

'Oh—er.' Rob thought for a few seconds, desperately trying to recall something—anything—from his ten years of school Latin. Without thinking he took another gulp of his beer, swallowing the liquid rapidly before its distinctive savour could reach his tastebuds. 'Er—all right, here's one: *dulce et decorum est, pro patria mori.*'

'That sounds good,' the barman said in approval. 'What's it mean?'

'Let me see, oh yes. Ahem. 'It is fair and fitting to die for one's country.' '

The publican nodded solemnly. 'That it is, true enough. Very good that. I done my bit you know. More'n twenty years ago now.' He reached for another glass. 'Tell us another.'

Rob hoped this ordeal wouldn't go on too long, or he would soon reach the limits of his knowledge. If only Dee was here, he thought, she's the one who excels at this sort of thing. 'Well there's always *Dieu et mon droit,*' he said. 'God and my right. The motto of our royal family.' And at that moment, inspiration seized Rob and leaning forward to speak very quietly he said, 'Miss Fenniston was a great one for languages, I hear.'

'Now it's funny you should say that, sir, I was just thinking the self-same thing myself. She was real good at languages; French, German, you name it, she could talk it. She brought a couple of them in here. Wanted to see a proper English pub, they did.'

Rob fought down a momentary alarm. 'They didn't have any of this beer, did they?' He held up his glass. The landlord immediately took it from him and refilled it.

'That they did. Most impressed they was. Broke out into foreign talk they did, as soon as they tasted it. One of them, the German, he was patting her on the knee and talking to her in Deutsch the whole time. A bit too friendly, he was, once he'd had a few. Not that she seemed to mind.'

'Just that one occasion, was it?'

'No, they was in here several times. He was only here a week or two, but she met him here for lunch a couple of times, and then at least twice they come in here in the evening. It could be two or three times, now I think about it, 'cos of course she come here with him *and* the French chap and his son one night, and once or twice with the German chap on his own, then one time, he had his missus with him too.'

'They *were* friendly,' Rob commented.

'Well, she said to me it was business. If you ask me he wanted to take her back with him when he went. He was poaching her for his own business back home, I reckon. Say summat else in Latin.'

Rob sighed and wracked his brain once more.

*

Chapter Twenty-two

The next morning, purely on impulse Dee knocked at the front door of the terraced cottage two houses along. Rob, well dosed up with aspirin for his headache, trailed along behind her in bewilderment. Cissie's cottage was one of the middle terraces, whereas the one belonging to Mrs Hunter's family occupied a more spacious end plot with a garden at the side of the house as well as at the back, currently producing a fine crop of tall messy weeds topped with flowers in purples and golds that hummed with bees and butterflies. As far as Dee was aware, no one lived in the other mid-terrace cottage, or in the cottage at the far end, and she wondered why that was. Rob had an idea about that.

'I bet they belong to weekenders, people who live in the city most of the year, but keep this as a getaway for weekends and holidays. The Prescotts own everything, so they probably rent them out to people coming down from London for the summer months.'

'In that case, it's a shame for the village that the people aren't resident all year round,' she responded, then after a moment's thought added, 'But then, if they did, we wouldn't be able to stay here either.'

Dee was a little alarmed by her own audacity. She hadn't planned what she was going to say, not really believing they would be invited over the threshold. But it was Marlene who opened the door and she simply grinned at them as if they were old friends as soon as she saw them. She invited them to step into the parlour immediately on their right. Rob glanced briefly down at the stone slabs that formed the floor at the foot of the stairs, and when he looked up, Dee knew he was picturing the old woman lying there on that morning, just as she herself was.

Marlene said, 'I'll just go and put the kettle on and let Mum know you're here.' Then she hurried along the dim hallway. Dee, only now realising she had been holding her breath, exhaled, and crossed the room to take a seat. The room was stuffy with lack of fresh air and the overwhelming scent of polish and mothballs. The heavy net curtains at the windows added to the inner gloom. It was a tiny room, and even the small amount of furniture present made it seem stuffed to the gills.

They sat in solid old armchairs of great age, and Rob looked at Dee, one eyebrow raised. She grinned and whispered,

'I was so sure we wouldn't be invited in, I didn't think about what I was going to say.'

Marlene returned with a massive tray of tea-things. She blushed with delight as Rob leapt up to take it from her and set it down on the table.

'Ooh, thank you ever so, Mr... er...' she giggled. Clearly she had already forgotten what her grandmother had told her about Rob and the likelihood of him being a possible 'boyfriend' type.

'Gascoigne,' he said, and executed a little bow over her hand, flashing her his most charming smile. 'Rob

Gascoigne.'

Dee was put in mind of a Regency fop, and decided she would tell him so later.

Marlene giggled again and didn't seem to know quite what to say next.

'I do hope we haven't put you to any bother,' Dee piped up as Marlene began to pour the tea.

'Not at all, Miss, it's very nice to see you again, I'm sure.' Marlene enunciated far more carefully than usual, batting her lashes at Rob.

Dee took a few extra seconds to place her handbag on the floor next to her feet, and only looked up when she was sure she wouldn't burst out laughing.

'I know it probably seems very rude of us to barge in like this, you may not know this, but...'

'You're a detective, miss, aren't you?' Marlene said. 'That must be really exciting. I bet you meet all sorts.'

Dee nodded, hoping Marlene wouldn't ask for too many details. It felt rather dishonest to let anyone think she was a detective when she was simply a very nosy woman. Especially since her cousin was telling people—telling his sergeant anyway—that she came from a long line of nosy women. Which wasn't true. It was rather unfair, she thought, losing her train of thought now that she'd started thinking about Bill, that he insisted on blaming all the women in his family for what was only his mother's failing. Not that it was a failing in Dee's view. But at the same time it was thrilling to be able to smile and nod sagely as if she really was an *actual* detective. And she had always admired her aunt's commitment to pursuing justice and—to be honest—her sheer determination to find out things. Things that were supposed to be the sphere of the police, who all too often weren't terribly interested in the crimes that Aunt Dottie uncovered. Besides, Dee silently reminded herself, whatever job you do, there's always a day you have to actually start doing it. This could be that day.

Marlene certainly seemed impressed and didn't think of questioning Dee's credentials. 'I expect you've come to look into Gran's murder,' she said. 'I knew someone would listen eventually. I told Mum they'd send someone to go into it, and now here you are. It just goes to show, don't it?'.

'We're not connected with the police,' Rob hurriedly explained, and from the way he sat up very straight and the change in his tone, Dee could tell he had his barrister hat on. 'But,' he added, 'The police from Scotland Yard have now arrived. I don't think I'm betraying any confidences by telling you that, as I'm sure it will be all over the village by now. They are here to conduct an official investigation into the recent sad events, but my sister and I are here in a purely private capacity.'

Throughout this speech, Marlene's eyes never left Rob's face. She seemed by turns in awe of him then determined to flirt. Dee was beginning to wish herself somewhere else, but she desperately wanted to know more about Mrs Hunter, and Marlene was the best person to tell her everything there was to find out.

'I saw the London coppers at the pub. The chief inspector is a close friend of yours, isn't he?' Marlene said.

'He's only an inspector, not a chief inspector,' Dee corrected her. 'But yes, he's our cousin. And an excellent detective, too, in his way,' she couldn't help adding, then felt terrible for undermining him. 'He and Sergeant Porter are staying at the pub, and obviously as it's early days, there hasn't been much they could tell us that we didn't already know.'

There was a moment's silence. No one said anything. Marlene was still staring at Rob. Dee wondered if she should begin to ask some more pointed questions, anything to break the silence. Marlene seemed inclined to view private detectives and police officers as more or less the same thing.

Just then the parlour door opened, and Harriet Grayson entered. She was clearly the common link between the generations, being a mixture of the youthful audacity of Marlene and the gummy, ghoulish malevolence of the late Mrs Hunter.

'Mum, this is the detective lady and gentleman come down from London with the police to find out about Gran's death.'

Like her daughter, Marlene's mother seemed in awe of Rob. How did he do it? He didn't even like women, Dee grumbled to herself, how was it they were drawn to him so much?

'We met at the fair,' Dee said as she rose and reached out her hand to greet Mrs Grayson.

Mrs Grayson said with a laugh, 'Ah yes, I remember. The magic worked for you, did it?'

'It certainly did.'

'I'm glad, dearie. And this must be your brother?' She turned to hold out her hand to Rob, saying, 'Harriet Grayson. Mrs.'

From the way she was smiling at them both, it seemed Mrs Grayson was also unlikely to demand that they left her house.

Seizing the opportunity, Dee said, trying to sound very official, 'Can you remember anything about either of the nights that Miss Fenniston or Mrs Hunter died?'

Marlene and Harriet looked at one another, then both shook their heads.

'I work most evenings until about ten o'clock,' Harriet said. 'I've got a cleaning job at the warehouse. I clean the offices and so forth, and sometimes I help out in the warehouse itself, stacking and so forth. I go out at about six and get back home again at ten.'

'And I used to stay in and look after Gran,' Marlene put in. 'When I wasn't working up at the manor house, which is normally only at the weekends.'

'Miss Prescott used to come in to read to Mrs Hunter, I understand?' Dee said, and the other two women both nodded.

'Mondays and Thursdays, it was,' Harriet confirmed.

Dee pondered this. Then said, 'Marlene, it was a Monday when Sheila died, wasn't it? So was Miss Prescott here that night?'

Marlene nodded vigorously. 'Oh yes, she came as usual. It was just a normal night.'

'And what time did she leave?'

'It was a bit before Mum came home. Might have been half past nine. Or just after.'

'You didn't see her outside at all, Mrs Grayson?'

Harriet was already shaking her head. 'No, she was long gone. I didn't see her at all on my way home. Sometimes I did, but not that night.'

'I see. Well, and what did you do after Miss Prescott left, Marlene?'

'I got Gran ready for bed. Well, she was already in bed, but I took her downstairs to the lavvy, then I got her back up to bed again, and made her a cup of hot chocolate, then she went to sleep.'

'And what time did you both go to bed?'

Again, they exchanged a look, as if making sure they were in agreement. Harriet said,

'I went just after I got home, I must have been in bed by a quarter past ten. And I was out like a light, I was that tired.'

'I listened to my radio quietly until I got sleepy, then turned it off and put out the light,' Marlene said. 'It wasn't that late, about half past ten?'

'Sorry, but what time would you normally lock the doors?' Rob interrupted.

Mrs Grayson looked sheepish. 'Well, it would normally be as soon as I got in, but I'm not sure about that night. I've got a feeling I might have forgot. I can't be sure. But in the morning,' She took a breath to compose herself. 'In the morning the back door was standing open. So, I wasn't sure if I locked it or not. We only use the back door,' she explained. 'The front door is for visitors, and it's kept locked. And it was only later in the morning, when someone came down from Prescott's to ask for her... I went up to check her room, and, well, that was when we found Sheila.'

'I hate to ask, but I've heard that the spare key for the back door is kept under the flowerpot outside?'

Harriet nodded. 'I know it's stupid, but I've always done it. You just don't think it's dangerous, not in a little place like this. I mean, we don't tell people, but I suppose it's the kind of thing people can guess, or...'

'Try not to let it worry you,' Dee said gently. 'I expect lots of people do the same.'

Harriet nodded then turned to her daughter and said, 'Have you shown them the rooms yet?'

'I was just going to, Mum, when they started asking questions,' Marlene said with more firmness than Dee's own mother would have permitted.

Mrs Grayson said to Rob, 'I'm sure you want to get on with your investigation, so Marlene will show you upstairs, if that's all right. Excuse me not coming with you, but I've got some towels to put through the mangle.'

Dee noticed how red and sore Mrs Grayson's hands looked. That the woman worked hard for a living was clear. Dee felt terrible for intruding on her when she was not only grief-stricken but busy. Small wonder then that when the fair was on, Mrs Grayson so readily embraced her other identity. Dee was almost on the point of apologising for imposing and suggesting they leave, but Rob got up to hold the door open for Mrs Grayson as she left the room, and this small courtesy made her giggle a little, lighting up her face and making the years fall away until she looked no older than her daughter.

Marlene conducted them to the stairs and led the way. The stairs loomed steeply in the semi-darkness, the panelled wood and the low ceiling making the stairs as dimly forbidding as the hall that led through to the kitchen at the back of the house.

Dee could hardly tear her eyes away from the floor. She didn't even want to step on the part where Mrs Hunter had lain. The frail, elderly woman, falling onto that cold, hard surface. What was it the vicar's wife had said, something about Mrs Hunter clutching at something to save herself as she fell. *Frantically,* that had been the word. Frantically trying to save herself. But there was no handrail to save her. Dee shivered. It was a certainty Mrs Hunter couldn't survive a fall of that kind. Seeing it so clearly now, it was just as much a certainty that someone else had been behind her death. But having lived in the house for years, she would know to be careful. Dee wanted to make sure, so she asked,

'How long has your family lived here, Marlene?'

'All me mum's life. Gran and Grandpa come here when they first got married. Forty years ago in August, it would of been. Except Grandpa died five years ago. His heart.'

'I'm so sorry to hear that,' Rob said.

At the top a dark corridor ran in either direction from the front to the back of the house. There were no windows and therefore little natural light. A dim bulb burned on the right, but not on the left, and Dee thought the bulb was so dim, it was as good as useless. Marlene led them past two doors on the right side and it was at the end of the corridor that she threw wide a door with chipped once-white paint.

It was a grim, low-ceilinged room. At one end, a narrow bed stood against the wall and beside it was an old chest on short spindly legs; the chest clearly served as a combined dressing table and bedside table. On top was a dusty doily bearing an old clock and a handsome oil lamp that had to have been at least sixty years old. A black plastic comb and a pair of nail scissors appeared to form the entirety of the late Mrs Hunter's beauty regime.

There was a cast iron grate, above which was a white-painted mantelpiece sporting a few knick-knacks and photos in grimy frames, the features of whose subjects were lost beneath the dust of countless years. Or perhaps not countless, but forty years in August, Dee corrected herself. She could quite believe they had sat there untouched all that time. After a while, she thought, you get out of the habit of noticing what's right under your nose. Either that, or there's not enough time to get to everything that needs doing when you're working two jobs, possibly more.

On one side of the grate was an elderly easy chair with embroidered cushions and on the other side, a rocking chair beside which stood the empty wheelchair. Behind the door was a narrow tallboy of some dark wood, obviously the mate of the chest by the bed. There was nothing else in the room.

Dee noticed a book lying on the cushion of the easy chair. She picked it up and turned it to the grimy window to read the cover. It was called *Mary's Heart* and depicted a miserable-looking woman in a headscarf. Inside the cover was a library label with dates written neatly in black ink.

'That's what Miss Prescott started reading to Gran last week, but it wasn't Gran's cup of tea. She liked something with a bit of action and excitement, but Miss Prescott had other ideas. Gran said it sent her off to sleep in no time. All about a woman who thinks she don't love her husband no more but she decides to stick with him anyway. More fool her, I say. Blooming boring stuff.'

There was a sound from below.

'Mum wants me,' Marlene said, and ran off, leaving

them alone.

'Gosh, this place,' said Rob in a low voice.

'I know. It's a bit grim, isn't it? Makes you realise how lucky we are. Cissie's cottage is so much brighter and homelier. If it was like this, it would just be too depressing.'

'It's awfully dark.' Rob crossed to the door and clicked on the light-switch. The naked bulb glowed dimly then suddenly dazzled them.

'Would it be terrible if I snooped about a bit?' Dee asked him. He shrugged.

'That's what we're here for, isn't it?'

Tentatively, Dee began to ease open the drawers of the bedside chest, trying to do it quietly so as not to give herself away to the people downstairs, but it wasn't easy as some of the drawers stuck horribly. She felt less like a detective and more like a nasty snooping, nosy-parker.

The first two contained Mrs Hunter's few clothes, already smelling slightly musty, although she had only been dead a week. The bottom drawer contained a pile of old magazines, dog-eared and thrust in at random, pushing each other out of shape, and so tightly jammed with the other things inside that Dee had trouble getting the drawer closed again.

The sound of Marlene's feet on the stairs made Dee give the drawer a last panicked shove, and as it slid home, a tiny tell-tale strip of newspaper poked over the top of the drawer. Dee ripped it off and put the strip in her pocket. She and Rob were looking at the photos on the mantelpiece when Marlene entered the room.

'I'm so sorry about that,' she said. 'My mother wanted me to show you Miss Fenniston's room whilst you is here. You are finding out about her death also, aren't you?'

Dee, trying not to smile, said they were. Marlene waved Dee ahead of her into the corridor, and when

Rob held back to allow Marlene to precede him, she giggled and blushed again, saying in her normal voice, 'He's such a gentleman, your brother, ain't he?'

Dee smiled back and said, 'He is indeed.' And that was when she saw it. A tiny brown streak on the chipped white paint of the edge of the mantelpiece.

She paused. She had an awareness of the other two watching her, but knew they were not seeing what she was seeing. Her thoughts whirled in her brain. Uppermost was a feeling of near-triumph. She had found something, she just knew it. A clue. A real clue. To a real murder. She felt elated at the find. Then ashamed to think of her own satisfaction at such a moment, and these two states were followed by a cold sense of dread. It was a mixture of emotions she would remember for the rest of her life.

All this passed through her mind in the space of a second or two, then with a sense of falling back to earth, Dee became aware of Marlene's stare, of Rob impatiently grumbling, 'Do come along, Dee.'

Marlene snapped off the light in the bedroom, saying, 'Mum'll kill me if I leave that on. Got to watch the pennies.'

'I saw Mrs Hunter's wheelchair in the bedroom,' Rob said. 'Did she need it up here?'

'Not really,' Marlene said over her shoulder. 'I mean, she could get about in her room by holding onto the furniture, but there wasn't room in the hall downstairs to leave it there, and she couldn't get down without it.'

'But how did you get her downstairs?' he asked.

'Just bumped her down each step. Of course, she had to hold on to the arms of the wheelchair like billy-o, and it had to be me doing it 'cos of mum's bad back, but that's the only way what we managed to get her downstairs.'

'I see.'

Rob said, 'Good solid construction, these old houses.

Not like those flimsy new houses going up everywhere. None of the floors or stairs creak in the slightest, do they?' He was talking to Marlene, but Dee knew that his message was for her: any careful person could have moved around the house in near silence at night, unlikely to wake the sleeping inhabitants. The thought made Dee shiver.

Marlene shrugged and said, 'I dunno about that. It's all right, I s'pose.'

They were continuing along the corridor, back across the top of the stairs, and on until they came to the first door, and Marlene flung it open and said, 'This were Miss Fenniston's room.'

Marlene shoved the door wide, and stepped back to allow Dee to enter. She did so, walking across bare wooden boards to stand in the middle of the room, the events of that awful morning flooding back. Marlene and Rob stood in the doorway, saying nothing, just watching her.

She knew it was fanciful, she had never been one to give way to maudlin thoughts, but as she stood there, she felt an almost overwhelming sense of sorrow. Such a hideous way for Sheila to die, she had been so alive, so ambitious with her plans on the day of the village fair, and her brave red nails and lips, the cigarettes, the smart suit. Then to die here, all alone, in that awful way. The chair may be empty now, but in Dee's mind, she still saw her sitting there, the demure white of her ankle-length nightdress with its satin bow at the breast, and the lace edging on the sleeves, the yoke and the shoulders. Sheila's hands had been cradled in her lap; there was the sticky mess of blood on the floor, darkening and pooling about her feet. And of course, there had been the razor. Sheila, dead, buried, already half-forgotten. She had few friends. The Prescotts were only too relieved she was out of their lives. Did anyone truly mourn her?

Dee shivered. Rob stepped forward, spoke her name—she thought he said her name as a kind of a question—and the strange spell was broken. The room was bare. This was a different day. She turned to him, and hauling up her courage from the soles of her shoes, she managed a smile. She nudged him with her shoulder as they had always done as children.

'It's all right. I'm all right. It was just as if for a moment...'

Marlene bustled in and noisily shoved up the old sash window.

'It's a bit stuffy in here, ain't it?' she commented, untouched by the clinging memories. 'We'll have it aired out in no time. As you can see, we had to burn the carpet, there was that much blood on it. We couldn't never get all that out, Mum said. And we tried turning it round, see if we could make it so the stain was hid by the wardrobe, but we couldn't quite do it. Shame. It were a nice bit o' carpet, too. If you look there, you can still see a couple of tiny bits where the blood seeped right through to the boards underneaf...'

Dee could hardly bear to look. Marlene's matter-of-fact manner was making her feel ill. Pints and pints of blood had spilled out of Sheila, enough for her to bleed to death. The smell alone... That morning it had hit her even before she came into the room. Now again, the memories were so strong. She clapped a hand over her mouth, but the nausea subsided without her having to run for the bathroom. Not that she even knew where that was in this house. It definitely wasn't upstairs.

Marlene was still speaking: 'There was one big patch either side of her, see, from her wrists. It were a bloody mess, I can... Oh but you remember, don't you, miss? You came in to see if there was anything that could be done for her. So I expect you saw it all over the floor.'

'Marlene!' Rob said, a little more sharply than he'd intended. 'I'm sure I heard your mother calling you just then.'

She turned and fairly ran from the room. As the sound of her boots on the wooden floor died away, Dee sank into the other chair beside the chenille-covered table. Rob knelt in front of her.

'All right, Dee? It's awful, isn't it?'

She looked at him with wide, troubled eyes.

'It's real. It's only just hit me. It's as if this whole time I've been playing a game. All this time. It's all been about me. About how clever I am, how I just 'had' to know what happened. But it's not a game, is it? It's real. I came in here and suddenly it just hit me. Not just the enormity of trying to solve a murder, but the sheer horror of what happened to Sheila. Rob, she was just sitting up here, in her bedroom, all alone, in her sweet old-fashioned nightie. She was ready for bed, and either something happened *to* her or she *thought* something or *felt* something. And it was something so terrible that the only way she could think of to fix it was to get a razor and rip her wrists to pieces and bleed to death on the carpet.'

She fished in her bag for a handkerchief, found none, but then Rob held out his own, pristine as always, and neatly ironed. She unfolded it to snuffle into the white cotton. Tears were filling her eyes. 'Oh Rob! I feel like some nasty little voyeur, coming in here like this. I'm so ashamed. I've been such a bloody fool. I can't really explain. It's as if, up to now, I never really thought about what all this was really about. Or what it was like for the victim. I met her. I liked her immediately. She had so much to say, she was full of plans for her life. She was clever, and proud, and brash, and funny. It's so awful that she's dead. And no one helped her when she needed them. Either she was desperately sad and all alone, or someone else, someone she trusted, did this terrible thing to her. It's just so—wicked.'

They could hear the rapid approach of boots again as

Marlene began to run up the stairs. Rob got up and crossed to look out of the window. Dee quickly wiped her eyes and put the handkerchief in the pocket of her jacket.

Very softly, as Marlene was approaching along the hall, Dee said, 'Rob, I can't do this. I'm out of my depth. And it's none of my business.'

But by the time Marlene came bounding into the room, Dee was smoothing the tablecloth, enjoying the soft feel of the ruby-red chenille, and the cool floppy feeling of the deep fringe running through her fingers. From sheer nosiness she lifted the cloth back to look at the table. It was a beautifully polished oak dining table. There was a little cutlery drawer in the side with a fat round knob to pull it open. She opened it now, just for something to do as she waited for the redness of her face to subside, hidden by her long tawny hair sliding forward like a curtain.

'Mum says, would you like another cuppa?'

Rob turned from the window. He beamed at Marlene. 'Oh that's very kind, but I'm afraid we need to be going very shortly. Please thank your mother for us.'

'I will, sir, thank you too. What you got there, miss? The police never looked in that drawer.'

'These kinds of tables always have drawers like this. They used to be used for storing cutlery and napkins, that sort of thing. That's why they're lined with felt,' Dee said, but her thoughts were on the papers she had found.

'Yes, miss, that used to be Gran's, from when she was in service. Mr Prescott's grandfather gave it to her as a wedding present in 1902.'

'Your grandmother was in service with the Prescotts?' Rob asked, coming across from the window.

At the same time, Dee said, 'You say the police didn't look in here?'

To Dee, Marlene said, 'I can't say for sure. They

might of, and just thought them bits and bobs wasn't important.' And to Rob, 'Er, yes sir, she was with the Prescotts from when she was fourteen until she got married at twenty years old. Not the Prescotts what's there now, but the one before. It was Mr Prescott's grandfather.'

Dee nodded. 'May I take these? I'd like to look through them, in case there is anything that might be of interest to the police. Now that the Scotland Yard men are here,' she added.

Marlene's eyes were round like saucers. 'Of course you can. Let me know what they say, won't you.'

'We certainly will. Thanks, Marlene.'

Dee stacked the few items neatly and put them into her handbag, glad she had a roomy one with her, and not the usual tiny one that only had room for a few coins, a comb and a lipstick. She got up, looked around, exchanged the slightest of nods with her brother, then said to Marlene, 'Thanks for putting up with us. I think we've seen all we need to see.'

At the door, as an afterthought, Dee said to Marlene. 'The razor that Sheila used to... You know... Had you seen it before?'

'No, miss, never. It wasn't the one she done her legs with, that was a proper safety razor like mine.'

Dee nodded. 'Thanks.'

They moved into the hall, hurried down the stairs as best they could given how shallow yet steep the stairs were. Moments later they were outside in the sunshine again, and the air felt clear and fresh. Marlene saw them going with disappointment in her eyes, whereas Dee felt as though she'd been reprieved.

'A stiff drink at the pub?' Rob suggested. He looked at his watch. 'Though it is only half past eleven.'

'All right, though I only want a cup of tea, if they'll do me one.'

They crossed the road and went into the peaceful

shade of the lounge bar.

'What were those papers you found?'

'I'll show you in a minute,' she said and went to find a corner table whilst Rob went to the bar for a pint of shandy for himself and begged a pot of tea for his sister, for which he paid the same as for his pint.

When he joined her, her handbag was lying on the table unopened and she was gazing into space. She still looked pale and distressed. He put his hand on hers.

'Dee, you can do this. I'm certain of it. We'll make a Miss Marple of you yet. You've got the knack. Everything will become clear.'

She smiled at him and leaned against his shoulder. 'You're so sweet. I can't think why some nice man hasn't snapped you up. You deserve to be happy.'

'I'd settle for being wined and dined at the moment. Or, you know, a bit of hanky-panky.'

That made her laugh. She pretended to slap his arm. 'Behave yourself. Anyway, I'm glad you're here. You've been fab.'

The tea arrived, carried over to them by the barman. He set it down and gave them an odd look. 'Not one of they teetotallers, are yer?' he asked Dee.

She smiled and shook her head. 'No. I just didn't feel too well earlier, and I really needed a cup of tea.'

'You know there's a caff down by the sea, don't yer?' He nodded in that direction.

'Er, yes, I did know, thank you.'

He wandered away grumbling to himself about people who went into a pub and didn't want to drink alcohol.

'Coming back to what we were saying,' Rob said, 'I know you've got what it takes to be a detective: you've got guts, you're determined, practical, and you're good with people. *And*, you notice things. I would never have noticed that drawer in a million years.'

'I only found it by accident. But thank you. Don't ever

leave me for a man, I will need you to bolster me up forever. Does it sound too melodramatic to say I want to find out who killed Sheila because I want justice for her?'

'Yes. But also no, because I wholeheartedly agree with you. That's why I'm training to be a barrister, after all. Our mission statement is, 'To uphold the law, to pursue justice and protect those in need."

'I thought you just liked the wigs and gowns,' she said with a grin.

Joan bustled over just then. 'I do hope you'll forgive my husband. He's that put about with tourists coming in at all hours wanting fish and chips and ice creams. Says all he wants to do is to run a proper English pub. But he didn't mean no offence, my dears. If you fancy having your supper here tonight, I'm doing a very nice hotpot, though I say it as shouldn't.'

'We wouldn't miss it for the world,' Rob said, adding, 'Will the policemen from London be eating here tonight as well?'

'They didn't say either way when they left this morning. Do you think I ought to keep some for them?'

'Definitely,' Dee said. 'They'll have been out all day, and who knows if they'll get any lunch? They'll be ravenous by the time they come back this evening.'

'Very good. I'll make sure I keep plenty back for them. Will the four of you be eating together?'

Dee and Rob exchanged a look.

'We probably shall, yes,' Rob said.

The landlady nodded and hurried away.

Dee poured out a cup of tea, added milk and half a teaspoon of sugar. When she had done this, Rob said, 'Right, come on. Let's have a look at these papers.'

*

Chapter Twenty-three

When Hardy and Porter returned to the pub at six
o'clock, the landlady came over, eager to pass on two
messages.

'There's a nice Lancashire hotpot booked for your
supper tonight if you want it. Miss Gascoigne booked it
for all four of you for seven o'clock.' she said, and
focusing on the senior officer, she missed the
brightening of Sergeant Porter's countenance at the
word 'supper'. She carried on, 'And Miss Gascoigne and
her brother said to tell you they would be glad of a word
with you at their cottage before you sit down.'

She retired with the relief of one now free of a heavy
burden, and so failed to notice that this time it was
Inspector Hardy's face that brightened—at the mention
of Miss Gascoigne's name. The two men turned on their
heels and left.

A minute later, Hardy knocked on the front door of
the cottage. The door was opened by Dee, and there was
a tense moment as they looked at one another before
she stood aside to allow them to enter. In the sitting-

room Rob explained why they'd asked them to call.

'We went to see the Graysons today. Actually it was more of an impulse to try and get a look at the scene of the crime,' Rob explained.

Hardy was already frowning, and Nat Porter was looking with great interest from one to the other and back again. This ongoing saga between the other three was like a posh version of *Coronation Street*. He was already addicted, looking forward to the next episode.

Dee handed over the papers from Sheila Fenniston's drawer.

She saw that Hardy was annoyed that the drawer had been missed; she instinctively began to apologise for her find, but he held up a hand to stop her.

'No, no. There's no need to apologise. I'm very grateful that you found it and let us know. It's not your fault,' he assured her. 'Now let's have a look. What have we... Ah! Interesting.'

He unfolded some small pale blue pages, and after rapidly reading them, passed them over to Porter. Porter took a look, exchanged a glance with Hardy and issued a loud whistle of surprise.

'So Miss Fenniston was getting poison pen letters, was she?'

'It seems a number of people in the village have been getting them,' Rob said. 'We knew Sheila had received some but didn't know what they said. Though they are fairly predictable: 'you trollop', 'you'll bring shame on your boss', and my personal favourite, 'no better than you should be'.'

'This is the first we've heard of any poison pen letters.' Hardy sounded annoyed. 'It's practically a cliché of traditional village life, it seems. Even so, I can't think why no one's mentioned it before now.'

'Dee heard all about it from Cissie Palmer in the post office.'

'Is that the same Cissie who used to work for your

parents?'

'Yes. She's a widow now, sadly, and she runs the post office here in the village. She lives in the flat above the post office and rents this cottage out. Not that the Prescotts are very happy about that, apparently. It's actually them who own it.'

Fishing in the pocket of her dress, Dee handed the other scrap of paper to Hardy, saying, 'I also found this in a drawer in old Mrs Hunter's room. There was a pile of old magazines in there. And a pair of scissors, and some glue.'

'Is that what I think it is, sir?' Porter asked.

'Yes, sergeant.' Hardy held the fragment up to the light for them all to see. It was clear that two letters had been cut out of the middle of a bold headline. 'It looks to me like a small piece torn from a newspaper. Put it in an evidence envelope, please, sergeant. And these poison pen letters in another.'

Hardy turned back to Dee. 'It looks as though you've both discovered and solved a mystery in a single day.' He grinned at her, and her heart sang as she stared at his mouth, curving upwards in that old familiar way.

'So the old woman was the writer of the anonymous letters, or rather, the maker of the anonymous letters?'

'It seems that way, sergeant. An old woman in poor health, someone so well known for gossiping that no one even bothers about it anymore.'

'In spite of her health problems, she always knew everything that happened in the village,' Dee said. 'Marlene must have helped her. They were always out and about together, watching everyone, noticing what went on. I think it would have been Marlene who did all the fiddly bits of the gluing, the cutting out and finding the letters and words in the magazines. Magazines and old newspapers no doubt given to her by Millie Edmonds or perhaps Meredith Prescott as part of her charitable visits. She used to read to Mrs Hunter what

Marlene described as 'improving' books. I daresay Mrs Hunter just told Marlene what to say and who to say it to, then they watched gleefully for the reactions of their victims.'

'We'll have to take all this,' Hardy said.

Dee nodded. 'Yes of course. Erm—and these were also in the drawer with the poison pen letters.' She handed him the final two items of her haul.

'Something else? Oh my word!' Hardy's surprise was everything Dee and Rob had expected.

'Sir?'

There was a pause whilst Hardy examined the items. Then, with a glance at Dee, he handed them to Porter.

'A passport and a plane ticket,' Porter commented. He opened the cover to reveal the ticket itself. 'In the name of Miss Fenniston. London, Heathrow to Frankfurt in Germany. The flight leaves Heathrow early on Friday the 4th June. The ticket's one way.' He let out a long, low whistle, shaking his head. 'I wonder if Jeremy Prescott knows about this?'

'He soon will,' Hardy said grimly. 'This could give him a motive for murdering Miss Fenniston. She was leaving him in the lurch. Is that everything? No more cats to pull out of the bag.'

Dee hesitated.

Hardy raised his eyebrows. 'There is, isn't there? What is it?'

'I don't know if it's anything... It could have been there for ages. I don't want to waste your time.'

They might have been alone. He said, very softly, 'You could never do that.'

She looked down at the floor for a moment, then said, 'I saw a smudge of something on the mantelpiece in Mrs Hunter's room. I think it might have been blood.' She saw the surprise in his eyes, and she hurriedly added, 'But it could have been there for years, or...'

He nodded. 'Thank you. I'll make sure that's checked. It really ought to have been before now.'

There was a brief silence. They all stood in the centre of the room looking at each other. On the mantelpiece, the clock chimed the half-hour.

'Half past six already,' Dee murmured.

'We need to go back to the pub for supper, the landlady said it would be ready at seven o'clock.' Porter got to his feet. 'I just want to have a quick wash first.'

Hardy placed a hand on his shoulder. 'Not us, sergeant. We've got to get up to the big house and speak to Jeremy Prescott. But first, I need to make a phone call.'

Disappointment was written all over Porter's face.

'But sir,' he said anxiously, 'It's Lancashire hotpot.'

The London policemen had been turned away from the manor house yet again: Mr Prescott was out for the evening.

As they walked back to the village, Porter said, 'Do you think he really was out, sir? Or are they just being awkward.'

Hardy shrugged his shoulders. 'I have no idea, to be honest with you. I wouldn't be the least bit surprised if he was there hiding behind the curtains. But if they won't let us in, we can't force our way without a warrant. And we're a long way from that just yet. Now then, I want to speak to the pathologist. No doubt he'll be at home having his evening meal.' Hardy turned to look at Porter, knowing he was worried about missing the Lancashire hotpot. 'Right, let's go back, get that dinner you're so excited about, then after we've eaten, I'll telephone the pathologist. I don't really want to leave that until tomorrow morning. Then, I'd like to confer with you about what we've discovered so far.'

'Or someone else has discovered for us.'

Hardy sighed. 'As soon as I saw her, I knew she was

going to mess about in my investigation.'

'She's done a lot better than us,' Porter said rashly. Quickly he added, 'Not that we haven't worked hard since we got here.'

Hardy sighed again.

*

Chapter Twenty-four

The next morning, Hardy and Porter were still unable to meet with Jeremy Prescott, so they paid a visit to Downhill Farm to speak to Eddie Higgins, farmer's son and boyfriend of Marlene Grayson.

His father wasn't very happy to see two London policemen in his barn wanting to speak to his boy when there was work to be done.

'What's he been up to?'

'Nothing at all, Mr Higgins, we would just like to ask the lad a few questions. We're hoping he can help us.'

'Good luck there then. If he can help you, it'll be more than he does me. Oi, Eddie, you're wanted!' Higgins bellowed up a ladder into the hayloft.

Eddie came down—a tall, skinny youngster of about seventeen. He wore a filthy overall, just like his father's, although unlike his father's, his buttoned up across the stomach. The boy's eyes were wary. He knew who they were.

'Eddie, we'd like to ask you a few questions.' Porter showed his warrant card. Hardy, standing further back, gave the lad a friendly smile.

'All right,' Eddie said, somewhat grudgingly. He leaned back against a rail, arms folded across his chest in a classically defensive pose. 'What's it about?' he demanded.

Porter took up his station against a vertical support beam. Hardy stayed back a little to allow Porter to start the questions.

'You're Marlene Grayson's boyfriend, aren't you?'

The lad's chin lifted up. 'What if I am?'

'Did you ever see or hear anything unusual at her family's home?'

'What sort of unusual?'

'Just anything you might have noticed. For example, on the night Miss Fenniston died. Or possibly when Mrs Hunter fell to her death. Take your time, have a think.'

'There's nuffink to think about. I never.'

'Did Marlene ever say anything that made you think perhaps she knew something or had heard something? Or possibly there was something she had seen or someone...?' Porter was trying hard, but Hardy could see he wasn't going to get anywhere. The boy just didn't want to co-operate.

'I told you, no,' Eddie snapped.

'Did you ever see Miss Fenniston in the company of a man?' Hardy asked.

'An old bird like her? No! She was like forty or fifty easy,' Eddie said scornfully.

'She was thirty-seven,' Hardy said. 'And from what we hear, she was an attractive and intelligent woman.'

'If you say so,' Eddie sniggered.

'Marlene told the lady staying in Mrs Palmer's cottage, two doors along from Marlene's, that she was certain her gran was murdered, that her gran couldn't possibly have fallen down the stairs the way she did by accident.' This was Porter again.

Eddie was looking back and forth from one to the other like a spectator at a tennis tournament. He shrugged. 'You'd best ask Marlene about that.'

Porter folded his arms across his chest, mimicking the boy's posture, and watched Eddie closely with an attention the boy seemed to find unnerving.

Hardy asked, 'Had you ever seen Mrs Hunter walk?'

'Don't think so. Couldn't swear to it.' The lad turned away and gripped a hammer and a box of nails.

'We know about the letters,' Hardy said suddenly.

Eddie dropped the box of nails, cursed and began to pick them up from the dusty floor. Then he turned to face them, and this time there was fear in his eyes. He attempted to keep his cool. 'I don't know what you mean. I don't know nuffink...'

'We know you do, Eddie, and I can see it in your eyes,' Hardy stated. 'So don't bother lying to us, you're not very good at it anyway. Tell us about the letters.'

There was a long pause. Eddie shuffled his feet, broke eye contact and addressed the floor. 'Yeah well. If you know, then you don't need me to help yer.'

'Marlene and her gran wrote them, didn't they?' Hardy said.

Eddie's head snapped back. 'I thought you said you knew!' he sneered.

Hardy could have kicked himself. 'We just want you to tell us how you were involved. I can see you're a decent lad. I don't want you to get into any more trouble than you have to.'

Eddie was outraged. 'That's police brutality, that is, I've a good mind to report you!' The police is always a instrument of the State to keep the Proletariat in their place.'

Hardy sighed. 'Just answer the question, Eddie, then we can be on our way.'

The teenager looked sulky, but said, 'I didn't have nuffink to do with it. It was them. Marlene and the old bat. Giggling together over it. Getting me to drive all over the place in the farm van to post 'em. My dad was that mad about how much petrol I used, I had to pay him back. That's all I did; I posted the letters for 'em. I didn't choose who got one or nuffink. I didn't do none of the cutting out nor the sticking on. They did it all. Used them magazines Madam Muck kept bringing round.'

Hardy decided that was enough. He told Eddie to behave himself in future or they would make life difficult for him. The two policemen went outside. Hardy told Porter to take down Eddie's formal statement.

'I've got to go back to Sandneath for a case meeting this afternoon, but you needn't come. I'll drive myself. You can take that little so-and-so's statement, then go and get yourself some lunch. Spend some time going over the statements we've got so far, if you will, just in case there's something we've missed. Then I'll meet you at the pub at about four o'clock and we'll go and have a little chat with Marlene.'

'Yes sir.'

Porter watched the inspector leave. As he went back into the barn to take down Eddie Higgins's statement, the main focus of his thoughts was that he was looking forward to having a nice working lunch at that pub.

While the police were on their way to see Eddie Higgins, Dee left Rob to get on with his studies at the cottage that same morning and went to enjoy a leisurely breakfast with Cissie Palmer. It made a very pleasant break after all that had been going on. It was so easy to simply pretend they were just two women having a cosy meal together and a good gossip over their tea.

Dee wondered if Cissie was lonely. She seemed to really relish the companionship and the chance for a bit of conversation before going into the post office to open up for the day, donning the brisk, business-like persona of an efficient post-mistress as if it were part of her uniform. At the kitchen table, in her light blue flannel dressing-gown, with her iron-grey hair still in curlers under a colourful scarf bearing the legend 'A Present From Eastbourne' along with a design of sandcastles and seashells, Cissie seemed like a younger, more carefree version of herself as she poured them another cup of tea. This was how Dee remembered her from her youth, working at Ville Gascoigne, always smiling and happy, taking care of everyone, especially Dee's mother, Flora, who was the same age.

'It always takes at least two cups to get me going in the morning,' she told Dee with a smile.

'Me too.'

Once Cissie's hair had been combed out and the severe dark grey dress had been put on, the front door of the post office was unlocked, the sign turned to show 'open', and then Cissie was occupied by a steady stream of patrons in and out for the rest of the morning. Dee tidied up Cissie's kitchen then called goodbye and left, stepping into the village street to the welcome but uncertain sunshine of a typically British late spring.

She had planned to call on Meredith Prescott. She didn't know if or how she would learn anything new, but she hoped that once she got going, inspiration would strike and she would manage to subtly gain some information.

Davies, as always, opened the door to Dee. It was difficult to tell if the woman had any personal feelings or emotions. Her face was habitually so impassive, her features schooled in preserving a polite and unchanging aspect, no matter who she was speaking to.

Today she merely registered that the caller was Dee, and led her to a chair in the entrance hall, saying, 'I'll just go and see.'

Feeling conspicuous and unwelcome, Dee sat

obediently on the chair and looked about her. The manor house really was very gloomy inside, especially after the glare of the morning sunshine. She had only been there after dark previously, when the interior was all lit up with lamps and bright electric bulbs. Now in the mid-morning gloom it was rather depressing. She felt vaguely ridiculous sitting there, like some discarded umbrella or a hat, or perhaps more accurately, like a naughty child sent out of class.

And here comes the headmistress, she thought, as she watched the imperious Mrs Smithies descending the stairs with a very regal lack of haste, leaning on her walking-stick. Lucinda Smithies approached, displaying no more of her feelings than her maid. Did she feel pleasure or distaste on seeing the visitor? Impossible to tell.

Dee stood, eager to show due deference and good manners. She wasn't sure whether they should shake hands, but in any event her outstretched right hand was ignored as Lucinda Smithies swept past her into the morning-room, saying over her shoulder,

'I hadn't realised we were expecting you this morning.'

Mrs Smithies took a seat, but Dee was not invited to sit. She hovered in the doorway, feeling rather pinned there by Mrs Smithies' chilly expression. She began to stammer an explanation, which to her own ears sounded rather like the old 'the dog ate my homework' variety of schoolgirl excuse.

'I—just—thought I'd call on Mere—er—Miss Prescott. That's all.' She knew she was blushing. This is ridiculous, she told herself. I sound so childish. I'm almost thirty, for goodness' sake. Mrs Smithies stared at her as if she couldn't quite believe her temerity.

'I'm afraid I have no knowledge of my niece's whereabouts or engagements for this morning. It may be that she will be home shortly. Though whether she will be able to spare you any time, I cannot say.'

Dee was still standing more or less in the doorway, with no idea what to do. Davies arrived with coffee; the tray bore two cups. Under the slight distraction of the coffee being poured, Dee slipped into the nearest chair.

There was no chance for Mrs Smithies to object, as Davies turned to Dee first. 'Milk, miss? Or sugar?'

For some reason Dee panicked and said 'No thank you' to both then found herself with a large cup of strong black coffee to get through. But at least she was now sitting down, all too clearly now a guest. Davies left them alone, and the hush of the room enveloped them.

Mrs Smithies, clearly making the best of a bad situation, said, 'I seem to remember something about you being a teacher, am I right?'

'Oh yes. I was a teacher at a private ladies' college until...' She faltered. She didn't want to expand on that, but she'd said too much not to finish the sentence.

Mrs Smithies was watching her closely, clearly all ears for some kind of scandal. 'Until?' she prompted.

Dee managed a smile. 'Until my marriage.'

Dee guessed this was just the kind of thing her hostess wanted to hear. Mrs Smithies raised her eyebrows in polite inquiry. 'I hadn't realised you were a married woman.'

There was no point in hedging. 'We recently separated.'

'Ah.'

Dee wondered about that unhelpful word. It was said not without sympathy. It led her to say, 'He was brute, as I quickly discovered after we were married. It was too much, so I recently left him. It cost me my job, unfortunately. And now I'm waiting to obtain a divorce.'

Mrs Smithies sipped her coffee. For a moment, Dee wished she'd kept her mouth shut, but then her hostess said, 'I don't agree with this attitude...'

Dee thought, here we go. She would have to sit there with a polite smile on her face and listen to a treatise on how the modern idea of divorce was the reason for the breakdown of society. Or that women should put up with being beaten or threatened, and accept that it was a part of marriage, and a man's right. How often had she heard such rubbish?

But Mrs Smithies continued with, '...This attitude of 'you've made your bed, you must lie in it'. There is nothing more destructive than living with a violent man. I should have left my husband. But as a young woman, I was too afraid of him, and of his mother. And my own mother if it comes to it. Why is it so often the women of one's own family who tell one to put up with things? You'd think, wouldn't you, that they would take your side, would support and assist you. Show a bit of solidarity.'

'Oh dear,' said Dee, astonished. 'I'm so sorry. What did you do?'

'I learned how to keep him happy. I learned to avoid making him angry. And—mercifully—he died young, and I was saved.' She shot Dee a wry look. 'Which is a terrible thing to say about a marriage. Or a human life, come to that.'

Dee nodded. She had no idea what to say. She sipped her coffee and grimaced. 'You know, I think I will have a little milk and sugar,' she said and leaned forward to make the necessary adjustments.

'Davies makes such strong coffee.' There was another pause, then she said, 'Will you go back to teaching?'

Dee shrugged. 'I don't think so.'

''You're not in need of finances, then.'

It was a statement rather than a question, but a little too personal to be comfortable. Dee hated discussing her financial situation with anyone outside her family. Nevertheless she gave a slight nod. 'I have a small income. I don't need to work to survive. And my parents would always help me if I was in dire straits. Or one of my brothers.'

Mrs Smithies nodded to herself, sipping her coffee again before saying, 'And are those London policemen still in the village?'

'Yes, they are.'

'What are they doing, exactly? I thought the inquests had already decided the natures of our recent tragedies.'

Dee said, 'The inquest into the death of Mrs Hunter was adjourned, I believe. It seems there was some doubt over the evidence. They are examining everything once more, but from the point of view of murder.'

Mrs Smithies' cup clattered in its saucer, and Dee could not have failed to note how upset the older woman appeared.

'Murder? Impossible!' It was said with an approximation of her usual vigour, but her eyes were wary, the puffy cheeks growing pale under her expensive rouge. 'You seem to know a lot about it,' she said, looking at Dee. 'What possible grounds could they have for such an incredible assertion?'

'I'm afraid I...'

'The whole idea is... No doubt some mischief-maker has been trying to make themselves appear important or clever, spreading rumours and falsehoods. It's too much, it really is.' She slammed her cup and saucer down on the tray.

Dee felt sorry for her, all shut away in the big house, unable to do anything when the mud was thrown at her family but deny, deny, deny. Where could she go, if she couldn't stay here?

But before she could think of a comforting word to say, Mrs Smithies said, 'Envy and greed,' she said, in what was almost an echo of the vicar's words. 'It thrives in a place like this. Oh yes, thrives. These days everyone thinks they should have what their betters have, and if they can't earn it, well it pleases them to take it, by force if necessary and tear down what those families have worked for, striving for hundreds of years to achieve. Greed and spite. That's what it'll be, mark my words. At the back of this whole affair will be some sordid little reason, some desire to have what someone else has. We—our family—have been targeted—for years! I can't bear it...'

'I'm sure no one is accusing your family...' Dee was on her feet. Mrs Smithies was gasping for breath in an alarming manner.

'Are you all right? Shall I call a doctor? Please, try to stay calm.' Dee's heart was pounding.

She was already halfway to the door even as Mrs Smithies gasped, 'Get Davies.'

Dee fled to the kitchen for the only woman who could manage Lucinda Smithies.

Davies took one look at Mrs Smithies and dropped to her knees, taking Mrs Smithies' flailing hand between hers and saying, 'There, there, my dear, and what are you doing, upsetting yourself like this? Sit back now and breathe slow. I'll go and fetch your pills.'

As she went past Dee, she shot her a venomous look and said, 'What have you been saying to upset her like this?' Without waiting for an answer, she ran from the room, and Dee heard her pounding up the stairs and along the corridor above.

As if there had been no interruption, as soon as Davies returned she said to Dee, 'You'd better get out, hadn't you? She'll not be in any state for visitors now. You've done quite enough, missy.'

'Will she be all right? Should I call the doctor?'

'She don't need no doctor. I can manage her. She'll soon be back to normal, with rest and care. Now, out you go.'

'But...'

'Out, I say!' No longer were Davies's emotions or

feelings hidden behind a mask of dutiful respect. With her eyes blazing, her mouth and nose pulled up almost in an animalistic snarl, she was the very attribute of hatred.

Dee snatched up her handbag and without a backward look, fairly ran for the door.

*

Chapter Twenty-five

Hurrying away from the manor house, Dee grew more and more agitated as her imagination replayed the scene in Mrs Smithies' morning-room over and over again. By the time she reached the green, she was convinced she was about to be arrested for—well, not exactly murder, because she hadn't done it deliberately, but—what did Rob call it? Manslaughter? Or woman-slaughter, in this case.

As she rounded the corner of the pub, the sight of Hardy's familiar broad shoulders and his dear face overwhelmed her already over-burdened emotions, and Dee flung herself into his arms, sobbing violently.

Not only had Inspector Bill Hardy been a boy scout once, and so was always prepared, but he had been in love with his adopted cousin since he was nine years old. With a brief but genuinely fervent, and silent 'thank you' to the higher power that had placed him in the right place at the right time, he wrapped his arms around her and held her tight against his chest, enjoying the sensation very much. He proceeded to gently pat her back and murmur something along the lines of 'There, there'. He did not fail to notice that her lovely chestnut-coloured hair still smelled of flowers and sunshine, as it had for as long as he could remember.

It was almost two blissful minutes before Dee was calm enough to feel embarrassed. And angry with herself, and, unreasonably, with him. She disentangled herself from the strong arms of the law, and dodged back two steps, opening her bag to look for a handkerchief, and to avoid meeting his eyes. She was horrified at her behaviour. What a good thing it was they were in a tiny village with scarcely a soul to be seen. After futilely searching, she accepted the large white handkerchief that appeared under her nose.

Bill Hardy folded his arms and waited. His brief moment of happiness was over, and order was about to be restored. He sighed inwardly.

'Is everything all right, DeeDee?' He used the childhood nickname without even thinking. He watched her with steady, concerned eyes, but otherwise his emotions remained hidden.

She was still wiping her eyes and nose. When she'd finished this, he took her gently by the arm and guided her down towards the sea. 'I've got some time before I meet Porter, let's go and get a cup of tea.'

They entered the café, and he led her to a table. Within a few minutes, they had a large pot of tea and a plate of Rich Tea biscuits in front of them. Once Lily had, with great reluctance, left them to it, Dee started to tell him what had happened at the manor house, along with her fears that she might have given Mrs Smithies a fatal heart-attack.

'That's easily found out.' Hardy got up, went outside, ran across the road and up a bit to the pub, and disappeared inside.

Dee quickly dabbed some powder on what her mirror

confirmed was a very shiny, rather pink nose. She was grateful to him for being there to sob all over. But irritated by his stupid, 'Is everything all right?' Because even he should have been able to see that obviously everything was *not* all right. Or why would she be sobbing all over him like a child? With detective skills like that, how on earth had he made it to the rank of inspector?

'Stupid man,' she muttered under her breath, shaking her head. She looked down at his handkerchief that she was still holding. 'Sweet man,' she said to herself, even more quietly. She was cross with herself for giving way and getting so hysterical. Because if there was one thing men thought, it was that girls—women she amended remembering her great age—*always* got hysterical. She had always prided herself on keeping herself under control, and not making scenes or giving way to tears. And now look at her. She was a sniffling weepy mess.

He was coming back. She could see him at the kerb waiting for a car to pass. The sun was glinting on his dark wavy hair. The cut of his suit emphasised his broad shoulders and slim waist. She sighed. Then so that he wouldn't know she had been staring, she quickly gulped a mouthful of hot tea, took a bite of a biscuit and generally ensured that she appeared completely at ease by he came back inside and sat down.

'The old lady's fine,' he said. 'Though the maid's trying to say you want locking up for tormenting the old girl, but no, nothing to worry about. Mrs Smithies is fine.'

'Thank you.' She didn't like the intense way he was looking at her. Here we go, she thought. Here comes the police interrogation. Well, she'd asked for it. There was a distinctly damp patch on the shoulder of his suit. A lovely suit, she thought. Aunt Dottie had made sure over the years that her sons dressed well. And along with the tall muscular build inherited from their father, not to mention those cheekbones and the dark slash of eyebrows, Bill and his younger brother James Joseph, or JJ as he was always known, both looked very good in a suit.

Sure enough, he said now, oh-so-casually, as he stirred his tea, 'So what did you say to upset the old lady?'

Dee told him everything, there was no point in not, he'd see through her immediately. He noted it all down in his little black notebook, which she found rather disconcerting. When she had finished, he closed the notebook and put it away in the inside pocket of his jacket.

'Is that evidence now?' she asked. She kept her tone light but deep inside, she was nervous. Had she inadvertently committed some other crime?

He smiled. 'No, love. But I just wanted a note of it. It's interesting, don't you think, the way the old woman got so upset over nothing.'

She looked at him.

'So you don't think I did anything awful?'

He took her hand, kissed her fingertips. 'No, love. It wasn't your fault. She's got something on her mind, and I intend to find out what. I shall go and have a little chat with her tomorrow. Don't want to seem uncaring, so I'll give her some time to compose herself. But I'll need to speak to her. I'm curious to know just why she was so upset to hear about the adjournment or the presence of police from Scotland Yard, and why she feels her family is being victimised. It sounds to me like she has a guilty conscience. Just in case it could be pertinent to my case, I want to find out exactly what it is she feels guilty about.'

Dee extricated her hand. Her fingers were tingling. She didn't know quite what to say. But he'd never taken much notice of her before when she'd told him to behave and not to do things like that. He was stubborn. He went his own way. He made no secret of his feelings. But what about this new woman he was seeing, whom he'd actually introduced to his mother? Busty Barbara, or Brenda, or something like that?

The silence stretched between them. For a while neither spoke. Then she glanced up at him, and suddenly he said,

'Three years?'

She pretended not to know what he meant. But couldn't help the slightest of nods.

He made a sound that was not quite a laugh. 'That's going to seem like forever.'

'Oh, don't...' She couldn't sit there and listen to that. She found herself blindly fumbling for her bag and heard the scrape of her chair on the floor as she stumbled against it in her hurry to leave, to get away from him, put some distance between them.

As the door closed behind her, she wondered if he had really called her name or if she had imagined it.

*

Chapter Twenty-six

'Michael Fenniston?' Porter asked.

Fenniston nodded, hesitant to emerge from behind the half-open door.

'We're police officers, Mr Fenniston, from Scotland Yard. We'd like to ask you a few questions if we may. Mind if we come in, sir?' And Porter stepped forward, leaving Michael Fenniston no choice but to step back allowing them to enter.

They followed him into a disastrously filthy kitchen and Hardy took the only other chair, that which was opposite Fenniston, leaving Porter to prop himself up against a tallboy whose door declined to remain shut.

Michael Fenniston was sullen. 'Now what do you want? Why can't you people leave me alone? I'm the victim in all this.'

'Surely the victim would be your late sister, sir?' Porter suggested. Fenniston glared at him over his shoulder, but then Hardy spoke, forcing him to turn his attention back to the senior ranking policeman, in his expensive suit and with his neat, perfect haircut and clean, shiny shoes of good quality leather. More at home in a posh club in a posh part of London, he would be, Fenniston decided. Just look at him, he thought. Posh suit. Nice tie. Smart hair. Keeps his nails neat and clean. Posh shoes, fancy socks that cost more than my dinner. He might as well be a blooming judge or a duke or summat. Speaking the Queen's English like someone off the BBC. A voice that could cut glass. And la-di-da, too, no doubt.

The other one, now he didn't look half so posh. And he looked more like a rugby player than a copper. Not a local lad to judge by the deep brown of his skin, and that Caribbean twang to his voice. As wide as he was tall. You wouldn't want to meet him in a dark alley. Quite a bit older, not so posh, but still well turned out in a decent off-the-peg suit and clean shoes, even if they were well-worn. No public school for this one, more like the school of hard knocks. Fenniston would rather both of them got out of his kitchen. Asking their fool questions. Checking up on him. He was sure they knew he'd been inside. Coppers always knew.

'Did you see your sister at all, in the days leading up to her death?' Hardy asked.

'I've already...'

'Told the others? Yes, I know. But we're here now, so if you could just humour me, I'd be grateful. So when did you last see Sheila?'

'Cup of tea might be nice,' Porter said.

Fenniston snarled at him like an injured dog. 'Get your own damned tea in your own damned time! You're supposed to be finding my sister's killer!'

'Actually sir, Sergeant Porter was offering to make you a cup of tea. But in any case, the coroner brought in a verdict of suicide, didn't he? So why would we be looking for anyone in connection with your sister's death?' Hardy enquired mildly, with a delicate raise of one dark eyebrow.

Fenniston felt the rage flashing through him. He forced himself to take a deep breath, fighting to control himself. It was a full minute before he said:

'I don't think she killed herself. They told me what she did. With the—the razor. She'd never do that to herself. That man—that boss of hers—he did it.'

Porter and Hardy exchanged a look over Fenniston's head.

'And why would he do that?' Hardy asked softly.

'What? I dunno, do I? That's your job, to find that out. I just know he did it. But in any case, if you're not looking for anyone 'in connection with her death', why are you here?'

Ignoring that, Hardy asked, 'So what did she tell you about Mr Prescott?'

Fenniston put his face in his hands. His voice was slightly muffled. He may have been weeping. He said, 'She was so bloody pleased with herself. I told her she should be careful. People like that, people with money, people who own everything and employ everyone locally, they close ranks don't they? And they think they can do whatever they want. They think they can have everything their own way, you don't have any choice, if you're not for them you're against them, and then you've got to get out. I told Sheila that—I'm always—I *was* always—telling her that but she just used to laugh at me. 'I'll show them all', she used to say. 'I practically run that place as it is. It's time I got the credit that's due me. Without me that place would go under in five minutes, then them up at the big house can kiss goodbye to being the Lords of the Manor'. I told her you can't never win with people like the Prescotts. She just shrugged and said they had two choices.'

'And what did you think she meant by that, Mr Fenniston?' Porter asked. He had been making rapid notes in his daybook.

'Well, she didn't tell me straight out. But the last

time I saw her she just said, 'I'm meeting him for a drink tonight at the pub in the village.' I was surprised. Prescott wouldn't normally be seen dead in the village pub. Not rubbing shoulders with the workers, like. Not that I said that to her. And she said, 'What if I was to tell you that in a months' time, I was going to get a big promotion. A really big promotion!' Then when I asked what she was talking about, she just laughed and tapped her nose, like, and said it was all still hush-hush. It was only later I realised what she meant. I'd got my wires crossed. The next time I saw her was at the village fair and she was cross with me for trying to talk to her when she was trying to find Prescott. I wanted her to introduce me, I was hoping to get a job at the warehouse. But Sheila didn't want him or his family to even know who I was. She was ashamed of me, I suppose. On account of I've...'

'Been inside?' Hardy suggested. 'Breaking and entering, wasn't it?'

'I got two years,' Fenniston nodded. 'She was worried I might ruin things for her. But I just needed a job, any job. We shouted at each other. I never spoke to her again after that. My baby sister...'

Fenniston's voice broke and he leaned forward onto the table and sobbed into his hands.

Porter put away his notebook and busied himself making a pot of very strong tea.

'Here mate, get that into you,' he said gruffly, setting a cup down on the table. There was silence for some time. Once Fenniston had wiped his face on the cuff of his jacket, his took a sip of the tea and settled back in his seat, his eyes fixed on some point halfway up the tallboy door, uncomfortable about his outburst of emotion.

Hardy said, 'So am I right in thinking your sister had either demanded promotion from Jeremy Prescott, or that she was threatening to leave to go and work for one of the wine growers, perhaps a German gentleman by the name of Herr Kostner?'

'Yes. That's what it seemed like. But I don't see how Prescott could have promoted her. She wanted full control, to do what she thought was best for the company. It took her a while to see it, but that was never going to happen. I mean, he couldn't make her a joint managing director, could he? A woman? And not a posh one, either.' Fenniston glanced from Hardy to Porter and back again. Porter shrugged. Hardy drank some tea, repressing a grimace at the stewed taste.

'Women do work in high positions in businesses these days,' Porter said.

'True,' Hardy said. 'But it's still the exception rather than the rule, I'm afraid. And certainly not in a traditional family company like Prescott's. Unless he married her of course, but...'

'Marriage?' Fenniston said. 'I suspected they'd had a bit of a fling, but I wasn't sure. But anyway the company's on its knees. She told me that. Their overseas wine-growers are all pulling out of their contracts. Prescott may think he's the bee's knees, but he's small fry compared to some of the big importers. Sheila said he's just not working hard enough to make new contacts or to make it worth their while.'

'Changing tack slightly,' Hardy said, 'Had your sister ever mentioned someone by the name of Norman Slough?'

'Oh, him! Yes she went out with him a couple of times. But she said he was useless, and not good enough for her. Slough was a nuisance though, after she gave him the elbow. He kept trying to see her, sending her flowers, asking her to meet him. She asked Prescott to get rid of him. Don't know if he did, though.'

'Oh yes, Prescott got rid of him all right, sacked him on the spot,' Porter said.

Fenniston looked at them. 'Well, there you go then.

That's another one could have had it in for Sheila.'

'It's a possibility,' Hardy admitted. 'You have my word that we'll look into it.'

'So you believe me then? That she was done in by someone? Because I'm telling you, she would never do that to herself. It's just too terrible.'

'We believe you,' Hardy said. He got up. 'Thank you for your time, Mr Fenniston. I'm very sorry about your sister. We'll be in touch as soon as we have some news.' He held out a hand and shook Fenniston's.

'I—I'm sorry I was—a bit short with you at first. I'm grateful you're trying to find out what happened.'

'No problem at all, sir,' Porter said, and clapped the smaller man on the shoulder so hard, Fenniston stumbled forward and winced. 'Take care of yourself. You know where we are if anything comes to you...'

At the door, Hardy paused. 'Sorry, I've just remembered. Did Sheila—excuse me—Miss Fenniston— ever say anything about her landlady?'

'The old girl that died?' Fenniston looked surprised. 'No, why? She's dead too, isn't she?'

'Yes sir, nasty fall in the night,' Porter said.

'Poor old girl. Sheila said she was a cantankerous old bat, but she kind of admired her too. Said she hoped she'd have the same guts when she got to that age. They got on pretty well.'

'So she wasn't afraid of Mrs Hunter, or angry with her for any reason?'

'The letters you mean? She told me about them, but she wasn't sure who was behind them. She thought it was probably the old woman, or her niece. But she wasn't too bothered about it. 'Let them have their bit of fun,' she said. 'Words don't hurt me. Anyway I'll be gone soon.' That's it, really.'

'Thank you, Mr Fenniston,' Hardy said.

They left, returning to the car they'd borrowed from the main police station. As Porter turned the car around and headed back into Sandneath, Hardy said,

'Well that's certainly given us plenty to think about.'

'Yes, it has. I wonder if the police here ever spoke to that German gentleman. It would be interesting to see what he could have told us. I wonder if Sheila really did have a chance of a job with him.'

'Hmm,' Hardy said. 'Well she was planning to go to Germany, so that seems very likely to me. If Herr Kostner can confirm that he'd offered Sheila a job that could provide our killer with a motive. And it's just possible Miss Fenniston confided in him. I need to speak to the Sandneath police again, see if they can shed any light. But before that, I need some lunch. Anything to take the taste of your tea out of my mouth.'

They returned to Porthlea on the local train which stopped at every field, barn and shepherd's hut or so it seemed to Porter, whose stomach was reminding him he was overdue for some more of the hearty pub food he'd been enjoying, and it tasted even better for knowing that it was all on expenses. He decided he could come to enjoy being in CID.

'I've been on to the Bishop's office; they gave me the new address for Callum Edmond's former curate, a Henry Harrison,' Hardy said.

Porter, attentive as always, nodded and automatically reached for his daybook and pencil. He took down the address that Hardy read out to him, and snapped his daybook shut, closing it securely with the elastic, thinking that was the end of it. But then, Hardy said,

'So I'd like you to go and see him tomorrow. See if he knows anything. Find out why he left. The real reason, not this rubbish about it being a policy to move staff from time to time to give them wider experience. Also, get his alibi for both deaths, just to be on the safe side. Let me know what you make of him. He might open up quite a bit now that he's out of the area.'

'Yes sir,' Porter said. He eyed Hardy with a mixture of wariness and respect. 'Anything else? Sir?' he added somewhat belatedly. If Hardy noticed, he said nothing, simply responding,

'I'm not sure at the moment. I'm going to tackle the major. Hopefully he'll be able to give me a bit of background on this place. Oh, and we've got an appointment to see Dr Bartlett at 2.45pm, so make sure you're back for that. In fact, we could endeavour to have lunch at that little café on the seafront. That will give us a chance to swap notes before we go to see the doctor. Shall we say one o'clock?'

'Sir.'

'You can take the car, obviously you'll need it, and I won't.'

'Sir.'

On the inside, Porter was full of questions and a quiet, burgeoning confidence. On the outside, his demeanour remained as calm and impassive as always.

Hardy gave him a nod and left.

'So what do we have?' Hardy asked four hours later when Porter returned with the tea and sandwiches.

Taking a seat, Porter began to flick through his daybook.

'Not all that much,' he said ruefully. 'I really thought I'd get something useful out of the curate. And I suppose I did. He was very open about why he left. Basically he has a problem with drink, and in a small place like this, it got round. He even had a couple of those poison pen letters.'

'In that case his drinking was clearly common knowledge. Enough for Agnes Hunter to get wind of it.'

'I felt sorry for the man,' Porter said. 'He said he's a lot happier in a bigger parish in the city. He feels less like he's being watched all the time. And he can go to AA meetings and he gets a lot of help where he is now.

He's ashamed of his time here and glad to put it behind him and start again.'

'Hmm. Good for him. It's not much help to our inquiry, but we can rule him out as a suspect. At least, I'm fairly sure we can.'

'I'd say so, sir. On the evening of Mrs Hunter's death, he was attending an AA meeting from eight o'clock until eleven. Meetings don't usually last that long, but it was some special event they were holding. And then on the evening of Miss Fenniston's death, he was staying with his married sister in Wakefield, in Yorkshire for a few days. It was their joint twenty-fifth birthdays—they're twins—and the whole family threw them a party. We could check, I suppose."

'We'll do that later if it seems necessary. I assume you've got the address?'

'I have, yes. I think he might be a homosexual, sir, but it wasn't something I asked about nor did he mention it.'

'He wouldn't mention something like that unless he was forced into it. The Bishop's Office didn't mention any concerns in that regard, but they mightn't know, or might want to ignore such a thing. That would probably explain him wanting to leave a small place like Porthlea, too. No doubt word got around.'

'True. If you want me to, sir, I'll check with his sister, but to be honest, if he is our man, he would probably give himself a good alibi.'

'Absolutely. Well that's that. Good work, sergeant, and thank you.' Hardy drank his tea. He noticed that Porter was glancing repeatedly out of the window. 'I didn't get anything much from Major Reeves,' Hardy said, bringing Porter's attention back to the job.

'No, sir?'

'He knew about the poison pen letters. But he didn't seem to have any idea that it was Mrs Hunter and Marlene behind them. Not until my cousins had drinks at his house recently, along with a few others, and it was suggested to him. Seems he had a couple of letters, accusing him of sneaking about with Meredith Prescott.'

'And was he?'

'He says not, quite emphatic about it. I get the impression he'd welcome the idea, but the lady is not in favour of them getting to know one another better.'

Porter nodded. 'Poor guy. He needs to move somewhere with a bit more scope. Not many single ladies to choose from in a small place like this.'

'True. I asked him if he had seen anything on either evening. He said no. But then he said that he remembered seeing Miss Prescott coming out of the Graysons' place on the Monday evening when Miss Fenniston died.'

'There to read to the old lady, I believe.'

'Exactly. He said she didn't see him, but walked along the road towards her home. He watched her until she was out of his sight around the bend of the road.'

'Did you find out anything useful from the doctor, sir?'

Hardy shook his head, and leaning back, he folded his arms. 'No. That was another complete waste of time. He didn't see anything on either night. You'd think, wouldn't you, that in a place this size, there'd always be someone who'd seen something, noticed something out of the ordinary, or just been gawping out of the window, spying on their neighbours. But no, he just saw the same as the major, Miss Prescott hurrying home after her visit to Mrs Hunter. But on the night Mrs Hunter herself died, the doctor was in bed all night, his first full night of sleep in over a week, he said.'

'I suppose it couldn't have been the doctor himself?'

Hardy shrugged. 'I doubt it. I mean, why? What would his motive be?'

Now Porter shrugged. 'Just clutching at straws, sir.'

Me too, Nat, me too.'

'We are not getting on very quickly, sir.'

'We're not, are we?'

For a few minutes, they concentrated on their food. When they got up to leave, Hardy said,

'Do you mind if we take a quick look at the sea while we're here?'

'Oh—er—not at all, sir.'

Hardy looked away, grinning to himself. Porter was almost skipping along the road now, and grinning broadly, looking about him to take in the scene. When they reached the beach, Hardy said, 'I might try to find a pretty shell to take back. Seems wrong somehow to come to the coast and not take back a shell as a memento.'

'Just what I was thinking myself.'

As soon as she opened the door of the cottage, Hardy said, 'Dee, would you help me with something? I need to send some telegrams to the wine grower in Germany. The one who was here recently.' He got out his daybook and quickly found the page. 'Ah yes, a Herr and...'

'Herr and Frau Kostner. Of course. You realise the post office is closed now?'

'I'm afraid I'll have to ask Cissie to do this for me out of office hours. Can we go now?'

'Of course,' Dee said again. She knew Cissie would be only too pleased—and very excited—to help with the investigation.

*

Chapter Twenty-seven

Over lunch, Meredith Prescott had a discussion with her brother.

'It's not that I've got anything against them as such, although they're not really our sort of people, if one is being brutally honest. But really, after this morning! That girl practically accused Aunt Lucinda to her face of being involved somehow in the death of—well—I don't know if she meant Old Mother Hunter or if it was Sheila Fenniston's death as well. It's completely unacceptable to be spoken to like that by some... what is she... a teacher at some inner-city secondary modern? They are not coming here and that's final. In any case, Aunt Lucinda is not up to hosting another of your dinner parties.'

Jeremy felt a strong sense of exasperation combined with the unfortunate urge to laugh. He dismissed these concerns with a terse, 'Oh for God's sake, that's utter rot! They are perfectly pleasant, and there's no need to take what they say seriously. It's pure idle speculation. And you know they most definitely are 'our sort of people'. They come from more money than we'll ever see and could be a useful contact. They could tell all their friends, then they could tell their friends. Just laugh it off, that's what I do. Anyway, they're harmless. In any case, you've got to go, Old Reeves will be desolate without you.'

Meredith flashed back angrily, 'I've told you before, stop joking about that. He's becoming too tiresome in his ridiculous pursuit of me. Anyone would think we were still in the last century.'

'Oh come on, Sis, at least have a little pity for the man. His poor passionate heart beats only for you.'

'As far as I'm concerned, his poor passionate heart can stop beating altogether. He's a boring little man with terrible breath. I just can't be bothered with him anymore. If he corners me at the front door one more time, and tries to kiss me, I'll... well, I don't know. I just wish he would turn his attention to some other wretched woman. But you're missing the point as usual. It's not a question of what Dee Gascoigne can do. It's the appropriateness of continuing the acquaintance if there's the ghost of a chance that some jumped-up nobody from Scotland Yard will pay attention to her.' She sank back in her chair and gazed into space for a moment or two.

Jeremy said, 'Even if they are exaggerating to make themselves seem more important, we can't afford to take the risk of offending them and becoming the subject of the Scotland Yard people's interest. The more I think about it, the better it will be to co-operate fully. Then the police will be on their way back to London, and we can get on with our lives. There's no real investigation here, it's just a question of dotting Is and crossing Ts. Make it look like everything has been properly looked into, taken seriously. I insist on you attending, Meredith. We can't have it said that you stayed away from our own dinner, people will start saying we have something to hide. You know how gossip spreads in a little place like this.

'We'll say Aunt Lucinda is unwell, and I'll phone Reeves and ask if we can have everyone round to his place instead of here. I'll send Davies down with the food and everything in the car, which will help Reeves out no end, he's only got that part-time charwoman who does a bit of cleaning for him, he's not really up to proper entertaining.'

Meredith would have liked to persist with her refusal but she couldn't deny the truth of what he was saying. In any case, Jeremy was showing signs of temper and she didn't feel up to dealing with one of his moods. If he said she had to go, then she would go, but she would make her feelings perfectly plain.

In a pondering tone, she commented, 'I wonder how they know that fellow from Scotland Yard? I mean the inspector, obviously, not the other one.'

'Can't remember. No doubt his mother was their nanny, or something. They've got so used to being treated as if they're special, they don't realise that no one wants to tell them they're just overindulged brats.'

'Well,' Meredith replied, 'Whatever is going on, it doesn't have anything to do with us, so let's just forget about it. I'll do my duty as far as entertaining the kiddies goes, and that's all anyone can ask of me. Is there any more tea? I'm going to need a top-up if I'm to make it through to half past seven.'

Meredith went out to the kitchen and gave Jeremy's directions regarding dinner to Davies, and asked for more tea to be sent up. Then she went to her room. She needed to be alone for a while if her patience was going to be sorely tested that evening.

At four-thirty Jeremy Prescott sent Rodericks to the cottage with a message for Rob.

Rodericks knocked softly on the front door then

waited, using the short time to smooth his hair and check his lapels were straight and his uniform tidy. Then he polished his shoes on the back of his trouser legs, one foot at a time, one hand on the wall to steady himself. It was important that he made a good impression. Prescott had told him of his suspicions regarding the young man from London, so Rodericks was doubly keen to see him again to make his own judgement.

It was Rob who answered the knock at the door, and Kelvin Rodericks felt a little tongue-tied for a moment. Rob Gascoigne was even more attractive than he had remembered.

'Good afternoon,' Rob said pleasantly.

Rodericks treated him to a warm but polite smile. 'Good afternoon sir. I'm Rodericks, Mr Prescott's chauffeur. He has sent me over with a message for you.'

Rob smiled. 'Yes, I thought I recognised you. What was it Prescott wanted you to tell me?'

'Mr Prescott's compliments, sir. He wonders if you—and your sister of course--would do him the honour of joining him and Miss Prescott for dinner at Major Reeves's home. Unfortunately, Mrs Smithies is unwell, and so the dinner has had to be moved to the major's.'

'What a shame,' Rob said smoothly. 'I do hope Mrs Smithies will be feeling better shortly. Is Mr Prescott certain it wouldn't be better to cancel the arrangement altogether?'

'No need, sir. Mr Prescott and the major have it all in hand. Just go to Reeves' cottage instead of to the manor house. Mr Prescott is looking forward to the pleasure of seeing you later.'

'I see. Well, thank you, please tell Mr Prescott that we'll be there,' Rob said.

'Thank you, sir. Good afternoon.' Rodericks nodded and walked back to the manor house, thinking that if Rob Gascoigne was indeed what Prescott suspected, he himself would very much like to get to know him better. Prescott might be good-looking, but he acted like he was doing you a favour just talking to you. He never stopped being the social superior. And he was inclined to turn nasty when drunk, which was often. Rob Gascoigne was far more—Rodericks couldn't even begin to think how to describe him. But he spent a long time that evening thinking about him.

Dee had gone for a walk. She went to the beach. There wasn't really anywhere else to go in Porthlea, apart from the churchyard, and she was already feeling introspective and dreary in her mood. She was ready to leave Porthlea and get back to London again and get on with her life.

With a sense of frustration at not being able to walk for mile upon mile along the strand, Dee nevertheless headed for the far end of the beach, a mere four minutes' walk away, where the trees at the back of the churchyard came down and met the upper slopes of the shingle. It was not until she was almost there that she noticed a woman sitting beneath a tree. Meredith Prescott.

Dee hesitated. She could feel Meredith's eyes on her, but Meredith made no sign of welcome although neither did she get up as if to leave. Dee decided to approach.

Meredith looked young and sorrowful. She was sitting on her jacket. The blue of her blouse complemented her skin and eyes, making her appear fresh and alive. Dee knew Meredith was older than she, but at that moment she could not have said if it was by five years or fifteen.

Still Meredith said nothing. She stared out to sea as if searching for something vital. Dee sat on the grass some six feet from Meredith. She too turned to contemplate the ocean. For several minutes, neither spoke. Then all at once Dee had the urge to get it over with.

'I'm so sorry about this morning. I didn't mean... I *never* meant...'

Meredith turned on a smile, holding up a hand to silence Dee.

'No, no. It is I who should apologise to you. I feel certain my aunt must have been very rude.'

'Not at all. She was very pleasant. Is... Is she—all right?'

Meredith laughed at Dee's anxious face.

'Yes, of course she is. She's as strong as an ox, that woman. Have you been worrying about that all day?'

Dee nodded.

Meredith laughed again.

'Oh you poor thing! Yes, yes, Aunt Lucinda is absolutely fine. Making a fuss as usual. But that's nothing to worry about. You needn't let it worry you a moment longer.'

Dee relaxed. 'That's such a relief, I honestly thought for a moment I'd killed her! And I still don't really know what I said to bring it all on. We had been talking so pleasantly up to that point.'

'Well, I should just forget about it, if I were you. It'll all blow over. Are you coming to dinner tonight?'

Seeing Dee hesitate, Meredith added, 'We've shifted the venue to Major Reeves's, if that's any help, and Aunt Lucinda is staying at home to rest. My brother sent our chauffeur to your cottage to let you know.'

Again Dee felt relieved. Her shoulders relaxed and she smiled. 'In that case, yes, I'd love to.'

'Very well, then, Cinderella, you shall go to the dinner,' Meredith said, and her own smile showed a charming dimple in her left cheek. If she had seemed young before, she was even younger now, Dee thought. No one seeing Meredith Prescott at that moment would take her for a day over twenty-five. What a pity she had never married. But then Dee had a fleeting thought of Martin and had to repress a shudder. She wasn't going to think about him just now.

'You seem to be really putting your heart and soul into this detective business I've been hearing about. Everyone seems to think you're a modern Miss Marple,' Meredith said. She was watching Dee's face closely. Dee hesitated, glancing away then back again.

'Well, yes, I suppose I am,' she said, but nothing more.

Meredith felt a rush of irritation. Why did one need to prise every little bit of information out of the girl? She really was the most annoying creature. With a bright smile, however, Meredith said,

'And apparently you have the ear of Scotland Yard?'

'Inspector Hardy is my cousin,' Dee said.

'So you're not going to be a teacher, after all?' There was certainly an underlying tone in Meredith's voice. It took Dee a moment to identify it as contempt.

Dee looked at her. 'Oh, I think I can manage both.' She made a show of looking at her watch. 'I'm afraid I need to be getting back. It was lovely to see you again and I'm so glad Mrs Smithies is not seriously ill. See you this evening.'

Meredith watched Dee walking away and felt a cold, burning rage inside her. How her hand itched to slap the silly girl. Instead, she got up and shook out her jacket. As she put it on, she could see Dee was almost at the part of the beach that led up into the village street.

Meredith sighed. Turning back to head for home, she began to wonder what the best course of action would be. Should she go to the dinner or cry off? She wanted to cry off, but it occurred to her she might miss something. Miss Gascoigne would be blatantly pursuing her enquiries, even at the dinner, of that Meredith had no doubt. It was laughable that the dratted woman should see herself as some kind of private investigator.

Hopefully she'd quickly get bored and go home.

*

Chapter Twenty-eight

The detective inspector at Sandneath police station was looking forward to getting off home nice and early. In fact, he was putting on his hat and lifting his raincoat off the coat rack in the corner of his office, when, to his dismay, a call came through from the front desk.

'It's that Scotland Yard fellow on the phone. He'd like a quick word, sir,' said the desk sergeant.

The inspector knew that if he put him off until tomorrow, it would just niggle at him all the afternoon and evening. With a sigh he said, 'Very well. Put him through.'

He hung up his hat and coat and resumed his seat—still warm—behind his desk. He knew that the men from The Met were determined to make him look bad. It came as no surprise to hear Hardy say, as soon as the call was connected,

'I'll make this quick, no doubt you're busy. I just wanted to let you know that in my view, both the recent deaths in Porthlea are suspicious, and I've submitted a report to my superiors to tell them why. I am treating these as two related murder enquiries.'

'Do I get the courtesy of a full report?'

'I'll have one with you by the end of tomorrow. I'm just on my way to speak with Jeremy Prescott. I now know that Sheila Fenniston was planning to leave Prescott's to work in Germany for one of the wine-growers who imported to Prescott's.'

'And I suppose you can prove that, can you?'

Hardy was conscious of an acute dislike of the man at the other end of the line. It was a struggle to remain polite, professional. He said, 'Yes of course. I have evidence, and the German gentleman's own testimony by telegram.'

There was an extended silence.

Hardy said, 'Right, well, that's all I wanted to say. Good evening.'

The other inspector said nothing, and simply put the phone down. Then he hurried next door to have a word with his sergeant.

'I've got a way to steal Scotland Yard's thunder,' he told him gleefully. 'Here's the plan. Now first thing tomorrow, we'll take some men with us, and go to the wine place in Porthlea...'

Davies opened the front door to the policemen. Really, she thought, it was getting like Piccadilly Circus round here. She left them in the hall whilst she went to speak with Mrs Smithies. Only a minute later, she was showing them into the drawing-room.

'Mrs Smithies will be with you shortly.'

'But it was Mr Prescott we wished to speak with,' Hardy stated.

Davies glared at him. 'He isn't here, is he? He never is this time of day. He is at the warehouse.'

'We've already been there. He isn't there.'

Davies shrugged. It was nothing to do with her where people were. 'So do you want to see Mrs Smithies or not?'

'We do,' Hardy said firmly, and sat down on the sofa to wait. Davies huffed to herself and left.

'Nice place,' Porter said, looking around him. 'I could do with a place like this. I'd eat my breakfast in a different room every day.'

Hardy grinned. 'It's very pleasant. I think you'll have to set your sights a little lower on what The Met pay, I'm afraid. Unless you make it to Commissioner and get a knighthood, of course.'

Porter wondered about Hardy. Had he grown up in a big place like this? He certainly had the posh boarding-school accent and he didn't seem particularly overawed or impressed by the manor house.

The door opened, and in swept Mrs Smithies, Davies in her wake with a shawl and a walking stick.

'Are you from the police?' Mrs Smithies demanded. Both men had leapt to their feet as she approached. Her tone was hostile, but nevertheless Hardy produced his warrant card and a pleasant smile.

'We are indeed, Mrs Smithies,' he said smoothly. 'It's nothing to alarm you, madam. I'd just like to ask you a few simple questions.'

He didn't bother with the conventional, 'If I may'. He was giving her no room to deny his request. As it was, she merely rolled her eyes in a very modern manner, and said,

'Oh, if you must. Is this about Agnes Hunter?'

'No, it's about Sheila Fenniston,' Hardy said. Porter already had his daybook out.

'Her? But why?'

Was she really so surprised, Hardy wondered. He felt certain there was a momentary fear in her eyes. She glanced away to settle her shawl about her, using it as a prop, he was sure, to manage her emotions.

'I have reason to believe Miss Fenniston did not take her own life. I am now investigating her murder.' He watched her closely. That she was shocked was evident.

'Murdered? Oh, but that's nonsense.' The pitch of her voice was higher, shrill, with the fear she was trying so hard to disguise.

'Were you aware that Miss Fenniston was planning to leave Prescott's in a few weeks' time?'

Her surprise at this was genuine. She quite clearly had no knowledge of Sheila's plans.

Mrs Smithies said nothing, but she was obviously thinking furiously. She got up to pull the bell, and when Davies came hurrying, ordered tea. But she had no real option other than to resume her seat. She did so now. Hardy thought she was considering—and rejecting—various alternatives. In the end all she said, in a low worried tone was,

'No. I didn't know that. May I ask where...?'

'She had been offered a position in Herr Kostner's business. She had her passport and a plane ticket ready.'

'It was a firm plan, then,' Mrs Smithies said to herself.

'And you did not know of this plan, Mrs Smithies?'

She shook her head but said nothing more.

'What about your nephew? Did he know, do you think?'

'I have no idea what knowledge my nephew or anyone else has. He said nothing to me. Therefore, I assume he knew nothing. Now if you don't mind, I must ask you to leave. I have a dinner engagement.'

Davies held the front door open for Inspector Hardy and the sergeant to leave, and no sooner had they reached the top of the stone steps outside than she slammed the door behind them. Inside, in the entrance hall, she gave a sniff and noting that Mrs Smithies was now back in her private sitting-room upstairs, Davies ran up to ask if anything else was needed. Her enquiry was met with a weary smile.

'Police gone? Thank goodness. To think of the police of all people, coming *here*. Davies, you're so good to me. What would I do without you?'

'It's my job, madam, that's all. And a pleasure to serve a proper lady as makes it seem no work at all.'

'How many years has it been?'

'I came to you when I was just fifteen, madam, which makes it twenty-six years this Michaelmas.'

'Twenty-six years, Davies! Where has the time gone? I wonder if I knew then how loyal and devoted you would be.' Mrs Smithies frowned a little as she tried to remember. 'But how was it you came to us at fifteen and not straight from school when you were fourteen?'

Davies looked at Mrs Smithies, somewhat dismayed. She hesitated, hoping her employer's memory would supply the missing details without Davies herself being forced to reply.

Surely Madam hadn't forgotten? Not something so—so *painful* as that had been?

But Mrs Smithies was clearly waiting for her to reply. Davies, fighting to remain composed, took a deep breath and in a lowered voice said, 'Perhaps you've forgotten about my—trouble, madam?'

'Your...?' Lucinda Smithies stared for a moment, surprised, then laughed, flapping a hand at Davies. 'Oh of course, yes indeed. Your 'trouble'. So silly of me. Well, well, not a very promising start to your career but you turned out all right in the end, eh? More than just a flighty little piece after all. Now then, a cup of tea will be just the thing, thank you.'

Mrs Smithies picked up a magazine and began to flick through it, and Davies, trembling, retreated to the kitchen.

The baize door fell shut behind her. In the gloomy kitchen, Davies filled the kettle and set it to boil, then she took out a tea-tray and wiped it with a cloth. She placed a large brilliantly white doily on the tray along with a cup and saucer. Then a sugar bowl and milk jug. A small cut-crystal bud vase with two pink carnations provided a dainty splash of colour. Lump sugar was piled into the sugar bowl, and fresh milk poured into the milk jug. Sugar tongs, a strainer and a teaspoon were placed side by side next to the cup and saucer. Davies added a plate of homemade biscuits.

By this time the kettle was boiling. She poured a little water in to heat the pot. After a few moments she swished the water around in the pot then poured it down the sink. Now she added tealeaves to the pot and poured boiling water on top. The lid of the pot was replaced, and the pot was added to the empty corner of the tray.

Gripping the handles of the tray, Davies made her way up the back stairs to the sitting-room, carefully negotiating the curve of the stairs at the top, where it was so hard to see where to put your foot, and more than once she had almost gone down the stairs backwards. She carried the tray into the room and set it down on a little side table next to Madam. Madam barely noticed, just gave a little murmur, not even an actual word, just a raise of the hand and a half-smile then she was lost again in her magazine. Davies bobbed a half-curtsey and left the room.

Back in the kitchen once again, breathing hard and trembling, and knowing full well she should be getting on with the vegetables for the dinner party, Davies sat herself down at the long table. Twenty-six years. She sat and she stared into space. And as she stared into space, her fingers automatically worked on the corner of her apron, folding it and unfolding it, then folding it again.

Twenty-six years. *More than just a flighty piece after all.* And no more caring about her after all this time than she did about her magazine or her shoes or... just... anything. *Your trouble,* Madam had said, with her lips tipping up at the corners, like it was something a little bit silly, like it was something *small* she'd made too much of. Like she'd been a nuisance and made too much fuss. Something unimportant, a minor annoyance.

Her father had almost killed her when he found out. He'd taken his belt to her. She could still see the look in his eye, his red face, the blue vein in his temple that had seemed to bulge as he lashed at her again and again with the full force of his fury. And her mother, sobbing in the corner, her tears wetting her needlework.

A flighty little piece. Davies bit her lip. The memories, so long held at bay, flooded back and she remembered the awful night that her whole world had seemed to die. She could still hear her own voice sobbing in her head, smell the man's breath, heavy and foul with alcohol. Feel his rough hands on her body. She'd sobbed and tried to fight. Terrified, she'd been.

Just fourteen, with no experience, no understanding of things like that. She was a poor innocent girl. She hadn't even known how babies were made. She'd been so naïve. And her employer's son had been so good-looking, she was that sweet on him, she would have done anything. She thought young Mr Prescott was such a romantic figure. Almost twenty years older than her and so sure of himself. She had so many silly girlish daydreams about him back then, when he was the doting uncle of young Mr Jeremy and Miss Meredith. To think he'd have been sixty now, if he'd still been alive.

But that night she had learned the hard way that good looks don't mean a good heart. And his heart had been blacker than most. Not that he'd given her a choice, just forced himself on her as if she was yet another part of his inheritance. His father—Madam's father too—had been the magistrate, so it all got hushed up. Five pounds to keep her mouth shut, and as soon as the baby was born it was taken away—she—*she* was taken away. And not even three weeks later, Davies had gone to work for the married sister of her 'fine champion', and now after twenty-six years of loyal service, that was what she got. *Your trouble,* and a little smile. *More than just a flighty piece after all.* A flick of her fingers, a murmur from behind her magazine.

When he'd been killed by enemy action just a year later, Davies was the only one who didn't mourn for him. She had been glad. Glad he was dead. Good riddance to him. He'd never hurt her—or anyone else—again.

Now the tears came. The emotion broke on her like a storm. She wept with the pain of twenty-six years and couldn't have held it back if she'd wanted to. Part of her mind was appalled by the noise she was making. What if someone heard? But the other part of her no longer cared. Damn them all. For twenty-six years she had been the devoted and loyal servant. She had given up on her youth, given up on romance, and served the family of *that man* with respect and faithfulness. She had been cautious, mature, reserved, for her whole adult life. Now she was once more the terrified kid who had been attacked by an adult man that should have known better.

Eventually her weeping subsided. She wiped her face and blew her nose. She tidied her hair and tried to calm herself. She drank a glass of cool water and then she looked about her. Twenty-six years of living in someone else's house, of caring for someone else's things. After all that time, what did she have to show for all her hard work? A bad back and bad knees. Less than a hundred pounds in her savings account at the post office. And everything she owned could all be fitted into her one small suitcase.

Courage—or perhaps recklessness—surged through her veins. This wasn't the 1930s or 40s anymore. The youngsters were always saying it was a new age. You could do what you wanted nowadays. Go somewhere else. Make a new life.

A new life.

She was breathing hard. All she was doing was just standing there in the middle of the kitchen. So why was she panting so hard? Thoughts were whirling in her head. She felt rather faint. Her knees shook. Did she dare? Did she?

She wrenched at the strings of her apron, then gave up and tugged it off over her head and threw it across the back of the chair. Already half-frightened by her daring, she ran quickly up the back stairs to her room. It took just two trembling minutes to put everything that was hers into that suitcase. She put on her hat and her coat and her outdoor shoes then took a last look in the mottled glass above the cracked basin with the hot tap that didn't work.

Her eyes were still red from her weeping. Her hair was coming down again. She quickly pinned it back into place. Her fingers shook. Her bottom lip trembled. She took a deep breath. She had to do it. She had to. Now, before her courage failed, leaving her cold and defeated and another twenty years to do in this house.

She grabbed the suitcase and hurried away down the back stairs.

At the same moment that Mrs Smithies was pouring herself a second cup of tea and turning the page of her magazine, Violet Davies was hurrying along the drive in the direction of the village. She hurried, suddenly afraid she would be seen and somehow stopped and forced to go back. Her state of mind was wavering between horror and euphoria, with the euphoria rapidly declining and the horror gaining an ascendance.

What have I done, she thought. I must be mad. She went into The Seagull public house for the first time in her life and slipped into a seat in a dim corner of the lounge bar. The landlady gazed at her in sheer astonishment.

'Can I have a gin and tonic, Joan, please?' Violet Davies asked when the landlady came over. Joan hastened to bring the drink to her. She set it down on the table in front of her and Violet downed it in one.

'Are you all right?'

Violet nodded. Then shook her head. 'I don't know. I've left. I don't... Have you got a room? I've just left and I didn't think. There wasn't time. It just came over me all of a sudden. And now I don't know what to do.' Her words ran out. She had reached the end of her impulse to action. She felt exhausted, frightened. She had her little bit of money she'd saved up over the years. But it wasn't much. Wasn't enough. It wouldn't last long; the days were gone when you could live on a hundred pounds a year. Her little bit of money wouldn't last long. If she was ever desperate—and how she hoped she would never be—she had her mother's wedding ring. But after that... After that... She pushed the thought away. Inside she was quaking. Her stomach churned and lurched.

The landlady started to shake her head, but she knew Davies, and she could see things weren't right.

'We've got a boxroom, it's nothing special, ever so small. It's got a few bits stacked up in the corner, bottles and glasses and whatnot. But I can make up the bed for you, it'll be all right for a night or two, if you're sure?'

'I am. Thank you,' Violet said.

'Do you want to go up now, Vi?'

Fishing in her handbag for her purse, she took out the money for the drink then nodded, adding,

'You won't tell anyone I'm here, will you? Please? Specially not the Prescotts or Mrs Smithies. Please.'

'No one will hear it from me, dear. Have you got all your things? I'll not charge you for the room, it's not a proper guest room really. But it should be all right just for a few nights, until your plans are more certain. Come and have a look.'

As they stood inside the door looking at the tiny room, Violet said, 'I'm sorry for what I said to you three years ago at the harvest festival. I didn't really mean it, you know, about your fruit cake. It really was delicious. I was just jealous.'

'It's all right, Vi. Water under the bridge, my dear. It wasn't one of my best, I knew it deep down. Will you have a bit of supper later? You can have it in the little dining-room if you like, or up here. Something hot inside you will make you feel better.'

'Up here, please.'

'You know we've got them London policemen here, don't you? And they are friends of the young woman and her brother who are in Cissie Palmer's cottage.'

'I haven't done anything to be ashamed of, only left it too long before coming away.'

Joan was silent for a moment then turned to take her leave.

'Just make sure and let me know if you need anything. Supper will be in an hour, if that's all right.'

The door closed.

Violet Davies sat on the narrow mattress, her suitcase at her feet. She could hardly believe it. Only an hour earlier everything had been just as normal, then suddenly, almost from nowhere, her whole life had been turned upside down. And all because she'd got upset and let things get to her. A madness had obviously gripped her, an uncontrollable—*something*—had risen up in her, destroyed everything she had spent her whole adult life building and now it had left her flat again almost immediately. She sat on the bed and looked about her at the quiet, crowded room.

What on earth was she going to do now?

As they approached the manor house for the second time that day, Jeremy Prescott's sleek Jaguar passed them on the drive. Prescott himself was in the back and gave them a curt nod. The policemen followed at a leisurely pace.

Porter said, 'Nice car.'

Hardy said, 'My father has one of those. I'm more of an MG man myself. Not that I run a car at the moment. I hardly need one when I'm in London.'

'MGs are nice cars too,' agreed Porter. 'But no good for a family.'

'True. Don't you find it odd that Prescott has such a grand car—and let's not forget a chauffeur too—when his place of work is only one hundred yards from his front door?'

'Now that you mention it...'

Hardy looked at his watch. 'Almost seven o'clock.'

'I wonder where he's been until now?' Porter said.

'You read my mind, sergeant. Is it likely he's been at his desk all this time?'

When they reached the front door, Prescott was already out of the car. He slammed the door, then addressed himself to Rodericks, who had the window down,

'Call for us in half an hour, will you.' He turned to face them, warily eyeing them as they drew closer. 'Gentlemen. What can I do for you?'

'Just a few questions, Mr Prescott. Nothing to take up too much of your time.'

'Good. I have plans for this evening.'

Porter thought sadly of his own plans—to eat a large plateful of a delicious meal at the very comfortable pub. 'Hopefully we won't keep you long, sir.'

Prescott's eyes flicked over Porter then away, but he said nothing. To Hardy, he said, 'Very well. Let's go to my office.'

They entered the house, and inside the door, Prescott

said a terse, 'Wait here.' He went into a nearby room; they heard the sound of voices, then he came out again and led them across the hall to a small dark room. He snapped on the lights, took a seat behind the desk, and said, 'Now then...'

Hardy pulled out a seat for Porter and another for himself. Receiving the slightest of nods, the sergeant produced his daybook and waited, ready with his pencil.

'What's this?' Prescott attempted a light-hearted laugh that didn't quite work. 'Taking down everything I say to use in evidence?'

'Not at all, Mr Prescott,' Hardy said with a broad, friendly grin. 'I expect you find this yourself, sir, when you're in a business meeting, for example. You talk to so many people, it's easy to forget who said what. This is just to refresh my memory later.'

Prescott seemed to accept that. He relaxed slightly.

'Now then sir, I just wanted to ask you about Miss Fenniston. Were you aware that she had plans to leave Prescott's for a position with your German wine supplier, Herr Kostner.'

'Rubbish,' Prescott said. 'Absolute rot, I'm afraid.' He sat back, now completely relaxed. Whatever he'd been afraid they would ask, it wasn't this. 'Whoever's been telling you that, they're completely wrong. No doubt Sheila was trying to make out that her life was an exciting one. Real life was a bit too mundane for our Sheila.'

'Interesting,' Hardy said. 'So you really didn't know?'

'As I said,' Prescott began, but something in Hardy's tone gave him pause. 'Wait. Are you saying you really believe...?'

'I'm saying that we *know* she was leaving. She had her passport, a plane ticket, and Herr Kostner has confirmed the details. Sheila Fenniston was leaving Prescott's.'

There was a silence. At length, Prescott seemed to rouse himself. 'Well, well. Lucky old Sheila.' Then, remembering she was dead, he added, 'What a shame.'

Before Prescott could fully recover from this, Hardy said, 'Have you ever given Mrs Harriet Grayson, or her mother Mrs Agnes Hunter a bottle of wine?'

'What? No, of course... Look what are you getting at?'

'No need to get upset, Mr Prescott,' Hardy said calmly. 'We are just trying to establish how a bottle of drugged wine came to be on the table in Miss Fenniston's room.'

Prescott's nose wrinkled across the middle as his lip lifted in a sneer. 'What? Of course, I didn't give it to them. Or to Sheila. As I said at the inquest...'

'Yes, we know what you said at the inquest. We have the transcript. I just thought that now you've had time to reflect, after the initial shock of Miss Fenniston's death has worn off, you might have recalled giving a gift of wine to someone in that household.'

'Then you thought wrong. Right, well, I'm afraid that's all the time I have, gentlemen.' He got to his feet and began to walk them to the door.

'Just one last thing,' Hardy said. He was standing in the doorway. Prescott could hardly slam the door on him, though it was clear he would like to do so.

Prescott heaved a sigh. 'Quickly then, Hendy. What is it?'

'The name is Hardy, sir. My question is just a continuation of the previous one...'

'I've already told you. It's perfectly clear...'

'Yes sir. Do you ever give gifts of wine to anyone?'

Prescott frowned. Hardy knew he was trying to decide if this was a trap of some sort. After a moment he said,

'Well yes, of course I give my friends wine sometimes.'

Hardy smiled his reassuring friendly smile. 'I thought

so, sir. Very generous of you. Do you remember the last time...?'

'Oh for God sake, man! It was probably at Christmas. I gave a bottle to all my friends.'

'And who would that be, sir?'

'Well, just, you know. Friends. My friends in the local area.'

'So the vicar perhaps? Or Major Reeves?'

'Yes, of course.'

'Anyone else, sir? Just cast your mind back, if you will.'

Prescott was close to losing his temper, Porter could see. Hardy was still giving him encouraging cheery smiles. It was odd, Porter thought, seeing the taciturn, somewhat gloomy inspector smiling so much. Like that crocodile in that children's book. It went something like, *How doth the little crocodile*...and ended with something about gently smiling jaws. That would continue to irritate him until he remembered the book.

Prescott huffed crossly. 'Let me see. The vicar, Major Reeves,' He was ticking them off on his fingers.

'Mrs Palmer at the post office?' Porter suggested. Prescott frowned.

'What? No. None of my...'

'None of your tenants, sir? Of course not. Any workers at the factory?' Hardy put in.

Prescott shook his head. 'I don't give them any, but at Christmas they can buy a bottle at half price.'

'Generous indeed, sir. Any other friends?'

'Jeremy? Jeremy!' A querulous voice issued from the drawing-room.

'My aunt wants me, inspector. If you don't mind?'

'What about Mr. Smith? Sir? Sonny-Ray Smith?'

'Oh yes, I did give him some wine. And the doctor chap, Bartlett. I think that's all.'

'Excellent sir. Thank you very much. What about Davies, your maid-housekeeper?'

'No. Definitely not.' Prescott was already beginning to walk away.

Hardy said, 'And Rodericks your driver?'

'What?' Prescott stood stock still. 'What? Rodericks? I... I...'

'It's all right sir, if you can't remember, we'll just check with him. Well, thank you for your time, we'll get off and leave you to enjoy your dinner.' Hardy began to button up his jacket, half-turning to leave.

'Ah yes, now you come to mention it, last Christmas I believe I did give Rodericks a bottle of wine. A thank you for all the extra driving he had to do for our guests recently.'

'Very good. Thank you very much sir, that's been a huge help. Goodnight, sir.'

Prescott's face, as he watched them leave the house, was a picture of consternation.

'You've given him something to worry about, sir,' Porter commented as they set off back into the village.

'Good. He really didn't want us to know about giving the wine to the chauffeur, did he?'

'I thought it was good of him to reward his driver almost six months before they had the visitors here,' Porter said.

Hardy laughed. 'Indeed. And now, I suppose you want your dinner.'

'If it's not too much trouble, sir.'

Hardy laughed again. 'I'm bloody ravenous too,' he said. He stopped in his tracks. He closed his eyes and shook his head for a moment. Porter watched him, his heart sinking. He was not in the least surprised when Hardy clapped him on the shoulder and said, 'You go on ahead, Nat, I've got one more task to do before I can join you.'

Relief flooded Porter's being, immediately followed by guilt. When Porter turned to go into the dining-room, Hardy headed to the bar to ask to use the phone.

'Dr Bartlett? It's Detective Inspector Hardy here. I have some questions to ask you.'

'Oh, er, very well. Make it quick, man, I was about to have my supper.' The doctor didn't sound at all pleased, and in the background, Hardy could hear a woman's voice, crossly calling him.

'Of course, sir. I won't take up much of your time. On the night of Miss Fenniston's death, I believe you said you were coming through the village? What time was that, approximately?'

'Well, it must have been about half past eleven, perhaps slightly earlier.'

'Could it have been ten o'clock, sir?'

'Oh no, it wasn't anything like as early as that. It was well after eleven, probably twenty past, half past, something like that.'

'Thank you, Doctor. Now, I want to know if anyone amongst your Porthlea patients have ever been prescribed sleeping pills?'

Irritably the doctor said, 'I said this at the inquest. I have never prescribed Sheila Fenniston with...'

'I'm not asking about her, sir.' Hardy cut in.

'Well then, who?'

'That's what I'm hoping you can tell me.'

'I can't possibly divulge confidential information.'

Hardy sighed. 'I understand. But as you may be aware, I am investigating two murders. It's your duty to help the police. I just want a—call it a hint.'

There was a heavy sigh at the other end of the line. Then Hardy distinctly heard a woman's voice saying, 'Your cod and chips are getting cold, Sidney.'

'Very well,' Bartlett said into the phone. 'Let's just say, there is an older lady in Porthlea who sometimes has difficulty sleeping. I have prescribed the lady sleeping pills within the last six months.'

'And is this lady a well-to-do woman, a widow?

Living perhaps with younger relatives?'
'She is.'
Thank you, Dr Bartlett. Now my third question is, does anyone in that woman's immediate household have the blood type A negative?'

*

Chapter Twenty-nine

Hardy stood beside Rob at the bar waiting to order their drinks. The landlord was still serving another patron, a good-looking young man Rob was stealing glances at.

Using the mirror behind the bar, Hardy watched Dee. She was alone at their table, as Porter was halfway across the bar on his way to the men's room. Suddenly alert, Hardy began to count under his breath, still watching her.

One. He saw her register that she was alone.

Two. She glanced across to where he and her brother were waiting.

Three. She noted that Porter was just entering the men's room.

Four. She turned her head slightly to read what was written on the cover of the top folder Porter had so carelessly left unguarded.

Five. Hardy held his breath. She glanced across again to make sure his back was still turned.

Six. His estimate was spot on. She 'accidentally' nudged the folders onto the floor, stooping below the table to very, very slowly pick them up. He could see that she had one open on her lap below the tabletop, and was glancing through it.

'Now then, gents, what can I get you?'

It pained Hardy to have to turn away from her to give his order to the landlord. When he was able to look back again, she was putting the folders back on the table, and Porter was just leaving the men's room and on his way back.

Hardy was torn. On the one hand, he was angry with himself for leaving the folders within reach, knowing as he did her penchant for prying into things that did not concern her. It went against everything he believed in and had been trained to do, to allow a private citizen to pry into police business, or private information, or to corrupt correct procedure. It was utterly and completely wrong.

But.

Time and again his father had justified allowing his mother Dottie to interfere in his work, stating that she knew people, and that she had an almost uncanny knack for spotting motives and detecting lies. Bill Hardy and his father, Bill senior, had argued several times about this, with the younger man claiming that he would never tolerate such interference from anyone who was not a serving member of the police force.

'You just wait,' his father had warned with a smile.

Hardy paid for his and Porter's drinks, two half pints of bitter, and he waited whilst Rob counted out the money for his brandy and Dee's Babycham.

He made the mistake of turning and looking back at the table. Dee glanced up, saw him watching, and gave him a radiant smile. God, she was beautiful. His heart seemed to flip inside him, and he knew the battle was lost.

Back at the table, he said to her, 'If you can wait, we'll come back to your cottage with you, then you can read these in comfort. He tapped the folders with his forefinger.

She had the grace to blush.

'I'm warning you,' Hardy said, throwing the folders down on the arm of her chair. 'Some of the photos of Sheila Fenniston are very distressing.'

'I saw her for myself,' she countered. 'So I already know how horrible it was.'

Rob came through with a tray of coffee just in time to hear Hardy say, 'And when were you going to tell me you were attacked in this cottage just three nights ago?'

'What?' Rob almost dropped the tray onto the coffee table. 'Why didn't you...?' and to Hardy, 'This is the first I'm hearing of it.'

To Rob, Dee said, 'I didn't want to worry you,' and to Bill, 'You and your big mouth!'

Porter, sitting in an armchair, observed all this. He was still not sure how he felt about Hardy giving confidential police information to these two. Information Hardy had been very clear that Porter himself was on no account to hand over. He was ready to see where these actions took both the case and Hardy himself.

Dee's first thought was that the pictures weren't quite as awful as she'd expected. Mrs Hunter really just looked as though she were asleep, even though she lay at an unnatural angle at the foot of the stairs, with a wound on the right side of her head. And the black and white photo of Sheila came nowhere near to equalling the shocking impact of Dee's own memory of that morning. She stared for several minutes, feeling only sorrow at the needless waste of a life. Two lives.

It took her no time at all to read through the meagre information the Sandneath police had gathered. The pathologist's reports were interesting.

Dee read aloud, "Bruises on the forearms that may

indicate another person held the arm to make the incisions, although this are not conclusive'. Why didn't they mention this is the inquest?'

Hardy was watching her closely. He felt proud that she had noticed this. Perhaps after all, he had been right to include her. 'Because it was not conclusive.'

Dee frowned but continued reading.

It was clear that although the pathologist had decided Sheila had taken her own life, and Mrs Hunter had died because of an accidental fall, he had made a note that small traces of blood had been found under the fingernails of both victims that did not match either woman's blood type. This was attributed to possible contamination by police or other officials.

Dee looked up once more. 'Sheila's blood group is shown as AB positive, and Mrs Hunter's is shown as O positive. But the blood trace found under the forefinger and second fingernails of both women is shown to be A negative. Do you know of anyone with that blood group?'

Bill smiled at her. 'I can't tell you that.'

'But it is significant?' she asked.

He nodded.

'Did you have that blood smudge analysed? The one I told you about on Mrs Hunter's mantelpiece?'

He nodded again.

'And?'

'It's fairly recent and is A negative.'

Her eyebrows slanted up. 'Interesting.' After another moment she added, 'And have you found out who in Porthlea has that blood group?'

He grinned. 'That's your lot. Sorry, Dee, I can't tell you any more than that.'

Dinner that evening at Major Reeves' was an odd affair. They had arrived a little early to find the major on the telephone. It became clear there was a problem with the food.

'The Prescotts' housekeeper has done a bunk,' Reeves told them, lowering his voice, and placing one hand over the receiver. Dee was astonished.

'Davies? Left?'

'Apparently. Not a word to anyone. Took Mrs Smithies her afternoon tea, then went upstairs and packed her things, and left without a 'by your leave'. Unbelievable. And of course she was supposed to be making dinner tonight. Prescott's had to drive off to some hotel. He's going to bring some food back with him. Otherwise, I could probably rustle up some scrambled eggs, but that's about the limit of my skills. A fine to-do.'

'Gosh, I bet they're furious,' Dee commented, and couldn't help feeling a little pleased at the thought of their discomfort.

'Anyway, Meredith's on her way here. She's walking down. Thought I'd pop out to meet her—don't like the idea of a lady out on her own at night. You two stay here and make yourselves at home. I've made a pitcher of some snake bite—it's in the sitting-room. Help yourselves. Back in a tick. The Edmondses and that crooner fellow should be here soon. If I'm still out, let them in, won't you?'

And looking excited at the prospect of some time alone with Meredith, the major hurried out.

Rob and Dee went into the sitting-room and found the 'snake bite'. Rob sniffing the jug, nodded in approval and poured them a couple of glasses.

'It's not exactly the middle of the night,' Rob said. 'Look, the sun's just as high as it was at lunchtime, and it's still warm out.'

'It's nothing to do with the time of day or lack of light,' Dee said. 'He's just mad about her.'

'Hmm. Shame she's not half as smitten with him. But he is a bit like a puppy, isn't he?'

'I do hope Davies is all right. It's a bit odd, don't you think?'

'Well she must have her reasons. Perhaps they've sacked her for—well I don't know what, but... Oh, here they are.'

Meredith entered first, hesitated in the doorway then smiled and came forward with her hand outstretched to Dee. She kissed Dee's cheek then Rob's and accepted a drink.

Major Reeves looked like a man who has been told off in no uncertain terms, but after a drink he rallied his spirits and was soon laughing and joking along with his guests.

By that time, the vicar and his wife had arrived, and finally, making the most of a grand entrance in a small house, Sonny-Ray Smith had walked in, holding out both hands to be greeted by the ladies, who did so without enthusiasm. It was almost nine o'clock before Jeremy Prescott arrived with baskets of hot food in the back of his car. Callum Edmonds and Peter Reeves hurried out to help bring in the food, whilst Millie and Dee crowded into the major's kitchen and prepared to serve it up, Rob running to and fro with crockery, cutlery, napkins and so on.

If the food was excellent, the conversation lacked sparkle. Dee desperately wanted more details of the disappearance of Davies, but was afraid to broach the subject in view of her unfortunate lack of subtlety on previous occasions. But it was Meredith herself who brought it up, although she added very little to what they had already heard.

'Just walked out of the house without a word. She's probably in London or Brighton or somewhere by now, living it up. Well, as I told Aunt Lucinda, Davies had better not think she can simply turn up again in the morning, asking for her place back. After all these years, this is how she repays our kindness! It's a shocking disgrace.'

'And where does she think she can go?' Jeremy added, equally incensed. 'A woman of her age? Unless she's got some relations we've never heard of... Otherwise, one shudders to think what might happen to her. Her own fault though. You don't go biting the hand that feeds you.'

'Quite. She needn't think she'll get a reference, either. Or her week's notice.'

'Quite so, Miss Prescott. Very annoying for you all. First your secretary gets killed then the maid goes off. Some agency's going to do very well out of you.'

Dee couldn't help feeling the major's remarks were poorly judged, and judging from Meredith's expression, she did too. Jeremy Prescott said,

'God, yes. I hope that's all, too. Replacing two people is going to be a royal pain.'

'Bit surprised you haven't already got a new secretary, as a matter of fact, old chap,' said the vicar.

Dee said, 'It will be pretty difficult to get another secretary as good as Miss Fenniston, I imagine. I mean, she knew all those languages, and she knew so much about the wine business, and was fabulous with people.'

'I think you'll find her rather basic office skills are ten-a-penny these days. And anyway, if people want to do business in England, they should learn to speak our language. It's just a shame Fenniston couldn't have spent a bit more time actually getting on with her work instead of flinging herself with abandon at every man she came in contact with.' Meredith's tone was caustic. Jeremy on the other hand, concentrated very hard on his plate and said nothing.

You could cut the air with a knife, Dee thought. She looked from one to the other and wondered about their blood groups.

The major made a little too much fuss giving everyone more wine they didn't really need, and the vicar's wife began to clear the dinner plates. Dessert was brought in and conversation turned to more conventional topics: gardening, cricket, and of course, the weather.

They were glad to get away by half past ten.

Dee had no real idea what she expected from a coffee morning at the village hall, but it turned out to be every bit as dull as she's imagined.

Only a handful of other women were present. Mrs Bartlett joined Meredith, Millie and Dee at the table bearing the urn. It was hardly a surprise, Dee thought. The concept of a mid-morning coffee event depended for its success on a large number of well-off women who were at leisure to attend. The majority of the women in Porthlea had to work for a living.

'Does your aunt sometimes attend?' Dee asked Meredith.

Meredith laughed as if Dee had told a joke. She shook her head. 'Oh no, Aunt Lucinda is not interested in village affairs.'

'What a shame,' Dee said, running out of ideas to chat about.

'Is your brother still staying here with you?'

'Yes, he's doing some work today. For his university course. Got a case file to read. He says it's a landmark case they have to know inside out, but it's also incredibly dreary.'

Again Meredith laughed heartily.

Dee paid her sixpence, wondering what on earth they could be raising funds for when they only earned a tiny amount of money each week. At this rate they could only be raising a couple of pounds a year. It seemed pointless.

Millie took a cup, let boiling water from the urn into it, then added a large spoonful of instant coffee powder and a splash of milk from a jug.

'There you are,' she said handing the cup to Dee. 'The sugar is on the end there.' She nodded towards the sugar bowl on a tray. 'And help yourself to a slice of cake. It's Madeira. I made it myself.'

'Lovely, thank you,' Dee murmured dutifully, and Millie preened.

'Got to keep up all these traditions, you know. Baking and homemaking. The family and the church are the backbone of village life. After the Lords and Ladies of the Manor, of course.' She directed a sycophantic smile at Meredith who beamed back, every inch the country lady. Dee turned away quickly.

After a few more minutes of this sort of thing, the four of them sat down together in an awkward little semi-circle on the hard wooden chairs that jangled everyone's nerves when they scraped the floor.

Dee, smiling at the others, thought they really might as well have been at the vicarage or the manor house, it would have been far more comfortable, and any ordinary sitting-room could easily accommodate such a small number. The vicar arrived, clearly at a loose end and in need of cake, to swell their numbers to five.

The usual comments were made about the weather, and everyone agreed they were very well, thank you. That seemed to exhaust the supply of conversation. They sipped their coffees. Dee repressed a grimace at the bitter taste, quite unlike the normal taste of coffee.

She began to enquire after Jeremy Prescott's welfare, planning to move on to his quest for a new secretary— and a new maid, of course—in the full knowledge that this could be a very sore point with Meredith, but just as she said, 'And how is your...' to Meredith, Callum Edmonds spoke over her to say,

'And how much longer do you plan to stay in Porthlea, Miss Gascoigne?'

All four of them stared at Dee. It was as if their lives turned on her answer.

'As a matter of fact, we return to London tomorrow.'

The vicar took a loud slurp of his coffee and gulped it down with an audible sound and a bob of his Adam's apple. 'Not trying to hurry you away, ha ha!'

There was a tension that Dee couldn't pinpoint. She felt a strong conviction that someone—at least one person—definitely wanted her gone.

Meredith said, 'Oh you must both come for coffee tomorrow morning, to say a proper goodbye to us at the manor house. I'm sure my aunt would like to say farewell to you, too, especially after your last worrying visit.'

Thinking that she would prefer to never see any of them again, Dee forced a smile and replied, 'That would be lovely, thank you.'

'In fact, you should all come. Let's make a morning of it.' Everyone accepted Meredith's impulsive invitation. To have coffee with this lot two days in a row would be hell, Dee thought. It was a good thing Rob would be there with her.

'I expect you'll be sad to leave here. You've almost become one of us,' Millie Edmonds commented.

'It is lovely here. I'm surprised that you're not flooded with tourists from Easter to Michaelmas.' Dee inspired a discussion amongst them about tourism and holidays. All she had to do was to sit back and observe. The sense of tension lessened, and she began to relax.

'Why anyone would want to live anywhere else is a mystery to me,' Meredith commented. Millie and Mrs Bartlett immediately agreed, Millie responding,

'Oh definitely. We're so lucky to live here. We have no heavy industry to pollute the air or make the place unattractive. No problems with immigrants or dropouts and the like. It's a perfect little piece of England.'

Dee busied herself with her cake, not sure any response she made to this breathtaking speech would be at all well-received.

'Sonny-Ray tells me that California is very beautiful,' Mrs Bartlett ventured to remark.

Sonny-Ray Smith was immediately dismissed as a negligible judge of what was or wasn't beautiful. Tempted to poke the fire, Dee asked,

'Has he been in the village long?'

'About a year,' Callum said, his wife adding,

'He arrived right after that big mess about that interview.'

'Of course,' Meredith said coldly, 'If we'd known who was renting the place, we'd have refused. But as it was, his agent applied and said it was for a businessman recovering from an illness. Clearly, it's our own fault for not interpreting this to mean a penny-ha'penny crooner with a drug problem.'

'And has he a wife or children?' Dee asked.

Callum huffed sadly and again Millie spoke for him:

'An endless procession of young tarts goes through that man's bedroom. How he's got the gall...'

'Millie, please, that's my mother's son from her second marriage you're speaking about,' Callum protested.

'It's not as though you're close. In any case, it's true. That's why none of us go to his house. Although for some reason Major Reeves keeps in with him, always inviting him along to things. But I think the Prescotts,' And here she directed a nodding smile at Meredith who did the same in response, 'and ourselves have made our feelings perfectly clear.'

'Oh dear.' Another topic ground to a halt. Inspiration caused Dee to recklessly say, 'And then there's poor Major Reeves, all alone. It's a shame you ladies can't introduce him to a nice single woman. I'm sure he's lonely.'

'Oh definitely. *Man shall not live by bread alone*,' Callum said in what Dee thought was the least appropriate Biblical quote he could have chosen.

'Er—very true.' She glanced across at Meredith to see her blatantly bored expression. And inspiration once again dared Dee to say, 'Miss Prescott, have you thought about what you will do now that you don't have to give up two evenings a week to read to Mrs Hunter?'

Meredith almost dropped her cup, setting it down too quickly on the rim of her saucer. Fortunately, it fell sideways into the saucer and not the other way onto the floor. But as it was, about a quarter of a pint of horribly strong coffee splashed all down her dress and all over the wooden floorboards.

Whatever Meredith might have said was lost in the operation of mopping down her dress and the floor. Millie ran for a cloth, Mrs Bartlett leapt up to relieve Meredith of her cup and saucer, and Callum Edmonds hovered, just generally getting in everyone's way.

Meredith's day got worse.

On returning home at ten minutes to twelve, she ran upstairs to pull of her wet dress and put it to soak in cold water to get the stain out. Something Davies would usually have done. Then she hurriedly dressed herself again and ran along to her aunt's sitting-room.

'I'm back, Aunt Lucinda.'

'So I see.' Mrs Smithies did indeed just barely glance up from her magazine. 'I could do with a cup of tea. What are you making for lunch?'

Meredith was momentarily astonished. But then, she thought, I should have known. Aunt Lucinda would hardly go to the kitchen herself. It was doubtful she even knew how to boil an egg. 'Oh—er. I'm not sure. I'll need to look in the kitchen to see what we've got. That dratted Davies woman! How could she do this to us?'

'Hmm.' Mrs Smithies was once again engrossed in an article about a theatrical director who had recently gone into a nursing home to recover from alcohol dependence. 'I wonder where she is now?'

'Dead in a gutter somewhere,' Meredith said. 'That's all she deserves.'

'By the way the police have arrested your brother.'

Meredith, about to leave the room, halted. She turned, clutching at the edge of the door. 'W-what?'

'Yes. He rang from the police station in Sandneath at half past ten. Absolutely furious, obviously. Asked me to get onto his lawyer.'

'My God!'

Mrs Smithies glanced up. 'Meredith, you don't look well.'

'I don't feel...' Meredith came over to sink down onto a chair. 'Why on earth...?'

'They say he killed Sheila Fenniston and that Hunter woman. I must say, I think they're probably right.'

Meredith felt faint. She leaned against the back of the chair, tears spilling down her cheeks. 'Rubbish. Of course he didn't. He wouldn't.'

'Well, he is a pansy, and with low morals like that, who knows how low he could sink? I saw him *canoodling* with Rodericks the other night. The chauffeur! Of all people! I almost wish it was still Sheila Fenniston we were worried about. At least that would have been a bit more red-blooded. I shall have to send him away before anyone finds out. If the police let him go, of course. And I've told Rodericks he's sacked. I'll not get in a car with someone like that.'

'Rubbish!' Meredith snapped again. 'That's complete and utter rot! How could you...? Jeremy *wouldn't!*'

'Don't upset yourself, dear. I'm sure the police know what they're doing.'

'Bloody Scotland Yard! That Gascoigne brat will be behind all this, you wait and see.'

'Oh, it wasn't that young man from London who took him. It was the local inspector. Took some constables with him and arrested Jeremy in front of all his staff at the warehouse.'

'Oh my God!' As an after-thought, she added, 'And how quickly did the lawyer say he could get here?'

'Oh, I don't know dear. You'd better call him and let him know what's happened.'

Meredith stared at her aunt and felt the rage building. Suddenly on her feet, she towered over the old woman, yelling, 'You stupid, stupid woman! Why didn't you do it yourself straight away?'

And without waiting for a reply, Meredith Prescott ran from the room.

The two police officers discussed their investigation over dinner, keeping their voices low to avoid anyone overhearing them. To Porter's disappointment, neither Miss Gascoigne nor her brother appeared. Porter couldn't help wondering about her and the young inspector. Perhaps he would be able to find out something useful about that situation from his colleagues when he got back to London. He wondered if Rob and Dee were somewhere about the village pursuing their own enquiries. Now that the case folders had been shown to them, it was perfectly clear that they had no intention of obeying the inspector's original, but now seemingly forgotten, demand to, 'Keep out of this investigation, I'm warning you!'

Porter's muffled laugh at this memory caused the inspector to glance up as he was about to put a large piece of casseroled beef into his mouth. A large blob of dark rich gravy rolled down the fresh white cotton of his shirt. Hardy cursed and blotted the mark with a napkin, making the stain worse rather than better. When they'd finished eating, he said,

'I must just go up and change my shirt, I can't go about like this. I won't be long.'

He excused himself and ran up the stairs to his room, quickly found a clean shirt, and left his room, still knotting his tie—mercifully unmarked. He turned to close the door behind him. On turning back again, there, coming out of the room directly across the corridor, was the unwelcome person of Martin Clarke.

They both halted, staring at each other. The air was heavy with animosity as Clarke's lip curled up in a sneer.

'Oh, now it all makes sense,' he jeered. 'So that explains everything. Silly me. I should have realised my darling wife had to be in this dreary backwater hole for a reason—she's been whoring it up with you!'

His laugh was cut off midway as, almost of its own volition, Hardy's fist connected with Clarke's nose. Blood spurted. Clarke gave a bull-like roar of rage and threw himself at Hardy, his momentum carrying Hardy off his feet, his cheekbone slamming into the edge of the door jamb, splitting the skin like a knife. But before any further punches could be thrown, Porter was there, dragging them apart, stepping in front of Hardy to say to Clarke,

'Now, now sir. Assaulting a police officer is a serious offence. I suggest you take yourself off for a little bit of fresh air before I arrest you.'

Clarke was furious. He wiped his bloody nose on his sleeve. 'He assaulted *me*! It's him you should be arresting, he threw the first punch, look what he's done to me.'

Porter just shook his head. 'I'm sorry, sir, the light up here isn't very good. I can't say I've noticed anything different about you.'

'That's it, bloody covering up for one another as usual. You're all as bent as each other.'

'A nice walk, that's just what you need, sir, just the thing for a headache.'

It was clear from Porter's stance that Clarke wasn't going to be allowed any further access to Hardy. He turned to leave, knowing anything else was pointless. As he went, he yelled,

'This isn't over. I'll do her for adultery, citing you, and drag you both through the courts. That'll be just perfect for your career, won't it?'

Hardy, blotting his cheek on his handkerchief, and seeing that his new shirt was spattered with blood, wisely kept his opinions to himself at this point, just glad to see that Clarke was going.

'Miss Gascoigne's delightful husband, I assume?' Porter asked. The ironic inflection in his tone even made Hardy smile, though he winced at the pain.

'Indeed. Thanks for stopping me from making a bad situation worse. I'm afraid I completely lost my head.'

'Ah well, sir, when you love someone, that happens. Why don't you go into your room and—er—tidy yourself up a bit? I'll make sure laughing boy doesn't take it into his head to annoy the lady.'

'Thanks,' Hardy said again. He returned to his room. Porter paused for a second then nodded happily before going downstairs. He saw Clarke going out into the street heading for the railway station. Giving the man a minute to get out of sight, Porter decided it would be a good idea to let Miss Gascoigne know that the inspector was in need of a little nursing care.

Luckily, she was in the cottage, and as predicted, gave a yelp of dismay before running off towards the pub, leaving the door wide open and Porter and Rob grinning at each other.

She dabbed the wound with the damp towel. He winced but was otherwise silent. She worked gently and rapidly. Then she lay aside the towel and said, 'This is going to sting a bit,' as she took up the iodine she had borrowed from Joan.

He hissed air in through his teeth as the antiseptic met the wound, then was silent again. She allowed it to dry for a second or two then applied the sticking plaster and stepped back to survey her work. The survey took in the man, as well as the wound.

'You have adorable ears.'

For the first time in at least a week he smiled. 'What? I have not.'

'Oh you have. They're small and neat, and they don't stick out for miles. I can't bear ears that stick out. Nor ears that are large and fleshy.' She shuddered at the thought.

'Clarke has huge ears,' Bill remarked.

She laughed, but the laugh had a rueful sound. 'I should have known the marriage was doomed based on that alone. On our honeymoon, at a dance, he stood in a doorway with the light behind him. His huge head blocked out the light but it shone behind him and lit up his ears like a Chinese lantern. It was most peculiar.'

Bill shook his head, closing his eyes briefly. He didn't want to think of her on her honeymoon with another man. His voice practically a whisper, he asked, 'Deedee, why on earth did you marry him?'

The old childish nickname brought a bright spot of anger to her cheeks. Anything was better than tears. She snapped at him, 'Because you had gone off with *her*, you idiot!' She had to turn away. She made a show of gathering up all the bits and pieces. 'Well, that's it. I think you'll live. Unfortunately.'

And she stormed out of the room, leaving him to stare at the floor, mentally kicking himself yet again.

Coming out of the room, Dee almost collided with a woman in the corridor.

'Why, Mrs Davies!'

Violet Davies almost corrected her then stopped herself. What did it matter anyway? Nothing mattered any more. But automatically she apologised, stepping back a little.

'Sorry, miss. I didn't see you there.'

'Oh, no, it was all my fault,' Dee assured her. Davies

was looking terribly pale. Dee wondered if she was all right. She hesitated but felt compelled to speak. 'I was—surprised—to hear you had left the Prescotts.'

'I expect everyone knows by now. Are they blaming me, miss?' There was a bitter tone to Davies's voice.

Dee nodded ruefully. 'I'm afraid they are not being terribly kind about it.'

Davies nodded and said nothing. Really, thought Dee, she looked shockingly pale.

'I hope it wasn't because of that silly scene I caused with Mrs Smithies?' Dee said tentatively. 'It rather played on my mind afterwards. I never intended...'

'No miss. It wasn't because of that. Don't you blame yourself. It happened after you left. Quite a bit after.'

Dee nodded, relieved. 'Oh, I see. And—er—do you know what you're going to be doing next?' she asked.

Davies looked exhausted and confused. She shook her head. 'No miss. I haven't really had a chance...'

'No of course not. I suppose these things take time.'

There was a brief pause. Dee couldn't just walk away and leave her, Davies was obviously not well. But it was Davies who spoke next:

'I expect you'll be going back to London yourself soon, miss?'

'Yes, we're getting the two o'clock train tomorrow afternoon.'

Davies nodded. 'Of course, miss.'

They looked at one another, neither quite knowing what to say next. Then a tiny spark of hope, an idea, an outrageous idea, came to Davies. Tentatively she began,

'Miss, would it be asking too much to ask you for a reference? I might—well, I might go to London myself. I'm probably more likely to find a situation there than here in this place. Besides, I think I'm due for a change. Somehow, I don't think anyone at the manor house will want to give me a reference. If you'll excuse my audacity, miss.'

Dee thought for a moment.

Davies took the silence as a bad omen. She began to move away. 'Oh, I'm sorry, miss, please don't worry about it. I wouldn't want to impose. It was wrong of me to ask...'

Dee put out a hand to make her stay. 'Oh no, it's not that. It's just that... Could you bear to work for us? My brother and me? We share a flat. It's not very big, but we really do need someone.'

Davies stared at her, and Dee couldn't quite work out what the emotion was behind her eyes.

'It's not very exciting, but there'd be no stairs to worry about cleaning, and no grates to clean either,' Dee quickly told her. 'But as I say, we really do need someone. The room is nice, newly decorated and with a big window, though the view isn't anything special. But we're in quite a nice part of London, not too busy, with a park nearby and... things...' She broke off, running out of ideas, and fearing that in any case, Davies had already made up her mind.

'Are you serious, miss? I mean, do you really mean it?'

'Absolutely! We really need someone. We only moved in a short while ago, so we haven't got anything fixed up yet. Erm, the only thing is,' glancing back over her shoulder, she lowered her voice. 'I don't know if you've realised. It's my brother. He's—erm—he's not a lady's man, if you catch my drift.'

Violet Davies's eyes rounded in surprise. At least there was still one person in Porthlea who didn't seem to know, Dee thought.

'Better that than some randy fellow who is always pinching your bum, begging your pardon, miss.'

Dee couldn't help laughing at that. 'Much better!' she agreed. She fished in her handbag for the poison pen letter she knew was there, and taking out the letter, she wrote the address and the telephone number down on the back of the envelope. 'Look, why don't you think about it, and then if you'd like to try it, perhaps on a month's trial to see how we get on? Why don't you let us know? Or if you'd prefer, I will certainly be happy to give you a reference.'

The hand that took the envelope was shaking, but its owner said nothing. Dee looked at Davies.

'Do you need any—help—now?'

Davies straightened her back and put her chin up. 'No indeed, miss, thank you. I'm quite all right.' Then she wondered if her pride had just cost her a new position, but Dee smiled and said,

'Oh, that's all right then. I just wanted to make sure. And regards the train fare to London...'

'I can manage that too, thank you, miss.' Davies looked down at the address. She had a sudden conviction that this was going to work out all right. At the very worst, it would do until she found something better. 'Thank you miss. May I call on you on Monday morning at nine o'clock?'

'That would be fab, Mrs Davies, thank you.'

Davies inclined a regal head. 'Thank you, miss.' And she turned and went on along the corridor to the tiny boxroom that Joan had so kindly let her use. For the first time in several days, she felt that perhaps everything was going to be all right. She packed the envelope bearing the young lady's address very carefully in her handbag.

London. Just imagine!

Violet began to feel excited about the possibilities.

*

Chapter Thirty

The next morning a police car brought a furious Jeremy Prescott back to the manor house. He dismissed them curtly at the door and slamming the door, marched inside to the morning-room to find the two men from Scotland Yard there, along with Dee Gascoigne, her brother, the vicar and his wife, and Major Reeves, sitting there having coffee with Meredith and Aunt Lucinda. Jeremy halted abruptly just inside the door, blinking in surprise at the crowd.

Millie hurried over and launched herself at him in a hug. 'Thank God you're back home safely.'

He patted her arm, and gently putting her away from him, he immediately turned on Hardy and snapped, 'I've just spent twenty-four hours in police custody. I shall be making a formal complaint. It is absolutely beyond the pale. I've never been so...'

Hardy nodded. 'I'm very sorry sir, your arrest was not carried out under my orders. And I would like to assure you that I do not regard you as a suspect in my investigation.'

Prescott's reply was not of the kind suited to the ears of ladies in a morning-room. Millie's hand was at her mouth, unconsciously trying to hold back the vile words.

Seeing this, together with the shocked looks on the faces of his aunt and his sister, Prescott took a pull on himself, pinching his nose at the bridge, and taking a deep breath. In a relatively calm manner, he said 'That's not good enough. I demand to know once and for all what you intend to do about this situation.'

Hardy did his best to sound reassuring, 'I'm afraid we're still making...

Prescott, 'As I said, that's just not good enough. Surely you've put us all through quite enough. I shall be writing to my MP.'

Dee's heart was pounding. She found she was setting down her cup and getting to her feet. Did she really have the nerve to do this? She looked at Rob, who nodded at her, saying, 'Go on, Deedee.'

Taking a deep breath, she said, 'I think I can explain what's been going on and who is behind it.'

Everyone turned to stare at her.

Mrs Smithies said sharply, 'Good God, child, you can't possibly...'

Dee replied, 'Oh, but I can. If you'll hear me out, I can tell you exactly what happened to Mrs Hunter and Miss Fenniston.'

Nat Porter was mesmerised. It was like something from a book. He was transfixed, his notebook in his hand out of habit rather than a conscious plan to make notes. Hardy rolled his eyes then, mentally throwing up his hands in surrender, and keeping his fingers crossed that this wouldn't turn out to be the stupidest thing he'd done, he gave Dee a nod. Everyone in the room watched in silence as she began.

'As soon as I came to Porthlea, I saw that its existence was largely dependent on Prescott's wine warehouse and the Prescotts themselves.

'I also quickly discovered that although Jeremy Prescott's secretary was despised and manipulated by him and his family, she had some exceptional ideas, was intelligent, farsighted, and ambitious, whereas the Prescotts recklessly refused to move with the times, unwilling to adapt to the modern era, determined to keep doing things the way they always had. The firm was failing badly, a thing Jeremy Prescott wanted to keep from his family, and they were happy to enjoy the benefits of the wine warehouse's legacy without doing anything to ensure its success.' Dee paused, expecting an outcry from the Prescotts and Mrs Smithies over what she'd just said about them. Although they looked far from happy, no one said anything, so she continued.

'At the same time, there was another problem in the village. The problem of the poison pen letters. It seemed as though anyone and everyone was getting these letters through their letterbox. Meredith Prescott had at least two. Major Reeves had one, Lily Glover at the cafe had some, Cissie Palmer, Norman Slough, the Reverend Edmonds here, even I had one. And those are just the ones I know about.

'But who was behind them? Usually these letters are written—so I'm told—by a single person, often a woman, who is embittered, lonely, and jealous. Although that wasn't the case here in Porthlea.

'Here, there were two perpetrators: Mrs Hunter and her granddaughter Marlene. There was no real spite to the letters, just a desire to cause mischief and enjoy having a little bit of power. They meticulously gathered intelligence, then with Mrs Hunter shall we say supervising, and Marlene doing the actual work, they cut out letters and words from a selection of magazines and newspapers, assembled them into a message on a piece of paper, put this into an envelope and simply posted it to their chosen victim.

'Some people thought Sheila Fenniston was behind the letters, but I believe there were a few who guessed it was Mrs Hunter and Marlene, and...'

There was a loud sob from the corner. Marlene, in her baggy staff uniform, was pretending to weep into her apron that she held up to her face, though Dee could see the corner of her mouth lifting up as she smiled.

'She made me do it,' Marlene wailed. 'I never wanted to... Honest... It was Gran. I was that scared of her...'

'Oh, nonsense,' Dee said impatiently. 'You adored your grandmother, and the two of you were as thick as thieves, as everyone here knows only too well. You were very much a partner in the crime, and you loved every minute of it.'

The girl began to shake her head. 'No, no, I never. I swear I didn't...'

'You couldn't wait to see the face on each new victim once they received your letter through the post,' Nat Porter pointed out. Dee noticed he had his notebook in his hand although he didn't appear to be writing anything down. Beside him, Bill stood, arms folded across his chest, watching the proceedings closely. Dee only hoped she wouldn't let him down.

Marlene was still shaking her head, but her conviction was waning. Dee continued:

'When Mrs Hunter died, and the police arrived from London, I think almost everyone still thought Mrs Hunter's death was an accident. A few people, including myself, and Marlene, wondered if Mrs Hunter had been killed because of the letters. And in fact, she was.'

'It was obvious, once the theory of accidental death had been dismissed, that the only other solution was murder, carried out by someone who knew the village and those living here very well indeed. As well as Mrs Hunter herself.

'It had to be someone who knew all about the poison

pen letters. For convenience, they had to live nearby, or possibly in the village itself. And they would have had to know about the spare key kept under the flowerpot by the back door of Mrs Grayson and Mrs Hunter's house. Not such a stretch, admittedly, it's often common practise in a small village, after all. And the other thing they had to know was, where to find a key to Mrs Palmer's cottage, so they could get in and attack me when I came home after the bingo evening.'

'On the face of it, a number of people had a motive to kill Sheila Fenniston. Norman Slough, who was rejected by her. Her own brother Michael Fenniston who asked her to help him get a job at the warehouse, but she refused him, afraid that if his background came to light it would make things difficult for her. Or perhaps Mrs Hunter, or her family, had cause to suspect Sheila knew about the poison pen letters and was about to expose them. Exposure might lead to Harriet Grayson and her daughter Marlene losing their jobs. Perhaps it was Millie Edmonds, who disapproved of Sheila and thought Sheila was the writer of the poison pen letters. Millie Edmonds who was so protective of her husband's reputation, of her comfortable position here, respected and looked up to as the vicar's wife, able to run everything, enjoying being in charge of her own little empire.'

Unsurprisingly, Millie and Callum Edmonds looked rather taken aback by this, and were clearly offended. But ignoring them, Dee continued.

'Most notable of all, however, was the strong dislike Meredith Prescott and Mrs. Smithies had for Miss Fenniston. She challenged their attitudes, their status, everything they held dear. She overshadowed them at their own dinner parties and provoked them by flirting with Jeremy. She was rapidly making herself indispensable to the business, wooing the overseas visitors, trying to make the business more competitive, and just not remembering her place as a mere secretary. At the same time, the village seemed rife with speculation about Sheila's supposed affair with Jeremy Prescott, and many expected Sheila to attain the ultimate prize: Jeremy himself.

'But what about Agnes Hunter? Perhaps she really did just have a horrid albeit completely accidental fall on the stairs in the middle of the night? Her family refused to believe it, citing her inability to get about without assistance. So perhaps it was murder after all? On several occasions people, myself included, asked who would kill an old woman, and why? Usually in cases of murder, the police immediately investigate those closest to the victim. But not in this case. In this case, the victim's family was small in number but very devoted. Mrs Hunter's daughter and granddaughter had no reason to cause her death.'

'They might if they knew they would lose their livelihoods because of Mrs Hunter writing those letters,' the major suggested.

'They wouldn't need to kill her, Major. She depended on them completely for everything. Not just her food, or her personal care, or to get about the house and the village, but for the creation of the letters, and for getting the letters to her chosen victims. Mrs Hunter was the brains behind the poison pen letters, she chose the targets, but it was Marlene who actually made the letters, and her boyfriend Eddie who helped her post them. If Mrs Hunter's family wanted to stop Mrs Hunter, all they would need to do would be to refuse to cooperate and remove the letter writing equipment: the magazines, the scissors, the glue, or to refuse to post them. Mrs Hunter had no control over those things, and without them she could not have sent any letters.

'Again the village was full of speculation. There was a lot of talk about the poison pen letters. Some people were slightly irritated by them, others were more deeply upset. It seems that most people assumed the letters came from Mrs Hunter and Marlene. It was common knowledge that Mrs Hunter was nosy, loved to collect gossip and had a malicious sense of humour. It was said that she knew everything that went on in the village. It was also common knowledge that wherever Mrs Hunter went, she was aided and abetted by Marlene who helped her gather 'intelligence' for the letters. No one doubted for a minute that Mrs Hunter knew everything about everyone. And that was why she had to die.

'The problem with Mrs Hunter was that she didn't keep her knowledge to herself. She liked people to know that she knew their secrets. I'm sorry to say that she enjoyed watching her victims suffer. She liked to see them squirm. She enjoyed other people's misfortune, that was why she—and Marlene—came up with the idea for the poison pen letters in the first place.'

'Marlene has already admitted helping her grandmother to make the letters, and it seems that for Mrs Hunter, the most enjoyable part of the whole thing was seeing the reaction on people's faces after they received one. It was Mrs Hunter who chose the victim, who knew the secrets, who told Marlene what the letters should say.'

'Oh, for goodness' sake, this is too ridiculous,' Mrs Smithies grumbled. 'Just tell us who it was and leave me in peace.'

Dee, disconcerted, glanced at Hardy. He shrugged and nodded, then he whispered something to Porter. Porter left the room, returning less than a minute later. He nodded at Hardy and took up his position by the door once again.

'Very well,' Dee was saying, 'It was your niece. Meredith killed both those women.'

There was a collective gasp about the room. All eyes turned on Meredith Prescott, reclining in her armchair. She said nothing, but her eyes were fixed on Dee with

343

undiluted hatred.

Up to that point at any moment, Dee had expected Meredith to laugh at her, or throw her out of the house, or just deny the accusation. But Meredith did none of those things. She just continued to stare. Almost in surprise, Dee realised she was right.

'You killed Sheila because she was, in your opinion, disruptive, determined to cause change and upheaval. You thought she intended to become Jeremy's wife and have control of the company. She threatened your comfortable way of life, where you were adored as a kind of Lady Bountiful figure, dispensing good works, admired by everyone. Then you killed Mrs Hunter because she knew what you did and threatened to tell the police. Marlene, did you and your grandmother send a poison pen letter to Miss Prescott after Sheila's death?'

From her corner, seemingly awestruck, Marlene nodded.

Dee looked at Bill, and took a step back, to sit on the sofa beside her brother. Her part was done.

Stepping forward, Hardy said, 'Well, Miss Prescott, I think you'd better tell us all about it, don't you?'

Porter, barely able to believe what was happening, had his pencil poised over the notebook balanced on his knee.

Meredith Prescott lifted her chin, haughty, unbowed. Her pride allowed her to view them all as lesser mortals. For a moment Hardy thought she would remain silent, but then she said, 'I don't see why I should do your job for you.'

'I would have thought you'd want us to know what you did,' Dee said. 'Surely you want everyone to know how clever you were.'

Meredith's nose wrinkled in disgust, her lip curling. 'Oh, stop being so ridiculous, you spoiled little brat. You're not important. You'll never be important. My family have lived in this village for centuries. We *are* the village. Without us there'd be nothing here.' She looked around the room, noticing for the first time the looks of horror on their faces. Even her brother...

'Why, Meredith?' Jeremy's voice was little more than a whisper. He shook his head. It was all too much...

His sister shook her head impatiently. 'You were always spineless, useless, lazy... You would have let that woman ruin us, ruin everything we had here.'

'No, she was trying to save us. The firm's going under. Nothing can save it now.'

This seemed to startle her. 'Going under? But how?'

'All our suppliers have said they will no longer work with us. They can get a better deal elsewhere. We can't compete. We're out of date, out of touch. We've been losing money for years.'

She spoke then, in a cold rage. 'After all I've done for you. And this... this is how you repay me. You've driven the whole thing into the ground. I tried so hard to save you but it was all for nothing. I killed that stupid bitch of a secretary, just to prise her paws off you, and then that foul old woman.

'Oh I was very clever about it. I took the wine with me when I went to read to that old hag. I lulled her to sleep then tiptoed out—but later I found out that she was only pretending to sleep. I didn't know until I got that letter. 'I know what you did while I was sleeping'. Gave herself away completely. I mean, I'd always had my suspicions about who was behind those letters, but that slip was the nail in her coffin. She'd seen me with my bag, probably even seen the wine bottle poking out. I had put some of Aunt's sleeping pills in it, then went to present it to Dear Sheila as a thank you gift for all her hard work. She was astonished, I can tell you, and didn't really trust me. I offered to drink some with her, even pretended to open the bottle so she wouldn't notice it was already open. She said she was going out, not that I believed her. At nine o'clock at night? In her nightdress? She just wanted to get rid of me. That didn't matter to me, she drank it all the same.

'Then all I had to do was go back later to finish her off. I'd taken an old razor from home. It was unpleasant in the extreme, she was very drowsy but not quite out. Luckily for me, she didn't put up too much of a struggle, and it didn't take long.'

'Unfortunately for you, Miss Prescott, we have two witnesses who saw you going home, and with almost two hours difference between them, that tells us that you went home once, then went out again some time later,' Hardy told her.

'I also saw her going out,' Mrs Smithies said from her armchair. Her voice sounded older, querulous and weak. Dee hadn't realised that shock could age one's voice. 'It's played on my mind so. I have always maintained that family should come first, but this... You did a terrible thing, Meredith. Two terrible, terrible things. I won't protect you now. I will testify in court if the police ask me to do so.

Meredith was not particularly perturbed by this, Dee noted. She simply swept on with her grand revelation of her own version of the truth.

'Oh of course, family only comes first when it suits you, Aunt. Well, I did this for our family. Not that it went as well as I'd initially thought. Because a few days later, the letter came, and I saw that I had the old woman to deal with. I'd hoped it wouldn't come to that. Or that she would just accept some money as a 'gift', but I realised she wouldn't let it go. She'd love having that power over me, and she'd never keep her mouth shut. I couldn't allow that. She had to go. It was easy to get into the house, we've got all the keys of the tenants' houses in the office.'

She paused to sneer at Dee. 'You were wrong about that, Daphne dear, I didn't need to use the key from under the flowerpot. Killing her was not so hard really. Just a quick bop on the head, and she was so woozy she hardly resisted. The stone floor did the rest. You should have gone the same way.'

She directed a hostile glare at Dee at that. 'All that hair, I suppose. Saved you. Shame. I took an instant dislike to you. But I searched that cottage and found nothing. Marlene had talked constantly about how you found evidence in Sheila's room. I assumed she was exaggerating, but I couldn't take the risk. Obviously, you'd already handed it over.'

'Yes, I had, I gave it to Inspector Hardy the same day I discovered it.' Dee confirmed. She ran out of words as she looked about her at the other people in the room.

Marlene, in the corner, was weeping softly, all her bravado gone. Millie and Callum Edmonds were sitting on the sofa as if turned to stone. And in the major's eyes there were tears, Dee saw. Her heart went out to him, standing there in the wreckage of his hopes. Mrs Smithies was white-faced, her eyes dry, but like the others, thunderstruck, every line etched deep in her face. And lastly, Jeremy Prescott sat like a half-deflated balloon, defeat heavy about his shoulders.

Nat Porter was a good deal shocked. In all his long years as a police officer he'd never seen quite such chilling malice. A sideways glance showed Dee's face, white, tense, her eyes glistening, her hands gripped together in her lap. Rob put his arm about her shoulders. Porter hurriedly stuffed his notebook in his pocket as Hardy moved forward to place his hand on Meredith's arm, saying,

'Meredith Prescott, you are under arrest for the murders of Sheila Fenniston and Agnes Hunter...'

Meredith said nothing, looking neither to the right nor the left. As she was led from the room, Jeremy said her name, and she looked at him as if he was a stranger. Outside, Porter and Hardy put her into the back of the newly-arrived police car. As it drove away she looked straight ahead, silent, impassive, as if nothing in the world around her existed.

Rob came over to put an arm about her, leading her out, saying, 'Let's go home.'

It was over.

*

Epilogue

The flat-warming party was in full swing. Violet Davies was enjoying herself even though she wasn't there as a guest but was working. But she had never worked anywhere that was so relaxed. She was really enjoying her new job. And to think at one point she'd considered begging Mrs Smithies for her old job back.

That good-looking policeman was here. He'd been talking to the pretty young girl by the window but now he came over, she thought he wanted a drink. Knowing she could say exactly what she thought to the man, she said now,

'She's young enough to be your daughter!'

'We're just talking, that's all,' Nat said. 'She's a very interesting lady.'

'I suppose you want a couple of these glasses of punch, then,' Vi said, leaning the tray a little closer to him.

He took the whole tray off her and set it down.

'No,' he said, 'I came to ask you if you would like to dance.' And with that, he swept her into the middle of the dancing throng in a *very* tight embrace.

'I can't do that!' She tried to push him away, a momentary panic gripping her.

He put some space between them, and apologised for startling her, adding, 'Sorry, I got a bit carried away.'

'I really mustn't,' she repeated. 'I'm sure they wouldn't like it, it's not right...'

'Nonsense,' Nat said, and making sure no one was looking, gave her a quick peck on the cheek. 'Time for you to live a little, Miss Violet.'

Violet Davies made a sound that was suspiciously like a giggle.

Later, when Vi was doing the rounds again with a fresh tray of drinks, Dee was gazing out of the window at night-time London, all shimmering streetlights and waving shadows. She began to think again about the events in Porthlea and grew pensive. At the back of the room, Rob put another record on, whilst Kelvin Rodericks held his drink for him. It was a slow number, and it seemed perfect timing that Bill joined her just then. She sipped her wine.

'Why so sad?' he asked.

She shrugged. But he continued to stare at her, so in the end she just said what was on her mind.

'I ought to have prevented Mrs Hunter's death. I should have got to the truth after Sheila Fenniston died, and then Mrs Hunter would have been safe.'

The haunting melody of The Righteous Brothers filled the room. Bill took her glass from her and set it down, he drew her into his arms for a close slow dance, saying softly,

'As a policeman, I've often wished I'd got to a solution sooner, or managed to prevent some tragic event. But it's no good undermining yourself, you can only do so much. The important thing for any detective is to be there for the victim and their loved ones, trying to find justice for them. That's all any of us can do.'

As they swayed to the music, she closed her eyes and let everything else go. He nuzzled her neck. And as the song drew to a close, he said,

'So, it's going to be three years?'

'We've already talked about this.' And she didn't want to go into it all again. Suddenly a lump in her throat stopped her from saying anything more. Rob put a new record on, another slow one: Peter and Gordon's *True Love Ways*, another of Dee's favourite songs. Clearly it was Rob's plan to keep her slow-dancing with Bill all the evening.

'It's going to kill me to wait that long.'

She nodded, wrapping her arms still more tightly around his neck and laying her face against his shoulder.

'But,' he said, 'I'd wait forty, fifty years for you, if I really had to.'

Through tears she giggled. 'I hope it won't be that long. You'll have forgotten what to do by then.'

'Rubbish,' he growled in a dangerous tone. 'I'll spend all that time planning my moves.'

THE END

*

About the author

Caron Allan writes cosy murder mysteries, both contemporary and also set in the 1930s. Caron lives in Derby, England with her husband and an endlessly varying quantity of cats and sparrows.

Caron Allan can be found on these social media channels and would love to hear from you:

Instagram: caronsbooks

Twitter: caron_allan

Mastodon social: caron_allan

Facebook: CaronAllanFiction

Also, if you're interested in news, snippets, Caron's 'quirky' take on life or just want some sneak previews, please sign up to Caron's blog shown below:

caronallanfiction.com/

Also by Caron Allan:

The Friendship Can Be Murder books:

Criss Cross: book 1
Cross Check: book 2
Check Mate: book 3

The Dottie Manderson mysteries:

Night and Day: book 1
The Mantle of God: book 2
Scotch Mist: book 3 a novella
The Last Perfect Summer of Richard Dawlish: book 4
The Thief of St Martins: book 5
The Spy Within: book 6
Rose Petals and White Lace: book 7

The Miss Gascoigne mysteries:

A Meeting With Murder:

Others:

Easy Living: a story about life after death, after death, after death

Coming Soon 2023/24

A Wreath of Lilies: Miss Gascoigne mysteries book 2

Midnight, the Stars, and You: Dottie Manderson mysteries book 8

Dirty Work: Friendship Can Be Murder book 4

The Refuge: a story about love, family and surviving a catastrophe

Made in the USA
Coppell, TX
02 October 2023